unforgettable romance by the author of Blue Waltz

D.A.

Titles by Linda Francis Lee

EMERALD RAIN
BLUE WALTZ
WILD HEARTS

Emerald Rain

LINDA FRANCIS LEE

JOVE BOOKS, NEW YORK

EMERALD RAIN

A Jove Book / published by arrangement with
the author

PRINTING HISTORY
Jove edition / December 1996

The Putnam Berkley World Wide Web site address is
http://www.berkley.com/berkley

ISBN: 0-515-11979-2

A JOVE BOOK®
Jove Books are published by The Berkley Publishing Group,
200 Madison Avenue, New York, New York 10016.
JOVE and the "J" design are trademarks
belonging to Jove Publications, Inc.

PRINTED IN THE UNITED STATES OF AMERICA

10 9 8 7 6 5 4 3 2 1

As always, for Michael

Love comforteth like sunshine after rain.

— SHAKESPEARE

Prologue

August 1899

The weight of solitude. Sometimes unbearable. Sometimes unnoticed. Though undeniably the aftermath of distant days of sunshine and laughter.

Sunshine and laughter.

The words shimmered through his mind, resonating like a siren's song, beckoning him into the dangerous waters of memory. Places he had no interest in going.

He took a deep breath and ran his strong, chiseled hand through his dark hair. His fathomless blue eyes narrowed against the spreading sunlight that drifted through the window. It must have been the way the long, early morning rays caught motes of dust in a timeless dance that brought the words to mind. Or so he told himself. Why else would the unexpected and certainly unwanted images of so long ago have filtered through his head?

Though perhaps, he reasoned, it was nothing more complicated than the season. Late summer in New York. Never a good time for him, at least it hadn't been for the last three years.

"Sir? Is something wrong?"

He stiffened momentarily before he sighed, then turned away from the mullioned window of his Fifth Avenue office. "No, Henry. Nothing's wrong. Where were we?"

After a moment, his assistant said, "The Vanderweer Agreement."

"Ah, yes."

The Vanderweer Agreement would affect his company's revenues for the next five years at the very least. Leaning forward, he picked up the document and read each line with an attention to detail that belied the fact that he had drafted the document himself only days before. When he came to the end he set it down. Carefully, though boldly, he signed his name. *Nicholas Drake.*

"Very good, sir. I'll send it out by messenger this morning." The assistant gathered the papers before pushing another in front of Nicholas. "Today's agenda, sir." Henry glanced down at his own copy. "Maynard Gibson is scheduled for nine o'clock. He's already here, early as usual. Then at ten . . ."

Henry's words trailed off into a vacuum in Nicholas's mind, never ceasing, swirling, but unheard, replaced by the sudden image of rain. All around. Like flowing, crystal draperies closing out the world. And her face. Porcelain white. His hands coiling in her long blond hair, carefully pulling her near. Her full red lips parting. But on that day, that day of early spring showers so long ago, her emerald green eyes hadn't closed. She had looked at him, startled but expectant, waiting, wanting, as much as he had wanted her. He had leaned forward, and when he gently tugged her full lower lip with his teeth, sucking gently, he had felt her rosebud nipples rise with desire beneath the thin, wet cotton of her chemisette.

". . . Fortunately, you speak after the mayor, and we all know how long-winded he is. I'm sure you'll have plenty of time to get there, providing you leave the office by twelve-thirty.

"Three o'clock, back here," Henry droned on. "You have an appointment with the Women's League. They asked for two hours, I gave them one. I suspect they want money."

Nicholas smiled, a half-smile that was gone before it

settled. In the seven months Henry had been there he had learned his job well.

"Four o'clock, you have an appointment with Thaddeus Matthews; five o'clock, Fielding Banks. I'm sure you've heard he's trying to sell that old dilapidated mess of brick and mortar he calls a hotel. He seems to be the only man in town who doesn't know you're no longer in the building business." Henry shook his head disdainfully. "Six o'clock . . ."

Nicholas pressed back in his chair, forgetting to listen. His mind drifted to the memory of her laughter, full-bodied like a fine French wine, wrapping around him, never letting him go, touching him in ways that reached beyond what he had expected, beyond what he knew. For a time he had stepped into life, embracing it as he had embraced her, instead of standing aside, a cool, detached observer to the vicissitudes of being alive. She had reached something deep and primal in him that even he didn't understand. And had no interest in studying.

Turning away, he looked out the window, watched as once again life passed him by.

". . . Needless to say, nearly every hour of your day is scheduled—as you like."

For a moment, Nicholas pressed his eyes closed against the women who strolled by on the street below pushing baby carriages, and against the men who laughed, slapping one another on the back, no doubt sharing some tawdry joke. Yes, he thought, his day would be just the sort of mind-numbing, body-exhausting day that appealed to him, days that emptied full-bodied laughter from his mind. Nicholas sucked in his breath.

"Sir?" Henry said uncertainly. "Is there anything else?" When he received no reply, Henry glanced about the elegantly appointed room of dark woods and leather-bound books, as if hoping to find someone or something to help. "Mr. Drake?"

Nicholas glanced back at his assistant.

"Should I send Mr. Gibson in . . . or should I have him

wait a bit longer? Perhaps give him some more coffee . . . or some tea?"

"No, no." Nicholas's soft, dark voice was shaded with regret as he leaned forward and pulled another file from the stack that waited on his perfectly organized desk top. "Bring him in, no reason to delay."

Seconds later, Henry led Maynard Gibson into the office. A secretary followed with a notepad in her hand.

"Nicholas," Maynard practically bellowed, his tone robust and jovial.

But before Maynard could utter another word, a man burst through the door and pushed past him. "Nicky!"

Nicholas jerked at the sight. His mind seemed to stop.

For all appearances, the intruder acted more like an overgrown child than an adult. His voice was at odds with his appearance, meek and awkward, contrasting with his looming, thickset form. His sweater was rumpled and his shirt askew. His breathing made it clear he had run a long way.

"Jim," Nicholas said, his deep voice guarded. "What are you doing here? Is something wrong?"

And of course, as soon as Nicholas said the words he didn't need an answer. Of course there was something wrong. Drastically wrong. He should have known. Why else would he have been so plagued today by thoughts of another time?

Jim appeared on the verge of tears as he tried to catch his breath. "It's Ellie."

Nicholas flinched. *Ellie.*

"She needs you!"

Nicholas pressed back into the soft leather of his chair. Rain and emerald eyes flared in his mind. Dear God, no. He couldn't. He couldn't go to her. He couldn't start this all over again.

Even though he had never forgotten her—and never would, he feared—the times when he suddenly thought he saw her in the street, or gazing in a shop window, or laughing with a flower vendor happened less frequently with each day that passed. If he hadn't forgotten her, at least he was achieving some success in stealing himself against her. He couldn't afford to undo what meager progress he had made.

He took a deep breath and started to turn away.

"Nicky, no!" the childlike giant wailed. "Quit being mad! She needs you."

"No," he said, the words tight, burning in his throat.

"Oh, Nicky." Jim ran his sleeve across his nose and his voice trailed off until it was almost a whisper. "You gotta come. You gotta." His voice caught. "Ellie's dying."

The words seared Nicholas's mind. His lungs tightened and he lost his breath. Ellie dying? Sunshine and laughter snuffed out like a candle flame? Impossible. Bright, vibrant Ellie with a flair for the ridiculous, dying? Never.

But in spite of his reasoning, he couldn't quite push from his mind the pressing heaviness he had awakened with that morning. Nor could he deny that dark, secret place in Ellie's soul that sometimes obscured the light, lending Jim's words a glimmer of truth. But most of all, after Nicholas had told himself once and for all that he would never see her again it had never occurred to him that a time would come when he couldn't.

The realization hit Nicholas hard. And without another thought for what was best, Nicholas tossed his pen onto the desk, splattering the crisp, clean files with midnight ink. "Cancel my appointments, Henry. I'll be back."

Henry stammered and stuttered, but in the end managed nothing more than a meekly uttered, "When?"

Nicholas hesitated, his chiseled features harsh with emotion. "Whenever I can."

With that he strode from the office, Jim on his heels, leaving Henry and the others behind with brows furrowed in confusion, staring, until the secretary shook her head and asked, "Who in the world is Ellie?"

Part One

❧

THE EMBRACE

But to see her was to love her,
Love but her, and love forever.

— ROBERT BURNS

Chapter 1

April 1896
Three years earlier

Guilty. *One seemingly* simple word, yet not so simple at all.

The verdict was greeted by a moment of nearly deafening silence as the word reverberated against the rich wood and cold marble walls, before pandemonium broke out in the courtroom.

Reporters scrambled about—the *Evening Sun* was there, as was the *Evening Post*, even *The New York Times* had made an appearance—as they stuffed their tablets of notes into satchels of tattered leather. Within seconds they were running each other down in their haste to get back to their respective publications. No newspaperman in the courtroom wanted to be left out or left behind. The conviction would be the biggest story to hit the papers since Theodore Roosevelt was appointed president of the Board of Commissioners of New York City's Police Department, setting the institution on its ear with all his reform.

Eliot Sinclair stared down at the chaotic scene from the courtroom gallery, and reluctantly concluded that as days went she'd certainly had better. Her favorite hat, a mind-boggling creation she had spent hours making just the week before, lay crushed on her lap, the feathers and bows dangling at odd, misshapen angles. The long skirt of her pale-green gown was splattered with mud and a few less than savory streaks of something she wasn't particularly interested in naming. She could only hope that with her dress in such disarray no one could see her stockings—her lucky red stockings.

Running late that morning, Ellie had been forced to dash madly down Broadway in order to get to the courthouse in time. But as was all too frequently her habit, before she could make it uneventfully through the dignified doors of the criminal building, Ellie had managed to get herself tangled up trying to settle an altercation between two hired hack drivers who were not particularly appreciative of her efforts. But what else could she have done? she wondered with a disgruntled grimace. She would have sworn the disreputable-looking men had been mere seconds away from killing each other. Only when she found herself plunked down in the mud, the unfortunate hat beneath her, and the men doing little to hold back their mirth, did Ellie realize that perhaps she had misjudged the situation. Negotiating, apparently, had not been necessary. But for mercy's sake, she thought defensively, her chin rising a notch, it certainly had looked like an altercation.

After realizing her mistake, Ellie had picked herself up as regally as any queen, pulled back her delicate shoulders, bid the men a polite if cool good day, then sailed up the front steps of the courthouse, looking far more disreputable at that point than either one of the drivers. It was amazing the uniformed guard had let her inside.

Though for all the good her mad dash had done, or for that matter, her lucky red stockings. Harry Dillard had been convicted after all.

If only she could go to him, she thought, plucking grimly at the ruined feathers of her hat, the gallery nearly empty. To feel him hold her close in the circle of his strong arms. If only he would have. Ever. But of course, he hadn't. Ever.

No gentle, warm embrace, or sweet, tender kiss. No words of love or caring. Even before the accident.

On the day that word had raced through the streets of New York that Harry Dillard had been shot, Ellie had bolstered her courage, told herself to be firm, then had gone to him at the house on Lafayette Place, regardless of the fact that most any other person with an ounce of sense wouldn't have gone. But even she admitted that *sense* had never been her long suit when it came to Harry Dillard.

The large, hulking man who had answered the door, looking more the bodyguard than butler, left her on the front steps when he went inside to "see if his boss was in." *See if he was in,* she had snorted into the bitter cold, biting back a number of less than complimentary epithets that came to mind. How in the world could he be out? He had been shot, for mercy's sake. Not the best of conditions in which to conduct business or make social calls. But she had held her tongue, barely, and simply waited for the inevitable.

"He's not in," came the answer. Nor had he ever been whenever she had tried to see him.

It was best this way, best not to forge relationships that could never be realized, he had said eight years before on the day he brought her to the house on Sixteenth Street, saying it was hers. Ellie had stood on the walkway, carriages rolling by in the street, stunned. Safer to remain apart, he had continued in his smooth, velvety voice. For her sake, he had sworn.

She had wanted to believe him then—still wanted to believe him.

Though for all it mattered. He was gone now. Dead. From the gunshot wound to his abdomen. Had been for the last three months. These convoluted proceedings in the courtroom today, made possible by some obscure law on the books, had been nothing more than a formality to convict Harry Dillard of fraud so the state could strip his estate of all he had gained.

Ellie had to admit, however, that his attitude *had* saved

her in the end. Or at least she hoped so. The house was hers, free and clear, with only one single piece of paper left that could lead back to him—a criminal overseer, a turf boss of one of New York's rougher districts up until that fateful day when he was shot down by the raging husband of a woman with whom he had trifled. Yes, Ellie told herself, in the end he had left her as safe as anyone could possibly hope.

Perhaps Harry Dillard had loved her after all.

She closed her eyes, and a gentle smile pulled at her lips.

Her house. And the people in it. Those were the people who loved her. Those were the people who cared. This proceeding didn't matter. Guilty, not guilty. In reality, it changed nothing in her life. Though deep inside she knew that a tiny bud of hope had been nipped. There no longer existed any possibility that things would be different for the two of them. No reunions where regrets and sorrows were left behind.

A man named Nicholas Drake had seen to that.

After a moment, Ellie smoothed her hair as best she could, gave a futile wipe to the now-dried mud on her skirt, then pushed herself up from her seat. She needed to get home. But when she stood, knowing she should hurry, she saw him. A man she had never seen before. With dark brown hair, almost black. Eyes that even from this distance she could tell were a deep shade of blue.

She was certain she didn't know him even though he was looking up at her, his brow slightly creased in apparent confusion, as if they had known each other for a lifetime, but he couldn't quite remember her name.

Her pulse slowed as a deep, stirring sense of awareness washed over her. Thoughts of trials and betrayals, mis-shapen hats and mud-splattered skirts fled from her mind. Her world in that second consisted of nothing more than the man and the odd way he made her feel, as if he could see into that secret place inside her that she had shut away so long ago.

He was extraordinary, this man. His face, his mouth

beckoned as he looked at her with a stillness in his eyes that cried out to her.

For a moment she nearly smiled and raised her gloved hand in response. But the urge lasted no more than one insane second before she remembered where she was and, of course, ultimately, inevitably, who she was.

Harry Dillard's illegitimate daughter.

"Congratulations, Old Boy!"

Nicholas was startled from his thoughts. When he turned away from the gallery he found a man his father had done business with, a man Nicholas avoided at all costs.

"Thank you," Nicholas said, glancing impatiently at the man.

"It's about damn time this whole mess was put behind you. You've worked damnably hard to bring that wretched Dillard low. Everyone's saying you missed your calling. Should have been a man of the law instead of a man of business. Either way, now you've done it. Perhaps other turf bosses will think twice about toying with the likes of us."

But Nicholas hardly heard. He turned back, feeling oddly desperate not to lose sight of the woman. But when he looked up into the gallery again she was gone. He searched the entire balcony. Nothing. No one with white-blond hair and eyes the color of an emerald sea.

"What is it, Old Boy?" the man asked. "What are you looking for?"

"Nothing. I've got to go." Nicholas retrieved his black leather satchel from beneath his seat, then walked determinedly down the center aisle.

"I say, Drake. What's the hurry?"

But Nicholas didn't answer, didn't even listen. He pushed through the courtroom door to the high-ceilinged, marble-floored foyer of the courthouse, intent on finding her.

Voices came at him from all directions in an echoing din, rolling around, the words caving in on one another until they were nothing more than a muddle of sound.

Nicholas was taller than most, well over six feet, making it easy for him to scan the crowd. He took in the many faces of people as they walked from the staircase to the courthouse doors. Women's faces, men's faces, some old, some young, but none that resembled the shimmering-haired angel who had gazed down at him from the gallery.

After a few bold strides he pushed through the wide, oak double doors, out onto the hard granite steps that led down to the cobbled street. His eyes narrowed against the harsh, bright white, cloud-filled sky, but found nothing, no one he could believe was the woman he sought.

"Nicholas!"

He turned with a start, thinking irrationally that it was her. But of course it wasn't. Instead, once his mind had adjusted and he had taken a deep breath, he found a short, squat man who had come up beside him. "Oliver," Nicholas said simply.

"I suspect you're quite pleased with yourself just about now," Oliver Wicks said with a beaming smile.

And of course he was. Harry Dillard had been a man who preyed on the weak. Most people knew he owned a saloon, a few knew he owned a disorderly house, but Nicholas had learned that the man's sins were much worse than even he had suspected. Getting Dillard convicted had been relatively easy to accomplish once Nicholas had ferreted out the details of the turf boss's life. It had been the ferreting, in the end, which had proved the most difficult.

But just then, all Nicholas could think about was the fact that he had lost the woman. And in a city the size of New York, more than likely he had lost her forever. The thought frustrated him. And that was absurd. He didn't even know her. She was a nameless face in a crowded courtroom. Up close no doubt her face was pox-marked and coarse, her hair unnaturally blond. Emerald sea eyes, indeed. On top of which, she wore no hat, her hair was askew, and now, in retrospect, he would have sworn there was mud on her gown. He shook his head. No doubt he had only imagined his pulse had slowed at the sight. There had simply been too many nights spent avenging his parent's honor to think straight.

He obviously needed a woman. Yes, a woman. To warm his bed. To sink his flesh into. To lose his mind in for a few blissful hours. Nothing more. And there were plenty of willing women for that.

Steadying himself, Nicholas turned his attention to his longtime friend. "Sorry, Oliver. What was the question?"

Oliver Wicks looked at Nicholas curiously. "The trial, my man. How do you feel?"

Nicholas ran his hand through his hair and nodded. "Good. It's been a long time in coming."

"Yes, that it has. Too bad that double-dealing Dillard had to get himself shot before they could send him up. I hear they hang fellows like him in Texas. I wouldn't have minded seeing that low-life scum swing."

Nicholas was inclined to agree. But either way it was done. An eye for an eye. His revenge was complete. Or at least almost.

Back at his Fifth Avenue office, with its wainscoted walls of dark-stained walnut topped by the finest silk wallpaper of hunter green and deep, rich red, the remainder of Nicholas's day passed quickly. The sharp jangle of the newly installed telephone never ceased, though he had stopped taking the calls less than a half hour after his return. No need to hear more words of praise and congratulations. He had simply accomplished what had needed to be done. Nothing more.

The handcrafted grandfather clock that stood against the south wall had just struck five o'clock when his secretary, Jane, knocked at his door. "Your sister is here to see you," she said, her manner apologetic.

Nicholas grimaced.

"I saw that, Nicholas," Miriam Drake Welton stated as she sashayed into his office, her long gown the height of fashion, her soft leather, Italian-heeled shoes sinking into the thick Persian rug. "A little brotherly love and affection wouldn't hurt."

"No, I suspect it wouldn't," he responded as he stood from his chair. Coming around the desk he kissed her cheek.

Miriam was a tall, willowy woman with dark hair much the same shade as her brother's, though her eyes were more violet than blue. A stunner, many called her. Miriam, Nicholas knew, was inclined to agree.

It took her no more than a second or two to pull out a long, sleek cigarette from a gaily beaded reticule that hung from a silken cord on her wrist. She waited, in what Nicholas was inclined to think a practiced pose, for him to offer her a light. Nicholas obliged, after which she inhaled deeply then dropped her sinewy form into a leather chair opposite his desk.

"Dreadful, I tell you," she said as she exhaled with a husky sigh.

Getting straight to the point as quickly as possible had always proved the best way to deal with his sister. So when she appeared disinclined to expand on her statement, Nicholas prompted her. "What is dreadful, Miriam?"

"This." Seemingly bored and dispassionate, she extended a single sheet of white linen stationery in her bejeweled and fingernail-painted hand which still held the smoldering cigarette.

After a curious glance at his sister who had turned her head to gaze out the window, Nicholas began to read. Seconds later he set the letter aside. "So what's new? Your husband has been seen with a French woman in Europe."

"More than once."

"Repeatedly, I believe it says here." He leaned back against the edge of the expansive mahogany desk. "Still, what's new?"

Miriam looked back at him with bored blue eyes. "You're a hateful man, Nicholas Drake. Hateful as anyone I've had the misfortune to meet."

"So you've told me, time and time again."

Miriam sighed, her countenance softening with what might have been genuine regret. "There was a day, dear brother, when you weren't so hateful. In fact—"

"Enough, Miriam." His tone was short. "Why are you here? What is it you want?"

"I'm going abroad," she stated defiantly, her violet-blue eyes once again hard like amethyst. "To France, actually. To bring my husband home."

The words surprised Nicholas, though no one would have known that he was. "You're going to Europe?" he asked, one dark slash of brow rising in question. "To bring William home? Good Lord, why? You don't even like the man, much less pine with love for him. You have done nothing but complain about that 'worthless pup' as I believe you call him, since the day of your ill-advised marriage. I would think you'd be elated that he was gone."

Miriam looked away and shrugged her shoulders. "Maybe I love him more than I thought."

"Like hell you do," he grumbled, impatient with the never-ending antics of his only sibling. "This is just an excuse to go abroad."

Defiance flared bright red on her high cheekbones. "So what if it is! That scoundrel can't get away with leaving me over here while he's in Europe, flaunting himself like a strutting peacock."

Pressing his fingers to the bridge of his nose, Nicholas sighed. "Just tell me when you want to go. I'll have my assistant make the arrangements."

"No need for you to bother yourself, or that little gnome of an assistant you have, either. I've already made the arrangements." She glanced down at her fingernails. "I sail this evening."

"This evening? Why didn't you tell me before? And what about Charlotte? Do you plan to drag that poor child around Europe with you?"

Miriam stood from her chair, pressing her cigarette out in an exquisitely cut glass ashtray on a small table. Nicholas sensed her sudden nervousness. But before he could react, she opened the door. And there was her daughter, a tiny little suitcase clutched in her tiny little hands.

"I'm not going to drag my daughter around Europe with me," Miriam stated with a tight smile. "I'm leaving her here with you."

"With me!?" Nicholas sputtered.

"Yes, you." She turned to her daughter who looked at Nicholas as if at any second he might lop off her head. "Charlotte, darling, come to Mother."

"Miriam," Nicholas warned, his voice like steel.

Ignoring him, Miriam pulled her young daughter into the room. The little girl looked like a miniature of her mother, though softer, her innocence still intact.

"Charlotte, my pet. Weren't you just telling me how much you love your Uncle Nicholas?"

The child looked confused, as if she had never heard of an Uncle Nicholas before. And rightfully so, Nicholas conceded. In the six years of her young life, he had been consumed with the single-minded purpose of bringing Harry Dillard down.

"Don't be shy, Charlotte." Miriam's voice was suddenly sharp. "Say hello to your uncle."

As if it took every ounce of courage she possessed, Charlotte raised her chin until her head tilted back and she looked him in the eye. "Hello, sir," she whispered, her tiny voice filled with a forced bravado that made Nicholas feel strange inside.

But more than that, somehow, something seemed wrong. Nicholas didn't know if it was the smudges of dark crescent moons beneath little Charlotte's deep violet eyes as if she were tired, or if it was the look of terror on her face that made his chest suddenly tighten. Either way, he knew one thing for certain. He had no business taking care of a child.

"Charlotte," he began, gesturing for his secretary to come forward. "Why don't you go wait with Jane. I'm sure she'll let you sit at her desk if you ask, maybe even talk on the new telephone. I'd like to speak to your mother." He glanced at Miriam. "Alone."

"No time." Miriam leaned down and kissed the air on the side of her daughter's cheek. "I've got to get to the ship."

"Miriam!" he barked. "You can't just leave a child in my care!"

"Mr. Drake! Mr. Drake! I got it!"

Nicholas, Miriam, Jane, and even little Charlotte turned with a start to the door. There, out of breath, stood Bert, Nicholas's assistant, the few remaining hairs on his overly large head plastered down with sweat despite the cool spring temperatures.

"I have it," Bert breathed heavily. "I have it all arranged."

"All of it?" Nicholas asked, momentarily forgetting his sister and his niece.

"Well, almost all of it."

Nicholas tensed. "What do you mean, almost all of it?"

"Apparently there is one piece of property in Dillard's section of the block that he didn't own. But I have everything else. Isn't it grand?"

"Grand?" The word sliced through the office.

Bert's buoyancy was instantly checked. "Well, yes, I thought so."

"I must have the entire section, Bert," Nicholas said, his tone unrelenting. "You know that."

The assistant grimaced.

"And where is this remaining house?"

The implication finally sank in and Bert cringed. "Right in the middle of the section."

"How am I supposed to raze the area and build something in its place if there is one lone, shared-wall town house in the way?" Nicholas turned away sharply, looking out into the rapidly darkening landscape without seeing. "Hell!"

"Really, Nicholas," Miriam said, her countenance more teasing than scolding, "not in front of the child."

"I'll deal with you later, Miriam." He turned back to Bert. "What did you find out about that piece of property?"

"Well, let's see." Bert rummaged nervously through his satchel until he found a tablet of paper and consulted his notes. "It looks to me that there hasn't been a transaction on the house in well over twenty years—long before Harry Dillard started buying up the rest of the section." He shook his head. "But the files weren't complete. Papers missing. I've never seen such disarray in all my life. All I could find out for certain is that the house is owned by someone named Eliot Sinclair."

"Never heard of him."

"I don't believe I have either." Bert shifted his weight uncomfortably. "What should I do? I was so excited about everything falling into place that I . . . didn't think."

Nicholas shot his assistant an impatient glare before he considered the dilemma. He had sworn he would raze the buildings Harry Dillard had owned, and build a towering structure over them, something that would forever wipe out all traces of the man. *Then* his revenge would be complete. Finally, after twenty-three years. But now, apparently, one brick town house stood in the way. And while he had nothing against this Eliot Sinclair, whoever he was, Nicholas needed the man's property to once and for all avenge his parents. "Find out everything you can about him. Then go over to the house and meet the man. We'll make him an offer based on what we learn."

"I'll start on it first thing in the morning," Bert said. "But for now we need to get over to the courthouse."

"Congratulations on whatever it is, brother dear," Miriam interrupted. "I'd love to stay and celebrate, but I've got to go. Be a good girl for your Uncle Nicholas," she added to her daughter.

"Miriam!" Nicholas snapped.

"Really, Mr. Drake," Bert interjected apologetically. "We have to hurry. You've got to make it official. The clerk is waiting for us. But it's already after five. He'll leave if we don't get there soon."

"But . . ." Nicholas turned from his assistant to Charlotte, then to Miriam, only to find his office door swinging shut, his sister gone.

"Really, sir. There are others who are probably thinking along the same lines as you. If you don't hurry you might lose it all."

Nicholas nearly growled, but when he saw the terrified look on his niece's tiny face, he uttered a muffled curse aimed in the direction his sister had fled, then lowered himself until he met Charlotte eye to eye. He cleared his throat, not realizing that his furrowed brow, which had intimidated a great many men, was now striking terror in his young niece's heart. "I've got to go back downtown, Charlotte." He pulled his lips back in what he hoped resembled a kindly paternal smile. "When I get back we'll deal with this . . . situation. For now Jane will take care of you." He glanced up at his secretary. "Isn't that right, Jane?"

Jane seemed as surprised as anyone by the turn of events, but quickly regained her composure. "Of course, sir. It would be my pleasure to look after young Charlotte."

With that seemingly accomplished, thinking he had done an adequate job of arranging things and reassuring his frightened niece, Nicholas straightened, grabbed his hat and headed for the door. Perhaps, he thought with an arrogant shrug of his broad shoulders, this child business wasn't so very difficult after all.

Chapter 2

"*Let me paint* you, love. Naked."

The knitting needles Hannah Schurr held in her plump, gently wrinkled hands clicked to a halt. Sitting very still, Hannah stared across the parlor at the white-haired, sixty-five-year-old man who stood in a little nook surrounded by neatly starched lace-covered windows overlooking Sixteenth Street. And all she did was stare. Didn't say a word, couldn't really, for what would she have said? Somehow, simply saying no seemed wholly inadequate.

"How about it, Hannah?" Barnard Webb persisted. "Let me paint you naked. On a huge four-poster bed covered with armloads of daisies. Big yellow daisies." His gray eyes sparkled. "I can see it now. *Woman in Flowers*. It'd be famous. Hanging in the Louvre." Barnard stood in front of his easel, a palette in one hand a paintbrush in the other, a devilish smile playing on his lips.

Hannah snorted. "*Old Woman Past the Flower of Life*, maybe, hanging in some carnival hall, no doubt," she admonished, before forcing her needles back into action. The man never failed to stir her—frequently to a fond memory of desire, but more often to anger. "Go get yourself a young nymph for your paintings, old man."

Barnard scoffed at this. "What do I need with paintings of girls young enough to be my grandchildren." He leaned his tall, straight form casually against the wall, and his smile broadened. "Let's go upstairs. To my room. I'll help you undress."

"Why, you libertine! You're too old for such nonsense."

"The day I'm too old for painting naked ladies is the day they plant me six feet under."

"Mind your manners. Even to speak of such things! You should be ashamed of yourself."

"Is it the planting that bothers you or the painting?"

She shot him a censorious glare. "Both."

Barnard only laughed. "Have you always been such a prim and proper little prude, Hannah, or did it come to you late in life?"

"I'm a lady, Barnard Webb, and I'll thank you not to forget it," she snapped, forcing her attention back to her knitting. "Though I suspect you wouldn't recognize a true lady even if she jumped up and bit you in the face."

His laughter rumbled through the room. "Such a ball of fire you are. If you'd let me paint you, naked that is, I'd capture that fire. It'd be beautiful. You'd like it, Hannah love."

Glancing over the rim of her gold spectacles with a raised brow, she said, "What I'd like is for you to keep that mouth of yours shut and leave me in peace, unless, of course, you mean that love business and there's a proposal ready to slip from your lips."

His boisterous laughter rumbled to a halt, and the deep lines in his face from long years in the sun deepened even more. "There you go again. Ruining everything." He pushed away from the wall with a disgruntled scowl, and turned back to his easel. "Marriage, bah! I'm too damn old for marriage."

"A minute ago you weren't too old for anything."

"Leave me in peace, woman," Barnard groused. "I've got work to do."

"Fine. Sulk all you like. But you know I'm right, Barnard. We should marry." Her voice softened. "I'd take care of you when you truly get too old."

"I'm already old! Don't you think I know that!" he nearly shouted, throwing his brush down onto the palette, splattering paint. "My body reminds me of that fact every day. I don't need you pointing it out with your attempts to get your claws into me." He turned away, muttering. "Besides, I don't have time to marry. My son is coming for me! To take me to live with his family in Ohio. Dogs and children. Family! Do you hear me, Hannah Schurr?" he demanded, his craggy countenance furrowed with raw emotion as he looked not at Hannah, but off into the distance as if he could see all the way to that state so far away. "Once and for all, do you hear me?"

"Yes, I hear you, as does everyone else within half a mile of here."

"Including me."

Barnard and Hannah turned with a start. "Ellie," they gasped in unison.

"What are you two fighting about this time?" Ellie asked as she pulled her latest creation of bows and fine netting from her head, and set it down on the smooth oak table with ball and claw pedestal.

"Arguing," Hannah clarified. "We're only arguing, dear, not fighting."

"Damn it, woman," Barnard barked, "call a spade a spade. *You* were fighting."

"Me?!"

"Yes, you. Before long, no doubt, you'll be resorting to sharp left hooks," he added with a contentious snort.

"Maybe that would knock some sense into that thick skull of yours, old man!"

Barnard raised his eyebrows at this and cocked his head ever so slightly as if he couldn't believe what he had heard. "She's a mean one, Ellie. I don't know why you took her in."

"A better question," Hannah interjected, "is why she took *you* in, you licentious old goat."

His disbelief fled and was replaced with anger. "She did not take—"

"Enough, enough," Ellie called, her hands extended like a referee. "Fighting, arguing, it's all the same. He obviously still won't marry you."

Hannah snorted much as Barnard had before. "Marry me? No. But the old goat wanted to paint me, I tell you— naked!"

Ellie turned with a surprised start to look at Barnard. "You asked Hannah to pose naked?"

"Well . . ." he hedged.

Hannah shot Barnard a triumphant glare over Ellie's shoulder which he would have returned had he not been under his dear Ellie's scrutiny. Instead, he offered his landlord an innocent smile, waiting to direct his wrath at Hannah Schurr for later. Perhaps he'd bang his ceiling with a broom handle throughout the night. That always drove the woman crazy since her room in Ellie's boardinghouse was directly above his. He nearly smiled in anticipation but caught himself just in time.

Hannah leaned forward. "Naked as the day I was born, is what he wanted. In a bed of flowers, at that. Who does he think he is? A painter?"

At this Hannah laughed, great whooping gales of laughter that wiped even the memory of Barnard's smile from his mind.

"Hannah," Ellie warned. "Let me deal with Barnard."

"Now, Ellie, love. I was just having a bit of fun with her is all," Barnard offered with a shrug of his still-broad shoulders. He had been a sailor in his younger days, sailing around the world to nearly every port of call.

"Then have your fun in another way," Ellie stated dryly. "Checkers, chess, even poker is preferable. I'll not have you asking Hannah to pose naked in my house."

"You tell him, Ellie."

Barnard's angelic face crystallized with anger. "Mind your own business, old woman."

And suddenly they were at it again. Ellie winced and shook her head. It was days like this that she thought she just might throw them both out. But of course she never would. She loved them as much as they loved her. And they didn't fight all the time. Just most of it, she conceded with a resigned smile.

She started to ask where Jim was. Even though her only other boarder was twenty-one years old, five years Ellie's junior, he was more child than man, and she worried about him. He had lived in Ellie's house since she had moved in, occupying the room next to Barnard's on the second floor. But before she could utter a word, someone knocked on the door.

The small household rarely received visitors. Rarely, that is, before the recent, repeated visits of a persistent little man named Bert who had been trying to buy her house in the two weeks since the trial.

Each time the man had come Barnard had answered the door, telling him the owner was neither in nor interested in his offer. One of these days Ellie knew she would have to face the man herself. But she would put it off as long as possible on the outside chance he might give up. But this day, as she began to turn away, to escape upstairs, her eyes grazed the murky glass inset of the front door. Her heartbeat slowed.

The slightly distorted image on the other side of the door was not that of the persistent little man. Her eyes narrowed and she inhaled deeply. While there was no doubt that whoever stood on the other side of the door was male, he was in no way small. This man was tall and looming. Chiseled, even through the glass. Hair dark. Eyes blue. Was it possible?

Though she should have continued on, up the stairs, should have let Barnard answer, Ellie reached out and turned the knob. The door swung open. Bringing her face-to-face with the man. Him. The one from the courthouse.

The sunlight drifted through the doorway, casting his hard, lean form in golden light. He was beautiful really, or so he would have been if his perfectly patrician nose hadn't clearly been broken, perhaps as a child. As it was he seemed darkly handsome, predatory, and certainly not a man to toy with.

Ellie told herself to turn away, to race up the stairs and let Barnard deal with him. Instead, she stood very still, then offered him a beautiful smile.

"It's you," the man said without preamble, surprise gentling the forbidding darkness of his face.

Ellie's smile faltered.

"I mean, I saw you at the courthouse. I tried to—" But then, as suddenly as he began, he cut himself off.

Ellie watched, amazed by the transformation that occurred before her very eyes. One minute, as if caught off guard, he seemed approachable, kind. But in the next, as if a curtain had fallen to obscure any emotion, his face once again became a hard, implacable mask.

The change snapped her thoughts into place. Red seared her cheeks. This was not a man who had come to call, not that she would have allowed it, she chided herself quickly. Clearly he had not even expected to find her there. He obviously wanted something else. She thought of the only other visitor they'd had of late, and her mouth went dry.

Barnard came up behind her then. "What do you want?" he asked, his tone gruff.

The stranger raised one dark brow. "I'm here to see Eliot Sinclair."

"Well, you're wasting your time." Barnard started to step around Ellie and shut the door.

"I'm Eliot Sinclair," she said.

Barnard groaned and the man in the doorway was yet again caught off guard.

"But you're a woman!" His implacable mask slipped slightly.

Barnard shook his head and made a noise that sounded suspiciously like a snort of disgust. "For all your fancy looks, mister, it doesn't appear that you have a brain in your head. Of course she's a woman! Ain't you ever seen one before?"

At this Barnard chuckled, seemingly pleased with his humor. But neither the man nor Ellie paid him any mind, only stared across the threshold, their eyes locked.

"A woman," the man whispered.

Hannah stepped forward. "Maybe he's feebleminded," she said to no one in particular as she eyed the visitor.

With that the man seemed to snap out of his stupor. "I'm sorry," he apologized. "I was just surprised. I hadn't thought . . ." He shook his head. "Well, no matter what I thought." He straightened formally. "I'm Nicholas Drake."

Nicholas Drake.

Ellie's racing heart froze in her chest as the simple words slashed through her mind.

Nicholas Drake.

It was all she could do to remain calm, much less standing. The man who had destroyed her father was here. In the doorway.

Looking for her.

Lord have mercy, the man she had seen from the gallery, the man who had plagued her dreams, was here. Did he know who she was? she wondered, her throat tightening. But then she forced herself to be calm as she reasoned that surely he didn't know. Her father had promised, made her promise.

"Miss Sinclair?" Nicholas broke into her thoughts. "It is Miss isn't it?"

"Why do you want to know?" Barnard snapped.

"Yes, it's Miss," Ellie said without thinking, her mind racing with myriad plans for how to deal with this unexpected situation.

Barnard groaned again. "Your mouth is running like a spigot, girl. Don't be telling this man such things. You have no idea why he's here."

Nicholas glanced at Barnard briefly. "He's right, you know," he said to Ellie, his dark countenance intense, somehow protective. "You really should be careful of what you say to . . . people you don't know."

The words surprised everyone in the room, including Nicholas Drake it seemed. His brow furrowed and his jaw tightened.

"Miss Sinclair," he said firmly, "I'm here about your house. I realize my assistant has been here quite a few times—"

"And we've told him what he can do with his offers," Barnard interjected with an emphatic nod of his head.

Nicholas gave Barnard a brief, dry look. "So you have." He turned back to Ellie. "I've come myself today because I felt certain Bert had not made it clear what a generous offer I am making you."

"Offer, schmoffer!" Barnard exclaimed. "We don't want to move. Don't you understand English, boy?"

Ellie watched, transfixed as the muscles in Nicholas's jaw worked. She was certain it had been a great many years since this dark, forbidding man had been called anything but sir, much less boy. If her heart hadn't been pounding so fiercely, she might actually have laughed at the look on his face. "Mr. Drake—"

"Look everyone! Look! Look what I found!"

Jim Angelo burst into the house, holding the hand of a tiny little girl dressed in a cloud of pink tulle and lace.

Silence reigned for one paralyzed moment before Ellie gasped, forgetting the house, the man, and the fact that he had been the downfall of her father. "Good God, Jim! Who is that?"

"I found her! A little girl!" The giant man who acted more the child than adult turned to the little girl. "Say something, please!"

"Release her." Nicholas's voice suddenly snaked through the foyer with a deadly hiss.

Jim turned to Nicholas with innocent eyes curious. "Who are you?"

Just then an older woman puffed through the doorway, her face red from exertion. "I'm so sorry, sir," she mumbled nervously to Nicholas who had pulled the little girl away from Jim. "One minute he was talking to her real nice like, then the next he was pulling her up the stairs into the house."

Ellie looked on. The little girl stood next to Nicholas, and Ellie couldn't tell if the child was overwhelmed by the proceedings or if she was simply intimidated by Nicholas. Regardless, one thing Ellie knew for certain, this child was not well. Ellie took in the dark half-moon circles beneath her eyes and the much too pale shade of her skin. Though perhaps, Ellie reasoned, she was simply tired.

When Jim took a step closer to the child, Nicholas moved forward protectively. Ellie had the fleeting thought that this man would protect those he loved to the death. She hated to think about the poor soul who would be on the receiving end of such wrath.

"Stand back," he stated, bringing Jim's clumsy steps to a halt.

"No need to get nasty," Barnard retorted. "Jim here wouldn't hurt a fly."

Nicholas didn't look as if he agreed.

"Is she your daughter?" Hannah asked, with a smile for the young one.

"No," he said tightly at length. "My niece."

Not a daughter, but a niece, Ellie thought unexpectedly.

Without thinking, she came to kneel before the little girl with a calm caring that she had long ago accepted would never be directed toward a child of her own. "Hello," she said, her voice soft and kind, infinitely patient. "My name is Ellie. What's yours?"

The little girl stood shyly, her chin tucked close, her tiny hands clasped tightly. "Charlotte," she whispered.

"Such a beautiful name," Ellie said, smiling. "I always wished I had such a beautiful name as yours."

"But yours is pretty, too." The words were offered hesitantly.

"Well, yes. Ellie is pretty enough. But my real name is Eliot," she offered with a knowing look.

Charlotte looked confused.

"Yes, a man's name," Ellie confirmed.

"Why do you have a man's name?"

Ellie's green eyes widened momentarily then darkened, and she wished she had never started down this path, couldn't fathom why she had. But something about this little girl, this dark-headed little angel cried out to her. Ellie forced a laugh. "Who knows? And just now, who cares? How would you like some tea?"

But when little Charlotte looked up in question at her uncle, Ellie nearly cursed. She had forgotten all about the man. And while she would love to have tea with his niece, the last thing she wanted was to have tea with him. For many reasons.

"How silly of me," Ellie said, pushing up from the floor. "Your uncle is most certainly a busy man. We'll have tea another day, Charlotte."

"I think tea sounds fine," Nicholas interjected smoothly, with a smile that said he knew exactly what Ellie was thinking. "Charlotte and I were just on our way to have tea ourselves. We'd love to stay."

Ellie watched as Charlotte's face brightened. At any moment, she thought, the child might actually smile. How could Ellie refuse? She couldn't. She'd have to brazen out the unsettling situation, she added silently with a grumbled curse beneath her breath.

"What was that?" Nicholas asked with an unexpected, teasing half-smile and a raised eyebrow.

Ellie returned his smile, if bared teeth could be called a

smile. She would serve tea to this sweet little girl, ignore her uncle, then send them on their way just as quickly as was humanly possible.

Jim came forward then and reached out his hand to Charlotte. "Come sit next to me."

Nicholas's hard gaze came down on Jim's head and he started to speak, but Ellie cut him off. "He won't hurt her, Mr. Drake. Truly he won't."

Nicholas glanced at Jim and Ellie, then finally at his niece, before he gave a brisk nod of his head.

Charlotte went to Jim willingly, easily, and for a second Ellie would have sworn that a glimmer of pain swept across this hard man's face. But then it was gone and Nicholas turned to Ellie. They stood for a time, much as they had that day in the courtroom, their eyes locked, making her forget everything—glimmers of pain, who she was, who he was—for a moment. Though only for a moment.

Sharply, Ellie turned away and showed her guests into the sitting room across the foyer from the parlor. Hannah went down to the kitchen to prepare the tea. After a slight hesitation, Nicholas followed, only to stop just inside the door.

"M. M. Jay," he said, his voice laced with sudden interest as he took up *The New York Times* which lay folded open to an article on page three.

Ellie looked back at him, her porcelain features marked with sudden confusion.

"M. M. Jay," he repeated, holding up the newspaper. "The artist. What do you think of Able Smythe's latest article on the man?"

She glanced heatedly at Barnard, then said, "I haven't read it," before she continued on into the room.

"Actually, they say he has some talent," Nicholas added, following Ellie. "Controversial, I hear, but promising. Nevertheless, Smythe seems to be quite intrigued by the artist."

Ellie sat on a tufted divan. "Really?" she said, as she smoothed her skirt.

Nicholas sat across from her in a winged back chair. He shook his head and smiled. "I wonder if they'll ever learn who this Jay fellow really is?"

Barnard smiled. "There are those who say *I* am M. M. Jay."

Just then Hannah walked into the room with a tray held in her hands. "Bah! Don't believe a word he says, Mr. Drake. This old goat couldn't paint a three-inch square of plaster wall white to save his life! Daisies indeed."

"Why you old—"

"Barnard!" Ellie stated with a meaningful look. "Please. We have guests."

After casting a scathing glare at Hannah, Barnard merely muttered beneath his breath, then folded his long form down onto the divan.

"Now," Ellie said, "for our tea."

With the tray set before her, Ellie served tea with a swiftness that had heads bobbing back and forth as they tried to watch.

"In a hurry, Miss Sinclair?" Nicholas asked, his cool eyes gleaming faintly.

His goading question and amused grin made Ellie want to toss the tea in his face. But that would have taken an extra few minutes, not to mention the time it would take to clean him up. And more than anything else, Ellie wanted him out of her house. He made her feel things she didn't understand, things she didn't want to feel, when she should feel nothing but hatred. It didn't matter that she had known for years that her father needed to be brought down. He was her father— whether he had acknowledged it publicly or not. And Nicholas Drake was the man who had destroyed him.

"Me? Hurrying? Whatever gave you that idea?" she asked with feigned innocence as she gave two brisk stirs to her own cup, then tossed back her hot tea like a sailor in a tawdry saloon.

Hannah, Jim, and Charlotte looked on with mouths agape. Even Barnard clattered his cup in its saucer. But

Nicholas merely gazed at her with a look so terrifyingly calm and considering that it made her want to work all the faster to see the back side of him just as the front door was slamming shut.

"There we go," Ellie chimed, delicately blotting her lips with a fine linen napkin. "All done." She stood abruptly, reaching out to gather cups and saucers that were still brimming with tea.

"Miss Sinclair," Nicholas interjected chillingly, what had remained of his humor gone as she swept his cup away. "About the house."

"There is nothing more to talk about, Mr. Drake. As Barnard said, I'm not interested in selling."

Nicholas's sudden smile didn't reach his eyes. "You must not understand—"

"I understand perfectly. You want to buy my house. I don't want to sell," she replied, as if she spoke to someone who dealt from a deck that was a few cards shy of being full.

"But I'm offering you a fortune!"

"A fortune to you perhaps. But not to me."

Clearly frustrated, Nicholas ran his hand through his dark hair, leaving ridges where his fingers had passed. "At least think about it—"

"No, Mr. Drake." She straightened, tray in hand. "I'm not interested in selling my house, not for any amount of money."

The muscles in Nicholas's jaw began to work. "I have never met a more . . . stubborn woman in my life."

"Stubborn? You say I'm stubborn just because I won't sell you my house?"

"Yes," he ground out. "Stubborn. And I might have added foolish, since that is just what you are being. Foolish. I'm offering you a great deal of money, Miss Sinclair. Much more than this house is worth. An amount that any man in his right mind would grab in a heartbeat. A man, Miss Sinclair, would accept my offer. You should be married. To someone with the modicum of intellect it would take to recognize what an extraordinary offer I am making you."

Ellie's cheeks flashed red with outrage. "Modicum of— Why you—" She visibly tried to calm herself, then said, "Don't hold your breath, Mr. Drake. It's me or no one that you'll have to deal with, because I'll never marry."

"Never marry," he scoffed. "Every woman wants to marry. You included, no doubt."

At this the red receded from her cheeks, and a mischievous smile sparkled in the depths of her emerald eyes. "True, I'd marry. A knight in shining armor who'd build me a silver castle by the sea."

Nicholas's brow furrowed as if trying to make sense of her words. "You've been reading too many dime novels, Miss Sinclair. America, in the latter part of this century, is sadly lacking in knights who do anything, much less build castles by the sea."

"My point exactly."

"Which is?"

"I'll never marry," she quipped obstinately.

Nicholas stared at Ellie without speaking. After a moment, his jaw tight with frustration, he stood, gathered Charlotte and her nanny, then strode toward the door. But just when Ellie thought she was done with the man, he turned back and met her eye.

"Don't think this is over, Eliot Sinclair. I want your house."

He left it at that, but his meaning was clear. A shiver of foreboding raced down Ellie's spine as he slammed out the front door. She couldn't afford to have Nicholas Drake, or anyone else for that matter, prying into her life, not in a world where being a criminal's daughter was bad enough, but to be illegitimate—she shuddered to think of the consequences. Maybe she should sell. But as she looked around her she couldn't imagine how she could possibly part with the first thing in her life that she had ever owned. The only gift her father had ever given her. But more importantly, in order to sell, documents long thought lost and hopefully forgotten would have to be revealed—one document in particular that tied her to Harry Dillard as clearly as anything could. The deed. So in the end, she knew, had always known, that she could never sell her house. Even if she wanted to. This house, like so many things in her life, was both a blessing and a curse.

"Well," she stated, foraging for a reassuring smile for her boarders as she set the tray aside. "I think I handled that rather nicely, don't you?"

Barnard grimaced, but didn't respond.

"I think I'll just go upstairs now," she said, overly cheerful, before she quickly took the stairs, up and around, to the fourth floor—her floor. Not until she had shut the door behind her did she sigh, pressing her back against the hard plank, thankful to be alone—in her sanctuary at the top of the world.

The ceiling was high, the walls painted white, with lots of windows to let in the sun. Minutes ticked by before she finally pushed herself away from the door and went to a folding screen that separated a corner from the large room.

Taking a deep, calming breath, Ellie moved the screen back, then climbed up onto a stool that sat in a stream of light, warm and comforting. At length she closed her eyes, searching her mind. Slowly, thoughts of houses and fathers, handsome men and little nieces faded away, freeing her mind.

And then she began to paint.

Chapter 3

Obsession. *Like talons* of disquiet clutching at his soul.

Nicholas stood at the dining room window, his deep blue eyes narrowed against the rising sun. Was he obsessed with Eliot Sinclair? he wondered as he had been wondering for the last six weeks. He had been obsessed with Harry Dillard since he was twelve years old—since he had been betrayed. He admitted that. Easily. Freely. But obsessed with a woman named Eliot Sinclair?

He thought about her constantly. She filled his mind, making room for little else. She was too bold, and much too headstrong for his tastes. But still he thought about her at every turn. He had always believed in *Will. Will it and it shall be*. But his Will, it appeared, had little effect when dealing with this odd woman with a man's name. Did he desire her because his Will had been thwarted? Because he couldn't obtain her house? He doubted it was that simple.

He drew a deep breath, then turned away from the window, breaking off his thoughts, once again containing himself forcibly within the parameters which he had defined for himself so many years ago.

His footsteps echoed against the hardwood floor until he reached the finely woven Aubusson carpet. The long expanse of mahogany dining table was set for two, as it had been since the arrival of his niece, who, in that moment, he found peeking out from around the fluted doorway. Her head was tilted and her long ringlet curls hung away from her heart-shaped face. Her violet eyes shone brightly against her translucent skin, and a tentative smile curved on her bow-shaped lips.

Though the table had been set for two every morning, she rarely joined him. As a result, he had seen little of the child in the weeks she had been living in his house. But he had noticed a change in her. She seemed more at ease. Her cheeks seemed rosier, and he would have sworn the half-moon circles beneath her eyes had begun to fade. She smiled more often, and he had even heard her laugh when she was upstairs in the playroom he'd had built, and had Miss Shamworthy fill with toys. Unfamiliar toys for an unexpected niece. He shook his head in wonder.

Today, as always when he found himself in her company, he was at a loss for words. What did one say to a child when not giving gifts or providing instructions?

"Good morning," he offered.

Seemingly encouraged, she straightened and revealed the rest of herself with a quiet graciousness fit for someone far older. "Good morning, Mr. Drake."

Mr. Drake, still. Not Uncle Nicholas, or uncle, or even simply Nicholas. But he couldn't quite bring himself to ask her to call him anything else.

With common courtesies exchanged, they came to an impasse, both growing silent once again.

"Well," Nicholas said, clearing his throat as he accepted a cup of coffee from Lucy, the serving maid. "Have you eaten, Charlotte?"

"No." Nothing more.

"Would you like to eat?"

Charlotte raised up on tiptoes and glanced from Nicholas to the long line of breakfast possibilities spread out on the sideboard. Her lips screwed up as she took in the sight of scrambled eggs, ham, and porridge. "Just a cup of coffee, please."

"Coffee?!"

Charlotte came further into the room and headed for a chair. "Yes, please. With a little cream and sugar, perhaps."

As if she were sixty rather than six.

Lucy started to pour another cup.

"Not on your life," Nicholas stated, bringing his own cup down with a clatter. "You can't drink coffee."

Charlotte's eyes widened. "Why ever not?"

After an unsettled moment, he simply said, "Because."

"Because why?"

Nicholas scowled and considered the little girl before saying, "Because you're too young to be drinking coffee."

"Mother doesn't think so."

Nicholas set his cup and saucer down on the table, then pulled out a chair for his niece, and instructed Lucy to bring a plate of food and a glass of milk. "Your mother rarely thinks."

Charlotte grimaced. "I don't especially care for milk, thank you."

"Nonsense. Milk is good for you. And some eggs, a few slices of ham and a bowl of porridge." He ignored her heavy sigh.

After a moment, she glanced up at him. "I had a letter from Mother yesterday." She pulled the missive out of an oversized pocket in her deep blue dress.

"Really," he offered dryly. "How is my dear sister?"

"Fine, I suppose," she replied, smoothing the paper out against the linen tablecloth with her tiny hands. "Busy, it seems."

"If I know my sister, she's busy with galas and luncheons, and other frivolous affairs."

"Glittering galas and grand luncheons," she clarified dreamily, "where everyone drinks coffee."

Nicholas eyed his niece and wondered if she was trying to make some kind of a point. "No doubt they are drinking more champagne than coffee. Next you'll be asking for a fine bottle of Dom Pérignon for lunch?"

At this she giggled, surprising Nicholas. But then she grew serious and dreamy once again. "And they'll dance, my mother and father. My mother is a wonderful dancer. Waltzes, minuets." She looked at Nicholas with great seriousness. "Have you ever seen my father dance?"

"Can't say that I have. And if he does, he certainly doesn't dance with your mother," he stated without thinking, as he snapped open the morning paper.

"What do you mean?"

He failed to notice that her smooth brow wrinkled, or that her violet eyes were both accusing and concerned. "Nothing, Charlotte. I meant nothing," he replied, turning his attention finally, firmly, to the newspaper.

His office was quiet an hour later when he arrived. A vague feeling of guilt had plagued him the whole way there. Charlotte had slipped out of the dining room much too quietly after his remark about her parents. But he had a business to run. Papers to sign. Plans to make. Buildings to build. Those were the things he knew about, he reasoned. He didn't know anything about children, he added just as he sat down in the soft leather chair behind his desk. And quite frankly he had no interest in learning. Besides, Miss Shamworthy came highly recommended as a nanny, it was the woman's job to see to his niece's needs. Nicholas didn't have time to take care of a child—he still had too much to do until he could put Harry Dillard behind him. Once and for all. So he could get on with his life.

Nicholas had considered before how his life was at a standstill, moving neither forward or even back while he pursued Harry Dillard. Twenty-three years of single-mindedness and determination had allowed him to lose sight of moving on. Sometimes he wondered if he knew how. But those ruminations came rarely, and when they did, not for long. He had learned how to block them out—lock them away. He had willed himself to forget. But there were times when he wondered if the forgetfulness hadn't had a price.

With a sigh, he forced the thoughts away, just as he always did, and turned his mind to more important matters. Eliot Sinclair and her house.

In his attempt to gain the one remaining property in the section he was determined to have, since the day they'd had *tea*, Nicholas had returned to the woman's home at least a half dozen times.

Each time that he arrived at her house, always uninvited, barely tolerated, he was greeted by the entire household. Barnard belligerent and demanding. Hannah talking ceaselessly. Jim wanting to see Charlotte.

And of course there was Eliot. Ellie. Always Ellie.

Bert had spent hours digging into Eliot Sinclair's past, finding out little more than the fact that in addition to owning the town house on Sixteenth Street, she had a milliner's shop a few blocks away on Broadway.

At present, Hannah appeared to pay her way by working with Ellie at the shop, Jim by making the deliveries, while Barnard cooked and took care of the house. Nicholas shook his head. That afternoon he planned to return to her house. And this time, by God, he wouldn't be turned away empty-handed.

"Make love to me, old woman."

Hannah glanced up from the book she was reading in her favorite needlepoint chair. "Not in this lifetime, you old goat, unless you're ready to get down on your knee and pop the question."

"I'll pop you a question," Barnard muttered, thrusting his hands deep into the pockets of his baggy gray pants. "How many times do I have to tell you I'm not getting married?"

"One of these days I'm going to believe you, and mark my words Barnard Webb, you'll be sorry then."

"The only thing I'll be sorry about is that you didn't believe me sooner!" But then he took a deep, calming breath, his clear gray eyes boring into her. "I've told you," he stated with tight control. "I'm not getting married. My son is coming for me."

Hannah heaved a long, heavy sigh, her head tilting to the side. "Oh, Barnard dear, when are you going to accept the fact that your son isn't coming for you, not today, not tomorrow, not anytime in the future."

"You don't know what you're talking about!" The words were angry, defensive.

"Of course I do. You've told me yourself you hardly know the boy."

"He's not a boy! He's a man! And I don't hardly know him 'cause I was workin', workin' hard, all my life, trying to make a livin'."

"You were sailing, Barnard," she clarified ruthlessly. "A hand-for-hire wherever you could get work. Running. Escaping a man's responsibilities to his family. Don't you think your son knows that?"

"That's not true! He doesn't think that!"

"You can lie to me all you like. But quit lying to yourself. You were a worthless father and your son knew it. Good Lord, Barnard, how many letters have you written to that boy of yours? I'd venture to say you've written hundreds to Martin just since I've known you. And how many replies have you received?"

Barnard's face went red.

"How many, Barnard?" she persisted, unwilling to let it go.

But Barnard merely turned and started away.

"Zero, zilch," she continued unmercifully, bringing his steps to a halt. "The boy doesn't want a thing to do with you. And the sooner you realize that the better."

"You're lying!" he bellowed into the room, as he swung back in a rage. "I'm his father! He loves me!"

"What's wrong, Hannah?"

Jim had come up from the kitchen and stood in the doorway unnoticed. "What's wrong?" he repeated, his rough-hewn features furrowed with concern. "Hannah? Barnard? Tell me what's wrong."

But Hannah and Barnard didn't notice. They railed at one another, oblivious to the distress of this sensitive man who didn't understand what was wrong and imagined the worst, as he sank down onto the bottom step of the stairs that led to the upper floors.

The clatter of hooves on the cobbled street echoed against the solid walls of house fronts as Nicholas stood before the oval inset of glass in the oak door on Sixteenth Street. When he turned the small brass knob that rang the bell inside, no one answered. After a moment the carriages cleared, the echoing din receding in the distance. And then he heard it. Loud voices raised in anger.

He knocked this time, hard, to no avail. Without thinking, he turned the doorknob, muttering a curse that indeed it was unlocked, then stepped inside.

"Excuse me," he said, first once, then louder, trying to gain the fighting couple's attention.

"Hello," he called, the late afternoon sun casting golden light in behind him, turning his hard chiseled form into a dark silhouette.

Barnard whirled around to the door midsentence, his craggy face distorted with anger. But at the sight that met his eyes, he stopped, his mouth left open, his words left unspoken. The red in his face drained away, and tears suddenly pooled in his eyes. "Martin," he breathed.

Nicholas stood nonplussed. Barnard took a step closer, only to stop, hesitant. "You came," he whispered.

But then Nicholas cleared his throat and stepped further into the room, shutting the door behind him.

"Mr. Drake!" Hannah called out loudly.

Barnard sucked in his breath, his nostrils flaring, his face ravaged, tears spilling over to stream down his withered cheeks.

"Is something wrong here?" Nicholas asked.

"No, no. Well, maybe a little." Hannah went to Barnard who had gone to the nook in the corner.

Nicholas could only watch, unsettled. Barnard was clearly upset, cursing Hannah who was trying to console him, for reasons that escaped Nicholas. The giant, Jim, sat on the bottom step crying like a young child. Nicholas was at a loss for what to do. Slip back out the front door? Demand explanations? Somehow, neither seemed appropriate.

First Charlotte, now this less-than-clear domestic situation which he'd had the misfortune to step into. But he was saved from having to do anything when Ellie entered through the front door. For a moment, unexplained shouting and a grown man's tears were forgotten. Nicholas could only stare. It was always that way when he first saw her. A strange tightening in his chest. An awareness that shimmered through his body.

She stood in the doorway, tall, proud, brave. As always, headstrong. And more beautiful than words. As usual, she wore a green dress that on most any other woman would have been plain. On Eliot Sinclair it was soft and graceful, accentuating rather than detracting from the fine curves of her form. And a hat. *Good Lord, her hats,* he thought with amused dismay.

"Ellie," he said softly, his eyes narrowing against the unwanted emotion.

But if Ellie noticed his tone, or even him it seemed, she didn't let on. She took in her surroundings—Barnard, Hannah, Jim—then for the first time she turned, very slowly, to Nicholas.

"What have you done now?" she demanded, her fists planted firmly on her hips.

Nicholas stiffened, his dark countenance darkening even more. "Your assumptions, I'm afraid, are ill-founded, Miss Sinclair. I didn't do anything."

"Sure you didn't," she said, her tone accusing. "No doubt you barged in here with your persistent offers followed by your threats."

"I've never threatened anyone." Nicholas's jaw set.

"And I'm the Queen of England."

"Are you calling me a liar, Miss Sinclair?" His look was meant to intimidate.

Ellie merely provided him with an extremely unladylike snort in response. "If you didn't, then why is Barnard upset?"

Nicholas glanced over at Barnard, feeling an unaccustomed need to defend himself. "For a second, he seemed to think I was somebody else. Someone named Martin."

Ellie groaned, then pulled off her hat, turned on her heel and headed for the little nook.

Nicholas watched as Ellie soothed Barnard and pacified Hannah, before convincing them it was a beautiful evening for a walk. Then she went to Jim who sniffled on the bottom step. She lowered herself next to the man with no apparent thought for her gown. She wrapped her arm around his shoulders as far as she could manage, then pulled him close.

"It's all right, Jim."

"No it's not. Everyone's mad."

"No one's mad, dear."

"But Barnard was yelling."

"You know how he is. Always hollering about something."

Nicholas looked on, strangely mesmerized. Soothed. As if she spoke to him rather than the others, her soft smile wrapping around his heart.

"He wouldn't be our Barnard if he wasn't yelling," she added kindly. "Can you imagine Barnard not hollering about something?"

Jim looked at Ellie through tear-filled eyes. "Well, no. I guess not." He dragged his shirt sleeve across his eyes. "But still, Ellie, he was *sooo* mad."

Nicholas saw fatigue and frustration suddenly push at her shoulders, as if everything was threatening to crash in on her. Without thinking, Nicholas cleared his throat. "Jim," he began, searching his mind, "I forgot to tell you . . ." Then it came to him. "Charlotte has been asking about you."

"Charlotte. Asking about me?"

"Yes. She wanted me to tell you hello."

Jim's face brightened. "Really?"

"Yes, really," he added, smugly pleased with the result.

"Gosh, do you think she could come over to play?" Jim looked at Ellie. "Can Charlotte come over to play?"

Ellie sat very still, then said, "We'll see. For now, why don't you go find Barnard and Hannah."

"You promise you'll think about it?"

"Of course, Jim," she replied softly.

Jim lumbered up from the step. "You tell Charlotte hello for me, too, Mr. Drake," he said, as he banged the front door shut behind him.

Once they were alone, Ellie turned on Nicholas. "Now look what you've done!"

Nicholas had expected relief, gratitude—maybe even a soft smile. "I'm certainly taking a good deal of blame for causing a fight I had nothing to do with, then doing nothing more than restoring a smile to Jim's face."

"And making him hope for something that's not going to happen!"

One slash of dark brow lifted, making him appear even more strikingly handsome. "Who's to say it won't?"

"I say," Ellie said, her mouth tightening grimly, taking refuge in anger. She wasn't in the mood to be gracious. She didn't like the tremor of excitement that raced down her spine whenever the man was near. Besides which, she was frustrated with Barnard, with Hannah, even with Jim. Moreover, she had hats to make. Bills to pay. And she certainly had no time to deal with the likes of Nicholas Drake. "Why are you here?"

"What?" he asked, his eyes alight with teasing warmth. "No offer of tea and cake? Biscuits at the very least?"

"Your humor, Mr. Drake, escapes me."

"Such a shame. But if it's business you want, then

business you shall have. I'm here to discuss the sale of your house."

"Again?" she asked sarcastically.

"Yes, again. Until you come to your senses."

"Come to my senses?" she demanded, her voice beginning to rise.

"Yes. And from everything I've learned about you I was led to believe that if nothing else, you were a sensible—"

"You've been prying into my life?" Her green eyes narrowed and her breath caught painfully in her chest.

"Researching, Miss Sinclair."

She stared at him long and hard, until finally she asked, "What else have you learned?"

Nicholas studied her, his head tilted in contemplation. "That you opened your milliner's shop seven years ago, that you have no note on your house or your shop." He looked at her, a surprising lightness creeping into his eyes. "And your favorite color is green."

Her head came back. "What are you talking about?"

"Green, as in grass in the summertime, pine trees at Christmas . . . or your eyes—"

"Spare me the poetics, Mr. Drake," she said crossly, despite her blush. "Why in the world would you think I like the color green?"

"Because I've looked around me. Green dress, green wallpaper—"

"The wallpaper is not green," she snapped.

"My apologies," he replied with a teasing bow. "White with green latticework."

Ellie glanced at the wallpaper in question as if seeing it for the first time. "Green isn't my favorite color."

Minutes passed in silence, Ellie looking at the wallpaper, Nicholas looking at her. "Then what is?" he asked quietly.

Her eyes grew dreamy. "Red."

At this, Nicholas laughed out loud. "No. Never red. Not for you."

Whirling around to face him, she demanded, "Who are you to tell me what is or isn't my favorite color?"

"I'm not *telling* you anything. I'm merely remarking on an observation. I've known you long enough to be certain you would never allow yourself to love red." His deep voice softened. "Just as I can tell you're tired."

High spots of color flared to life on her cheeks. Tired. Was she tired? she wondered unexpectedly, turning away. Down to the bone, it seemed. Tired beyond the need to sleep. "I'm fine."

His blue eyes darkened, and lines of emotion suddenly etched his brows. Touching her cheek, he forced her to look at him. "No you're not."

The simple touch. The look in his eyes. She felt a stirring of awareness, but more. Again she felt as if she had known this man for a lifetime. A kinship. A knowing.

The sounds around them seemed to cease. No rattle of carriages out in the street, or bark of a dog in the distance. Just Nicholas, there, strong and solid, like so few things she had known in her life.

Common sense told her there were no two more dissimilar people in the world. He was arrogant, and too pompous by half. Nicholas Drake, undoubtedly, would never find himself caught in the middle of an altercation between two hired hack drivers.

"You've been making too many of those damn frilly hats," he said, his words a caress, "and taking care of too many people besides yourself. I can see it in your eyes."

She bit her lip against his words, caring and unfamiliar. "I'm not going to sell my house, Mr. Drake."

"Good, don't sell."

Ellie eyed him suspiciously. "You don't mean that."

"True enough," he conceded with a soft, devilish smile and a shrug. "But we can discuss that another time." He reached out and took her hand without asking, pulling her up from where she sat on the bottom step. "Come on," he said, dispelling her thoughts. "I'm going to make you some soup."

"You're going to make me soup?" Her look grew incredulous.

"Yes, soup," he added grandly. "Since you're feeling low."

A traitorous smile wavered on her lips. "I think you must be thinking of hot cocoa. Soup is for sick people, Mr. Drake. Chicken soup to be exact."

His smile evaporated and he shook his head, a troubled frown creasing his forehead. "I shouldn't be surprised. I'm not so good at this 'caring for' business."

"Ah," she said, surprising herself by immediately understanding. "I take it things aren't going so well with Charlotte?"

He considered for a moment, then shrugged his broad shoulders, before pulling Ellie down the stairs to the kitchen as he spoke. "Oddly enough, she seems happier now than when she arrived. At least happier when I'm not around."

"What do you mean?"

"I never know how to deal with her. Hell, this morning she wanted coffee!"

"Coffee?" Ellie asked in amused disbelief, disregarding his indelicate language as she pulled to a halt on the staircase.

"Yes, coffee," he muttered. "Can you believe it?"

Ellie remembered the little girl, so sweet and so young, but with a worldliness in her eyes that was well beyond her years. "Actually yes, I can believe it. So let her drink coffee. What can it hurt?"

"A six-year-old child drinking coffee? She needs to be drinking milk and eating porridge."

Porridge.

The word startled Ellie. How long had it been since she thought of porridge, she wondered, her heart suddenly hammering in her chest. "I hate porridge."

She looked away, looked at the green latticework wallpaper without seeing. "Actually what I hate most about porridge is cleaning the bowl. Not the bland taste or the lumps, but the cleaning," she said to no one in particular. What made it stick so? she had wondered so often as a child, taking her turn at the orphanage sink to scrub her dish. "The nuns made us eat every bite."

"Nuns? What nuns?"

She looked up at him with a start, her mind churning as she tried to make sense of her surroundings. It was frequently that way. Even after all these years there were times when she found it hard to believe she no longer lived within those thick, dank walls of the orphanage. It was hard to believe that this house, every inch of which she loved and cherished, was hers. All hers, to share with the people who had become her family.

At length, she forced a laugh. "Nuns who served porridge . . . at school," she equivocated, for indeed the orphanage had been a sort of school. She had learned a great deal there.

With all due haste, she turned away and hurried down the remaining steps to the kitchen. "It's time you should go, Mr. Drake," she called back to him, disconcerted. "Our business is finished. I won't sell you my house . . . and I certainly don't need any soup."

Nicholas merely sauntered down the steps behind her. She could feel his dark blue eyes boring into her as if he could see into her soul. At any second she was certain he would question her. The man was too clever by half. She wouldn't be able to get away with some glib story if he was intent on answers. But she was saved from answering when, after what seemed like a lifetime, he merely said, "To think they say you're sensible."

"I *am* sensible," she laughed, relieved, as she busied herself with a box of market items left on the table. "Sensible enough to send you on your way."

"Too sensible is my guess."

Ellie's hand froze. *Too sensible. Could* he see into her

soul? "Can anyone be too sensible, Mr. Drake?" she asked quietly, looking back at him.

He met her gaze, his dark eyes suddenly fierce. "Before I met you I would have said no."

And just like on that first day he had arrived on her doorstep, she saw his surprise at what he had said. Abruptly, he looked away.

"Where were we?" he said, his tone suddenly gruff. "Soup, I believe."

"No," she replied, forcing the simple word. "You were leaving."

A hint of his smile returned. "Actually, I think I'll make coffee," he continued as if she had said nothing. "That, I know how to make."

"Mr. Drake, really . . ."

A slow, roguish grin broke out across his face. "Yes, I *really* know how to make coffee."

She knew she should be incensed and demand that he leave, but couldn't quite form the words. It had been so long since someone else had tried to care for her. Not that he truly did, she knew. He only wanted her house. But just then that hardly mattered. She wanted to lock reality away. She wanted to feel cherished. Life as make-believe. Without worries.

He began rummaging through her cabinets as if he owned the place. Strong, self-assured, confident, but most of all, at ease. "Where do you keep the coffee?" he asked.

"Really, I think—"

"Found it!" He turned back to her with a flourish and the tin coffee can. "How do you like it? Thick, thin . . . ?"

Despite herself, Ellie couldn't keep her amused grin back. "I didn't realize thick and thin were choices when it came to coffee."

"Ahhh, you never lived with my grandmother. She liked it thick, though I swear she drank it that way only because being so strong it curled her hair." He smiled. "Easier than those hot hair irons you women use."

Ellie gasped, trying not to laugh.

"Yes, thick as molasses she used to like it." He grimaced, searching for a spoon. "I made it for her every day from the time I went to live with her when I was twelve, until I left seven years later."

"You lived with your grandmother?"

His large, strong hand stilled, though only momentarily. "Yes," he said simply, then scooped the already-ground grinds of coffee.

The lightness dissipated, not completely, but enough to remind Ellie that beneath his relaxed exterior there was a carefully restrained power that could be unleashed at any moment. He had smiled and laughed today, but she had learned that Nicholas Drake was a ruthless man. She didn't think there was a person in New York who hadn't heard the tales of his obsessive pursuit of her father. Others had given up long before. But not this man. It was common knowledge that he hated everything about Harry Dillard, and she had no doubt that if he ever found out who she was, this strong, self-assured man would as easily bring her down as he would smile at her and make coffee.

"Now, where are the cups?" he asked, interrupting her thoughts.

She opened her mouth to speak, but what ultimately would have come out she'd never know because just then the kitchen door swung open.

"Ellie!"

She turned with a start. "Charles!"

She could feel Nicholas's gaze grow heated on her, and she sensed as well when he finally turned to the doorway.

Charles Monroe came to a precipitous halt, his blond hair perfectly groomed, his brown eyes lighted by a smile. But as he glanced between Ellie and Nicholas, his smile began to falter. After a moment, he pulled back his shoulders, forced a smile, and stepped over to Nicholas. "Charles Monroe," he said politely, extending his hand.

"Nicholas Drake," he replied, his angular features once

again hard and cold, no trace of the teasing man who had put coffee on to boil.

Charles's eyes widened. "Really? The builder?"

Nicholas gave an impatient nod.

Charles's smile became genuine. "I can't believe it! Everyone's talking about the new building you're going to construct."

Ellie glanced between Charles and Nicholas. "What are you talking about, Charles?"

"A building. Eighteen stories from what I've heard. Any day now he'll be razing the existing properties. Rumor has it that everything is ready to go." He glanced back at Nicholas excitedly. "Where is the building site?"

Nicholas, however, only looked at Ellie. He saw something in her eyes, unguarded, that he didn't like. Panic, yes, but also something deeper. A profound pain that he hated to see. "Ellie," he said, ignoring the other man.

She looked him in the eye, what tiny flash of acquiescence he had seen only moments before replaced by a growing anger.

"I think you should leave," she said to Nicholas, her tone clipped.

Charles's brow creased. "Is something wrong here?"

But Ellie and Nicholas ignored him, only stared at each other. At length, Nicholas broke the gaze. "No, nothing's wrong here. I was just leaving. Miss Sinclair," he added with a crisp nod of his head. "Mr. Monroe."

And then he was gone, up the stairs, the front door closing with finality.

"What was Nicholas Drake doing here?" Charles asked, clearly amazed.

With a start Ellie turned back to him, and could see that he was as intrigued as he was concerned. "Nothing, Charles."

"What do you mean, nothing? How can a man like Nicholas Drake be here for no reason?" He drew himself up. "He has a terrible reputation with women, Ellie. I hope you're not . . ."

Ellie skewered him with a scathing glare. "What, Charles? You hope I'm not what? Swooning at his feet? Melting in his arms? Falling for his notorious charms?"

"Well, I . . . It's just . . ."

"Rest assured, I hate Nicholas Drake. I'm not in the least danger of becoming one in what is no doubt a long line of his conquests." But of course she knew that was not entirely true. For a moment, for one crazy second of insanity, she had wanted the man to stay, to talk, to laugh, to . . . What would have happened had Charles not burst in?

"Then why was he here?"

"Because he wants to buy my house," she stated grimly.

"That's right! Drake is trying to build here, on Sixteenth Street. I can't believe I didn't put it together before. How much is he offering you?" He seemed to pause to consider something, then stated, "As your future husband, I should be dealing with this."

"Charles," she said, as if speaking to a child, "I've told you I'll never marry—you or anyone else."

"That hardly makes sense. You need to marry, Ellie. It's in your best interest. I can protect you," he said importantly. "Protect you from men like Nicholas Drake. How much has he offered you?"

"I think you should leave, Charles."

"I'm only trying to help. You can't possibly know a good offer from a bad one. You haven't signed anything yet, have you?"

"No, Charles. And I'm not going to."

"Good girl, not until I've looked it over. I'll show the offer to Father. Perhaps his solicitor should get involved. This place might not be much, but if Nicholas Drake wants to build here, it's worth something."

"This place," she said tightly, "is not going to be sold."

"Good. Hold out. You'll get more money."

"No, Charles. You don't seem to understand. I'm not selling my home. Now or ever."

"That's ridiculous. From everything I hear, Drake has big

plans. You could make a fair amount on this place, more than it's worth, certainly."

"This isn't about money. It's about the only home I have ever had. A home I love and cherish." A home, ultimately, that she couldn't afford to sell, for reasons she could never tell him.

"You'd buy another house somewhere else."

"You know as well as I do that I can't afford to buy anything of this quality anywhere else in Manhattan."

"Then you could live in a boardinghouse and put the money away." He smiled. "You'd have a little nest egg for when we marry. Money all your own. Money that I would allow you to use as you saw fit."

Her patience was running dangerously short. "I don't want to live in a boardinghouse. And I certainly don't want a nest egg," she snapped unkindly.

"But—"

"No, Charles." She sighed, regretting her harsh tone. "No buts. I'm not selling. Now, I think it's best if you leave."

"I think we should talk about this, Ellie. You're obviously distressed."

Distressed? Distressed! You bet I'm distressed, she nearly squeaked. Suddenly she thought of the red stockings she had begun to wear almost daily. At this point she was ready to hurl the unseemly things into the trash pail for good. What in the world, she wondered dismally, had ever led her to believe they were lucky? Good Lord, she had never had so much rotten luck in all her days.

"Charles, just go. Please."

After a deep, angry sigh, Charles abruptly strode from the room.

Ellie felt no desire to follow him, placate him. She knew she had been unforgivably rude, had insulted him, but she was only glad he was gone—not the sort of emotions a *sensible* woman would feel.

She remembered Nicholas's stinging words. Was she too sensible? Could a woman be too sensible? Unexpectedly, she had the irrational desire to shed tight, restricting Victorian clothes, and pull on a loose-fitting cotton shift. She imagined the feel of the soft fabric brushing across her skin. Like fingers trailing along her shoulder. Never had she longed so to be free, without responsibility, without the need to constantly juggle her life. But most of all, she thought suddenly, she was tired of being sensible.

Chapter 4

Weeks passed and the wide granite slab and cobbled streets of New York began to shimmer with the heat of summer. But on this day the sky overhead was dark. Threatening. Like a cold, blustery day in the dead of winter.

Nicholas walked the streets of Manhattan, his mind spinning dangerously. If he thought about walking, it helped. If he concentrated on first one step then the next, he was able to numb his mind. At least for a short while until he was forced to stop by the warning shout of a dray wagon driver—or when he heard the sound of a young child's laughter.

He had taken Charlotte to the doctor earlier, then had dropped her off at home, and had managed little more than a grim smile when she looked at him with her violet eyes luminous and her tiny voice barely a whisper. "Please don't worry, Mr. Drake. Everything is going to be fine."

A six-year-old child reassuring him.

He swore savagely in memory as he continued on, his head down, hands thrust deep in coat pockets, his hat forgotten back at the house. The ear-shattering noises of the city which normally echoed against the cobbled streets and stone buildings were oddly muffled by the air, heavy with the impending storm. His heart ached in a way he didn't understand. He wanted to lash out, pound his fist against a wall. Anger he understood. This—fear, was it?—he did not. But of course he wouldn't lash out. Countless years of an ironclad control couldn't be washed away like winter-dried leaves on a windswept day, or so he believed. Had to believe.

He was unaware of the first few sprinkles that began to fall. Not until he felt the bite of heavy rain did he think to step into a tile-roofed pavilion. The back wall of the structure held another doorless entrance, the sides lined with large, gaping glass windows. Leaning his shoulder into a post near the front, Nicholas stared out into the rain, out into the cool, desolate day which reflected the feelings he couldn't seem to shake. He pulled a cheroot from the breast pocket of his raincoat, clipped the thick, binding tobacco leaf, then pulled heavily as he held a match to the end.

His father had smoked. The aroma always reminded him of family and home. The early years. Before everything had gone wrong. Nicholas rarely smoked. Very rarely wanted to be reminded.

He had thought that destroying Harry Dillard would finally allow him to get on with his life. Allow his mind to settle. Instead, he had found that suddenly his life was more unsettled than ever. He blamed it on the fact that he had lost what had been the sole focus of his life for the last twenty-three years. Tying up the loose ends of obtaining all the man's property hadn't proved nearly as consuming. But when he allowed a hint of truth to creep into his mind, Nicholas realized that his life was unsettled for two very different reasons. Two very different females. One young, one older. Neither of whom he had any interest in dealing with, but was drawn to nonetheless.

Charlotte and Eliot.

A tiny little girl who stared at him with a look he couldn't define, and a mysterious woman who filled him with a longing he couldn't name.

Ellie.

What did she make him feel? Was it simply her house that drew him to her? Or was it an obsession as he had assumed? Would holding her in his arms, or feeling his lips pressed to hers finally exorcise her from his mind? Would obtaining her home purge the yearning?

The questions continued to plague him. Circling. Madly. Seemingly unanswerable.

He continued to seek her out—with the regularity of a milkman, she had remarked one day, though not nearly as welcome, she had added in her smart, dry voice, tempered with a smile.

Oh God, how she made him laugh—or groan in frustration when yet again he lay awake in the middle of a sleepless night, images of her filling his mind with a kaleidoscope of color. The shell pink of her ears, the nearly white of her hair, the red of her lips—which he longed to nip and lick, regardless of the fact that now that he had gotten to know her, half the time he was convinced he didn't even like her. Sharp tongue, sarcastic retorts. A hard outer shell. But he had seen the cracks. Had unexpectedly felt the softness.

Ellie.

Oh, Ellie. If only you were here now to make me laugh.

An unexpected gasp interrupted his thoughts. With his mind circling, he glanced over his shoulder.

And found her.

She stood in the doorway of the pavilion, her white-blond hair darkened by the rain, her clothes damp, wet in places, as if she had been carrying her wrap and only tried to pull it on after the rain had begun.

"Mr. Drake," she breathed, her porcelain features washed suddenly with what he would have sworn was desire. Desire that matched his own.

The scent of lilacs wrapped around him as he took in her eyes. Of course he had noticed her eyes before, clear and green, but he had never noticed their intensity. Deep and rich, like jewels, the hue shifting to match her moods. Making him want to look, to watch—to wait for however long it took to see them change.

"Miss Sinclair," he responded carefully, sternly maintaining control.

But he forgot about control when she took a deep breath, her breasts rising beneath her open coat. Her rain-splattered chemise was wet, clinging, and a stab of yearning snaked through his body with a severity that made his chest tighten. His brow furrowed, and without thinking he started to reach out, to damn all else and pull her into her arms. As always when he was around her he wanted to touch her, hold her. To find the softness. To find solace in her arms, he thought unexpectedly.

But then she stepped further into the building, closer, and he found that her porcelain features had shifted . . . into a polite blank. That hard outer shell. No softness. He stiffened imperceptibly and dropped his hand away.

"Terrible day to be caught outside," she said, shaking the rain from her hair, no hat in sight.

Her words were spoken without emotion, an inanity one would share with a stranger. A dismissal. Nicholas leaned back against the post and studied her. She was calm, self-possessed, her eyes now an undisturbed sea, making him suspect he had imagined her desire.

In truth, every time he had seen her she had taken great pains to make it clear that she wanted nothing to do with him. There were times even when he was certain she wanted to hate him, though he couldn't imagine why.

Because he was determined to buy her house? Was that reason enough for hate? He doubted it.

He thought of the trial and Harry Dillard, the man who had so callously and indifferently made women his own, then cast them aside like so much rubbish. Nicholas's hand clenched at his side. His throat tightened as it hadn't in so many years—years since he had allowed himself to remember. But remembering didn't do any good. Never had. He concentrated on Ellie instead.

In all of Nicholas's search, he had learned that Harry Dillard had never married. No wife. Or children. No relatives still living that he could find. But he'd had mistresses at every turn. Could this woman have been one of his paramours? Nicholas's mind recoiled at the thought. No. Eliot Sinclair was no man's mistress. No doubt she had been at the courthouse like a hundred others. Curious. Drawn by the downfall of a notorious man.

She pushed damp hair away from her face, seemingly unaware of his scrutiny, or if she was she didn't appear to care.

He cared, and he had no idea why. He shouldn't. Didn't want to. But like that day he had looked up into the courtroom gallery and found her, she made him feel things he didn't understand—things he didn't want to feel, but couldn't seem to control.

He closed his eyes. The anguish he'd felt earlier returned, stronger. The need to lash out. Relentless. Irrational anger mixed with the pain and desolation that pulled at his heart, overwhelming him, making him speak. "Charlotte has consumption."

Then silence, save for the relentless staccato of rain against the roof tiles.

The calm, indifferent sea of her eyes grew stormy, disturbed. "Oh, no," she whispered, her hand stilling.

His heart tightened against the genuine distress and sympathy which only served to confirm the need for both.

"Little Charlotte," she said, disbelief etched across her features as she dropped her hand to her side. "Are you certain?"

"The doctor is," he replied, as he turned away, not wanting her to see his despair.

Ellie shook her head and sighed. "Her parents must be crushed."

Her parents. Gone. Far away. Unwilling to be reached. "Her parents are unaware of her condition."

"No!"

He looked out into the rain-laden sky. "Yes. My sister is off gallivanting about Paris," he said, his voice sharp. "And who knows where that husband of hers is. That's why Charlotte is staying with me. My sister dropped her daughter off at my office in April. I haven't seen or heard from her since."

Ellie shook her head as if in disbelief. "That poor child. To be so ill. Is it possible she might have something else? Maybe it's just a bad case of croup. Or even diphtheria. They are constantly being confused."

He pressed his lips together and didn't answer.

"Or even if it is consumption, isn't there something the doctors can do? They've learned a great deal about the disease in the last several years. Surely there is someone who can help her."

"They say it's some rare form of consumption. And it has progressed too far," he replied, his voice flat.

"Oh, Mr. Drake," she sighed, "I'm so sorry."

"Don't call me that!" he ground out as he looked back at her. "My name is Nicholas, damn it. Why does everyone call me *Mr. Drake?*" His voice softened with pain. "Even Charlotte calls me Mr. Drake. Am I such a tyrant?"

Ellie's eyes filled with sympathy and her full lips pulled into the soft smile he had longed to see weeks before. "No," she said, "I'm sure you're not such a tyrant."

He scoffed at this, angry at the need he heard in his own voice. "How would you know?"

"They say anyone who loves children and animals can't be all bad."

Looking out into the rain, he grumbled, "Who's to say I love either?"

Nicholas could feel her eyes taking him in, as if assessing.

"Because you clearly care very deeply for your niece.

I've seen that today. And no doubt if she wanted a pet you'd find her one and treat it quite well."

The muscles in his jaw worked as he searched for that place in his soul which had no feeling. "She's so young. She deserves life. A long life. She deserves outings and beaux, and one day children of her own. It's unfair. God," he swore, "I've always believed that seemingly insurmountable obstacles could be surmounted with hard work, determination, and perseverance." His eyes narrowed as if a blazing sun raged in the cloud-laden sky. "For the first time in ages I feel nothing but defeat. I'm defeated by a young child's illness."

Ellie sighed and leaned back against the opposite post from Nicholas. "You're only one man, Mr. Dra—Nicholas. You can't solve all the world's ills or even little Charlotte's. And if there is one thing I have learned in my twenty-six years it is that frequently life is more tragedy than comedy— and is certainly not fair."

He turned back to look at her, his eyes troubled. "You're too young to be so cynical."

"You know as well as I do that twenty-six is not so young. And as you pointed out yourself in my kitchen not so long ago, I'm sensible. Not cynical. Just sensible and practical. My world is my world. My place in it set."

Nicholas shook his head. "There you're wrong, Eliot Sinclair. Despite what I feel today, I know anyone *can* achieve whatever they put their minds to. It's a matter of Will and hard work. Most people simply don't want to work that hard." He looked deep into her eyes. "You don't strike me as the kind of person who is unwilling to work."

Ellie scoffed, the sound echoing against the wall of the tiny building. "Next you'll be trying to sell me snake oil."

A sad smile flickered across the nearly perfect features of his finely chiseled face. "Would you buy?"

Their eyes locked, neither speaking.

At length, Ellie looked away. "Absolutely not."

"Too bad. I was hoping I could sell you anything—lead you anywhere."

Ellie sucked in her breath and started to push away from the post, to leave. But the sudden, warm strength of Nicholas's hand stayed her.

"Don't go. I'm sorry. I shouldn't have said that. It's just that . . ."

His words trailed off, his thought unfinished. What would he have said? she wondered. The hard, ruthless man had faded away, making it harder than ever to hate him. He looked at her, his blue eyes suddenly aching, desperate. In that moment, he looked hurt and vulnerable as she never would have imagined this man could be. His strength had intrigued her from the beginning, but this . . . this vulnerability of the soul drew her in a way that made her forget all that she needed desperately to remember. Her heart tightened with something she didn't recognize. Panic, perhaps, but more.

His strong hand curled gently around hers. "Nicholas?" she said uncertainly.

He didn't respond, merely looked into her eyes, making her heart flutter. Ellie knew she should pull back—for so many reasons. Propriety, decency. Her father. Instead, when he pulled her close, she went to him, as she knew she shouldn't. But somehow pavilions in the rain seemed to wash away shoulds and shoudn'ts—freeing her from all the restrictions that bound her life.

"Why is it," he whispered, his breath warm against her skin, "that I'm drawn to you?"

She opened her mouth to speak, a shiver of feeling running down her spine at his words. But Nicholas pressed one strong finger to her lips.

"Shhh. Don't try to explain," he said, his voice quiet, mesmerizing. "You can't." His fingers trailed down her chin to the smooth column of her throat, pushing her lace collar aside. "You can't explain why suddenly I dream of fair-haired, emerald-eyed maidens in castles by the sea."

Castles by the sea. She never should have told him her dreams. She needed to flee, but thought only of his fingers burning a path across her skin. She made a feeble protest and started to step away. But he pulled her back, against what little Will she possessed to resist. And this time, where his fingers had passed, he pressed his lips.

She realized she had been waiting for this. Her dreams had been filled with him—Nicholas by a castle, Nicholas by the sea, his lips on hers, setting her on fire. He pushed her coat away and looked down at her, wet from the rain. "So beautiful," he said, the words a ragged breath.

She should have been incensed, outraged, embarrassed at the very least. She only felt a wave of pleasure when she saw the deep appreciation in his eyes.

A moment passed, their gazes locking, before he closed the distance between them, then touched his lips to hers once again. The kiss was tender but oddly desperate, as if he wanted something more from her than simply her embrace. More than she could provide, she thought fleetingly.

The kiss deepened. She was startled by the intimacy.

"Shhh," he murmured against her lips. "I won't hurt you, Ellie."

His tongue slid into the depths of her mouth. He tasted of smoke and spice, making her senses reel. With a soft, defeated cry, she raised her arms and clung to his shoulders.

His hand coiled in her hair, gently pulling her head back. He opened his mouth on her neck as he pulled her inside his coat. Closer. His strong hands trailed down her back to her hips, cupping her, pulling her up until she felt the evidence of his desire hard against her body.

Rain surrounded them, washing over the windows, leaving them murky. For the moment, their pasts were forgotten. They stood together in a world apart, suspended. It was no longer before, and not yet after. Time only to savor the moment, stolen from a store of moments filled with battle whose lines had been drawn long ago.

But then he spoke, his words taking her breath away, shattering the spell.

"Who are you, Eliot Sinclair?" he whispered against her skin. "Where did you come from?"

Reality returned like a wave crashing back from the sea, the undercurrent pulling, threatening. It took her a moment to truly comprehend what she was doing—standing in a public place in the arms of a man—in the arms of Nicholas Drake.

"Though somehow," he continued, brushing his cheek against hers, unaware of her sudden distress, his voice deep and low, "I find that I don't care."

But she cared. Very much. Dear God, what had she done? Her mind jerked away, much as her body tried to.

"Ellie?" His brow furrowed, the deep timber of his voice laced with concern. "What's the matter?"

She only tugged harder, desperate to get away. "Let go of me, Mr. Drake. The rain has ceased, and I've got to go." She drew a deep breath, then faced him, her chin rising a notch. "I have acted shamelessly. You'll have to excuse me." Then she pulled her coat tight, and moved away.

Nicholas nearly stopped her, nearly reached out once again and sought whatever it was that she made him feel. But in the end he let her go. Without looking back, she stepped free, away, out onto the slabs of granite that lined the cobbled street.

He took a deep, calming breath as the scent of lilacs dissolved in the thick, rainswept air. Ellie was gone. Once again, the doorless entry was empty.

Nicholas stood for long, endless moments until he realized with a start that the tiny, unexpected cracks in the foundation of his life had sealed over as if they had never been. He pushed from his mind the thought that Ellie had soothed him, that indeed he had found solace in her arms. The Nicholas Drake he knew had returned, strong, resolute. Determined.

He could help Charlotte, he knew suddenly. There were

doctors all over the world who studied the lungs. There had to be someone who could cure her.

The sun broke through the darkened sky. When he stepped outside, the air was crisp, washed clean by the rain. He glanced down the walkway in the direction Ellie had fled. Yes, she was gone.

Nicholas told himself he was glad. He had no interest in dealing with her any longer. She distracted him. Proof of which was the fact that he still didn't have her house. She made him forget his plans. He had become remiss, and that had to stop. He would tell Bert to deal with her in the future. His assistant was perfectly capable of closing the sale. Then Nicholas would never see her again.

But as he stepped away, no longer having to concentrate, he had the sudden thought that whether he ever saw her again or not, he would only have to hear a gasp, or unexpectedly glance over his shoulder, to see rain flowing like crystal draperies and emerald green eyes washed with desire.

Chapter 5

Light is color. But her life had been shadowed by darkness. How did she think she could paint?

The question was always the same, circling in her mind, faster and faster, until it became a blur and she forgot. Only then did the paintbrush in her small but steady hand begin to move. Sometimes fast, sometimes slow, her imagination taking shape on the canvas.

She left behind the stark white walls lined with long, wide windows and lost herself in the comfort of tints and hues, curves and lines—images which she savored like dreams of a man she could love.

Finally, thankfully, she was alone, at peace, with no other demand than capturing emotion and essence. No other responsibility than to convey what she saw.

The lines and colors changed as her imagination evolved, assimilating new ideas, discarding some of the old. What ultimately ended up left in the corner to dry rarely resembled what had begun in her mind. But this day, with its rain-washed sky and bright sun streaming in through the windows, the seed had been planted so firmly, so fully in her soul that her hand seemed to work independently of her mind.

The brush filled the canvas with sculpted lines and flesh-colored curves. Hair down, cascading. Damp and wet. Arms entwined: Solace mixed with desire, visible, tangible. More real than the touch of chiseled fingers to her skin.

But then, without warning, her mind came spiraling down as the bang of pots and pans unexpectedly crashed through the house. Her hand stilled; the stroke incomplete. She stared at the canvas and realized with a start that tears streamed down her cheeks. She didn't bother to wipe them away as she stood back and took in the world she had created. The image was unfinished, but clear. *Desire inherent in the embrace.*

She pressed her eyes closed. A surge of guilty joy swept through her, and a dazzling smile broke out on her lips. She had painted. Again. Finally. Stolen moments to make the time. But it was enough for now.

With a contented sigh she turned away, then pulled the screen back in place to hide her work.

Chapter 6

UPROAR IN DOWNTOWN GALLERY
by Able Smythe

The art world is in an uproar this fine summer day over the showing of the rapidly becoming *in*famous M. M. Jay's latest work, *The Embrace*. But uproar or not, that didn't stop New York's elite, both layman and expert, from lingering before the painting that admittedly both takes the breath away and outrages.

On a purely technical level, the man is quite good, has the potential even to become masterful. His technique is beyond reproach. The depth he achieves in his work as well as his use of color is brilliant. A fundamental principle of art, that light is color, fills his art.

And while I do not agree with other critics who tend to lessen the importance of Jay's work, solely in my opinion due to the content rather than the technique, I do feel that the artist ultimately holds back. M. M. Jay's work seems unfinished. One is left with the impression of underlying restraint in every line and curve on the canvas. No doubt it would be a sight to behold if the artist could bring himself to let go, free himself from the confines of whatever it is that holds him back as surely as reins hold back a thoroughbred.

Admittedly, his subject this time around—a barely clad man being boldly embraced by a fully dressed woman in what appears to be the rain—makes even the most liberal of critics wonder at the man's sense of decency. Not since Manet's *Luncheon on the Grass* has there been such a stir in the art world.

But where other critics would like to shut the door in M. M. Jay's elusive face, I would say to the man: Step through the turnstile to another world, beyond constraints. I dare you, Mr. Jay, wherever you are.

The article went on. But Nicholas read no further. He lowered his hands, crumpling his neatly pressed copy of *The New York Times* beneath them as he sat back in the hand-carved Chippendale chair behind the huge expanse of mahogany dining table.

The Embrace.

An unsettled feeling ran down his spine, though he wasn't certain why. Rumor was rampant about the painter who no one, apparently, had ever seen or met. The paintings arrived, it was said, on the doorstep of one of Manhattan's preeminent galleries, no note, no explanation, no one even to retrieve the work after it was shown.

Nicholas had never been particularly interested in art before. But since the first M. M. Jay article appeared a few months before, he had been intrigued. However, he was not intrigued by the rapidly growing number of art schools and clubs that were turning up at every turn and corner of the City. It was M. M. Jay alone who had captured his attention. And for the life of him, he couldn't imagine why.

"Excuse me, sir."

Distracted, Nicholas looked toward the door. "Yes, Albert."

"Your carriage is here."

Nicholas glanced out the window at the clear blue sky. "I think I'll walk today, Albert. Send the carriage back."

"Yes, sir."

Minutes later, Nicholas came out the front door, down the flagstone walkway, then out through the wrought-iron fencing to the street where unexpectedly he found Jim.

"Hello, Mr. Drake," Jim said with a shy smile.

Ellie's tenant wore neatly mended wool pants, starched shirt, and a heavy sweater, regardless of the already rising temperature.

"Good morning, Jim."

"Is this where you live?" he asked, awe lacing his voice as he turned away from Nicholas and stared through the fence to the house.

Nicholas turned as well as if somehow he would see something altogether different than expected. "Yes, this is my home."

"Does Charlotte live here, too?"

"Yes, she does." He eyed Jim. "Is Ellie all right?" he asked, concerned despite himself.

"Sure, she's fine," Jim replied simply, then looked back at the house without another word.

Nicholas didn't like the flash of relief he felt. "Jim?"

"Huh?"

"If Ellie is fine, why are you here?"

Jim glanced at Nicholas curiously. "No reason."

When Nicholas realized he was getting no further explanation he shook his head, then started down Fifth Avenue. Only seconds later, Jim ambled up to his side. Nicholas glanced over, expecting some other question, but Jim simply walked along next to him, taking in the passing scenery. They walked, block after block without a word.

"It's a pretty day," Jim said, breaking the silence.

"A fine day," Nicholas confirmed.

"I'm going to work."

"Yes, I would imagine you are. Aren't you late?"

"No, Ellie said I could go up and see the park this

morning. I like to go to the park. Barnard showed me how.
I went last week and when I was going home I saw you go
into that big house." Jim smiled. "I remembered. I walked
all the way back this morning, early, and remembered the
right house."

They came to Nicholas's office. "Well then, good for you.
Now, if there's nothing else, I'll be going in." Nicholas
waited a curious half second, before he gave a swift, crisp
tug to each of his shirt cuffs, then walked through the
entrance held open by a uniformed doorman.

Jim watched him go, standing there until Nicholas was
swallowed up by the building. Once the door swung closed,
Jim turned to study his own well-mended cuffs, gave each
an awkward tug, smiled, then hurried down the side street to
work.

Jim always went the same way. The way Ellie had taught
him. It never varied. Routine. And routine was all-important.

Just when he came to the middle of the block, three large
men stepped out.

"Well, well, well. Look who we have here, boys."

"Hi, Rudy," Jim said with a hearty wave. "Hi, Billy. Hi,
Bo."

Rudy, Billy and Bo leaned casually against the wrought-
iron railing that led up to a doorway.

"What's your hurry? Why don't you stay awhile and chat.
Aren't we your pals, Jim?"

"Well, yeah, Rudy. My best pals. But if I don't hurry, I'll
be late. Ellie said I had to be at the shop at nine o'clock."
Jim pulled out an old and worn pocket watch. "See, it's
already almost nine now. She doesn't like it when I'm late."

"I guess we should let you go then," Rudy said, pushing
away from the banister. "But first Jim, we have a little
business we need to discuss with you. Isn't that right,
boys?"

"Yeah, boss," Billy and Bo chimed in unison with hearty
smiles.

"What kinda business, Rudy?" Jim asked, leery.

"Well it's like this, Jim," Rudy began, wrapping a large ham of an arm around Jim's broad shoulders. "You know how we've been lettin' you get through the street every afternoon only paying five cents?"

"Yeah," Jim said carefully.

"Unfortunately," Rudy continued with a shrug of shoulders, "the rate has gone up. We've let you get by for only five cents for a long time 'cause you're our . . . pal. But everybody else is paying ten cents."

"Ten cents?" Jim looked around. "Are you sure, Rudy?"

"Now, Jim boy, would I lie to you?"

Billy and Bo laughed.

Jim sighed and stepped away. "No, Rudy. But ten cents is too much."

Rudy shrugged once again. "Then I guess you'll have to come and go to work another way."

If Jim had to go another way he would have to get Ellie or Barnard to show him how. And if he asked them to show him another way, they'd ask him why. And then he'd have to tell them about using his tip money to pay his pals. He knew Ellie wouldn't like that. But Jim liked Rudy, Billy, and Bo. He liked his pals. "All right," he mumbled. "I'll try to get ten cents."

"Good, good, glad we came to an understanding. We'd hate to lose our best pal," Rudy said, slapping Jim on the back. "Now, you'd better hurry. Wouldn't want you to be late."

Nicholas was sitting behind his desk when Bert knocked on his open door. "Come in."

"There's a gentleman here to see you." Bert's tone grew apologetic. "He doesn't have an appointment, but he's interested in selling you some property. I thought you might want to speak with him."

"Where is the property?"

Bert came forward with what proved to be a hastily drawn map. "It's here on Sixteenth Street."

"I thought we had everything on Sixteenth except Miss Sinclair's home."

"Everything in that one section, which was all you wanted. But as you know, there is an alleyway that divides the entire block into two sections." He shrugged. "I thought since Miss Sinclair was proving so difficult, you could purchase the properties on the other side of the alleyway and build in that direction. No doubt you can get variances to build over the alley."

Nicholas leaned back and considered. It wasn't perfect. Perfect was obtaining Ellie's house. But for now even he had to concede that it wasn't looking likely. Perhaps if he could obtain the rest of the street, Ellie being the only one left, he could convince her of the wisdom of moving. "Bring him in."

Seconds later, an older gentleman wearing his Sunday best was ushered into the office. His overly long gray hair was neatly combed back, and his face cleanly shaven. His shoes were worn but held a high polish. Extending his hand, the man came forward. "Grady O'Shea, Mr. Drake. Pleased to make your acquaintance."

"Have a seat, Mr. O'Shea," Nicholas offered. "I understand you're interested in selling a piece of property."

"Yes, sir. My home on Sixteenth Street, where rumor has it you're going to build some big, tall building."

"Perhaps," was all Nicholas said.

"Well, yes," the man said uncomfortably. "Given what I had heard, I thought . . . well . . ."

"Mr. O'Shea, even if I wanted to build there, how does buying one house in a long line of shared-wall houses do me any good?"

Grady brightened at this. "I've taken the liberty of gathering up the folks involved. We're having a meeting. I thought you could come and talk to them. Convince everybody to sell."

Nicholas stared at the man across the desk. "All right. When is your meeting, Mr. O'Shea?"

"This Thursday. I'll leave the address with your assistant." With that, Grady O'Shea stood and quit the room.

Nicholas was left alone. Why wouldn't Ellie sell her house? he wondered, as he had wondered a thousand times since meeting her. She was steadfast in her refusals, and while in the beginning he had simply assumed she was holding out for more money, it had soon become apparent that he could offer her the moon and she wouldn't sell.

Offer her the moon.

He smiled at this. It sounded just like something Ellie would say, fanciful and impossible. And on the heels of that thought, he had the urge to see her—despite his promise never to see her again. He wanted to see her laugh, see her smile, see her turn those emerald eyes on him, taking him in, out of himself.

But he got no further than the thought when voices filtered in to him through the door.

"But Mr. Drake is a busy man," he heard his secretary say.

"I'm sure he is. Just like I'm a busy woman." The voice was deep from age, but melodious and undoubtedly female. It sounded familiar but Nicholas couldn't place it. "Orders to take," he heard the woman continue. "Orders to fill. Day after day, with no end to it, let me tell you. No life of luxury for this woman. I'm busy, yes I am. So just show me into your Mr. Drake's office and I'll be quick."

"As I said," his secretary continued with a sigh, "you don't have an appointment."

"All right, dearie. If that will make you feel better, then make me an appointment."

Another sigh, this time in relief. "Very good, madam. When would you like to make an appointment?"

"For ten o'clock, Monday the thirteenth."

"But that's today, right now!"

"True enough. Now that I have an appointment, it is terribly rude for you to keep me waiting. Look," he heard the woman say, and no doubt was pointing at the grand-father clock against the wall, "it's after ten already."

Nicholas couldn't help but smile. Who was that woman? he wondered as he pushed up from his seat and went to the door.

"Mrs. Schurr," he stated when he saw her.

"Ah, there you are, Mr. Drake. Good of you not to keep me waiting. I have an appointment, you know," she added with an emphatic nod of her gray head.

"Yes, so I heard," he replied, his blue eyes sparking with humor as he held his smile at bay. "Come in, please. What can I do for you?"

Hannah allowed herself to be ushered into the office. "Ooooh," she said, running her plump hand along the high-backed leather chair.

"Please have a seat, Mrs. Schurr."

"Miss," she corrected. "Though hopefully soon to be Missus."

"Really. And who's the lucky fellow."

Hannah blushed. "Barnard Webb."

"Really? I didn't realize the two of you were engaged."

"Truth to tell, he doesn't realize it either," she replied, her tone heated. "But he will, the old goat. Mark my words. But enough about me. I'm here to talk about you."

Nicholas straightened in his chair. "Me?"

"Yes, you sir, and the distress you're causing my dear Ellie."

"Ellie?"

"Are you deaf? Of course Ellie. Who else would I be here about?"

Who else indeed? He leaned back.

"She's a wonderful woman," Hannah continued, "saved me and Jim and even that old goat, Barnard. She'd fight tooth and nail for us, and she has. She gave me a job when no one else would. Thankless relatives. Throwing me out on the street when their children no longer needed a nanny. Where was I supposed to go? Had never learned to do anything but watch after young ones. Ellie had to teach me herself how to make those blasted hats. Then took me into her own home to live when she found out I had no place to go. Then there's Jim. She saved him, too. Brought him with her from the—" Her paper-thin skin stained red. "Well that hardly signifies. What's important here is that she will fight for those she cares about, but she's not so good at fighting for herself."

"And that's why you're here," he stated, studying Hannah over steepled fingers. "To fight for Ellie."

Hannah eyed Nicholas carefully. "Fight? Well, no. Simply to reason with such a fine gentleman as yourself."

An unease began to spread through his limbs. First Charlotte's illness. Then Jim coming to see him. Now this woman arriving here to defend Ellie. Defend. Protect. To save loved ones.

"Leave her alone, Mr. Drake," Hannah said, her gruff voice having softened to nearly a plea. "She's good and kind, and she loves that house. You can have any house you want. She only wants the one."

"I'll give it some thought, Mrs. Schurr," he said tersely, suddenly wanting her gone. Abruptly he stood.

After a moment Hannah rose from her seat, too. "Well, all right then. I'll just be going."

Nicholas could tell that she didn't feel she had finished, and was on the verge of launching into another speech. "I appreciate your coming by. Truly, I'll think about what you've said."

This seemed to pacify her. She extended her hand, shook his, then departed.

Nicholas went to the window and looked out over the landscape covered with buildings. No doubt thousands of buildings, hundreds of town houses. Most nicer than Ellie's. But, of course, niceness had nothing to do with his desire for her house. He had to have hers. No other would do.

No sooner had he sat back down than the hushed atmosphere outside his office erupted, washing away the silence. A loud voice, a voice this time he was sure he recognized, boomed beyond the door.

Pushing up from the chair, Nicholas came around his desk to open the door. He grimaced at the sight. "Barnard," he said simply. "Did you come with Hannah?"

Barnard whirled around, his head nodding in triumph. "I knew you were in there. Wasn't about to be thrown out like vermin. And what do you mean about Hannah? Why would I bring her? It's you I want to see!"

Barnard came forward and, when he reached Nicholas, he simply passed him on his way into the office. Nicholas's staff stared in silent disbelief. Nicholas raised one dark brow then followed the older man inside. Barnard stood very still as Nicholas returned to his chair.

Nicholas's smile was humorless. "Have a seat, Mr. Webb."

"I'm not sitting down. I won't be here long enough to bother."

"All right then. What can I do for you?"

"You can leave my Ellie alone." The words were spoken with determination and not a little venom.

"What do you mean, leave Ellie alone?" But of course Nicholas knew. Hannah had already told him.

"You know good and well what I mean. Ellie's told you she doesn't want to sell her home. Quit badgering her. You've upset her, and if Ellie's upset then the rest of us at the house are upset for her."

"And why is that, Mr. Webb? She's a grown woman, and one clearly determined to be independent."

"Damn it man! We love her! She's good and decent, qualities you certainly aren't familiar with. But that's no fault of hers. She cares about people," he added gruffly. "She hired me to do repair work around the house. Sure I acted fine, well off. But hell, I wasn't. I had one decent pair of clothes. I was living like an urchin on the street. She'd insist I come early for breakfast, and stay late for supper. The house was practically falling apart. Needed all kinds of work. And then one day she says, 'Barnard, why don't you just stay here, there's an extra room next to Jim's.' Course, I couldn't afford to pay room and board, and before I could say a thing, she says, 'Room and board for work done on the house.' I moved in that night, have been there ever since. She saved me, Mr. Drake. And I'll not sit idly by while you make her life miserable."

Nicholas pressed back in his chair. His gaze grew cold and uncompromising. The old man's words were absurd. How could he possibly make Nicholas do anything he didn't want to do? But still, Nicholas's head began to ache.

Making him remember.

"I think you should leave," Nicholas stated, his voice taut, strained.

"Not until you give me your word that you'll leave my Ellie alone!"

Nicholas eyed the older man with barely held control. "I will have her house, Mr. Webb. If obtaining it bothers her, then so be it."

Barnard planted his hands on his hips. "You can't do this!"

"Really?" Nicholas said, his voice deceptively calm. "Who's going to stop me?"

Barnard raised his chin and started to speak. Nicholas cut him off. "I'm a busy man, Mr. Webb." His dark countenance grew darker, revealing the hard, ruthless man he had been for so long. Nicholas watched Barnard's bravado begin to waver. He wanted Barnard gone. Out of his office. He didn't care how it was accomplished.

"Don't think this is over, Drake. Ellie saved me. I'll not let you destroy her now."

"Get out, Mr. Webb."

At length Barnard shook his head and turned to go. But just when he reached the door, he turned back. "You're a heartless bastard, Drake. No doubt your own mother didn't even love you." Then he was gone.

Nicholas's hands pressed against the smooth mahogany desk.

Mother.

He turned away, toward the window, as if he could turn away from unwanted memories. But the streets and buildings outside held no refuge.

Oh, Mother.

Chapter 7

New York 1873

"Mother!"

Young Nicholas raced through the front door, and slid to a halt on the black-and-white marble entryway floor in the palatial home on Lafayette Place. The guys were waiting out front. They were going to catch the crosstown omnibus, and Nicholas wanted to go along.

Ted and Maynard were older by two years. Fourteen. Nicholas knew his parents didn't like his new friends, and perhaps with good reason, he conceded. They talked and laughed about things that gave Nicholas pause. But still, they were going fishing, and he wanted to go.

He found his mother standing in the middle of the long curving stairway, beautiful beyond words, staring off at nothing Nicholas could see. She wore a fairy-tale dress of blue and gold. And around her shoulders he was proud to note that she wore the gossamer thin scarf that had been the first gift he had ever picked out on his own.

But while she was as beautiful as ever, something seemed wrong. "Mother," he repeated, concern tingeing his words.

Startled, his mother turned to him. "Nicholas, there you are. I was just going out."

She seemed uneasy, not herself, as she took the remaining

steps to the foyer. She headed for the door, then stopped. When she turned back to him, her violet eyes seemed suddenly desperate, almost pleading. "Nicholas. Let's go out. You and me. For lunch, or shopping."

Her impromptu invitation was unexpected. Her days were filled with plans and parties. Whenever he wanted to do anything with her he had to ask well in advance. He glanced at the door. What would he tell Ted and Maynard?

"If we hurry," she added, her chime of laughter forced and hollow, "we might even make it to the park."

Nicholas grimaced. "I can't, Mother. I'm going fishing."

"Of course," she said with a sigh. "Boys and fishing. Innocent days of childhood. If only I were a child again."

Nicholas gave his mother a curious look. "Does that mean I can go?"

His mother laughed, a sad, hollow sound. "Of course you can go, my love. Have fun."

Then before he could race out back to gather his fishing gear, she slipped out the front door. It wasn't until he sat along the shore of the Hudson River that an uneasiness began to creep over him. She had left the house without calling for a carriage, he realized. No carriage for a woman who never walked. Where was she going dressed as she was in the middle of the day?

Without a fish in his basket, he left Ted and Maynard, and caught the crosstown omnibus that would take him back home. He arrived at two o'clock, had his gear cleaned and put away by two-thirty. By three his mother still hadn't returned.

He paced the house, each floor, until he went outside and dropped down onto the front steps. He wished more than ever that his father was home. But Nicholas knew this was a futile wish. His father was rarely home these days. And when he was, he was busy, upset, his normally laughing demeanor harsh and angry, snapping unexpectedly at the servants or at anyone who caught him at a bad time.

It was four-thirty when an unfamiliar black-enameled

landau with fine matching horses finally pulled up alongside the wrought-iron fencing. When the small black door pushed open, Nicholas's mother slipped out. And she was crying. Silently. Sun catching in the tears that streamed down her cheeks.

Mother, Nicholas breathed silently.

He stood, paralyzed by the sight, uncertain what to do. His mother, crying. He could hardly fathom the sight.

He started to speak, to say something, anything. He wanted to offer comfort. But how? He was scared and confused. But most of all he simply didn't want her to be weeping.

She didn't seem to notice him as she dashed up the steps. Not a word of greeting or explanation. He was only offered a glimpse of milk-white skin where her scarf had been earlier, but wasn't any longer.

Chapter 8

"How could you?"

Barnard came to an abrupt halt in the middle of the staircase and cringed. It was the following morning and sun streamed in through the windows. At the sight of Ellie, but more importantly, at the tone of her voice, he turned as quickly as he could manage and started back up to the second floor.

"Too late, Barnard. You're not going to escape this time." She hadn't seen him since yesterday's *Times* had arrived— since Able Smythe's latest article had appeared. "You owe me an explanation."

"Ah, Ellie," he said with a groan, as he trudged down the remaining steps. "You're not going to yell, are you?"

"You promised!" she burst out, venting her fear and frustration. "You promised not to take another painting out of my room."

Barnard had the good grace to look chagrined. "I know, I know. But that last one was just too good to let gather dust."

"That's not what Mr. Able Smythe said! Restrained, he wrote. Restrained!" She fought back silly tears, hating that she cared that some man she didn't even know had said her work wasn't good enough.

She had wanted to be an artist since Sister Beatrice had given her a bundle of colored chalk as a child. After that, Ellie had drawn on everything she could. It was what she could do. Draw. It defined her in a way that she loved, even if it was something she only did in secret. And "in secret" was the only place she would be able to paint. There was no place in the world for a woman artist, especially one who had to support herself.

"What does that little prig know about anything?" Barnard added, interrupting her thoughts.

"A lot, and you know it. That's why you take them to him."

"I do not take them to him," he stated indignantly.

"Excuse me," she said with considerable asperity. "You simply drop them off at the back door of the one gallery in town that you know he frequents."

"Your work needs attention, doggonit! How many times do I have to tell you that?"

"Why is it that all of a sudden everyone feels compelled to tell me what I need to do?" She threw her hands up in the air. " 'You need to sell your house, Ellie!' 'You need to marry, Ellie!' 'You need to marry *me*, Ellie!' 'You need to show your work, Ellie!' I'm on the wrong side of twenty-five, for heaven's sake. Old enough to make decisions for myself!"

"Now, Ellie," Barnard said, his voice cajoling, "of course you're old enough, and capable, too. It's just that we're concerned, is all. We love you."

"Speak for yourself. Charles doesn't love me."

"Hell, you met the man years ago, and he's been askin' you to marry him ever since. You keep saying no, and still he keeps askin'. How can you say he doesn't love you?"

"Because he doesn't." She looked away. It was true. Charles had been pursuing her for years now. He was a decent man from a family of hard workers who were trying to better their lot in life. Ellie knew that in his own way Charles loved her, but not the way she wanted to be loved, she thought, her eyes unexpectedly burning. Loved and touched and cherished, she added silently, as she remembered the sweet feel of Nicholas Drake's hands brushing against her skin.

"You're just feelin' low, Ellie love. Why don't you go upstairs and rest."

"I'm not feeling low!" she blurted. "And I don't want to rest." She wanted to live. She wanted to throw caution and good sense to the wind, she wanted to dance in the streets in her red stockings. She wanted to go to the Palette Art Company herself. Not Barnard, but her. On her own. To walk through the crowded aisles, to pick out her own brushes, to smell the varnishes and linseed oils. She wanted to run her hands over unstretched canvas. Meet other painters. Perhaps go to one of the nearby cafés where artists of all kinds gathered to talk about their work. But most of all, she wanted to paint without hiding. To touch people with her work.

"Now, Ellie, you worry too much."

"Worry! Of course I worry. And I worry with good reason. They call my work scandalous, and that's when they think I'm a man. This society that has become so enamored of art approves of portraits and landscapes, still lifes and hunting scenes—*not* the kind of things I paint! Good Lord, I hate to think what would happen if Mr. Able Smythe got wind of the fact that M. M. Jay is a woman."

"Able Smythe isn't going to find out who you are."

Ellie gave the older man a searing look.

"He's not!" Barnard added stubbornly.

"You better be right, Barnard." She didn't know how she could survive the scandal that would no doubt ensue if she was found out. Women, if they painted at all, were relegated to disciplined still lifes or watercolors of innocuous summer landscapes. They did not create paintings that caused scandals. But still lifes and landscapes had never appealed to her, had never made her feel.

She started toward the front door, then turned back. "And

one other thing. Don't you dare take another painting out of my room, do you understand?"

Barnard shook his head and moaned, but nodded just the same. "Yes, I understand. Though it's a waste, I tell you. A terrible waste."

"The articles have to stop, Barnard. The interest has to cease."

"Given time," he muttered, clearly disgruntled, "no doubt Able Smythe will forget all about you."

Ellie started again for the door, but before she could leave for work Hannah came up from the kitchen.

"Morning paper's here," the older woman said, her cheerful yellow cotton day dress at odds with the uneasy creases on her normally gentle face. She dropped the paper on the table. "You might want to glance at page three."

Barnard's ruddy complexion blanched. Ellie froze. After glancing back and forth between Hannah and Ellie, Barnard snatched up the *Times*.

Ellie didn't move, couldn't move. Another article? she wondered, panic hammering in her brain. She had lived for years with the fear that at any moment she would be found out as Harry Dillard's daughter. Now, with Barnard's clandestine efforts, whether well-intentioned or not, she lived in fear of being found out as the scandalous artist M. M. Jay.

"What does it say?" she asked finally, not sure she really wanted to know.

Barnard smiled, snapped the paper shut, then slapped it beneath his arm. "Nothing. It has nothing more than a discussion of an artist. An artist, in fact, that you might be interested in seeing. I'm sure that's why Hannah mentioned it. Isn't that right, Hannah," he said with a meaningful glare in the woman's direction.

"Oh, my, I forgot to tell you, Ellie," he continued, without giving Hannah a chance to respond, "I heard there's some kind of a meeting this Thursday at Grady O'Shea's."

"You're lying, Barnard."

Barnard's eyes widened, and his hand came dramatically to his chest. "I am not lying, there *is* a meeting."

"I'm not talking about a meeting. I don't *care* about a meeting. I want you to hand over the newspaper."

"Now, Ellie," he lamented.

"Don't you, 'now Ellie' me, Barnard. Give me the paper."

Barnard groaned at the same time he shot Hannah a venomous glare. "Now look what you've done, old woman," he snapped as he handed the paper over.

With dread racing through her veins, Ellie opened to page three. And there it was. Headline blazing.

WHO ARE YOU, M. M. JAY?

By none other than Able Smythe.

Ellie walked out the front door, a newly designed hat of bows and bells pulled on loosely, her gloves forgotten. All she could think was why was this happening now, after so many years of relative peace and anonymity? The house. The articles. Why now?

To make matters worse, when the door shut behind her, she found Nicholas Drake sitting next to Jim on the front steps.

"What are you doing here?" she demanded, etiquette and niceties swept clean from her mind.

"Good morning to you, too," Nicholas offered with a devilish smile.

"I'm not in the mood, Drake," she warned, coming down the steps like a military man.

"Drake, is it?" Nicholas glanced at Jim with a look of commiseration. "Do you live with this every day?"

"Yes," he nodded.

"Jim!"

"I mean, no," Jim amended, looking confused.

Ellie provided Nicholas a withering glare. "Now look what you've done."

"Why is it that I get blamed for everything that goes

wrong around here?" Nicholas asked with a shake of his head.

"Because you're the *cause* of all the problems around here."

Nicholas pushed up from the cool granite steps, his crisp, light-wool trousers falling beautifully into place. "I forgot. Your life was a veritable feast of peace and tranquillity before I arrived on the scene."

"Close enough," she muttered ruefully, bringing a full-bodied laugh from Nicholas.

Jim stood, too, next to Nicholas. As if on cue, both men gave a brisk tug to their cuffs. Ellie watched the movements curiously before she shook her head and headed for the street.

After a few easy strides, Nicholas was beside her, Jim on his heels. "We need to talk."

"No we don't, Drake."

"I really wish you wouldn't call me that. It has such an . . . unfriendly ring to it."

"The unfriendly ring, as you put it, is intentional," she said, looking straight ahead, her step determined.

"Temper, temper," he teased. "Did we get up on the wrong side of the bed?"

"*We* didn't do anything. Nor will we."

"The least you could do is call me Nicholas, or sir if you prefer," he added with a mischievous glint in his eye.

Ellie scoffed at this. "In your dreams, Drake." Then she seemed to consider. "Though, Nicky has a nice ring to it."

"I like Nicky," Jim announced. "Nicky," he said to no one in particular. "Nicky. Nicky."

Nicholas groaned. "Now look what you've done."

Ellie only responded with a satisfied grin and continued down the street.

They walked in silence for several blocks before Nicholas spoke. "I have a new offer for you. One I think even you will agree is more than fair. It's certainly more than your home is worth."

"Do you think to change my mind with sheer persistence?" she demanded, as she turned with a start, causing her loosely tied-on hat to flop to the side.

Without responding, Nicholas reached out before Ellie could stop him and straightened her hat. They had come to the shop, and Jim proudly raced up the steps with Ellie's keys, unlocked the door, then slipped inside. Nicholas and Ellie stood alone, so close that their breaths tangled in the early morning air.

"I'm not sure what I think anymore," Nicholas replied, the nearly perfect lines of his face shifting with emotion. "I'm not sure why I can't forget you—why I can't walk away and never look back. Yes, I want your house, and if sheer persistence is what will convince you, persist I will." He sighed then, his deep blue eyes raging like stormy skies. "But beyond that, I seem to want you more, more than your house. I want more from you than hardly a glance and sharply tossed out barbs."

Ellie hated the shiver of feeling that raced down her spine, much less did she understand it. Even if she didn't already hate the man, she couldn't imagine ever liking him. Hard. Cold. Ruthless. And the last thing she wanted in her life was another hard, cold, ruthless man.

But still, as his eyes drifted to her lips, she wondered if he thought about how his lips had pressed against hers, how his hands had caressed her body that day in the rain? She had thought of little else since.

As if in answer, he reached out and took her hand, pulling her close until they stood scant inches apart.

"What are you doing?" she whispered, struggling to get the words out of her suddenly dry mouthy.

"I'm going to kiss you."

"You can't."

"But I am," he murmured, before his mouth hungrily descended on hers.

A tiny moan spilled from her. And with that sound he wrapped his arm protectively around her. He touched her lips with his tongue, coaxing her lips apart, until he tasted her sweetness. He kissed her then, deeply, thoroughly, his groan rumbling in his chest. His lips on hers were more than a kiss, seeming to pull at her, pulling at that place inside her that yearned to know more.

Startled, she pulled away.

It was a moment before he spoke, and when he did his voice was strained. "I promised myself I wouldn't see you again."

"If only you had kept your promise," she breathed.

His sharp features filled with regret. "There are so many 'if onlys' in this world. But 'if onlys' are just that, useless yearnings for something that didn't happen. I find it best to deal with reality." He ran his knuckles gently down her cheek. "And the reality is that you wanted my kiss as much as I wanted to kiss you."

The truth was laid out before them, her acquiescence making his words impossible to deny.

But then Jim called out from the doorway. "Ellie! What are you doing?"

Ellie jerked back. What *was* she doing? Kisses and truths? Ellie pressed her hands to her face. She could still feel Nicholas's touch as if his fingers were still there—as if he had branded her in some way as his own. She felt his heated gaze on her, felt the blood singeing her cheeks.

"Are you coming inside?" Jim asked. "Are you coming inside, too, Nicky?"

She started to go. She needed to get into the shop, through the door, inside—safe. But her steps faltered when Jim asked about Charlotte. Sweet little Charlotte. So ill. So alone.

Of all times! When she wanted, needed, to escape. But even through her own turmoil Ellie could feel the sudden tension in Nicholas's body. "How *is* she doing?" she asked softly.

He was quiet for a moment. "I don't know how she is," he answered truthfully. "I want to believe Charlotte is better.

Truly she seems happier. But the very same doctors who lavish her with attention in their offices wait for her to leave before telling me there's no hope."

"No hope? How is that possible?"

"I don't know," he repeated, this time brusquely. "One minute she's asking for coffee, the next . . ." He shrugged, creases suddenly etching his brow. "The next, the doctors are less than encouraging."

"I'm sorry."

"I haven't given up, though," he stated, his eyes growing hard with determination. "I plan to find someone who has answers."

"Ahhh, answers. Answers that you like, no doubt. This must be the infamous 'Will' you spoke about. *Willing* things to be." Ellie sighed, her head tilting with concern. "Perhaps it's time you looked in another direction."

"As in?" Nicholas stared down at her, his eyes filling with a formidable darkness.

But Ellie stood her ground. "For all their great discoveries and cures, the medical world doesn't have what *you* can give Charlotte."

"Which is?" The simple words were icy.

"Love. You can give her love."

He shifted his weight and his jaw cemented. "Love? My niece needs a cure, Miss Sinclair, not some useless emotion that no doubt doesn't exist."

"Doesn't exist?" she demanded, startled. But as she looked into the depths of his eyes, she realized with a certainty that he meant what he said. *This* was his truth. Not kisses that made her want to know more. Not fanciful dreams of being cherished. This man was as hard and cold as the chiseled sculptures he resembled. Coldly intent, uncompromising. Stark and grim. Not even a glimpse of the vulnerability she had sworn she had seen in the rain.

What secrets hid in his soul, she wondered, that made him believe in a world without love? And without thinking better of it, she asked, "What happened to you that cast your heart in stone?"

Her question clearly took him aback. She could see it in his eyes. His jaw clenched, his hand worked. Emotions clearly waged a war within him.

"You're a romantic fool, Miss Sinclair," he said at length, his features once again under control. "Knights in shining armor. Hearts cast in stone. Love instead of science. Love is a figment of a romantic fool's imagination. Science is fact."

For reasons she didn't understand, Ellie refused to back down, couldn't afford to back down. "There *are* people who love," she stated with conviction.

"No, Miss Sinclair," he said, suddenly looking far older than his years. "There are only people who desire. You'd do well not to forget that fact."

With that he turned and walked away, leaving Ellie alone on the walkway, knowing he had spoken of himself.

Chapter 9

New York 1873

"We're ruined!"

Nicholas sat at the dining room table, staring at his father who stood in the doorway.

"We're ruined, I tell you," his father raged. "Ruined!"

The dropping clatter of silver on fine bone china drew Nicholas's attention. His mother sat in her chair at the foot of the table, her violet eyes wide, her porcelain cheeks blanched of color.

"What are you talking about, Pierre?" his mother asked, the normal calm of her voice strained. "How can we be ruined?"

"Everything is gone! Lost!"

Nicholas couldn't seem to breathe. His narrow chest felt oddly tight and his head felt light. Not because of the actual words his father spoke, he hardly comprehended them. Nicholas's world seemed to be falling apart around him. First his mother with her unfamiliar tears and missing scarf; now his father, a man so tall and proud, slumped against the doorjamb, his strong features crumpling into a hideous mask. Nicholas neither knew why it was happening, nor what he could do to stop it.

Pierre Drake, from the long line of aristocratic New York

Drakes, was a highly respected man for more than his lineage. An upholder of justice and a man of the highest standards, he and his family lived the quiet, peaceful life of the well-to-do. Pierre Drake had married the young Louise Whitmore, of the highly regarded Boston Whitmores, thirteen years earlier. A love match, it had been said.

"Explain, Pierre!" his mother cried. "What are you talking about? How could everything be lost?"

"It was a certainty," he groaned, shaking his head. "Just as I told you and Nicholas. I invested in the pipes the city will need for the sewage system they plan to overhaul. I bought them, damn it! And when I went to the city, they had already purchased them from someone else."

"This is terrible, Pierre. But one investment? How can one investment ruin us? What about my inheritance from my family? The inheritance from your family?"

"Gone. All gone!"

"But how!? You said right here at this table, one risky, but small investment."

"I put it all in. Enough pipe work for the entire city. I invested it all!"

"No," his mother breathed. "No."

"No one else knew of the city's plans. I was sure to succeed. I would have tripled my money. But someone found out and swept it out from beneath me. Someone came in ahead of me. And not only that, they sold their piping at an outrageously low cost. I never could have competed even if I had gotten there sooner. This seller is surely going to lose money. It's as if someone did it to me on purpose!"

His mother gasped.

"How could this happen?" Pierre cried, half in anger, half in despair. "How could anyone have found out?"

When Nicholas looked back, his mother sat at the table, one delicate hand to her chest, the other pressed to her mouth as it to stifle a scream.

"Mother, what's wrong?"

Her eyes darted to him, and Nicholas saw the fear. But before he could ask another question, she pushed up from the table, her chair tumbling to the floor, and fled from the room.

Chapter 10

At nearly three o'clock on Thursday, the day Grady O'Shea had set up the meeting for Nicholas, Ellie stood completely unsuspecting in her shop. The bell over the door rang, announcing someone's arrival.

Ellie's hats were in demand. The most stylish as well as the wealthiest society women shopped in her store. "Mrs. Roberts." Ellie greeted a short, well-dressed woman with primly styled brown hair. "How good it is to see you."

"Miss Sinclair," Maisy Roberts said, her voice atwitter. "I would like you to meet a dear friend of mine, Miss Deidra Carlisle."

"I'm pleased to meet you, Miss Carlisle."

The woman was tall and lithe, with deep brown hair and dark brown eyes. She was beautiful and knew it, Ellie assessed in a moment, as she generally could when she met a new customer.

Maisy twittered. "She has just returned from her father's plantation in the Caribbean and needs an entirely new wardrobe, including hats. I've told Deidra about the stunning creations you make, and insisted that we come."

"How kind you are, Mrs. Roberts." Ellie turned to Miss Carlisle. "I'd be happy to show you a few things."

Ellie directed Miss Carlisle to a chair in front of a mirror. After she considered the woman's coloring, face shape, and had asked a few questions, Ellie began showing off an array of hats in multiple hues and styles. Miss Carlisle was considering one hat from several angles, when Ellie went to a side counter to retrieve a length of black voile that Deidra had requested. Maisy followed.

"Miss Sinclair," Maisy whispered, glancing surreptitiously at Deidra. "Miss Carlisle has spent a great many years in that . . . shall we say, less-than-civilized region of the world." She glanced back once again. "As a result she is . . . less than knowledgeable about what should and should not be worn in polite society. She's here to find a husband, after all, and we can't have her looking like a widow . . . or a woman of lesser virtue."

"Ah, and you'd like me to steer her in . . . more appropriate directions."

Maisy sighed in relief. "Yes, if you could."

Knowing that the task set before her would take some time, Ellie sent Jim on to make his deliveries. Loving the challenge of the task at hand, she turned back to Maisy. "Now, let's see what we can do."

Nicholas pulled out the Sinclair file. In it he found the latest offer. The woman drove him crazy. But then a slow, reluctant smile pulled at his lips. She was an infuriating little baggage. But amusing. And kind. He glanced at the clock. Five-fifteen. If he hurried he could be at Ellie's shop before it closed, and finally present her with the offer that surely even she wouldn't decline.

Nicholas set off through the streets in his black-enameled landau, directing his driver to take a side road in hopes of missing some of the heavier traffic. They hadn't gone more than a few blocks, however, when Nicholas caught sight of a huddled form. Upon closer inspection, he realized with a start that it was Jim.

Nicholas muttered a curse, then called for his driver to

stop. Jim sat on the bottom step of a town house, his head in his arms on his knees. Nicholas would have sworn the man was crying. "Jim?" he called, looking around as if he might find someone to help.

"Go away," Jim muttered brokenly.

Nicholas wanted nothing more than to do just that. Instead he sighed, climbed down from the carriage, and with no thought for his Saville Row suit, sat down on the bottom step next to Jim.

"I told you, Nicky. Go away."

Nicky. Nicholas held back a grimace.

"Come on, Jim. Tell me what's wrong."

Jim raised his head and looked at Nicholas through tear-filled eyes. "Nothing's wrong."

Nicholas grumbled another curse. "Are you sure?"

Jim raised his head and wiped his face with his sleeve. "Sure I'm sure."

Nicholas hesitated and considered. Should he leave? Should he just sit there? He didn't know. Why was it, he wondered irritably, that every time he turned around these days, he was faced with some peculiar . . . domestic situation. He shook his head. But he was relieved in the next second when Jim asked, "Is that your carriage?"

"Yes," Nicholas replied. "How about a ride?" Anything to keep the man from crying again.

"Sure, Nicky. I've got to get back to the shop."

"Perfect."

Once in the carriage, with the exception of Jim's occasional oohs and aahs over the fine leather interior, they rode in silence. When they pulled up in front of the shop, Nicholas saw Ellie standing at the door with two women. Ellie appeared distracted despite her customers.

"There you are," she practically cried, when Jim jumped down to the street, a mix of worry and relief etching her brow.

"Mr. Drake!" Maisy called. "How good it is to see you."

Nicholas reluctantly pulled his attention away from Ellie

and noticed for the first time that Harvey Roberts' wife, Maisy, stood on the steps. "Mrs. Roberts," he nodded.

"Mr. Drake, I'd like to introduce you to a dear friend of mine, recently arrived from her father's plantation in the Caribbean, Miss Deidra Carlisle."

Nicholas gave a slight formal bow. "Miss Carlisle."

Deidra extended her gloved hand, seeming to purr as she watched him. "Mr. Drake."

"I hope you are enjoying New York," he said, taking her hand politely.

Her smile grew sultry. "Why yes, Mr. Drake. In fact, it is becoming more enjoyable by the second."

They exchanged a few more pleasantries, before Nicholas bid the women good day, then turned to Ellie just in time to catch her watching the exchange.

Hastily, she turned to Jim, seemingly flustered. "This is the third time this week you've been late," she said after a moment.

Nicholas eyed Jim more closely.

"I know, Ellie," Jim said apologetically. "I'm sorry. I don't mean to be late."

"Of course you don't." She pressed her hand to Jim's forearm. "Is something wrong? Have I given you too many deliveries to make?"

"Oh no, Ellie!" he said, his eyes wide and beseeching. "Really, I'm sorry I'm late. I'll do better tomorrow, I promise."

After Jim stepped inside the shop, Ellie turned to Nicholas. "Thank you for bringing him back," she said stiffly, hating that she felt anything over the way Nicholas had talked to Deidra Carlisle.

"I was waiting for you to blame me for him being late."

Nicholas's smile was broad and wonderful, melting Ellie's anger. "You probably *were* the reason he was late," she quipped, unable to keep a reluctant smile from softening her words.

Nicholas chuckled. "Well, whatever the reason, he's back now. You can stop worrying."

"Me? Stop worrying?" She shook her head ruefully. "I swear I've been worrying about Jim for as long as I can remember."

"Since school?"

Ellie looked confused. "School?"

Nicholas smiled. "Nuns who serve porridge," he stated with a casual shrug, ". . . at school, remember?"

Exhaling slowly, Ellie sank down onto the steps. "Yes, of course, since school."

Unexpectedly Ellie chuckled, but her eyes were sad. She looked for all the world like a lost little girl, and Nicholas felt an unaccustomed need to gather her in his arms and rock her gently. He shifted his weight against the feelings. And then for reasons he would never fully understand, she began to talk.

"Jim was six years old when he . . . enrolled. He was so cute and sweet." Her lips pursed. "But he was a target the minute he stepped through the door."

"Ah, and you became his champion?" Nicholas speculated, his voice gentle and soft.

"Of sorts, I guess. I was eleven, and I did the best I could for him."

"You've been a fighter for a long time then."

"A fighter? Who knows." Her gaze grew troubled. "The other children were so mean to Jim. Teasing, taunting, stealing what few possessions he had. I just did what anyone else would have done. I was older. I tried to protect him."

"No, Ellie, not what anyone else would have done," he said tenderly, pointing out the fallacy of her statement. "The others were the ones who taunted him."

She smiled suddenly, as if he hadn't spoken. "There was one boy, a thirteen-year-old named Clive. He was particularly mean to Jim. And no matter what I said to him I couldn't get him to stop." Her emerald eyes lighted with heart-stopping mischief.

"Why do I get the feeling that somehow you finally managed to get the boy to stop?" he asked, captivated in spite of himself.

"Because you are too smart by half, Mr. Drake," she chuckled. "I've rued that fact more than once since I met you." She started to push herself up from the step.

"Wait a minute! Where are you going? You can't leave me hanging. I want to know what happened to the no-account Clive."

Relaxing back onto the step, Ellie shook her head with a chime of laughter. "No-account Clive," she mused. "Well, Clive had a penchant for slipping all sorts of . . . unsavory items into Jim's clothes, his desk . . . his food. And no matter how often Clive pulled a stunt, Jim never learned to expect it."

A sadness flickered in her eyes, and Nicholas had to forcibly keep his hands at his side.

"And no matter how hard I tried," she continued, "I could never get everything checked for Clive's mischief before Jim happened upon it. But then one day I had an idea." Her smile returned, more devilish than ever. "If there was one thing that happened at the . . . school with clockwork regularity, it was the rice pudding served on Fridays. A special treat which Jim loved with all his heart. But Clive liked it too, or at least he liked taking Jim's away, switching his empty bowl with Jim's full one." She scrunched her delicate shoulders. "As it happened, Jim loved worms, always had some with him. You know, little white worms. Soooo, I slipped a few in Jim's pudding one day."

A curious twist pulled at Nicholas's lips.

"Yes," she continued. "And sure enough, Clive reached over and took Jim's bowl. I had hoped that Clive would merely eat the pudding, get sick as a dog, then never want to eat rice pudding again."

She paused and somehow Nicholas found he had to know what happened to Clive, what happened to Jim, but most of all, he had to know what happened to a brave little girl named Ellie. "You killed him instead," he stated, only half teasing.

Her burst of delighted laughter wafted up into the sky. "No, but one of the worms chose to make itself known just as Clive scooped up a big spoonful. Of course his eyes went wide and I swore right then and there that both Jim and I were dead. But as luck would have it, two things conspired to save us. Clive happened to have his usual contraband drawing of a very . . . undressed female that he had drawn hidden beneath the bowl of pudding."

"And the other thing?" he prodded, when she suddenly went silent.

"Mother Superior walked right up to Clive. 'You're not finished, Clive,' she said when he tried to push his tray aside."

Nicholas couldn't help his burst of laughter at Ellie's rendition of an undoubtedly stern and dignified nun's voice.

"'I'm not hungry,' Clive mumbled. 'Nonsense. Eat up this instant.' Well, what was Clive to do? Everyone there was scared to death of the Mother Superior. To defy her was to defy God himself. But to tell her of the worms was to invite an inspection, and ultimately to reveal his drawing." Ellie grimaced. "Clive ate the worms. Knowing they were there. Every last one." She shook her head. "I've often wondered if Mother Superior hadn't actually known. It's hard to say. But all that matters, is that for reasons only Mother Superior, Clive, and God are aware of, Clive never bothered Jim again."

Nicholas looked on, an odd poignancy washing over him. Ellie had tried to defend Jim with whatever means her young mind could devise. Nicholas felt a deep stirring of protectiveness within him that went beyond simple desire, making him uncomfortable. He wanted to beat the derelict Clive to a pulp, find an entire vat of rice pudding for Jim—and keep Ellie safe. "Perhaps I should've talked to old Clive," he managed, "before I tangled with the likes of you. Maybe then I'd have learned a thing or two and would have your house by now."

His words shattered the magical spell that had surrounded them. And he was almost thankful when her features flashed once again with impatience and anger, wiping clean that look that made him want to pull her into his arms and damn all else—damn her house, damn his vow of vengeance. Because that was impossible.

"How many times do I have to tell you, Mr. Drake, that I'm not going to sell my house?" she said tightly.

But he was given no opportunity to answer when Hannah bustled out behind them, Jim at her heels. "Come along, everyone," Hannah said, handing Ellie her reticule and wrap. "Time to go. You know how Barnard hates it when we're late." She stopped and gave Nicholas a calm, considering look. "Hello, Mr. Drake," she said with stiff politeness.

He knew she was remembering her visit to his office. He wondered if Ellie was aware of the visitors he'd had that day. He doubted it. "Hello, Miss Schurr," he drawled with a charming smile that made Hannah chuckle despite herself.

"A rogue you are, Mr. Drake. If you're not careful, I just might give up on Barnard and set my sights on you."

"And I'd be honored."

At this, Ellie snorted.

"Ellie!" Hannah exclaimed.

"What?" she demanded. She couldn't believe that she had just told this man anything about her past. The one person in the world she shouldn't tell! What was happening to her?

Hannah tsked, then glanced out to the street. "My oh my, such a fine carriage. Fast too, I suppose. As long as you're here, why don't you offer us a ride home, Mr. Drake."

"Hannah!"

"Now Ellie, we need to hurry," Hannah stated.

"I realize that Hannah, but no doubt Charles will come by at any minute. He can give us a ride."

"Charles won't be by and you know it. He's been busy

with his father opening that new publishing business of theirs. We've seen neither hide nor hair of that man in days, and no doubt won't for weeks to come with all the work they have ahead of them. A publishing business, for mercy's sake," Hannah chided, with a shake of her head. "But Mr. Drake is here and has kindly offered us a ride. A simple ride, dear."

"We'll walk, Hannah."

"I may not be the . . . gallant Mr. Monroe," Nicholas interjected with an exaggerated bow, "but alas, as Miss Schurr has pointed out, I am here and I have a carriage."

After that, Hannah and Jim ignored Ellie and strode down the steps to the black coach. Ellie cast Nicholas an angry glance. "You just love getting your way."

Nicholas's smiled broadened. "If only I could have my way with *you.*"

Ellie's cheeks scorched red. The thought of doing him bodily harm filled her mind with heady delight. But before Ellie could respond, Nicholas took her keys from her hand and slipped it in the lock. "Hannah's in a hurry, love. We don't want to keep Barnard waiting."

His taking her keys caught her off guard. So simple, yet so tender. Someone else being strong.

She sucked in her breath, then snatched the keys away, hardening herself against this man who turned her world upside down at every turn. "Believe it or not, Mr. Drake, I am perfectly capable of inserting a key and locking a door."

"I never said you weren't. I was simply being polite."

"Save the etiquette for someone who's interested. Like Hannah . . . or Miss Carlisle."

One slash of dark brow rose and his roguish smile returned. He studied her for a moment, before he gave her a crisp, seemingly satisfied nod, then trod down the steps to help Hannah and Jim into the carriage. When Ellie came alongside Nicholas, he merely stepped aside, offering no hand to assist her.

Ellie fumed silently as she narrowed her eyes, gritted her

teeth, gathered her long skirts, then put her daintily shod foot on the step and attempted to climb in. For a second she thought she might actually make it. But in the next, her balance, precarious at best with her hands all tangled up in her skirts, faltered. She tried to free her fingers from the coil of fabric with little success. But before she could topple to the ground, though not before she gave an undignified shriek, Nicholas reached out with surprising speed and caught her against his hard, solid chest.

Hannah gasped, but after one startled then relieved moment, Jim cheered. Nicholas smiled and bowed, with Ellie in his arms.

"You probably wish I had fallen flat on my face," she muttered petulantly. "A swan dive into the pavement . . . a nose dive into the mud—"

"If I had wanted that I wouldn't have caught you."

"You probably hoped that I'd fall so you *could* catch me," Ellie persisted stubbornly.

Nicholas raised a brow. "Don't we think highly of ourselves today?"

"There you go again with your 'we's', when *we* don't do anything together. *I* nearly fell because *you* were a mannerless clout."

Nicholas only smiled. "You can't have it both ways, Miss Sinclair. Either you allow me to offer common courtesies or you don't. Now get in."

"Really, Mr. Drake," Hannah said when Nicholas followed Ellie into the carriage. "One might believe you're intentionally trying to goad our sweet Ellie."

Nicholas chuckled, but when he responded he looked only at Ellie. "Did you ever think, Miss Schurr, that your *sweet Ellie* is intentionally trying to goad me?"

Ellie raised a brow of her own. "*Now* who thinks too highly of themselves?"

Nicholas's smile widened. "*Touché*, Miss Sinclair. Might we call a truce?"

"Not on your life, Drake, not on your life."

Chapter 11

At seven o'clock that same evening, Nicholas arrived at Grady O'Shea's home on Sixteenth Street. Though he was right on time, the house was already filled with O'Shea's neighbors.

"Mr. Drake," Grady enthused. "Good of you to come."

Nicholas was duly introduced to each and every person present. Many were of advanced years, some were younger but with children out of the house. Though a few, like the Widow Walsh, were young, husbandless, and with many children.

Nicholas took the time to discuss each person's home, explaining how a sale would be transacted should they choose to sell. By the time he was offered a makeshift podium at the front of the parlor to address the group at large, there really was no need. The mood was almost festive as everyone was well in favor of selling.

The mood, however, took an abrupt turn for the worse when the glass-paneled doors of the parlor banged open.

"How dare you, Drake!"

Heads swiveled around to the back of the room. Nicholas muttered a curse beneath his breath, but didn't say a word.

Grady leaped up from his seat. "Miss Sinclair," he said,

his smile forced. "What brings you here this fine evening?"

Ellie only stared at Nicholas. "This . . . this . . . scoundrel is what brings me here."

Several gasps of outrage along with a few of excitement wafted through the room.

Nicholas eyed Ellie, his eyes boring into her, dark and cold. For one uncomfortable moment, Ellie considered turning on her heel and fleeing. But only for a moment. She couldn't afford to leave. For the first time since meeting Nicholas Drake, she had come to realize that simply saying no wasn't enough. He wasn't a man to be deterred. Foolishly, she had underestimated his determination to acquire her home. And that couldn't happen. She couldn't afford for Nicholas Drake to ever see the deed to her house. It had been locked away in her drawer for years now. If she could have, she would have burned it long ago.

What would he do if he learned who she really was? Destroy her as coldly and callously as he had destroyed her father? In truth, she was no longer certain anymore. One minute she would swear he was actually kind and caring. But then the next, he showed the ruthlessness he was known for. Which would he turn on her if he ever found out that she was his most hated enemy's daughter? She didn't know, but knew she couldn't afford to find out. A deep sense of self-preservation that had served her well through so many years in the orphanage told her that Nicholas Drake's pursuit went beyond the simple need to see justice done.

Taking a deep breath in an attempt to bolster her flagging courage, Ellie smoothed her skirt, then as slowly and calmly as she could manage, walked up the center aisle formed by seats and sofas, until she stood in front of Nicholas. She forced herself to hold his gaze. For a second, all else fled from her mind. What did she see in his eyes? she wondered. A flicker of pride mixed with frustration? But when she looked more closely all she saw was the unreadable depths of dark blue.

Before what little courage she had could desert her, she

turned to face the crowd. "Ladies and gentlemen, I've come here this evening to tell you that if you sell to this man or any other, you'd be a fool."

More gasps. Mrs. Lambert who lived in the first house of the next section over from Ellie's leaned over to her neighbor and said loud enough for everyone to hear, "And to think I always thought Miss Sinclair was a lady."

Ellie felt the blood rise in her cheeks, but she refused to be daunted. This was her only chance. She had learned of the meeting from Barnard who had been waiting for her at the door after Nicholas dropped them off.

At first, Ellie had been paralyzed by the thought that Nicholas Drake could not be dissuaded from his goal, realizing that if he couldn't obtain her house one way, he would get it by buying every house in both sections until hers was the only one left. But then she had galvanized herself into action. Her only hope was to appear at the meeting and explain why selling was not in her neighbors' best interests. By calling the group fools, she wasn't off to a good start. But frequently her mouth worked before her brain had a chance to kick in.

"Think of me as you will," she stated to the sea of angry faces, "but I'm entitled to my say."

"You're entitled to nothing! You weren't invited here!" a man in the back of the room shouted.

But another man said, "Let her speak."

Latching on to whatever encouragement came her way, she said, "Thank you, Mr. Priori. I will be brief. I simply felt compelled to share with you a few simple facts. If you sell your home to Mr. Drake for what it is worth, or even a little more, you will be in no position to go somewhere else in Manhattan and buy anything remotely as nice as what you already have."

"What are you talking about, missy?"

"We all own our homes here on Sixteenth Street. Granted, our neighborhood isn't the best in town, but *we* have kept our street up. We have cared for it. Nurtured it. Kept thugs and hooligans from taking over."

"Harry Dillard kept the bad element out," Grady stated.

Ellie fought to retain her composure at the mention of her father.

"Now that Dillard's gone," Grady continued, "no telling what kind of thieves and cutthroats are going to start running our neighborhood."

The crowd murmured in concern.

"No thieves and cutthroats are going to move in," Ellie demanded. "Mr. Roosevelt has cracked down on such elements. He will make our streets safer—*is* making our streets safer."

Mrs. Lambert scoffed. "I'll believe that when I see it."

"Then start believing it. Police corruption is down. Turf bosses are having their stranglehold on the city loosened. Theodore Roosevelt has come here to do a job and he's doing it."

"What are you, missy, his campaign manager?"

The crowd laughed. Everyone, that is, but Nicholas who stood silently with what Ellie had learned was a deceptive calm. Nicholas Drake was mad as Hades. But she didn't care. Couldn't care.

"The kind of homes," she persevered, "that we can afford elsewhere are in neighborhoods not nearly as nice as our own. Mr. Drake would have to pay you double or even triple what your homes are worth in order for you to go somewhere else and buy into a decent neighborhood."

The crowd eyed Nicholas. "Is that true?"

Slowly, Nicholas turned his attention to the crowd. "Miss Sinclair exaggerates, I assure you."

"Exaggerates!" Ellie exclaimed. "If you don't believe me, go out and look around. Go out and see for yourself what you can afford to buy with what Mr. Drake is willing to pay. He's not concerned about you. All he's thinking about is his own self-interest."

"Ellie." The simple word was spoken as a command. Dark. Forbidding.

Steeling herself, Ellie turned to face Nicholas. Their eyes locked in combat, and she saw the searing savagery she had seen only once before—when he had spoken of a world without love.

"If you are going to tell them of *my* self-interest," he said, his deep voice marked by a deceptive calm, "I think it only fair you tell them of yours."

Her eyes narrowed. She should have expected this, but hadn't.

When she didn't speak, Nicholas turned to the crowd. "Miss Sinclair doesn't want *you* to sell because *she* doesn't want to sell. It would seem she wants to make the decisions for all of you, whether it suits your needs or not."

"Yeah," another man grumbled from the back. "Some of us might need to sell."

"But Mr. Drake won't buy just single houses," Grady supplied. "It's all or nothing."

"And you heard for yourself what Miss Sinclair said. Our neighborhood is not so good anymore. This is our chance to get out and make some money while we can."

"I demand a vote right now," Mrs. Walsh announced.

Ellie began to panic. This couldn't happen. They couldn't sell. "Mrs. Walsh. How could you even think about selling? Where would you go?"

"She could sell her home and move into a boardinghouse and live comfortably for the rest of her days," Nicholas offered with a kind smile for the woman in question.

"She has seven children, for God's sake," Ellie retorted. "No decent boardinghouse will take a woman with seven children."

"That's true," Mrs. Lambert said with a confirming nod to Mrs. Walsh. "If ye can't afford to go and buy yerself another home, then you'll no doubt end up in a tenement."

"On the Lower East Side?" Mrs. Walsh gasped, fear and dread washing over her features.

"Mrs. Walsh will certainly be able to afford to go some place besides the Lower East Side," Nicholas interjected.

"Where?" Ellie demanded. "To the Lower West Side?"

Mrs. Walsh didn't wait for an answer. "I vote no."

"But you said yes earlier," Nicholas said, irritation seeping through his cool exterior.

"Well, now I say no. I may not own any mansion on Fifth Avenue," she said pointedly, "but my house is clean and sturdy, and my Orville, God rest his soul, left it to me without a penny owed."

"Me, too. I vote no."

"Yeah, me, too."

And so it went, around the room, the yeses mostly turning to nos. Ellie felt a mixture of relief and guilt. Relief for herself, but guilt at having deterred Nicholas. And that was absurd. He certainly felt no guilt about trying to ruin her life. She turned to look at Nicholas. His face was a blank, but she knew as she knew her own name that he was furious. He turned dark eyes on her that were all the more scathing for their lack of emotion.

"Well then," she said, turning away, "I'll just be going now."

She hoped to escape through the front door and return to her house without having to speak to Nicholas. But her hopes were dashed as soon as she closed the front door, when it opened again.

"Ellie."

Her steps faltered, though only for a moment. With head down, she hurried along, down the walkway, determined to reach the safety of her home. But no more than a few steps away he caught up to her.

"Ellie!"

Reaching out, Nicholas took hold of her arm and wheeled her around. "Damn it, Ellie, you're doing this just to make me angry."

Her mouth fell open. Any guilt she had felt earlier vanished. "Why you arrogant, single-minded, selfish man.

This is not about you. This is about saving our homes. Saving our independence from unfair landlords."

"*You* are a landlord!"

"I may own the house, but Barnard, Hannah, Jim, and I are family. We depend on each other. We love each other. Things you don't know the first thing about."

His jaw tightened, she saw it. But she had come too far and couldn't stop. "You know nothing about creating, only destroying, and you don't care who gets hurt in the process."

She knew she was pushing him to some limit. His anger was barely contained, lethal. She felt a frisson of fear. But still she couldn't stop. Not now. All her anger and fear surged up like a raging tidal wave. "You talk about trying to help Charlotte. The only reason you want to help her is that you hate that you can't control the situation. You hate that she is ill and the all-powerful Nicholas Drake can't fix it. It's all about power and control with you, Drake. Not genuine grief over a little girl's illness."

The look in his eyes grew deadly. His grip was painful on her arm, but he didn't speak. Instead, with an abruptness that gave her pause, he guided her along the street.

"Where are we going?" she demanded when they passed her house.

Nicholas simply continued on.

Ellie tried to tug free, fear replacing all of what had been her anger. "Where are you taking me?"

They traveled no more than a few blocks from Sixteenth Street until they came to a tall granite building with an outside staircase that wound its way up to the top. Ellie would have stumbled as they took the first steps if Nicholas hadn't held her securely.

"Let go of me!"

But he wouldn't. They climbed, up and around, up and around. Ellie could hardly breathe, though as Nicholas climbed, the rhythm of his breath was barely broken. When they came to the top he released her precipitously, disdainfully.

He took a deep breath, but she could tell it wasn't to steady his breathing, but to steady his mind. Then he just stood silently, without moving, looking out over the land. She followed his gaze and could see the Hudson River to the west, the cliffs of New Jersey just beyond, and to the east the East River with what everyone said was soon to be incorporated into Greater New York City. On the long narrow strip of land between the two rivers that was known as Manhattan, she could see more buildings than she could imagine in every direction.

Looking back at Nicholas, she was half worried, half intrigued. All she could think of at seeing the look on his face as he looked out at something else altogether, was that this was how she felt when she painted. Lost in another world.

She watched him standing there, as the anger drained out of him, though she was certain he was not left in peace. Had this man ever known peace? she suddenly wondered.

And then she saw it again, the vulnerability. His dreams, perhaps his unattainable dreams, danced in his eyes. Desire mixed with doubt. How well she knew the look. And how rarely this man showed it. This man of strength and power—this formidable man.

"I don't want to destroy," he said quietly. "I want to create. To build. I have it all planned. The building. The interior. Even the magnificent gala to announce my intentions—my grand plans. The wheels have been set into motion, Eliot. The party will be the first week in September." He pressed his eyes closed, though only briefly. "Moreover, believe it or not, I don't want to control Charlotte. Truly, I just want her to be well," he added, never looking away from the view.

"I know, and I'm sorry. I shouldn't have said the things I did." She looked back into the darkened night with a sigh. What remained of her anger and her fear faded into the star-dusted sky. "How is it that when I should hate you the most," she said softly, "first in the rain, then again right now when you want to take away the one thing I . . . need, I only want to reach out and comfort you, to tell you that everything will be all right."

Though they stood more than a foot apart she could feel the tension in his body. Oddly, she did want to comfort him. She wanted to reach out. But before she could, he spoke.

"Sometimes I wonder if everything can be all right. Lately I've begun to wonder if I'm chasing moonbeams in a midnight sky of darkness that will one day swallow me whole."

She couldn't stand to see other people hurt, especially those she cared about. And standing there, despite everything, she was afraid that somehow she was growing to care about Nicholas Drake. "Wasn't it you who told me all things are possible?"

Nicholas grimaced.

"You did. And you can—you can catch your moonbeams."

He turned to her slowly. "That would mean I'd have to find a cure for Charlotte . . . and you'd have to sell me your home."

Her heart began to hammer, her eyes grew intent. "Find another house, another block, another street to realize your dreams."

"There is no other house, Ellie. Only yours."

"Why? You can build anywhere you want. There are hundreds of other streets, just like mine, where people would love to sell. Rows of houses that need to be razed and built over. Revitalize a neighborhood that needs to be rebuilt."

"I can't. I have to start here."

Ellie's frustration grew. "Why, damn you?" But of course, she knew, or at least suspected. Harry Dillard.

"That is none of your concern."

"Of course it's my concern."

He looked at her, his eyes boring into her. "Don't thwart me in this, Ellie."

"Someone has to!"

"No, someone doesn't have to. You could sell, and I wouldn't bother the rest of them. I only want your section of the block."

"Why? Why is it so important to you?"

"Because I want to build."

"Why here? Tell me." She wanted, once and for all, to hear the words from his lips. Not rumors. Not speculations. "Tell me the truth."

He looked at her forever, until slowly, quietly he spoke. But the words he finally uttered were not what she expected.

"I have to build here . . . for my parents' honor."

Chapter 12

New York 1873

The house on Lafayette Place was quiet. Still and silent. Nicholas's mother was upstairs, locked in her suite of rooms. His father had left for his office, though to do what, Nicholas had no idea. The nanny had taken Miriam to the park. Even the servants were gone for the afternoon. Based on what he had overheard his father say, soon the servants would be gone for good.

Dear Eva, solid James. Nicholas couldn't imagine life with them gone. But then again, he couldn't imagine the life that he suddenly found himself living.

Days had passed since his father had come home announcing that they were ruined. In that time Nicholas had moved about the house without notice. He was free to come and go as he pleased, could have taken the omnibus across town to fish every day without a word. But Nicholas didn't want to go fishing, didn't think he would ever fish again. He wanted his old life back.

The heavy brass knocker came down impatiently, the sound echoing through the house. Nicholas knew no one was there to get the door, so he pushed up from his place in the library.

"Good afternoon," a man said, his smile revealing straight white teeth.

The man was tall and well-dressed, though he was dressed differently from Nicholas's father. Was that a purple waistcoat? Nicholas wondered, intrigued.

"Hello," Nicholas responded to this man who somehow seemed familiar.

"Is your father in?"

"No, sir," he said politely. "He's at his office."

The man stepped into the house without being asked. Nicholas felt a trickle of concern. On closer inspection, though the man's hair was full and blond, it was longer than his mother would have thought proper, and his hazel eyes had a look in them that made Nicholas uncomfortable.

"I said my father is not home . . . sir."

The man hardly seemed to hear as he glanced around the foyer, his eyes taking in the paintings and furniture, antique vases, and oriental carpets.

"I think you should leave, now," Nicholas demanded, trying his best to make his voice sound commanding, "before I have one of the servants call for the authorities."

Laughing, the man said, "There are no servants here, little boy. Do you think I would have come if there were? No, no. Only a foolish man would do something so careless." He looked Nicholas in the eye. "And I am no fool." His chuckle resounded against the high-ceilinged entryway. "No, other men are foolish. Men who tell secrets to their wives. Wouldn't you agree?"

Nicholas's heart pounded. "I told you to leave."

The man raised a brow. "A boy trying to be a man." His muted laughter was ominous. "Not to worry. I'll be on my way," he said, looking around one last time. "I've seen enough. I just wanted to see what would soon be mine."

Nicholas's heart hammered against his chest. "This is our house!"

The man looked down at Nicholas with a sardonic smile. "For now." He took a deep breath, then sighed, the look on his face full of contented pleasure.

With that, seemingly satisfied, the man turned to go. But

at the door he stopped and stepped back. With a forbidding smile, he pulled a gossamer thin scarf from his breast pocket, long and beautiful, more gold than blue. Nicholas recognized it immediately.

"That's my mother's," he blurted out.

"Yes. So it is."

The man's perfect smile grew less perfect. "Give it to your father. A message, if you will . . . to a foolish man," he added with a chuckle. "With my thanks." He started to go, then stopped in the door frame. "Tell him it's from Harry Dillard."

Harry Dillard.

The name swirled around in Nicholas's mind as he stood alone in the foyer. Though he might have been young, he wasn't so lacking in years that he didn't know that Harry Dillard was not a man who should have his mother's scarf. He also wasn't so young that he didn't know that his father hated Harry Dillard.

Nicholas stood dumbfounded, the sheer material of his mother's scarf shimmering against his fingers, as he tried to make sense of his thoughts. Pushing the curtain aside, Nicholas looked out the window. The man, Harry Dillard, stepped into a long stretch of black carriage pulled by matching grays.

Suddenly he remembered the day his mother had wanted him to go out with her. To lunch. To the park. Anywhere. But he'd already had plans. A sickening dread washed over him. The carriage that pulled away today was the same carriage that pulled away the day his mother was crying.

It all became clear then, even to his young boy's mind. _His mother had told Harry Dillard the secrets._

Good God, what should he do? Confront his mother? Tell his father? Nicholas didn't see how he could, not with the angry and hurtful way his father had been acting lately.

Nicholas didn't know if it was hours or merely minutes later when he heard his mother at the top of the stairs.

"Was someone here, Nicholas?" she asked, her voice teary.

Quickly, surreptitiously, Nicholas shoved the scarf in his pocket, then opened his mouth to speak. But before he could utter a word the door fell back on its hinges, crashing into the wall. For one startled moment Nicholas wondered if Harry Dillard had returned. But it was his father who stood in the open doorway, his face suffused in red, his rage clear on his face. His hair was a mess, his clothes disheveled, his eyes wild as he took in the sight of his wife and son.

"I must have been cursed the day I was born," Pierre Drake raged. "Cursed! For now I have learned the truth of who betrayed me."

Chapter 13

One single sheet of fine linen stationery, old and yellowed, lay on his desk. Not a letter, or a missive, just his name, one neatly written line, and a signature.

> *My dearest Nicholas,*
> *Forgive me.*
> *Mother*

Nothing more.

Nicholas took a deep breath and closed his eyes against the clatter from the street below his Fifth Avenue office. He ran his large hand through his hair before leaning his head down to press against outstretched fingers, attempting to hold memories at bay.

He had dealt with the reality of his mother by sealing off the memory and never thinking of her again. Until recently. Why now? Why after all these years?

Was it because of Ellie?

Ellie. Ellie in the courtroom, streaked with mud. Ellie revealed from behind the oval inset of glass. But most of all, Ellie in the rain.

He shook his head. His tastes had always run to the

dark-haired, dark-eyed variety of women. Sophisticated, their deep voices as smooth as the full curves of their bodies. How ironic that he had been felled by a blond-haired, green-eyed, sharp-tongued female whose feelings towards him were anything but cordial or inviting, much less encouraging.

What did he feel? Was it the obsession he had considered before?

No. It was need. A need he didn't like, didn't want. He had been bound to no one in years. A person couldn't afford to need. He had learned that lesson long ago. Those you need ultimately disappoint. And of course, betray.

Trying to force himself to concentrate, Nicholas picked up a report and read the opening line. The buildings men made from his plans were becoming known far and wide. One of the largest bankers in the country wanted Nicholas to design a new bank. Bigger. Better. More beautiful. Nicholas should have been pleased. But as he sat alone in his office, the clock ticking the minutes away, all he could think about was Ellie and her house on Sixteenth Street.

It didn't matter that the house meant more to her than he understood. What he understood was what it meant to him. Closing the circle. Bringing that chapter of his life to an end. Finally forcing Harry Dillard from his mind. Then, surely, the memories would cease. Only Ellie stood in the way.

Frustrated, Nicholas tossed his pen aside, then headed out the door.

The day was beautiful and Nicholas chose to walk. The intersection of Fifth Avenue, Broadway, and Twenty-third was nearly at a standstill. Just like yesterday, he continued south on Fifth Avenue past the Western Union Telegraph building, until he came to Twenty-first Street where he turned right, telling himself he would hop over to Sixth Avenue and catch the elevated train. He was unwilling to admit where he was actually heading.

His step faltered, however, when half the distance to Sixth Avenue he found Jim, once again on the bottom step, his head in his arms. Nicholas grimaced, but he knew there was no help for it.

"Hey, pal," Nicholas called out, then lowered himself to the granite step beside Jim.

Jim's head jerked up, his eyes wide, staring at Nicholas.

"It's me, Jim. Nicholas."

It was a moment, Nicholas was certain, before Jim recognized him.

"Nicky," he said finally, confusion marring his brow. "What are you doin' here?"

Nicholas shrugged. "Just out walking."

"Are you really my pal?"

The question surprised Nicholas. He had used the word without regard for its meaning. "Sure," he said.

"Really?" Jim looked concerned.

"Really. I don't have any pals to speak of. If you'll have me, I'll be your pal."

Jim sighed. "Does that mean I have to pay you money, too?"

"Pay me money? What are you talking about, Jim?"

"Rudy, Billy, and Bo are my pals. And I have to pay them money every day."

"You pay people money?"

"Yeah," he sighed, his massive shoulders slumping.

"How much?" Nicholas asked, his eyes narrowing.

"It used to be five cents. But now it's more. Ten cents," Jim groaned, shaking his head. "It's too much."

"Hold on, Jim. Who are these . . . pals you're talking about. What are their names?"

"Like I said: Rudy, Billy, and Bo. They're good pals. They've only made me pay five cents for a long time even though everyone else pays ten."

Nicholas slowly took in the information Jim provided. Without warning, Nicholas thought of the day before. Jim in the very same situation he was in now. Nicholas remembered Ellie saying that it was the third time Jim had been late. He also remembered her story. His eyes narrowed against the thought of a young bully named Clive—and Jim sitting alone crying. A slow, burning anger began to build. "And where is it that you see these pals of yours?"

"Back a ways," he said, gesturing down the block in the direction from which Nicholas had just come. "They already left though."

"Did you pay?"

"Yeah," he said, despondent. "All my tips from deliveries. Nine cents." He cringed. "I still owe a penny."

"What does Ellie say?"

Jim's eyes went wide again. "She doesn't know. Don't tell her. You can't." He suddenly fumbled with his pocket watch. "I gotta go."

Jim pushed himself up awkwardly from the step and started down the walk. A couple of yards away he stopped and looked back at Nicholas. "Are you really my pal, Nicky?"

Nicholas stared at Jim, a strange feeling tightening in his chest. "Sure, Jim. Sure we're pals."

Jim smiled, then turned back. But this time it was Nicholas who called out.

"And Jim."

. "Yeah, Nicky?"

"Tomorrow, just go down two more blocks to Nineteenth Street, then cut over to Sixth. Real pals don't take your money."

"What do you mean?" Jim looked crestfallen, his faith in many things seeming to waver.

Nicholas stood on the walkway, his hands thrust deep in his pockets. "Nothing," he said finally. "Just talking to myself. You better hurry."

For some time after Jim disappeared, Nicholas just stood there, his jaw clenched, his shoulders tense. Then suddenly he hung his head and groaned, but when he straightened and started away, it was in the direction from which he had come. He had some business to take care of—with three fellows named Rudy, Billy, and Bo.

• • •

It was five-thirty the following evening when Nicholas's butler flew into the office, his normally impeccably groomed gray hair wild about his head.

It had been a lousy day and Nicholas was in an even worse mood than usual. He'd had little sleep the night before, though not for lack of trying. He had arrived at the office early that morning, and had cancelled all his appointments. Now it looked as if his day was going to get even worse.

"Sir!" Albert said, gasping for breath as if he had run all thirty-six blocks from the house, then bypassed the elevator and ran up all ten flights of stairs to the office. "Charlotte's missing!"

Nicholas's mind went blank. For one second he couldn't comprehend. "Missing?"

"Yes, sir. We can't find her anywhere."

With Albert at his side, Nicholas whipped the sleek black gelding which pulled his two-seater calash into a dead run. Despite the late day traffic, they galloped up Fifth Avenue, mindless of dray wagons five times their size, and pulled up in front of the house within minutes of their departure.

Miss Shamworthy was frantic. "Oh, Lordy, I didn't turn my back but a second, I swear it on my dear departed father's grave. Miss Charlotte wanted tea, she did. I went to the kitchen to have Cook put some on. I came back and she was gone. Gone I tell you like a—"

"How could she just be gone? Did you look upstairs in the playroom? The yard? The carriage house?"

"Of course, of course. Many times. She must have gone out into the street. Wandered away."

"Why would she just wander away? She had just asked for tea." Dread began to fill him.

"I know. I know."

"Did you see anything unusual. Anyone unusual?"

"Well, there was a man standing out in front of the house earlier."

"What did he look like?"

"Kind of clumsy-looking, I'd say. Looked familiar, now that I think about it."

"A big man?"

"Well, yes."

"Brown hair, flannel shirt even in summer."

"Yes! That's him."

Nicholas's dread receded, though only somewhat. Without another word, he dashed back out the door, leaped into the calash, then headed back down Fifth Avenue. He drove as if the devil were on his heels, along Thirty-fourth Street to Sixth Avenue, then south on Sixth. He was angry, furious, in fact. But mostly, he was scared. And he hated that.

He took the corner of Sixteenth Street practically on two wheels. Suddenly traffic thinned out, and he saw them. His heart hammered. No sooner had he reined to a stop than he leaped out of the carriage.

"Charlotte!" he bellowed, the word echoing against the house fronts.

Charlotte turned with a start, and she nearly lost her balance. He stared, trying to make sense of what he saw. She stood on the sidewalk, her arms out on either side of her body like wings, Ellie sitting on the front steps watching her.

"Uncle Nicholas!" Charlotte exclaimed, clearly oblivious to his anger. "I'm roller-skating!"

A wholly unexpected start of pleasure washed over him at the sound of "Uncle Nicholas." But then he quelled the absurd pleasure, and his gaze dropped to her feet where somehow crude metal wheels were attached to her shoes with straps of leather. Very carefully, she took a step toward him and when she did, she wobbled, causing Nicholas to leap forward, only to make Charlotte laugh when she regained her balance, and she rolled right up to him.

"Isn't it wonderful! I'm skating!"

Taking a hold of his niece, Nicholas turned a deadly glare

on Ellie, who still sat on the steps, looking rather pleased with herself. And more beautiful than she had a right to be.

"What do you think you're doing?" he demanded of Ellie.

He watched, fascinated despite himself, as the perfect lines of her face shifted and changed.

"What do you mean, 'What do I think I'm doing?'" she snapped back at him insolently.

Abruptly, he turned to Charlotte, dropped down on his haunches, then proceeded to unfasten the skates from around her ankles.

"I'm not ready to stop, Mr. . . . I mean, Uncle Nicholas."

Nicholas shot Ellie an irritated glance, knowing she obviously had said something to the child about using his name. Somehow even that added to his anger.

"I only just got the hang of it," Charlotte continued. "I want to practice so I can be as good as Ellie."

Nicholas looked back at Ellie. "You were skating, too?"

Ellie grinned proudly. "Of course I was." She considered him for a moment, her grin turning impish. "And if you're very, very nice, I'll teach you how as well."

His eyes narrowed. "I'll pass," he replied dryly.

With an economy of movement, Nicholas had Charlotte unstrapped and on her way inside the town house to wash up, while he "had a word" with Miss Sinclair.

Ellie didn't like the sound of that, but she braced herself to hold her ground. She'd not be undone by a ranting Nicholas Drake.

Once the door shut, Nicholas turned back, his blue eyes dark, accusing. But Ellie was ready for him.

"Who do you think you are charging over here?" she demanded. Of course she knew that her question made no sense, but it had the right tone. For a second she could tell Nicholas was taken aback. But he recovered himself quickly. Too quickly.

"What are *you* talking about?" he demanded. "What are you doing taking Charlotte away from my home without so much as a word to me or anyone else, sending us out of our minds with worry, all so you can teach her to skate!"

"I didn't take anyone anywhere. She came with Jim." The words died in her throat. "Oh, no. He took her?"

"Yes. Jim took her. Anything could have happened along the way."

Ellie rubbed her temples. "Well, nothing happened to her. She's fine. And I'll talk to Jim. Besides, she was desperate to play."

"She has a playroom filled with toys."

Ellie rolled her eyes. "She wanted to play with someone . . . and don't say she has a nanny to play with. She wanted to have fun. She's a child, Drake. Your Miss Shamworthy apparently doesn't know the first thing about having fun. Good Lord, when I asked Charlotte what her favorite Mother Goose fairy tale was, the child had no idea what I was talking about. A six-year-old child not knowing Mother Goose!"

Nicholas looked at her as if she had lost her mind. Ellie only continued. "So we all trudged upstairs to the attic and rummaged around until I found *my* book of Mother Goose!" Ellie's eyes softened as she remembered. "Charlotte loved Humpty-Dumpty." She looked at Nicholas earnestly. "If you'd like, I'll lend you my book."

"No, I would not like to borrow your book."

"Why am I not surprised," she scoffed.

The dangerous glitter in Nicholas's eyes spoke volumes. She watched him as he ran his hand through his hair. And for the first time she noticed his knuckles.

"What happened to you?" Ellie asked at the sight of his cut and scraped skin.

Nicholas looked at his knuckles and seemed as surprised as she by the sight. "Nothing," he said, dropping his hand to his side.

"That is not nothing. It looks like you hit something, something jagged." She peered closer. "And your jaw! Were you in a fight?" she asked, incredulous.

"It's nothing."

"That is not nothing," she said, reaching out without thinking to touch his jaw.

Nicholas flinched.

"See! You've been hurt. Good heavens, tell me what happened!"

"It was nothing. Really. I had a little . . . business to take care of on Twenty-first Street."

A teasing smile broke out across her lips. "Why Mr. Drake, you ruffian you. Someone could have told me the sky was orange and I would have believed *that* before I would have believed that you would ever engage in fisticuffs." Her amused laughter rang into the air just as the front door flew open.

"Ellie!" Jim called, but stopped at the sight of Nicholas. "Nicky! What are you doing here? Did you see Charlotte? She's here, too. We skated. Ellie showed us. Do you want to see me skate?" But then he seemed to remember something. "I forgot. Look, Nicky." He dug deep in his pocket, then pulled out his fisted hand. With great ceremony, he opened it, palm up. "See!"

Nicholas looked on. A reluctant smile pulled at his lips. "Yes, I see, Jim."

"Ten whole pennies!" Jim glanced at Ellie surreptitiously, then added in a near whisper, "And I even went on Twenty-first Street."

Ellie's smile froze as she looked at Jim. Very slowly, she turned back and took in Nicholas's wounds. Silent moments passed before she looked deep into Nicholas's eyes.

"Where did Charlotte go?" Jim asked, looking around.

"She's inside with Hannah," Nicholas said, his gaze never wavering from Ellie's.

Jim shoved his pennies back into his pocket, spun around to the door awkwardly, then raced inside.

The sounds of the city wrapped around them, the clang of brass bells, the echoing din of metal wheels over cobbled stone.

"I guess I owe you my thanks," Ellie said, her throat suddenly tight and aching.

"It's not what you think."

"Isn't it? I should have suspected that Jim was late because he was running into trouble. Apparently his trouble ran into some trouble of its own. I can only guess that they look worse than you," she said, a smile trembling on her lips. But the smile collapsed before it ever wholly materialized, tears burning in her eyes. "You kept him safe."

"Ellie," he said softly, coming closer.

But Ellie jerked away. "You kept him safe," she whispered. "I didn't."

Then she fled into the house, leaving Nicholas on the stoop watching her as she raced up the stairs before the door slowly swung shut.

Nicholas stood there, silently, staring at the closed door. He didn't know why he had gone after the thugs who had bothered Jim, any more than he knew why he found himself standing at Eliot Sinclair's front door over and over again. He told himself to go and find Charlotte, then take her home. To put Ellie firmly from his mind. But when Nicholas pushed through the front door, he didn't call out to Charlotte. He followed Ellie up the stairs instead.

He found her on the fourth floor. There was only one door, firmly closed. He could still turn back. But when she didn't answer his knock, he simply turned the knob.

She stood at one of the large multipaned windows, looking out, her forehead resting against the hardwood frame. As always, she took his breath away.

He was certain she was aware that he had entered, his reflection danced in the glass.

"What do you see?" he asked quietly.

No response, only silence as carriages rolled by in the street.

He stepped closer. "Ellie, what is it? What's wrong?"

Very carefully, she traced her finger along the glass in

some image only she could see, and he could tell she fought back tears.

"You kept Jim safe," she whispered brokenly.

"Ellie—"

"I didn't. I can't really."

"You're being too hard on yourself."

"No. Just truthful. I can keep Jim fed and clothed, but I can't keep him safe."

"You've kept him safe for years."

She laughed, but it was a hollow echo of sound. "No I haven't. Not like you have in one easy swoop." She met his gaze. "He obviously told you about his troubles. He didn't tell me."

"He didn't want to worry you," he said tenderly.

"Yes, but it's more. He needs a man in his life."

"He has Barnard."

She laughed again. "What kind of an influence is Barnard, bless his cantankerous old soul? Jim seeks you out. A man. A strong man. Something I can never be."

"You may not be a man, but I've never met anyone, man or woman, stronger than you." He realized with a start that his words were true. Her strength was deep, bone deep, not the kind that was fleeting or circumstantial. She was a survivor.

"He may seek me out," he added, forcefully turning his thoughts onto safer ground, "but he only wants to be my friend. Clearly he cherishes you."

"I know he does," she said, choked. "But it all comes back to one very important issue. In this day and age, in these dangerous streets, I can't keep him safe if for no other reason than I'm too busy. Too busy to keep an eye on him." She shook her head, her porcelain features ragged. "I'm doing so many things, but none of them well."

Drawing closer, he saw the same fatigue he had seen the day he had tried to make her soup. But he realized now that it was a fatigue that went beyond mere lack of sleep. He wondered for the first time what it must be like for her, a woman unmarried in a world that catered to men, as she tried to survive. What money came into this house was generated at her shop—again, her responsibility. He had felt many things about her up to today. And now he added respect.

"You do many things well, Ellie. You've put me off quite nicely."

He expected a laugh, a chuckle at the very least. But she only pressed her eyes closed.

"Ellie, what about your hats? They're . . . in demand."

"I don't want to make hats," she stated with sudden heat.

He shook his head, trying to understand. "What do you want, then?"

Her voice grew impassioned. "I want to live."

"Live? What are you talking about?"

"I want to climb the highest mountain, dance the Flamenco." She drew a deep breath. "I want to see the ocean."

"You've never seen the ocean?" he asked, surprised.

"No. I've never been off Manhattan Island, surrounded by rivers all leading away to the sea. So close, yet so far to travel."

"It's not so far, Ellie."

"Maybe for you, with your horses and carriages or, if need be, fares you can pay to get there."

"You can go to the ocean, Ellie."

"No I can't. Just as I can't keep Jim safe. For all my words about being practical and sensible, I see now that I've been looking at the world through a murky haze, refusing to see or accept the realities of supporting and keeping safe three adults besides myself."

"I don't understand."

She sighed. "It's like looking at my face in a candlelit room. I like what I see. But that's only because everything is softened by candlelight. I can forget that in daylight twenty-six years show."

"That's absurd. I've never met anyone so beautiful, candlelight or not."

"It's not beauty I'm talking about," she said, her stunning features troubled. "What I don't see in the candlelight," she continued, her voice growing soft, distant, "is the three-year-old little girl who was desperately lonely, and the eighteen-year-old who was determined to make a new life for herself . . . or the twenty-six-year-old who still feels like she's three, simply wanting someone to hold her, to let her cry . . . and tell her everything is going to be all right."

Her words seared his heart, and without thinking about possible consequences he reached out, slowing pulling her back into his arms. "Everything *is* going to be all right, Ellie."

He could feel the tension in her body, as if she waged a war, wanting to give in, but not knowing how. "Let me hold you, sweetheart . . . it's all right to cry."

And then she did, surrendering, the hard outer shell crumbling as she broke down in his arms. He could feel the wet heat of her tears soaking through his cotton shirt. And he knew as if she had uttered the words, that she cried for the three-year-old and the eighteen-year-old. But it was the twenty-six-year-old, he realized with unexpected certainty, who felt so right in his arms.

Gently he rocked her, murmuring gentle words into her ear. After long minutes had passed, her tears began to subside.

"Oh, Ellie," he whispered, wanting to comfort her, needing to comfort her, "you do so many things well. How many women hold together the life you do? The fact remains that whether you like making hats or not, you make them well."

"You hate my hats," she sniffed into his chest.

Nicholas smiled. "I never said that."

"You didn't have to."

For the first time, Nicholas glanced around the room, noticing the menagerie of headwear hanging along the walls. Hats of every shape and size, in every color of the rainbow, but not a single one that could be called subtle. Outlandish, outrageous, perhaps, but never subtle. Unfortunately, at just the very second that Nicholas grimaced involuntarily, Ellie looked up.

"See," she groused accusingly. "You hate them." She pushed away self-consciously, then walked over to the long line of her handiwork.

Nicholas followed, stopping in front of several hats dangling from a single peg. On impulse, he took down a jaunty wide-brimmed affair, and without ceremony, tied it on his head. Rakishly, he turned back to her. "What do you think?"

Ellie's eyes widened in surprise. But then a slow, teary-eyed smile broke out across her lips. "I think you look rather dashing actually. Most women don't look half as good in my hats as you do."

Nicholas stepped closer, his eyes narrowing. "I don't think I'm flattered, Miss Sinclair. Dashing wasn't what I had in mind."

"What *did* you have in mind?" she asked, her eyes drifting to his lips.

"Peculiar, bizarre." He voice deepened sensually. "I was trying to give you a run for your money in the outlandish department."

"Me? I'm sensible, remember, you told me so yourself."

Nicholas chuckled. "It's hard to believe that I ever said that about you, a woman who makes very . . . imaginative hats, roller skates in the streets, and slugs back nearly scalding tea like a drunken sailor."

Ellie blushed and looked away. But Nicholas reached out, and with the tips of his fingers, turned her face up to his. "You, I'm afraid, are the most maddening, unpredictable, and stubborn woman I know." Very gently he traced her ear and cheek, lips and throat, his fingers trailing back into her hair. His strong hands tilted her head back ever so slightly. "Ellie," he breathed against her lips, the hat falling back to hang on his shoulders.

He kissed her then, carefully, as not to scare her. His tongue caressed her lips, gently parting them to taste the sweetness within.

He felt her sharp intake of breath when his hands trailed from her hair to her shoulders, down her arms to her fingers, entwining them with his. Slowly, he brought her hand up to his lips, kissing her knuckles and finally her fingers. But just before he pulled one delicate finger into his mouth he saw it.

Paint. Under one half-moon nail.

"What's this?" he asked with a curious smile, setting her hand a distance away to get a better look.

Ellie sucked in her breath, pulling her hand away to study her fingers. With a quick shrug of her shoulders, she dropped her hand and said, "I must have gotten into the paint when I was helping Barnard," she stated, pushing away. "And I think it's best that you go."

"But—"

"No, Mr. Drake. What just happened between us shouldn't have happened."

"What? That I asked you questions about paint under your fingernail?" He reached out and took hold of her hand. "I won't ever ask you again," he teased softly.

"You know that's not what I'm talking about." Her voice was strained.

"Ahhh. Then you're referring to the fact that I kissed you?" He pulled her back to him. "That, I'm afraid, I can't promise not to do again."

He pressed his lips to the nape of her neck, gently, softly.

"No," she breathed. "You can't. We can't."

"Why not?" His lips trailed up to her ear.

Her body trembled. But then she jerked free, and turned back to face him. Her stained cheeks belied her outer calm. "Because nothing good can come of this."

"Ellie . . ." he began, then stopped when unexpectedly he caught sight of his reflection in the glass window. Tall, dark, the man he had known for so long—with an absurd hat hanging from his neck.

The sight jolted him, seared him. Not because he looked foolish, not because he would never live it down if anyone else saw him, but because of the sight, the proof, of how far he had strayed from who he had been for so many years—the man he had taught himself to be. Hard. Cold. Ruthless when he had to be. Nicholas Drake was not a man who teased a stubborn woman by wearing foolish hats.

Unexpectedly, the memories started to swell in his mind. Punishing. His jaw cemented, and he took a deep, bracing breath, untying the silken cords with measured movements. "Well, then," he said at length, "I'll bid you good night."

*C*hapter *14*

New York 1873

"You! You betrayed me!"

Nicholas stood perfectly still, his thoughts reeling as he tried to make sense of his father pointing at him. Him. Nicholas.

His father blamed him.

He was barely aware of his mother's gasp. He tried to concentrate instead on the clock as it tolled the hour, the sound deep and low, swirling around him like turbulent eddies in a violent sea.

His father blamed him.

His father whom he worshipped. His father whom he had tried so hard to emulate.

His father blamed him for a wrong he didn't commit.

"Flesh of my flesh, blood of my blood," his father raged, his face suffused in red, a telltale vein bulging on his forehead. "Betrayed! By my own son!"

Nicholas couldn't speak, didn't know what to say, how to defend himself. He pressed his hand to the pocket which held the scarf Harry Dillard had delivered. His head swam as he turned to look at his mother. What did he see? Fear? Panic?

Mother please, Nicholas pleaded silently with wide innocent eyes, *tell Father it wasn't me.*

"I cannot believe a son of my loins would tell his damnable friends of my plans. Who else could it have been? I trusted you. My son. My heir. I have made you a part of most every discussion. So you could learn."

"But, Father—"

"Don't 'but, Father' me, boy. There are no excuses for what you have done." He shook his head. "Your mother told me that Ted and Maynard were no good. I should have listened to her."

Nicholas's head swam, his heart seemed to have ceased beating. His father hated him, he could see it in his eyes. One last time, he turned to his mother, his eyes beseeching. He didn't think about the consequences that would undoubtedly follow when she told the truth. He didn't think about the deadly results that would certainly follow. He merely looked into his mother's eyes, and only started to breathe again when finally, thankfully, she started to speak.

Chapter 15

Nicholas stood in the window of his study, staring out into the rainswept night. He had never looked more dangerous. Tired. Menacing. He was impatient with himself for letting the memories affect him. Again.

Control. He needed control.

Turning away, he decided to retire for the night. Perhaps in sleep he would find a few hours of peace.

Upstairs, his footsteps were muffled by the thick carpet. On impulse, he checked on Charlotte.

"Uncle Nicholas?"

Uncle Nicholas. He nearly smiled. "Yes," he replied.

"I'm sorry if I upset you by going to Ellie's house with Jim. I didn't mean to make you angry."

Leaning against the doorjamb, he sighed. There were times when it was so easy to forget she was ill. "I wasn't angry."

She hesitated. "You looked angry."

"Well, yes, I suppose I did. I was . . . worried."

Then silence. A surprisingly comfortable silence as if all was right in the world.

He was just on the verge of pushing away and saying good night when her voice sounded through the room once again, suspending the perfect silence.

"Is my mother ever coming back for me?" she asked uncertainly.

He stood for a second. What was he supposed to do? Tell her the truth, that he didn't know? Tell her that his letters to his sister had gone unanswered? Should he lie? He hadn't wanted to tell Miriam of her child's illness in a letter, so he had simply said she needed to return home. To no avail.

Damn, Miriam, he muttered beneath his breath. How could she do this to him? he raged, then amended, how could she do this to her daughter?

His life had been nothing but black and white for so long. Now, with Charlotte waiting expectantly for an answer, his life was shaded with myriad shades of gray. It was one thing to feed a child, or clothe her to keep her warm, and he was barely managing with that. But talking about mothers coming back, especially a mother whom Nicholas was concerned indeed wouldn't return, was well beyond his nonexistent child-rearing skills.

Nicholas cursed his sister yet again. Miriam had been irresponsible for years, for as long as he could remember, actually. As children they had moved together to their grandmother's house. Miriam had only been seven years old. By age ten she had turned into a terror. From a terror she had grown into an outrageous adolescent and finally, an irresponsible adult. But it had never bothered Nicholas as it did now when faced with the quiet questions of her little girl.

After a moment, he came over and sat down beside Charlotte on the bed. Reaching out, he awkwardly smoothed back her mane of lacquered hair, trying his best to muddle through the predicament. "Of course your mother's coming back," he stated with what he hoped was a convincing smile.

"With my father?"

He hesitated. "With your father." Even if he had to tear Paris apart to find them, he thought suddenly, then drag the two errant souls across the Atlantic Ocean himself.

At this, Charlotte beamed. She believed him, trusted him. Nicholas felt a wave of surprising satisfaction.

"Thank you," she sighed contentedly, then turned over on her side, pulling a rag doll that Nicholas had never seen before into her arms, and closed her eyes. "Good night, Uncle Nicholas. I love you."

Nicholas grew very still, paralyzed by emotion he didn't want to feel. "Good night," he whispered, unable to say more, unable to tack on a simple "I love you" of his own.

In the hallway, he leaned back against the closed door. How long had it been since he had said those words, I love you? How long had it been since he'd heard them?

He had loved his mother—his beautiful mother with her dark hair pulled up and away from her face, tendrils escaping to curl against her forehead and cheeks.

Oh, Mother.

Why had she been crying? he wondered, just as he had wondered so long ago. But this night he hoped for a new answer. A different answer. One that would negate what he had eventually learned.

If only he had gone to lunch with her as she had asked. If only he had asked what was wrong when she had returned. But he hadn't. He had dashed out of the house to go fishing with his friends.

Nicholas took a long, deep breath, then pushed away from the wall and went to his room. Standing at the glass-paned doors that led to a terrace off his bedroom, he knew sleep would be impossible. He tried to read, but couldn't. With a sigh, he pulled on a raincoat from a cabinet, then walked out onto the terrace and down the curving granite steps to the yard below. Out into the night. Through the streets.

Until he found her.

Chapter 16

Ellie stood quietly beneath the night sky, exhilaration filling her mind. She had walked out into the night, despite the late hour. Pulled. Drawn, to the art gallery. The one. The place where Barnard took her paintings, or so she assumed, given what was displayed on the other side of the glass.

Her work. *The Embrace*, as Able Smythe had called it. Framed and hanging. Bold and brazen. Surprising her with the unexpected emotions she felt at seeing something she had created shown somewhere else besides her room.

Her closed umbrella hung at her side, her raincoat hanging loosely from her shoulders. She hardly felt what was left of the rain. Hesitantly, she reached out and pressed her fingertips to the smooth glass window, taking in her work. Just then, it didn't matter that Able Smythe had said it wasn't perfect. His words were gone, replaced by the sheer joy at seeing the painting displayed. For anyone to see. For the world to see.

She had lived a lifetime for this.

"Hello, Ellie."

She closed her eyes at the sound. She wasn't startled, she wasn't scared. It was as if deep down she had known he would come.

Her eyes opened. "Mr. Drake," she said, looking at his dim reflection in the window.

"You really shouldn't be out in the rain, much less out alone at this hour of the night."

She glanced back then, past him, to the night sky. "The rain has all but ceased. A mist really. Nothing more." Her eyes drifted to his, a wry smile tugging at her lips. "And now, unfortunately, I'm no longer alone."

She felt a pang of remorse at the grimace that fluttered across his face, but then it was gone—if it was ever truly there, she admonished herself.

"You're really too nice to me." His deep voice held equal measures of teasing and sarcasm. "You should be careful. One of these days, I just might get the wrong idea."

"As a court jester, Drake, you are sorely lacking."

"Ah, back to Drake and majestic analogies, are we?"

She gave him an irritated look. "How I rue the day I ever mentioned anything about . . ." She searched her brain for an innocuous word to ease the melodrama of what she had said to him that first day they had met.

"Knights in shining armor, wasn't it?" he supplied. "Building silver castles by the sea?" He shook his head. "It's hard to imagine such a sharp-tongued woman as you having such . . . romantic notions."

She would have been insulted if just then he hadn't noticed the window, and she saw the startled look in his eye.

"*The Embrace*," he whispered, astonished.

Ellie's breath caught. How did he know? *What* did he know?

"I read about it in the paper," he added, answering her question as if she had spoken it aloud. "This has to be it."

When Ellie didn't respond, he added, "M. M. Jay. Remember? I asked you about the article on the artist in the *Times* that was lying out the first day I came to your house." He turned back to her. "Here he is. This has to be the one that everybody is talking about." He looked back, and took in the painting, much as Ellie had earlier.

She knew she should slip away, escape while she could. Instead, she found that she could do nothing more than study him as he studied her painting. She couldn't move, could only watch, marvel at the emotions that drifted across his hard, chiseled face. Surprise, intrigue. And ultimately, she was certain, awe. Finally, truly, she had touched someone with her work.

Ellie felt as if she had consumed an entire glass of champagne in one long, sweet swallow. The feeling was heady. But then she watched as his features grew troubled—as if there was something about the painting that he should recall, something he was certain he should remember.

"Come on," she stated quickly, wanting to distract him before he could remember. "Since I shouldn't be out alone, why don't you walk me home."

But Nicholas wasn't listening.

"Nicholas! Come on!"

He looked down at her then. Gradually his darkened features lightened. "Nicholas," he repeated. "You've only called me Nicholas one other time, that day in the pavilion—"

Without warning, he turned back to the painting, as if something had just come clear.

Ellie cursed silently.

"That's what this reminds me of," he breathed, almost reverently. "The day you came in out of the rain. The first time you called me Nicholas." Slowly he turned back to her and added in a voice deep and roughly sensual, "The first time I kissed you."

The rain had ceased altogether, and the normally busy street was deserted. And like that day in the rain, all else was forgotten when Nicholas reached out and slowly pulled her into his arms. For a moment they hovered close but didn't touch, as if they could still pull back, not plunge down a path that could lead nowhere either one wanted to go.

But then he touched his lips to her forehead, a delicate flutter of feeling, and all was lost. As always, she knew she should flee. But seeing her work combined with seeing the awe in Nicholas's eyes made fleeing impossible. The touch of his lips to her skin in that moment was as necessary to her as fresh water to a man lost at sea.

His hands lined her jaw. Slowly, gently, his lips trailed down her temple, his fingers sliding back to tangle in her uncovered hair.

"Ellie," he breathed against her ear.

His breath sent tremors of anticipation through her body, and when he pressed her back into the little alcove formed at the entrance to the art gallery, she went, willingly, shamelessly.

"You've tipped me over," he whispered, his breath labored as his hands trailed down her back. "Tipped me over as surely as a chess player tips over the king."

"Then what is my prize?" The words rang in her ears. Bold and brazen, like her painting. Part of her couldn't believe what she had said. But another part of her, the part that bade her to shed tight, restricting clothes, to dance in the streets in her red stockings, demanded she wrap her arms around his shoulder as he pulled her up against the evidence of his desire.

"Prize?" he murmured as his bare hand touched the sensitive skin on her neck.

She sucked in her breath. "Nicky." She exhaled the word without realizing what she had said and was confused by his low chuckle.

"No sooner do I get a Nicholas out of you than you resort to something else. What is it about my name that bothers you?"

She met his gaze, her body alive with sensation. "You've been Nicholas for far too long, I think. Always Nicholas. Even as a child, no doubt." She ran her finger down his cheek with an aching tenderness. "Such a ponderous name for one so young. Someone should have called you Nicky long ago."

She saw his dark blue eyes flicker. With what? she wondered. Anger? No, not anger. Yearning, perhaps. But whatever it was, she knew that he was unaccustomed to the emotion. She recognized as well when he once again resumed his ironclad control. "Let go, Nicky. Let yourself feel. You told me to live. So should you."

The emotion flickered again, his eyes intense, a battle raging. But this time he failed to regain control, and when she timidly reached up and touched her tongue to his lips, he opened his mouth to her, pulling her tight in a crushing embrace.

This wasn't what she had been talking about when she had said let go. Not passion, not desire. Rather she had meant letting go of the need to control every emotion. But when he kissed her, again, pulling her out of herself, she forgot.

She clung to him, yielding, willingly, letting herself feel. He pushed her coat aside, his arms like bands of steel as he lifted her off the ground, pulling her legs up to his hips. He pressed her back against the window frame, the wood and thick glass all that separated them from *The Embrace*.

He ran his hand up her legs, over her stockings. Unexpectedly he stilled, pulling back ever so slightly to look down. A shimmering golden ray from the gaslight illuminated his sudden smile and shake of his head. "You told me your favorite color was red and I didn't believe you."

Ellie's brow furrowed with confusion.

"Your stockings," he said.

A tiny wisp of breath escaped her lips. Her lucky red stockings. How had she forgotten? But then his fingers slipped beneath the much-mended red wool, and she forgot.

Her head fell back and he sucked at the pulse in her throat. When he found her lips she returned his kiss, this time her tongue boldly seeking entrance to the hidden recesses of his mouth. Clinging to his shoulders, she groaned at the taste of him. Smoke and brandy. Light and heady.

She felt as much as heard his sweet murmur when she entwined her tongue with his, a primal dance led by instinct.

She gasped in delight when she felt the bite of rain-cooled air against her skin as he pushed her chemisette away. And then his mouth. Sucking. Biting. So gently.

He pulled back, his bold glance taking her in. "God, you're beautiful," he breathed, his hand coming up to cup the weight of one full breast, his thumb brushing over the swollen bud. "You keep your charms well hidden. Plain dresses. Plain shoes. Everything plain except for your hats."

He smiled suddenly, and she remembered why she had once thought him almost beautiful. "I think perhaps you're fond of my hats, after all," she murmured.

"Yes, I suppose I am." His smile disappeared, as he took in her rose-peaked breasts. "Just as I am fond of you."

Leaning down, he pulled her nipple deep in his mouth, his tongue laving. When he pressed her more securely to the wall, she felt his fingers against the soft flesh of her inner thigh, and she tensed.

"Shhh. It's all right, love. I won't hurt you. I couldn't. Let me love you."

And then his fingers found the secret folds between her legs. Her gasp mixed with a sigh.

"Yes, Ellie. Feel. Just as you told me to feel."

She didn't respond, couldn't respond, at least not with words. She buried her face in his hair. He kissed her ear when he slid his finger deep inside her. Instinctively, she tried to close her legs, but couldn't as they were held captive on either side of his hips. She was a prisoner to her own surrender.

But then the wave of uncertainty receded, replaced by an intensity she could hardly imagine when his finger began to move in a rhythm as old as time. She began to move, too, against him, wanting more, though what exactly she wanted she couldn't say.

"Yes, love," he murmured.

Her body was on fire, her face flushed, her heart erratic. She flew toward something, something that no longer could be denied. She wanted it, craved it, and when he widened her thighs every so slightly, his thumb this time brushing the terribly sensitive bud, she willingly obliged, seeking just as he sought.

"Reach, Ellie," he demanded, his voice hoarse.

And then she did, crying out when the startling waves of body-racking intensity crashed through her slim frame.

She was certain she couldn't breathe. It was too much as he pressed the palm of his hand against her flesh, no doubt able to feel her release. But finally it subsided, and she collapsed against him, weak, spent.

Long moments passed before he spoke. "Why is it, Eliot Sinclair, that when it comes to you I seem to have no Will of my own." He whispered the words against her skin, a desperate caress of breath. "It's as if some greater Will draws me to you with the inevitability of the tide rising with the moon."

Her mind could barely grasp his words. She felt so many things. Pleasure, certainly. Her body tingled in the aftermath of what she had experienced. But there was also an aching emptiness that she didn't understand. The need to cry. The need to be held. By this man. For a lifetime.

But she was given no opportunity to make sense of her thoughts when out of seemingly nowhere, an unfamiliar voice filtered into her mind.

"What the hell is going on here?"

She felt Nicholas's instant response. He held her closely, protectively, but didn't move.

"Nothing, officer," he said in a voice that managed to be both respectful and commanding at the same time.

Ellie kept her head in Nicholas's shoulder, but she peeked out into the darkened street and could just make out the blue-uniformed, leather-helmeted roundsman. A policeman, the broad mustache, so common to his profession, full and thick on his lips. Ellie thought she would die of embarrassment.

"Nothing, you say? I find that hard to believe," the

policeman replied sarcastically. "Unless, of course, you've got a little *green* that might make me see things differently."

Nicholas turned every so slightly, enough that his cold, penetrating gaze and his fine gentleman's clothes were caught in the cascading street lamp light. "Perhaps, sergeant, we should take this matter up with Lieutenant Reynolds. Perhaps I should discuss it with him at next week's commissioner's meeting."

The officer's demeanor instantly changed. Every roundsman knew that Lieutenant Reynolds was working very closely with Theodore Roosevelt to root out police corruption.

"The commission, you say," the man said. "I was just teasing, of course, about the green, that is."

"Of course," Nicholas ground out.

"I'll just be going now." And then he ambled on, down the walk, his tuneless whistle carrying back to them.

Ellie felt the tension in Nicholas's shoulders lessen. Her long skirt covered her legs, no one could see what exactly had transpired beneath the heavy folds of material. But Ellie knew. And now that the immediate danger had passed, the enormity of what had just happened between them hit her. Hard.

Mortification racked her body, much as passion had earlier.

"Let me down," she demanded through clenched teeth.

"Look at me, Ellie."

"Let me down." Her breath hissed through her teeth, her eyes locked on a place on the wall just behind his head.

"Ellie, damn it. Look at me. I refuse to have what we shared ruined because I was fool enough to forget where we were. You deserve better. I know that, and I curse myself. But I can't say that I regret what happened. I only wish it had taken place somewhere more appropriate. Next time, I promise, it will be better." He waited a moment, then tilted his head to the side and smiled. "In the kind of place a knight would take a damsel."

Her eyes shot daggers at him. "Don't flatter yourself, Drake. You're no knight, and I'm certainly no damsel in distress. Now let me down."

With a sigh, he released her legs, but he didn't remove the iron band of his arms from around her shoulders. "Don't do this, Ellie. Don't ruin what we share."

"*We* don't share anything. When are you going to get that through your head." Mortification made her tone overly sharp.

"There you're wrong, sweetheart. We do share something." He shook his head, as if just then realizing the truth of his words. "And we are going to share more of the kind of passion we shared tonight. We are going to make love, Ellie. Not yet. You're not ready. But mark my words, we will. We *will* make love."

Her heart raced. An intensity that made her want to give in, to concede the battle, maybe even the war, washed over her. And that made her angry. She couldn't give in. It didn't matter that her nights were disturbed by dreams of him cherishing her, loving her, because her days were filled with a stark reality. He might want her, and she might even have come to want him, but he had told her himself that he would never love. Anyone. He could only desire. And Ellie knew with a deep conviction of soul that once the flame of desire had burned itself out, there could be nothing left but ashes.

"Who are you to tell me what I will or won't be doing, Drake? You are *not* a part of my life and never will be. You'd do well not to forget that."

Despite her harsh words, his fingers caressed her cheek like a gentle breeze. And when she tried to brush him away, he held firm, tilting her chin until she was forced to look into his eyes. "Whether you accept it or not, I have become a part of your life. And we *will* make love, Ellie. Don't you forget *that*."

She went to lash out, to strike him. But he caught her fisted hand easily.

"Don't fight it, Ellie. Don't fight me."

"Why you arrogant—" She cut herself off, then visibly tried to calm herself. With a jerk, she broke free, hurriedly straightened her gown, then headed down the walkway, hoping to escape. But only seconds later, Nicholas was at her side.

"I'll see you home."

"I don't need you to see me home, Drake," she replied through gritted teeth as they made their way through the deserted streets. "Just like I don't need you."

They came to the steps that led to her house.

"Everybody needs someone, Ellie."

Her body stilled. Faint nocturnal sounds floated through the silent streets. "Who do you need?" she asked him quietly.

The question took him aback. Her, of course. The thought shimmered through his mind before he could stop it, leaving him unsettled. Forcing a smile, he said, "I'm the exception to the rule."

"You're wrong, Drake," she replied with a sigh, taking the steps to the front door. "You were right when you said that we all need someone. Even you."

"What if I needed you?"

Her fingers froze on the door handle. His heart froze as well as he waited for her answer.

After what seemed like a lifetime she pressed her forehead against the door frame. "You don't need me, Drake. Just as I don't need you, can't need you. If we are destined to be anything, you and I, it's enemies. You spoke of chess before. A game, Drake, where only one player can win. Unfortunately, I don't know how to play. I spend all my time simply trying to fend off your moves, lessen the damage. You may want me now, may want to make love to me, but only because it is one move closer to gaining your goal."

"That's not true, Ellie."

"Isn't it? Isn't your pursuit of me simply a means of

obtaining my house? Well, I won't sell, Drake. Now or ever."

Their eyes locked, and despite everything that she knew to be true, Ellie found herself willing him to denounce his need for her house, deny his hatred for a man he didn't even know was her father. But after long, silent minutes passed, she chided herself for being a fool. "Please, Nicholas. If I have to I'll beg, but please, just leave me alone." Then she pushed through the door, leaving Nicholas on the hard granite steps.

The nighttime sky was clear now. Cool and crisp. Nicholas stood, unmoving. Surprisingly calm. The memories he had fled out into the night to escape were faint and distant. He realized as he stood there that he had sought her out, to hear her voice, to look into her emerald green eyes. To calm his soul. And she had. Like nothing else in his life ever had. A droll smile pulled at his lips.

Leave me alone. Her words. Her plea.

Nicholas knew that with some people it was a split second that changed their lives forever. If they had gone another way or waited a second longer, their lives would have remained unchanged. But Nicholas realized then, standing alone in the blackened night, that it wasn't that way for him. Certainly his life had changed the second he had seen Eliot Sinclair in the courtroom gallery. But he realized now with startling clarity, that having gone another way or having looked up at a different time wouldn't have changed a thing, just as he realized that he couldn't do as she asked and leave her alone.

He had told her they would make love. But he knew now that while this was true, he knew that they would share more than that. Sinking his flesh into hers wouldn't finally purge her from his mind. Nor would finally gaining her house. They were destined to be together. She was part of his soul. To fight it was futile.

He shoved his hands deep in his pockets and looked away. He realized as well, that he had known it since they had met, but had tried his best to deny what he felt. He had lived so long swearing he would never need another person.

How had it happened to him—strong, capable, a man to contend with? But he knew the how made little difference. Eliot Sinclair had entwined herself around him like ivy on a tree. He was whole in her presence. Maybe angry or amused, he thought with a wry shake of his head. But whole. And suddenly he felt certain that she was the one person in the world who could cease the memories forever.

Only one thing stood in their way.

He took a deep breath, knowing in that instant what he had to do. Despite the past, despite all his promises and vows, if he wanted Ellie, if he wanted to move forward in his life, to finally exorcise his haunting past, he had to forget her house.

He had to forget Harry Dillard.

And for the first time since he was twelve years old, his skin still tingling with the memory of sweet Ellie's passion, he felt that he could. A soft chuckle escaped his lips, a joyousness and odd relief he had never known filling him. Little did Ellie know that she had won the game without even knowing how to play.

Chapter 17

Nicholas woke slowly to the nearly dark room. Heavy green velvet draperies hung open as they always did, regardless of the hour. A lightness he could hardly comprehend filled him.

Ellie. Sweet, passionate Ellie, giving more of herself than he had dreamed possible. Her soft, intimate heat. Her burning sensuality. Her sweet thighs spread. For him. Just him. Remembering made his body stir, making him want her. And he knew now with a certainty that she wanted him, too. If she wasn't so damned headstrong and determined to be independent she would have known it long ago.

Minutes later, Nicholas was shaved, bathed, and dressed. He was pulling on his tie when a noise gained his attention. "Charlotte," he said in surprise when he found his niece at the door. "Good morning."

She stared at him for a minute without uttering a word, as if considering something of grave importance, deep half-moon circles beneath her violet eyes, her breath painfully short. Nicholas hated the stab of helplessness he felt. He had contacted every doctor between Boston and Philadelphia. But not one had offered encouragement.

After another minute she took a tentative step forward

and slowly extended her hand. "For you," she said gravely, holding out a long, thin box to him.

"For me?"

"Yes. I hope you like it."

Nicholas had no idea what to do. After a moment's hesitation, he took the box and opened it with strangely clumsy hands. Pulling the top free, he stared down at the gift. He wasn't certain what it was.

"Do you like it?" she asked tentatively, biting her lower lip.

He glanced up, and even Nicholas in his unknowledgeable way knew that her eyes were lighted by hope. Clearly Charlotte wanted to please him. The sentiment made him uneasy. "Of course I do," he said brusquely.

He saw her flash of disappointment, and he would have cursed himself aloud had he been alone. "Truly," he offered awkwardly. "I think it's . . . wonderful."

The disappointment receded slightly, and her tiny face brightened. "Really? You like my tie?"

Ah, a tie. "I love it." He set it aside and began to finish the intricate knot on the one he had chosen to wear that morning.

Tangling her hands in her skirt, she said, "I think my tie would look ever so lovely with your pretty suit."

Nicholas's hands froze. She wanted him to *wear* the tie? "I'm sure it would," he lied. Good God, it had a huge orange flower painted down the middle. "But this tie goes better."

Her face fell, but then she mustered a brave smile. "Of course, my tie is a silly old thing. Miss Shamworthy was right. She said you wouldn't wear it."

She turned to go and Nicholas hated the feeling that stabbed at him. Anger at the nanny, but, more importantly, guilt. Guilt for disappointing someone who had taken such pains for him. He groaned at the realization of where that left him. Either he disappointed her . . . or he wore the blasted tie.

"Well, Miss Shamworthy was wrong," he was amazed to

hear himself say. "I love your tie. I'll be the envy of every man about town," he added as he tossed his own tie aside and pulled Charlotte's from the box.

His fingers stilled over the sheer size of the accessory, but the squeal of delight issuing forth from his niece set them back into determined action. Racing forward, she leaped up onto the bed. "I can do it," she announced excitedly.

And she did, with amazing dexterity for one just six years old. Nicholas didn't want to consider why she knew how to tie a tie. Her father certainly was never around long enough to allow her any practice.

"It's perfect," she sighed dreamily. Stepping back clumsily on the thick mattress, she took in his appearance. "Yes, perfect."

Nicholas had his doubts. But doubts and ties fled from his mind when suddenly Charlotte looked him in the eye with a heartfelt seriousness. "Thank you," she whispered, before she reached up on tiptoe and wrapped her tiny arms around his neck.

Nicholas stood, paralyzed not only by the unexpected embrace, but by the strange way it made him feel as well. His hands were extended on either side of his body, elbows bent uncertainly.

"Next to my father," she said softly, "you are the very most beautiful man in the world."

Emotion tightened in his chest, and he pressed his eyes closed. Then slowly, awkwardly, he brought his hands up and wrapped her in a warm embrace.

"Find my sister."

The words were a command, spoken as soon as Nicholas set foot in his assistant's office.

Bert looked up from his paperwork, his glasses sliding down on his nose, the long strands of his thin hair falling onto his forehead. But before he could respond, his small eyes widened at the sight of his employer's neckwear.

Nicholas looked down at his chest and seemed as

surprised as Bert to find the flowered accessory. He had
intended to take the tie off as soon as he left the house. But
when the door had clicked shut behind him, he hadn't been
able to pull the blasted tie free. A reluctant smile flitted
across his lips, bringing another startled moment to his
assistant. Nicholas's smile evaporated, and he grumbled.
"Find my sister," he repeated.

"Your sister, sir?" Bert asked, raking his hand through his
hair to smooth the strands back down on top. "Your sister in
Paris?"

"Yes, Bert," he snapped impatiently, "that sister. My only
sister. Get her back here." He headed for his office, then
paused. "And find that worthless husband of hers while
you're at it. I might not be able to do much for Charlotte,"
he added, more to himself than any other, "but by damn I'll
get her parents back for her."

After scrambling up from his desk, Bert followed Nicholas into his office. "I'll get on it right away, sir. Also, I think
I might have finally come up with an offer that Miss Sinclair
will actually consider."

Bert looked pleased with himself. But his inflated chest
deflated when Nicholas said, "Forget it."

"Forget it, sir?" Bert asked incredulously.

"Yes. Forget it. I've decided not to pursue Miss Sinclair's
property any further."

"Not pursue it any further!? Why ever not?"

Nicholas glanced at his assistant and smiled. "Because
I'm going to marry her instead."

Marriage.

The word had slipped out. But Nicholas realized as soon
as he said the word that it was what he wanted. And not so
he could gain her property.

Nicholas imagined Ellie, the way she smoothed an errant
strand of blond hair back into her chignon when she was
concentrating, the insolent way she called him Drake, the
courageous way she stood her ground, the wistful look that
came into her eyes when she had talked about the ocean.

No, it had nothing to do with her property. He wanted to fill her days with happiness and her nights with desire. And having admitted that, Nicholas couldn't imagine a life without her.

He hadn't allowed himself to get close to anyone since he was twelve years old because, of course, people ultimately disappointed—and betrayed. But Ellie wouldn't betray him. For all her stubborn ways, he had never met a more loyal person to those she cared about. Just the thought of an eleven-year-old little girl trying to defend Jim against an urchin named Clive astounded Nicholas—and filled him with a need of his own, to protect. And he wasn't going to allow her fear of her feelings blind her to what they shared.

The emptiness that normally shadowed his life faded. After only one day of telling himself he would put Harry Dillard behind him, Nicholas mused, amazed, his life had moved forward as it hadn't in years.

Marriage.

But first, he knew he had to court Ellie. Show her that he no longer cared about her house. Prove to her that they weren't the enemies she had clearly convinced herself they were. Then, only then, he would ask her to be his wife. He was going to show her the kind of life she dreamed of, the kind of life she deserved. And he would start by taking her to the ocean.

"I can't go to the ocean!"

Ellie stood in the front parlor, the swinging door that led to the dining room swinging to a halt after she had walked through.

"Why not?" Nicholas asked.

"I have a business to run." Her eyes drifted to his hands—hands which had touched her so intimately, so passionately. Did he think about what they had done in the doorway of the art gallery? Had he felt any of the emotions she had felt when afterwards she lay alone in her bed? Or did he return home and give it no other thought?

"Ellie, you're not listening."

Red surged in her cheeks. "Of course I was," she lied. "You said it was August." Hadn't he?

"That's right. It's August. And you know as well as I do that no one who lives in Manhattan is in town this time of year, much less buying hats."

"People who have money, you mean."

"People who buy hats," Nicholas responded with a pointed shrug. "I have a cottage on Long Island. You need a vacation, as do Hannah and Jim. Even old Barnard stands to benefit from a bracing ocean breeze."

"I heard that!" Barnard's voice carried to them from his nook where he sat painting. "And don't believe a word of it, Ellie. We don't need to go anywhere."

"Of course you do," Nicholas replied, as if it had been Ellie rather than Barnard who spoke. "As does Charlotte. The brisk air and drying summer sun will do Charlotte a world of good. Besides, you told me yourself you wanted to see the ocean."

"I lied."

He sighed. "Why is everything a battle with you, Ellie?"

She hated the words. And she hated that they were true. She had thought before that she was damnably tired of being sensible. Good Lord, she had worn a gaping hole clear through her red stockings these last months. And now here was her chance set before her like a gift on a silver platter, she thought with a tremble of excitement racing down her spine. Here was her opportunity to throw caution to the wind. To go to the ocean. But when actually faced with the possibility, could she? Did she dare?

The swinging door fell open, revealing a startled Hannah and Jim, who clearly had been leaning against the door in an attempt to hear better. Jim straightened. "I'd love to see the ocean, Ellie. Do you think we could really go?"

She opened her mouth to speak.

"Just imagine," Hannah interjected. "The ocean. Just like rich folks."

Another reason to say no. Ellie, however, couldn't quite get the simple word out of her mouth. She stood there, shifting her weight, her lip caught between pearl-white teeth. August truly *was* a slow month for business, she found herself reasoning, her heart beginning to hammer in her chest. And she *had* wanted to see the ocean for as long as she could remember. But still . . .

Hannah cleared her throat, then said pointedly, "And just think, Ellie, how good and beneficial it would be for little Charlotte."

"Cottage!" Hannah exclaimed, holding her gently lined hand to her ample chest. "You call that a cottage?"

Ellie stared out the carriage window and down the long drive that led to the looming structure of granite and marble which Nicholas had called a cottage. Was it possible, Ellie wondered ruefully, that in a matter of hours she had closed her shop, packed her clothes, and run off to the ocean with a man she had told herself she needed to hate? She groaned silently, then fell back against the fine leather seat cushion.

"I haven't been here in years," Nicholas said.

Charlotte leaned forward, a blush of excitement coloring her pale cheeks. "We call it Waverly. Mother and I come every summer." Her excitement abated. "Every summer until this one," she amended, her voice fading away in a wheezing cough.

Ellie saw the pained look pass through Nicholas's eyes, then he surprised her when he reached over and pulled his niece close. "Your mother will be home soon, princess. I promise."

With a sigh, Charlotte leaned easily against his side and took his large, beautifully sculpted hand in her own, lacing her tiny fingers with his.

After a moment Nicholas looked up and his glance caught Ellie's. He smiled softly. Ellie turned away, uncomfortable, not understanding why tears suddenly burned in her eyes.

Only minutes later, everyone piled out of the carriage.

Ellie had never seen, much less experienced, such grandeur. Ellie was led to a room down one long hallway, while Hannah, Barnard, and Jim were led down another. Charlotte settled into what was obviously her room, her nanny next door, down the hall from Hannah. Ellie's heart skipped a beat when she realized that the only person whose room was close to hers was Nicholas's.

Intentional?

No doubt.

She tried to be angry. Her heart fluttered instead.

But then she stepped up to the window, and for the first time saw the wide expanse of the Atlantic. Her breath caught in her throat. So blue. Going on forever, until the water fell off into eternity.

Pushing open the paned windows, Ellie breathed in the smell of sand and seawater.

"Is it all that you expected?"

His voice wrapped around her, much as the breeze did.

"More," she said. "It's even more than I expected, everything that I hoped."

"Ah, hopes and expectations that differ." He came up behind her. "You expect little so you won't be disappointed. To protect yourself, I wonder?"

He saw the subtle tensing of her shoulders. He wanted to reach out and pull her back to him. But he didn't. It was too soon. He thought of the interlude they had shared in the doorway of the art gallery. How foolish he had been. How inconsiderate. Especially in light of the fact that now he intended to marry her.

So yes, he would wait. He would court her, as he had told himself. He would move slowly so her defenses would ease—so that the hard outer shell could crack away altogether. He wanted the softness. But more than for himself, he wanted it for her.

They stood at the window silently, surprisingly at ease.

"I'm glad you came," Nicholas said quietly.

"I must be insane."

Nicholas chuckled. "One of the many things I admire about you. Your honesty."

"I thought that was one of the things you hated about me."

"Hate? I don't hate anything about you. I might not always . . . agree with you, but never hate, Ellie. Never hate."

Ellie wrapped her arms around herself, holding tight. "If you act the way you do *without* hating me," she said softly, "I shudder to think how you would act if you did. You'd be ruthless."

His face grew troubled. "Perhaps. But I think even my harshest critics would agree that I'm only ruthless with those who have betrayed me."

Chapter 18

August on Long Island.

Never in Ellie's twenty-six years had she imagined she would have reason to string those four words together, much less be able to add idyllic, blissful — more than she could have imagined. Unfettered sun against her face, the ocean breeze caressing her skin. But most of all, Nicholas. She went to sleep each night and woke up each morning praying it would never end.

As hard as she tried, Ellie was unable to hold on to her resistance against Nicholas. Though in truth, she wasn't certain that she had tried so very hard, at least not since the wheels of his carriage rolled across the majestic expanse of the Brooklyn Bridge, taking her, for the first time in her life, away from the urban confines of Manhattan.

Barnard still seemed to be holding on to his dislike of the man, but Hannah had softened altogether, and Jim . . . well, Jim had given in long ago, tossing his heart into the ring of Nicholas Drake's unpredictable affection. If there was anything that had given Ellie pause over the days they had been on Long Island, it was that. She didn't want Jim to be hurt. But just as with her resistance, it was hard to hold on to her concern. All traces of the dark, formidable man had faded away. He had melted back into the charming, even playful man who had told her his grandmother drank strong coffee to curl her hair. And as he did, he effectively destroyed every seed of disquiet Ellie had managed to sow.

It had started the first night when Nicholas had shown his guests around the house, pulling startling white slipcovers from piece after piece of furniture, using one sheet as a matador's cape, another as a king's robe. Charlotte had laughed, delighted. Ellie had smiled despite herself.

But then, as Nicholas and his guests had continued on, they failed to notice that Charlotte disappeared. Not until they came to the last slipcover did Nicholas finally look around.

"Charlotte," he called, looking behind him. His brow furrowed in question. And with his questioning gaze rapidly growing to concern, he pulled the last slipcover free distractedly.

The sight of little Charlotte revealed from beneath the sheet, her smile luminous, her hair standing on end from the static, gave everyone a start. Including the ever-composed Nicholas, whose deep blue eyes would have given him away even if he hadn't jumped at the sight.

"I scared you!" Charlotte announced with a cheer.

Everyone had laughed; everyone, that is, but Nicholas, whose indulgent smile, Ellie knew, didn't quite reach his eyes. Instead, when she had looked closely, she found what she would have sworn was a depth of love and caring that Ellie could hardly believe possible in this man. But she saw it. It was love. She was sure of it.

And as Nicholas methodically went about charming her each and every one of the magical days they spent on Long Island, rooting out each seed of concern, he left behind seed after seed of hope that began to grow in the soil of her soul, the roots spreading, crumbling the walls she had built seemingly so securely around herself years ago.

• • •

"A walk, Miss Sinclair?"

Ellie stood in the library, her finger gliding along the gold-leaf-lettered spines of more books than seemed possible. "A walk? If I'm not careful, I'll be one big freckle by the time we get back to Manhattan," she said, turning back to the door with a smile.

Nicholas strode across the room. "I happen to like your freckles."

He stopped just before her. Close enough that if she reached out she could touch him. Her heart beat oddly, and she blushed.

"I also happen to like the way you blush . . . seemingly for no reason at all."

"Heat flash," she countered, stepping back, afraid at any moment she would forget propriety and reach out and run her fingers down his arm. But she didn't dare. Not only because it was forward beyond belief, but because Nicholas hadn't done more than brush her hand accidentally in passing since the day he had found her staring at *The Embrace*. Not a touch. Not a kiss. Not even a glance that said he wanted to.

"Heat flash?" His smile quirked up on one end. "You are a horrible liar, Eliot. Your face betrays every emotion you feel. And heat flash was not what you just betrayed."

"Really, Drake? A master of face reading, are you? What emotion *did* I display?" Her eyes widened when she remembered what she *had* been thinking. "Never mind. I'd love a walk."

Nicholas didn't question her, though the look in his eyes told her he knew exactly what thoughts had been swimming in her head. Instead, he took her hand and led her from the room.

After that, they shared a slow, heady walk along the beach every day, her shoes and stockings left behind on the smooth, flagstone steps, the feel of warm sand sifting between her toes. Every night there was a languorous candlelight dinner on the terrace, Nicholas regaling her with lighthearted tales of the young boy he had been or heartfelt visions of the future. Days of simple pleasures, nights of hopes and dreams. And still Nicholas never touched her . . . until the night he found her in a room at the top of the house.

"It's my favorite."

She turned at the sound of his voice to find him in the doorway, fresh from an early evening swim. He swam every day. Laps in the rocked-off portion of the ocean, then the trek up to the garden house. A quick wash. Returning to the "cottage" smelling of fresh summer grasses. Warm summer air. Nothing of the city.

Ellie took a deep breath, wondering how she could breathe at all. When he entered the room, he seemed to consume the area, leaving no space for anything else but him.

"You like it up here don't you?" he stated.

She turned away from him and studied the room of high ceilings and many windows. "Yes, I do," she said, exhaling slowly, "very much. It's special . . . magical." Turning back to the window, she looked out. "It's as if I'm on top of the world." The perfect place to paint, she thought fleetingly. A place where she felt surprisingly whole, peaceful and calm, but amazingly powerful—oddly, a place that seemed to have been made just for her. White with hints of green. A tiny red laquered chest in the corner. But most of all, a view of the ocean reaching out forever.

Ellie felt as if she had come home, as if finally she had found the one place on earth where she belonged. In this room, with Nicholas, by the sea.

"After seeing your apartment in your house I thought of this room. I've never done much with it. But I used to love to come up here as a boy and just stand in the window. It was always so quiet. I could see the sun rise in the morning, then watch it set in the evening." He hesitated as if lost in memory. "It took me a year to buy the house back from the people who had bought it from my father."

"Your father sold it?"

"Yes." Just that.

"Why?" she prodded.

He had come inside the room by now, to stand behind her, just to the side. She had turned slightly and looked up into his chiseled features, once so fierce, now softened as he looked out at the darkening sky. "Because he needed the money," he answered quietly.

How this man had changed, Ellie thought. It hardly seemed possible that this man could be the same furious man who had practically dragged her up those flights of granite steps after she had thwarted him in obtaining the other properties on Sixteenth Street. For the first time since she had know him he seemed at peace. "You've changed," she said without thinking.

She saw the slight tensing of his neck, but then he relaxed. Very slowly he looked down at her, and his fathomless eyes suddenly filled with emotion, written as clearly as words in a book.

"You've changed me," he said, reaching out, caressing her cheek with one finger.

A soft smile curved on her lips. "No one can change someone else. The change comes from within."

"Perhaps. But through you I saw things about myself that I had never seen before. I have been a hard, ruthless man because I had to be. Because it was necessary. I realize now that it was consuming me." His finger trailed down her cheek, then jaw, until he tilted her chin. "You have changed my life, Eliot Sinclair."

Her breath caught when he leaned down ever so gently and kissed her.

There was never a thought that she should push him away, that she should flee. There was only the feel of his lips on hers, gentle though demanding, claiming her as his own. Her life had brought her to this. A moment of perfect joy. Moonlight drifting in over the ocean, this man she was afraid she had come to love pulling her close. Yes, love, against all reason. Dear God, how had she let it happen? But like that day in the rain, the past was forgotten, at least temporarily.

She wound her arms around his neck as he pulled her against his hard-muscled chest. "Nicky," she breathed.

His deep chuckle rumbled through the room. "At least you've stopped calling me Drake."

"It's not that I've stopped," she responded, her eyes closed as he brushed his lips against hers, "it's that just now I'm not mad at you."

Abruptly he stilled and pushed back. It took a moment for Ellie to realize he had. Her eyes opened and slowly cleared. And when they did she saw the teasing glint lurking in his eyes.

"You like this, then?" he said.

"Careful, Drake."

His chuckle rumbled through the room. "You're priceless, Sinclair." His laughter fled. "That's one of the many things I love about you."

Love. Not *I love you,* but it was a start. A giddy elation washed over her. And when a twinge of thought about who she was—who her father was—tried to push its way into her mind, she forced it aside. Not now. And for the first time, she thought, perhaps not ever again.

"Hold me," she whispered.

She had never asked anything of him before, and she saw his flicker of surprise. But she saw as well the flicker of satisfaction that followed close on its heels.

"I want to hold you forever," he murmured, as he did what he was asked. But this time his kiss was a demand, seeking, intense.

Ellie gave herself over, seeking as intently as he. Boldly, she sought to touch him, slipping her hands beneath the loose folds of his shirt. She felt his rough intake of breath as her fingers ran up his chest, entwining with his crisp, dark hairs.

His breath growing ragged, he swept her up in his arms, then carried her across to a bed, not so big as most every other in the house, older than the rest. They sank down into the soft, downy folds as he pushed her chemise aside. He pulled his shirt free, tossing it aside.

"I want to touch you," he breathed. "I need to touch you. Day after day of being close, without touching."

"Why haven't you?"

"I promised myself I would be the perfect gentleman. Beyond that, I knew I had to give you time."

"And you think I've had enough time now?" she teased huskily.

He buried his face in her hair. "Enough? I don't know. But it's all that you're going to get."

And then he lowered his head and pulled one rosebud nipple deep in his mouth.

Ellie cried out at the intensity, though when he started to pull back, she tangled her fingers in his hair.

"Yes, sweet Ellie. Let me love you."

His voice was thick with wanting. She knew it, she had come to recognize the sound. She gave free rein to her hands as his lips traveled across her body, licking, nipping. His hand found the hem of her skirt, then made a slow, torturous journey up her calf, to the inside of her thigh. Higher and higher, pushing her undergarments aside until his fingers found her nest of curls, entangling in the mass. His fingers grazed her womanhood, barely, though enough to send a frisson of feeling through her body. He sucked her breast, before sliding his finger deep into the moist wetness of her, and she gasped. But he had no mercy as he continued his tender assault. His lips began a journey of their own. Lower. Her heart began to pound, harder, the sound echoing in her ears.

But as suddenly as it began, it stopped. His body stilled. He pulled her tightly against him as if he would never let her go. And then he sighed and pulled back, looking down at her body, regret filling the dark pools of his eyes.

"Dear God, you make me lose control." His voice was ragged, his face troubled.

Dread filled her, pushing at the passion. "And you hate that," she whispered.

But then his tormented features softened. "No, I don't hate it. In some ways I even like it. Giving in to desire with you is more than a man could ask for." A gentle smile curled on his lips. "I told you before that we would make love."

Ellie glanced down at their nearly naked bodies and blushed.

"We nearly made love now." He kissed the tip of her nose. "But not this way. Not now. Not yet."

Her brow furrowed, not understanding.

He was on top of her, his weight supported on his elbows, the palms of his hands cupping the sides of her face. "Not until we're married."

Married.

Stunned, she sucked in her breath. He kissed her at that moment, and she felt his breath, inhaling him, his life. Her eyes fluttered closed.

"Yes, Ellie. I am a part of you," he said as if he could read her thoughts. "Just as you are a part of me. Since the day I saw you in the courthouse we were destined to be together. Forever. It just took me a while to understand."

She pulled him close, her throat tight, her eyes burning as she pressed her cheek to his. Oh dear God, her most secret wish. To be cherished, by this man and no other. To have and to hold. To share.

But could she?

"And now that I do understand," he continued, "I know I can't live without you, and I won't. At the grand gala that I had planned to announce the plans for my building, I want to announce our engagement instead."

He must have seen her start of surprise and read it as reluctance. "I won't live without you, Ellie," he said with quiet determination. "I won't. I want you to be my wife."

Chapter 19

What was supposed to be a few days at the ocean turned all too quickly into a few weeks. Hats and bows, responsibilities and schedules, even her cherished painting had all ceased to exist in Ellie's mind. In their place she had found sunshine and laughter, moonlight and passion, though more amazingly, she had found love—from the very man she swore she would hate, from the very man she swore could never love.

Oh, Nicky, she murmured silently as she stood by the window of the room at the top of the house, looking out to the sweep of sand below where Nicholas walked. How can I marry you? she wondered. How can I not?

She took a deep, bracing breath. Nicholas walked along the edge of the water line, the breakers spending themselves just at his feet. As he progressed, his strength and power emanated from him like waves of shimmering heat in the hot granite streets of Manhattan. His hands were shoved deep in his pants pockets. She knew that something weighed heavily on his mind. But what?

Did he regret his impetuous proposal of marriage?

A week had passed since that night, without another word spoken on the subject, as if both of them were avoiding the issue. In some ways she knew she was, though perversely she wished he wasn't.

Nicholas walked along the beach toward the house. She didn't know what weighed on his mind, but knew it was something troublesome. The change had occurred one night during the week when Jim had found an old painting. "It's my mother," Nicholas had replied, his tone suddenly short when Jim had asked who it was. Nicholas had been troubled ever since.

Ellie took a deep, calming breath as she looked down at Nicholas on the beach, wondering if she would ever know what was bothering him.

Just then, Jim appeared in her line of vision as he ran across the terrace, then out to Nicholas. She couldn't hear what they said, but she could see Jim's happiness, and she could see Nicholas's slow easy smile. Nicholas, despite his cold facade with so many people, had softened the most with Jim and Charlotte, and had genuinely come to love them both.

Nicholas and Jim walked along, companionably, Ellie thought.

"I suppose he's not as bad as I thought."

Ellie jumped, turning back to the doorway. "Barnard! You scared me half to death."

Barnard came up closer to the window, beside Ellie, who turned back with him, so they both looked out at the sea.

"He's good to Jim," Bernard said with a shake of his head. "I never would have believed it had I not seen it with my very own eyes."

"I'm not sure I would have believed it either."

"No, I don't believe that's true. You saw something in Nicholas Drake from that first day he came to the house. The day your mouth—"

"Ran like a spigot, I believe you said," she finished for him when his words broke off.

"Well it did," he said defensively. "Never seen such a display. A perfect stranger standing in the doorway, and you practically telling him your life's story." He shrugged his shoulders. "You obviously knew he was good from the start."

Suddenly Charlotte appeared on the terrace below them. Jim must have seen her because he ran back the whole distance, while Nicholas waited in the sand. As if he was entrusted with a delicate china doll, Jim walked Charlotte back to the beach. Nicholas lowered himself on his haunches and said something to Charlotte, who wrapped her arms tightly around her uncle's neck and he pulled her up into his arms. The sight made Ellie's eyes burn with emotion.

"No," Barnard said quietly, "he's not so bad after all."

Barnard wrapped his arm around Ellie's shoulders as she leaned into him. He was more a father to her than she had ever known.

"I never thought I'd say this," he said, "but I'm glad he found us."

Ellie sighed and started to speak. But Barnard cut her off. "Go to him, Ellie. Tell him who you are. He loves you. I've seen it in his eyes. He hasn't mentioned anything about your house in weeks. My guess is that he has finally put Harry Dillard behind him. Tell him, Ellie. He seems to have moved on with his life." He hesitated. "It's time you do the same."

Barnard left the room then, leaving Ellie alone with her raging thoughts. *Tell him who you are. He loves you.*

But did he love her enough?

The sun lowered on the horizon, casting the world in riotous shades of yellow and orange. Ellie walked out to the pier where Nicholas stood at the end like a beacon drifting just above the sea. He stood alone, clearly still troubled. Jim and Charlotte had gone inside long ago.

Nicholas never turned even though Ellie was certain he must have heard the tread of her low heels against the whitewashed wooden pier. She came up beside him, resting her hands on the railing. They stood side by side, facing forever. Silently.

The air smelled of wet sand and sea, salt and brine. Happiness, she thought, amazed.

"Have I told you yet that I love you?"

His words were spoken softly, slowly. She had to strain to hear. "No," she breathed.

"But you knew."

"Yes, I suppose I did." Ellie hesitated. "And you?" she asked.

"Me what?"

"Do you know that I love you?"

She sensed a faint flicker of a smile as he gazed out across the water.

"Sometimes," he replied.

"And now?"

He reached over without turning away from the sea and placed his hand on top of hers. "Yes. I hear it in your voice. I feel it in my soul. It amazes me that I know things about you. I feel your feelings. I share your thoughts. I have suspected it for some time. But it has been confirmed by your stay here." He glanced down at her then, and ran his finger down her cheek. "We were meant to be together, Ellie."

Stated simply, plainly, as fact. But would he still feel the same once she told him about her past? She didn't know. Couldn't guess. She wanted to throw herself into his arms and hope he never learned the truth. But she couldn't do that, because she needed to be certain that his love, a love she had never dreamed possible, couldn't be snatched away if ever she finally gave in to it.

"Nicholas," she began.

He smiled. "What happened to Nicky? Or simply Drake?"

"I have something to tell you. Please."

He must have seen the look in her eyes, for his mischievous smile washed away, replaced by an intensity that made her suddenly breathless. The look she hadn't seen since they arrived. Dark. Forbidding.

"I know," he said. "We do need to talk." He turned back to the ocean and the sun, now lowered, the yellows replaced by deep reds, in all their blazing glory.

But before she could speak, tell him of her past, he spoke instead, stilling the words on her lips.

"I thought I could forget Harry Dillard," he said quietly. "For you, I told myself, I would put him behind me."

Her breath caught in her chest.

"I've tried. Truly I've tried." He took a deep breath. "But I can't. I can't get on with *us* until I've finished with Harry Dillard."

"Why?" she breathed, unable to say anything else.

"Why?" he repeated. "How to answer that question? Where to start? But I suspect you deserve the truth. Then maybe you'll understand." He glanced at her. "Maybe then you'll understand why I have to have your house, Ellie. Not O'Shea's. Not Mrs. Lambert's. Yours. Only yours. The only thing I don't have so I can finally wipe Harry Dillard from my life."

Her breath stilled in her chest. She wanted to run. To hide. To flee.

But then he began to tell his tale, his voice flat, as if the lack of emotion would somehow lessen what she couldn't deny was his racking inner pain. His words held her captive as he spun his tale around her. Of being twelve and seeing his mother run into the house crying. The scarf in Harry Dillard's possession. His father entering the house, standing like an all-powerful tower of rage, announcing he knew who had betrayed him. Nicholas waiting, afraid for his mother, desperate for his mother, wanting to protect her. For he knew. Yes, he knew that it was his mother who had betrayed his father's secrets. But then the accusation had come and his father had blamed him.

Ellie's mind reeled. How could his father have blamed him? "No," she breathed. "What did your mother say?"

Then silence. Long, painful silence as water lapped against the weathered wooden pilings that held the long white pier that stretched out toward the endless horizon.

"Nicholas, tell me. What did she say?"

Chapter 20

New York 1873

"Oh, Nicholas."

Nothing more.

Nicholas stood frozen. Shocked.

"Mother," he whispered, trying to catch his breath.

"Oh, Nicholas," his mother repeated, her eyes wild, desperate, like a caged animal, not knowing where to turn.

His father burst into another fit of rage then, but Nicholas hardly heard, hardly noticed. He stared at his mother, their eyes locked.

She had all but laid the blame neatly at his feet. He pressed his hand to the scarf which he held tucked in his pocket. In some recess of his mind he knew that all he had to do was pull out the scarf and deliver Harry Dillard's message. But even at his age, so young, and only days before so innocent, he held his silence.

How could he betray his mother to save himself? It didn't matter that she had done just that to him. She was his mother.

He stood quietly, his father's rage buffeting against the high-ceilinged foyer, Nicholas's silence sealing his fate. What little worldliness he possessed shaped, in that moment in the foyer of the house on Lafayette Place, into what would become the foundation of his life—all he knew, all he would know.

The next morning, Nicholas sat silently at the dining table, Miriam relegated to the nursery, his father in his usual place at the head of the table, his mother upstairs. The house screamed its silence. His father had no more words for his son, neither conciliatory nor cruel. Servants moved about more unobtrusively than ever. Even the clocks failed to toll the hour.

Silence. Utter silence.

Until the shot.

Once. Reverberating through the high-ceilinged, palatial home. Deadly.

Signifying an undeniable end.

Chapter 21

"She killed herself."

Nicholas's words rang cold and desolate, as the sun attempted to extinguish itself on the horizon. "Her secret went with her to the grave. She never told, I never told, until now."

"Oh, Nicky," Ellie whispered. "How could your mother do such a thing? Blame you, then kill herself, leaving you alone to deal with the consequences."

Nicholas stood very still as he stared out into the distance. Without warning he thought of his mother's note. The only thing she had left behind. *Forgive me.* For what? he demanded silently, pressing his eyes closed, emotion slipping through his implacable facade. For killing yourself, Mother? Or for betraying me?

"Later I learned that Harry Dillard had seduced her," he finally continued, his voice tight with emotion, "slowly, methodically, to get back at my father."

"Why?"

"Harry Dillard used to be a man of society."

Ellie's shock deepened and she nearly gasped. Her father, turf boss and criminal, was once a man of society? What had gone wrong?

As much as she ached for Nicholas, as much as she knew the words caused him pain, she had to hear more, didn't think she could stand it if he stopped.

"Apparently," Nicholas continued, "Dillard was a man of expensive tastes. He depleted his estate. Rather than tell his friends, he turned to less honorable, and certainly less gentlemanly means of making money.

"Gambling," he explained. "Selling opium." He hesitated. "Exploiting boy whores for profit."

The cool ocean breeze seemed to still in the darkening sky. The sound of breaking waves disappeared as Ellie's mind froze. Her stomach recoiled. *Boy whores?*

The trade in boy whores was one of the most heinous of exploitations in New York's underworld. Wretchedly poor young boys, unsuspecting children really, with no hope of surviving on the streets, drawn in by brothel owners whose clientele had a penchant for young boys dressed up and painted like girls. Harry Dillard had done this? No, her mind screamed. Please, God, no.

Ellie had heard the rumors of her father's criminal ways, but in some naive place in her heart she had always held on to the hope that he wasn't as bad as people implied. To hear it now, to hear a list of crimes more horrid than she had ever imagined stated as fact from a man she respected, was like a fatal blow. The man who had fathered her was beyond contempt, she realized, stricken. She was born of a base man—boy whores, for God's sake! And she was his daughter.

"As it happened, my father was the one who exposed him. After that, society ostracized Dillard." Nicholas shrugged his shoulders. "And he wanted revenge. He gained it by seducing my mother, a woman who, by all accounts, had loved him before she married my father. And Dillard used that love. Showering her with gifts. Showering her with attention. Making her feel loved at a time when my father was working frantically to save his own fortune. The pipe works had been his last resort."

"And your mother told Harry Dillard of your father's plans," she whispered brokenly.

"Yes. So Dillard got there first, selling low, leaving my father with nothing more to his name than warehouses filled with pipes that no one would buy."

"That's why you said you lived with your grandmother."

"Yes, Miriam and I went to live with my maternal grandmother in Boston. And I studied. Keeping myself alive with the promise that one day I would avenge my parents' honor. I studied and learned. I studied like no one has ever studied in his life. Graduated from Harvard. And after that, after my father had passed away without a word or note to me, I moved back to New York, ready to make my fortune, ready to destroy Harry Dillard." He looked at Ellie then, his eyes fierce. "I almost have. But only almost. Can you see now why I can't give up? I can't give up until he's gone."

"But he *is* gone, Nicholas!" she stated desperately, what life and happiness she thought she could have slipping away from her. "He's dead."

"He won't be dead to me until I've razed his properties and built one of my own in its place—until I've destroyed everything that Harry Dillard had to do with." He looked deep into her eyes. "At the gala, I still want to announce our engagement." He hesitated. "But I also want to announce my plans for the building. Your house is the only thing that stands in my way. Sell me your house, Ellie. Then we can get on with our life. Together. The past finally wiped clean."

Wiped clean. She almost moaned her bitter laughter.

"Don't answer me yet, Ellie. I know what I'm asking is difficult for you. Please, just think about it. And know that I'll make it up to you. I promise."

His nearly black hair shone red from the setting sun, his deep blue eyes filled with intensity and sincerity. Stunned and heartsick, Ellie knew that Nicholas believed he would make it up to her, make it right. But he didn't know the whole story. He didn't know the rest of the tale that he thought was only his.

A tentative smile wavered on his lips as he took a deep calming breath. "You came out here to talk to me, to tell me something of your own. And I did all the talking. I'm sorry. Tell me now, Ellie. What did you want to say?"

How odd, she thought, her head light, her thoughts drifting dangerously. They had built a deep and trusting relationship—against every ounce of her resistance they had built a bond. The kind of bond that allowed him to reveal his deepest secrets. A bond so strong that he could give of himself what he had given to no one else. His story. But in the giving, in Nicholas's ultimate gift, the story of his past, he had made it impossible for her to give a gift of her own. In a matter of a few minutes he had made it impossible for her to accept his love, or give hers in return. For she knew now that Nicholas Drake would not rest until everything that was Harry Dillard's was destroyed. Nicholas would never be able to forgive Harry Dillard. Or his daughter.

"Ellie," he said, the word a caress. "What is it? What's wrong? Talk to me."

Devastated, she took a deep breath, wondering what to say, how to extricate herself from this position—and ultimately, extricate herself from his life.

But she was saved from answering when they heard the shouts, "Nicky! Ellie!"

Startled, they turned toward the house. Jim raced toward them, across the sand, tripping and crying. Instantly, Nicholas ran down the pier toward Jim. Ellie followed, dread racking her heart. When they reached Jim, his face was covered with sand and tears, his eyes wild.

"What is it, Jim?" Nicholas demanded.

"It's Charlotte. You gotta come quick."

Part Two

∞

INNOCENCE LOST

The wounds invisible
That love's keen arrows make.

— SHAKESPEARE

Chapter 22

The hospital was unnaturally quiet. Nicholas paced the stark halls, while Ellie looked on, dread gripping like a vise around her heart. They could do little more than wait and pray that Charlotte would survive.

The ride back to the city had been harrowing. Nicholas and Ellie had taken Charlotte in the brougham and raced at breakneck speed to get back. Barnard, Hannah, and Jim had been left behind with Miss Shamworthy to pack and close up the house, a carriage hired to return them.

Just then, the door burst open. "How is she?" Hannah called from across the room, as she, Barnard, Jim, and Miss Shamworthy arrived.

"Charlotte's going to be fine," Nicholas stated, wrapping a strong arm around Ellie, pressing his lips to her hair. "She is," he murmured fiercely.

Ellie felt her determined calm crack, because she knew that as much as Nicholas was trying to reassure the others, he was trying to reassure himself. As long as Ellie lived, she knew she would never forget the image of Nicholas, larger than life, strong but desperate, racing through the hospital doors, clutching Charlotte, limp and lifeless, in his arms.

How had this horrible nightmare came to pass? Ellie

wondered, wishing desperately that the clock could be turned back. How was it possible that in no more than a few hours life could fall apart? First Nicholas's story, then Charlotte. Please, dear God, she prayed silently, if nothing else, let Charlotte survive.

Charlotte's critical condition remained the same for two days. It was on the third day that things changed. Charlotte, thankfully, began to show improvement. And her parents returned from Europe.

Ellie knew instantly that the woman who strode into the waiting room was Nicholas's sister. The same hair, the same shape of eyes; only hers, like her daughter's, were more violet than blue. Miriam Drake Welton and her husband, William, who followed in her wake, were the very picture of elegance.

"Nicholas," Miriam called.

Nicholas turned slowly from where he stood with Ellie by the window. "Miriam." The word was short, clipped.

A shadow briefly crossed the woman's eyes, then was gone and she smiled. "I missed you too, dear brother."

William had stopped in the doorway, looking as though he wanted to be anywhere but in a hospital. "How is she?" he asked Nicholas.

"Better. They've been able to relieve most of the congestion in her lungs. I've brought in a specialist from Boston, by this afternoon we should be able to take her home."

Miriam's eyes widened. "I'd best send word to have the house cleaned up."

"Don't bother. She'll continue to stay at my house. I've already arranged for medical equipment and a 'round-the-clock nurse. I want her out of here."

Miriam raised a brow. "For someone who had little interest in taking care of Charlotte you've certainly warmed to this parenting task."

A murderous look flared to life in Nicholas's eyes before he turned away sharply. In a cold, bitter voice he said, "Someone had to."

Guilt, and what Ellie would have sworn was pain, flashed through Miriam's eyes, but then it was gone.

"Yes," Miriam laughed, "someone has to be the responsible one."

Did the woman truly care as little as it appeared? Ellie wondered, stunned. Was the guilt and pain a figment of her imagination because she wanted to see it, needed to see it for the world to make sense?

For the first time Miriam took in Ellie. Her delicate brows piqued with interest. "And who might you be?"

"I'm Ellie Sinclair. A . . . friend of your brother's."

"A friend?" Miriam glanced back at Nicholas with a coy mien. "I didn't realize my brother had any friends."

But Miriam's interest was short-lived, and she turned on her heel, then glided to her husband's side. "I see Nicholas has everything under control here. Why am I surprised?" she added, her smooth tones suddenly caustic. "I guess we can go back to the hotel now."

Ellie watched a shudder of violence pass over Nicholas, but when he spoke his voice was deadly calm. "Don't you want to see your daughter, Miriam?"

Miriam flinched, though whether it was due to Nicholas's harsh tone or her gravely ill daughter Ellie couldn't tell.

"Nicholas, really. You act as though this little episode is something new."

"You knew about this?" he demanded, whirling back, rage contorting his features. "Good God, why didn't you tell me she had consumption?"

"Consumption?" Miriam's tall form stiffened perceptibly. "Charlotte doesn't have consumption. She has croup every now and again."

"Dear God, Miriam! Your child has a rare form of consumption," he said derisively, failing to notice that his sister's cheeks suddenly went white. "How could you have left her?"

"Consumption?" she repeated, her hand coming to her chest. "Are you certain?"

"Of course I'm certain."

Tears burned in Miriam's violet eyes before she turned away with a start. "I have to go."

"Miriam!"

"I'll visit her this afternoon, at your house," she added, her voice nearly pleading. "I'll meet everyone there."

Nicholas ran his hand through his hair, his control shaken. "No, Miriam," he ground out. "You won't *visit* your daughter. You'll stay with her. In my house. With your husband."

William Welton straightened indignantly. "You can't tell us what to do. It's bad enough you had us dragged all the way back here. I will not allow you to command our lives any further."

Nicholas crossed the floor in a few angry strides, what little patience he had at an end. He grabbed his brother-in-law by the collar and pinned him to the hospital wall. "You bastard," Nicholas hissed. "Your daughter thinks you are the most wonderful man alive. Well, as long as I am alive, by damn, you are *going* to be wonderful. Do we understand each other?"

"Get your hands off me," William uttered through clenched teeth. "I will do as I please."

There was another thud, as the man's breath was knocked free, then Nicholas, his tone deadly, said, "Only if what you please is being with your daughter. Charlotte may be ill now, but she *is* going to get better. And you are going to help." Nicholas's eyes glittered dangerously, and it was clear that in a second he could seriously hurt the other man, looked in fact as if he relished the prospect. "Do we understand each other?" he repeated.

Once William's breath returned, he pursed his lips, then said, "Yes, I believe we do."

Nicholas slowly released William's now-crumpled jacket, gave a few brisk, sarcastic dustings to the man's lapels, then said, "Good. I'm glad to hear it."

• • •

The afternoon passed slowly. Minutes turned into hours until finally Charlotte was allowed to go home. Traveling up Fifth Avenue, Ellie and Jim faced Charlotte who rested in the crook of Nicholas's arm. Safe and secure. Love and concern softening the hard lines of the man's face.

Miriam and William were waiting when Nicholas carried Charlotte into the Fifth Avenue mansion. At the sight of her parents, Charlotte's eyes widened and filled with tears. "Mother! Papa!" she breathed, clearly weakened. "You came back."

"Of course we did, darling," Miriam cooed, standing up from the settee in the parlor.

"And Papa—" Her sentence was cut short by a violent bout of coughing.

Ellie could see the tension in Nicholas's shoulders. If only she didn't feel so helpless. Ellie was used to taking charge. But here, in this instance, in this house, it was clearly not her place.

"Let's get you up to bed, little one," Nicholas said with a reassuring smile once Charlotte breathed easier.

But Charlotte reached out to her father, who was clearly surprised by the act. "Please, Papa. Come talk to me."

After one startled moment and a look from Nicholas that brooked no argument, William followed as Nicholas took Charlotte upstairs to her room. Miriam, Jim, and Ellie remained in the parlor.

Knowing there was nothing they could do, Ellie took Jim's arm. "It's time for us to go home."

"But I don't want to leave," Jim protested.

Miriam looked on curiously, a long cigarette held smoldering in her fingers. Someone else wouldn't have noticed the slight tremble of her hand. But Ellie noticed, and she wondered if this woman was hurt that her child hadn't asked for her?

"I want to stay here," Jim added.

"I know you do," Ellie said, dragging her attention away from Miriam. "But Charlotte needs to rest."

Nicholas came downstairs and returned to the parlor just as Ellie spoke. With a weary smile, he wrapped a strong arm around Jim's shoulder. "You need to get some rest too, Jim. You can come back tomorrow."

"Really?"

"Of course." He put his other arm around Ellie and leaned down to kiss her on the forehead, his touch lingering as if drawing strength. After a moment, he straightened. "I want you to take Ellie home and make sure she gets some rest. Can I count on you?"

Jim straightened importantly. "Sure you can, Nicky. Come on, Ellie. We gotta go."

Miriam's look grew curious and Ellie knew the woman was wondering just what kind of friends she and Nicholas were. And with that look, with the feel of Nicholas's desperate kiss still burning her skin, all that Ellie had been holding at bay came crashing down around her. Her chest tightened and her eyes suddenly burned as she remembered Nicholas's story, his past, and his undoubtedly insatiable need for revenge against her father. The only answer to Miriam's questioning gaze could be that she and Nicholas were enemies—from the start—no room for anything else. Ellie had told Nicholas that weeks before, before the ocean. At the time, the words had slipped out without thought. How prophetic that it had been truer than even she had realized. And now with Charlotte out of danger, Ellie knew that she had no choice but to break the ties, break the bond. No matter what her relationship was with Miriam's brother now, it had to end.

Ellie's heart pounded in her chest. Her eyes locked with Nicholas's, and she clung to his hand. Suddenly she didn't want to leave, she didn't want to walk out the door and out of his life. She wanted to throw herself in his arms and have him tell her everything would be all right. But everything wasn't going to be all right. And standing there in the home of the man she loved and was about to lose, she was afraid nothing would ever be right again.

• • •

Jim returned to Nicholas's house every day, arriving early, returning late. At first, Ellie went as well, each day trying to catch a moment alone with Nicholas. But he was so busy with Charlotte's progress and his plans for his building and gala that she rarely saw him for more than a brief, urgent embrace.

It was a week after their return from Long Island when Ellie determined that no matter what, she had to talk to Nicholas. His plans were going too fast and too far. She had to make him stop.

"Nicholas," Ellie said, arriving at his office, determined to see him. "We need to talk." She hesitated. "About our relationship."

Nicholas looked up from the papers before him on his desk. "I'm sorry, love. What did you say?"

He looked so handsome, though tired. Long hours of work etched his brow. She wanted to reach out, to comfort him. But couldn't. She took a deep, steadying breath, renewing her resolve. "We need to talk, Nicholas."

"Of course we do." He pushed up from his seat and came around the desk. His walk was smooth, no wasted energy. Leaning back against the desk, he pulled Ellie into his arms.

As soon as he touched her she could feel the tension in his body ease.

"I'm glad you came," he said.

She was surprised to realize that in some way he needed her. He had been so busy that she had assumed he had given her no thought. How could she do this to him, she wondered, now of all times? But how could she not?

"No!" She broke free.

"Ellie, what's wrong?"

She closed her eyes, searching for the steely resolve that had carried her to his office in the first place. "You're moving too fast. Building plans, engagement plans, as if all were set."

He tilted his head in question. "I thought everything *was* set."

"No!"

He stared at her for a few long, curious minutes, his penetrating blue eyes searching her own. "I thought you understood."

She didn't want to say the words, but knew she had no choice. "The only thing I understand is that . . . I can't marry you, Nicholas. Truly I can't."

The room grew silent. Ellie held her breath. She waited for his blue eyes to turn cold and icy, waited for him to demand that she leave. She raised her chin, determined to take whatever he doled out with dignity.

Instead, Nicholas very gently pulled her close, leaving her speechless. "I've had so little time for you since our return," he said.

The look in his eyes was part teasing, part desperate, breaking her heart.

"I'm sorry," he added. His lips curved into a smile, making him look for all the world like an errant schoolboy as he leaned down and kissed the tip of her nose. "You're just nervous. And who could blame you? I've hardly seen you. Now that Charlotte's out of danger though, I'll have more time."

"But—"

"No buts. I love you, Ellie. And I plan to spend the rest of my life showing you how much."

"Nicholas—"

"Excuse me, sir."

His assistant's knock and words interrupted Ellie.

"I'm sorry, sir, but Mr. Healey is here. Says it's urgent."

Nicholas pressed a kiss to Ellie's forehead, holding her tight for a frozen moment. "I promise," he repeated softly, "everything is going to be just fine. Now, let me meet with Bill. Hopefully I'll get out of here early. Then I'll come by."

Ellie returned home in a daze. Nicholas had totally disregarded her statement that she couldn't marry him. She felt a sense of panic. What was she going to do? What else could she say to convince him?

The next day Jim came into the kitchen. "Ellie! There you are!"

"Hello, Jim," she said, distracted.

"Charlotte was asking why you haven't been to see her."

"I'm sorry, Jim. I had promised Charles that I would let him show me his new office." It was true that Charles had shown her his office, and the day after that he had insisted he take her to Delmonico's for a celebratory lunch with his father. The Monroes' publishing business was beginning to show signs of a great success. But deep down inside Ellie knew that the only reason she had agreed to go either day was to keep herself occupied, to keep the panic from dominating her mind.

Jim's brow furrowed. "You need to go, Ellie. It's not nice."

Guilt welled up inside her. Indeed it wasn't nice, and she was ashamed that she had been so wrapped up in her own problems that she had failed to think of Charlotte. "Let's go now."

Thankfully, the nurse and servants were the only ones at home with Charlotte when Ellie and Jim arrived.

"Ellie!"

Charlotte looked up from her bed, excitement dancing on her features. But the excitement couldn't conceal that her eyes were glassy, and her breath was much too short. Ellie's eyes narrowed in confusion. Nicholas had said Charlotte was out of danger.

Forcing a bright smile, Ellie crossed to the bed and sat down on the edge. "Hello, Charlotte." Ellie smoothed back the child's hair, so soft and silky, though damp. She had a fever.

They talked for a while, Charlotte telling her of the pleasure of her parents' arrival. "I told them," Charlotte wheezed, "that I would show them how you taught me to skate."

Skating. Ellie's heart clenched, and suddenly she wondered if Charlotte would ever skate again. "How marvelous," she said over the lump in her throat. "Of course you will."

"Are you sure?"

The little girl's eyes unexpectedly beseeched her, as if she, too, wondered if she would skate again. But what was the truth? Ellie asked herself silently. Nicholas had said Charlotte was going to be fine. And Ellie certainly was no doctor. She merely had suspicions. And Charlotte clearly wanted to believe. "Of course I'm sure, love."

Charlotte sighed, clearly relieved. "Tell me the story of Humpty-Dumpty again, Ellie," she murmured, relaxing back into the pillows.

Ellie remembered telling Charlotte the Mother Goose fairy tale the same day she had taught her to skate. Suddenly, with Charlotte lying so ill, asking if she would ever skate again, Ellie wished she had never told her the story.

"Please," Charlotte pleaded.

"Why not another tale?" Ellie asked with feigned levity.

"No, Ellie. Please. I want Humpty-Dumpty."

"Well, all right. But just once." She drew a deep breath. "Humpty-Dumpty sat on a wall . . ."

Charlotte's giggle was washed away by a rumbling cough and aching breathlessness. When Ellie stopped, Charlotte only motioned for her to continue.

". . . Humpty-Dumpty had a great fall. But all the king's horses and all the king's men, cannot put Humpty-Dumpty back together again."

Charlotte chuckled, clearly wrapped up in the cadence and funny words. "I'm glad you came, Ellie."

Ellie smoothed Charlotte's hair, a tender smile gentling her features. "So am I."

Charlotte rolled her head to the side and found Jim in the corner. She sighed, seemingly in relief at the sight of him, as if somehow she needed her giant friend to be there for all to be right in the world. Then she drifted off to sleep, tiny purple veins showing through the white of her eyelids.

Ellie sat for long minutes, realizing then that just as the past couldn't be undone, Charlotte couldn't be saved. Ellie didn't have to be a mother or even a doctor to see the reality. Very clearly Charlotte was deteriorating. Despite what Nicholas had said yesterday, this child wasn't getting better. The realization was like a blow. Strong and hard. And she wondered why Nicholas had not told her the truth.

After smoothing the covers, Ellie pulled herself up, leaving Jim in the corner, and walked downstairs. When she reached the bottom step, the front door opened.

"Nicholas," she breathed, wanting to run into his arms, have him hold her, comfort her, let her cry for the tiny child upstairs.

As if he sensed her thoughts he closed the distance that separated them and swept her up into his arms. "I love finding you here when I come home." He held her close. "Will you be waiting for me every day once we're married?"

His words washed over her, making her ache even more, because there would be no marriage. But before she could speak, he kissed her, then looked upstairs. "How is she?" he asked, his furrowed brow belying the calm of his voice. "Did you notice how much improved she is?"

Improved. "I thought . . ."

"She just needs a little more time. She's tired now. But she'll be fine."

Ellie wondered if he truly believed his words, or if he simply couldn't afford to believe anything else. Oh, Nicholas, how will you survive once you finally accept the truth about Charlotte?

"Come back upstairs with me. I want to see her," he said.

"No. No, I've got to get to the shop. I was worried I'd have no business left when I returned. Instead, I have appointments every day."

"Then I'll come over later, though it might be late."

Tell him now, Ellie demanded of herself. Be firm. But just then, with Charlotte upstairs so ill, she couldn't bring herself to say the words.

Maisy Roberts was waiting at the shop with her friend from the Caribbean, Deidra Carlisle, when Ellie arrived.

"There you are," Maisy called from the upholstered settee. Hannah had offered the women coffee in delicate cups with tiny green flowers.

"Mrs. Roberts. Miss Carlisle. It's good to see you," Ellie said, pulling her hat from her head. "What can I do for you?"

Maisy twittered. "Hats, dear. Or rather headwear. Something grand. Nicholas Drake is having a grand gala. Everyone will be there."

Ellie forced herself to be calm as she set her hat aside.

"Deidra dear, tell Miss Sinclair what you had in mind."

Deidra glanced in the mirror. "A sheer veil that will flow down my back, secured on my head with pearls."

Maisy's mouth flew open. "A veil! With pearls! I thought . . ."

"What did you think, Maisy?" Deidra asked sharply.

"Well, I . . ."

"Ladies," Ellie interjected. "I can't make anything in time for the gala. It's only a week away."

"So you're aware of the party!" Maisy cried. "Obviously every woman in town has already been here. Miss Sinclair, please. You just have to fit us in."

Ellie's knowing had nothing to do with other women placing orders, it had everything to do with the fact that she was supposed to attend, as a guest of honor. But she wasn't about to tell Maisy Roberts that. Especially since she was doing her best to think of a way to get out of going at all.

Deidra smiled at Ellie, and her dramatic features grew stunning. "Miss Sinclair. The veil will be easy." She picked up a length of fine French, buttery voile. "This would be perfect. And I'll supply the pearls."

"But Deidra, a veil?" Maisy whined.

Deidra ignored her. "Underneath the pearls you could attach little combs. Truly it will be easy. And I'll pay double what you normally would charge."

Ellie wanted to groan in frustration, but didn't. The job really would be easy and quick. Hannah was well underway with every other order they had taken on. And nothing was due within the week.

"Please, Miss Sinclair."

The order was taken. Ellie worked on it every day, her normally assured stitches agitated as she tried in vain to take her mind off the rapidly approaching gala. She had been certain she would find the opportunity to convince Nicholas that she couldn't marry him. But every time Ellie tried to talk to him, his days were filled with meetings about building ordinances and doctor's appointments for Charlotte, leaving no time to see Ellie for more than a quick "I can't talk now. I'll come by later." But "later" never materialized.

The sense of panic began to grow. Anxiety laced all her thoughts. What was she going to do? She had to come up with a plan, and quickly. Her time was running dangerously short. And though for a short while she had thought that even if the announcement was made she could always back out of the predicament later, she knew that was the coward's way. It would also make a bad situation worse, embarrassing a proud man in front of the world. She had to do it before Nicholas had a chance to announce his intentions.

It was very early on the morning of the gala when Ellie arrived at Nicholas's office building, her heart pounding, her stomach tied in knots. She wanted nothing more than to escape back home. But meekness had gotten her nowhere. She needed courage, for she had to make Nicholas accept the truth of her words. Today. In his office. Without Charlotte upstairs. Without his assistant in the outer office. But when the doorman of the tall structure pulled open the door, she hadn't taken more than a single step when Nicholas appeared.

"Nicholas!"

Nicholas stopped abruptly. "Ellie," he said, surprised. "What are you doing here?"

She glanced between the curious doorman and the passersby in the street. "I have to talk to you. Could we go upstairs to your office?"

"I can't, sweetheart. I have a meeting downtown at the mayor's office."

"Nicholas!" She knew her voice was shrill and she tried to calm herself. "Please, we have to talk."

Nicholas tilted his head in question, before he glanced down the street, transferred his leather satchel to his other hand, then took her hand and pulled her inside the building, away from prying eyes. She stood perfectly still, training her unruly thoughts. His simple touch was like heaven. She wanted to touch him, hold him, but couldn't. She withdrew her hand and forcibly held it at her side.

"What is it?" he asked, drawing her close despite her attempts to stand away, making her heart pound erratically. Her eyes were drawn to his lips. And before she could answer, his arm came around her and his lips claimed her own.

The kiss was long and deep, a primal call that beckoned her to forgetfulness.

"God," he murmured against her lips, "I've missed you."

He ran his hand up into her hair, his thumbs outlining her jaw. Her body began to pound with wanting, drowning out the pounding of her desperation. She returned his kiss, having leaned his way. He sucked at her upper lip, before he pulled its mate gently between his teeth.

"God, you make me forget all that I have to do," he groaned against her mouth, his hand trailing down her back to grasp her hips.

He pulled her closer, tighter, and she could feel the evidence of his desire. He brought his hand up, capturing her breast, his satchel long forgotten on the floor. She felt the sensation down to her core. If only he would touch her skin.

But then she broke free, of the kiss, of him. "No, Nicky . . . I mean Nicholas."

A rueful smile sliced across his face. "Just when I've grown used to Nicky." He tried to pull her back.

She pressed her eyes closed and gathered what remained of her waning courage. "No, Nicholas! Let me go."

She could feel when he realized that she was truly serious, and his grip loosened.

"What's wrong, Ellie?"

His normally unfathomable gaze darkened with emotion. She knew he had been pushing himself for days, forcing himself to persevere in the face of Charlotte's illness when he had a business that still had to be run. How could she add to his heartache? How to tell him? But she had no choice.

"Nicholas, I can't marry you." Just that, relief mixing with her breaking heart. She was perilously close to tears, but held them back. There would be time enough to cry later.

"Now, Ellie—"

"No, Nicholas," she said forcefully, putting her hand out when he reached out to her. "I *can't*. I can't marry you."

The lines of his face hardened until his sharp features were etched with concern. "If you're not careful, one of these days I'm going to believe you."

"Oh, Nicky." She inhaled sharply. "You *have* to believe me."

"Why? Why do you keep saying you can't marry me?"

But of course that was the one question she couldn't answer. Instead she started down a path she hoped would suffice. "We're from two different worlds. Worlds that don't mix."

"That's absurd—"

"No, Nicholas! Not absurd. Just last week Maisy Roberts

and a friend of hers were in the shop wanting something to wear for your party."

"Our party."

"No, not ours! Yours! Just yours, for your friends and acquaintances. When I mentioned the date they assumed I knew it because I was making hats for other women, not because I would be invited."

"Soon they'll learn otherwise," he said, reaching for her.

But Ellie stepped away. "Nicholas, please. You're not making this easy."

"I have no intention of making it easy. You're uncertain now, but—"

"No! You're not listening to me, haven't listened to me for days." The fight drained away, her porcelain features quavering with despair. "I can't marry you, Nicholas."

When she tried to turn away, he caught her arm and turned her back toward him. Their eyes met and she could tell he was looking deep, looking into her soul. She tried to move away, but he held her chin still. He stared at her for an eternity. She was certain that he could see the truth, or rather the truth that she wanted him to see, the inevitability of their situation. The impossibility of a life together.

"Do you love me?" he asked.

So simple. So unexpected. She wanted to say no, needed to say no. But while she might not have told him the entire truth about herself, she had never lied. Ever. She didn't know how she could now. She couldn't lie about something so deep and essential to her soul—something she knew would never change, no matter how many years she lived after today.

She tried to break free, but he held her secure.

"You love me, Ellie. Fact. You can't deny it." He pulled her to him, fiercely, as if relieved.

Ellie felt as if her heart would shatter into a million tiny pieces.

"You love me, Ellie," he repeated, his breath a desperate whisper against her skin. "And I love you. I won't let you go. Ever. I'm so close to once and for all putting the past behind me. I want you at my side. I need you, Ellie."

He hugged her one last time before setting her at arm's length. "No more talk like this. Please." A hint of a smile surfaced.

"Mr. Drake," the doorman called, pushing open the door. "Your carriage is here."

Nicholas glanced back at Ellie. "You won't regret marrying me." He stepped away, picking up his satchel. "I promise."

"Nicholas—"

"I'll send the carriage for you tonight at eight."

And then he was gone, leaving her alone in the high-ceilinged vestibule, her thoughts echoing madly in the hollows of her mind.

Moments passed as she tried to make sense of what had happened. But no sense would come. She only knew that she had failed.

As if she were a hundred years old, sick with failure and defeat, she stumbled out onto Fifth Avenue, oblivious to the dray wagons and carriages, hired hacks and horsecars, all vying for right-of-way on the street. She had failed. Because she had no courage. Eliot Sinclair. Strong. Fighting to survive. Deep down a coward.

She was unaware of the tears that streaked her cheeks, unaware of the dray wagon driver who shouted a furious warning, and in the end had to jerk the reins, swerving to miss her. When she felt the whoosh of air flutter her long skirts and she realized what had happened, she wished with all her might that he hadn't missed.

Dear God, what was she to do? Marry him? Lord how she wanted to. But to tempt the fates? To tempt the gods? Who would be struck down? Plain and simple, she couldn't marry Nicholas as she had known since the second he had told her his story. If she went through with it no doubt she would only end up destroying them both. For in the end she knew it was impossible to keep the circumstances of her birth a secret forever. Her house, the one thing that Nicholas had to have, connected Ellie to her father as nothing else could. And when the truth came out, Nicholas would learn that she was the daughter of the man who had destroyed his family—the daughter of the man who had been responsible for the death of his mother.

With that thought, her heart breaking beyond repair, Ellie knew what she had to do.

Chapter 23

The ballroom was ablaze with light. Candlelight, gaslight, even some electric light filled the house like hundreds of glittering diamonds. Ellie saw Nicholas the moment she entered. There were no words to adequately explain how striking he looked talking to one person, laughing with another. So tall, so handsome—so at ease. He belonged to this world of lights shining like diamonds. He was good and pure. A knight who tried to save dying little girls, his armor shining as he tried to avenge his parents' honor. A wonderful man. How she wished things could be different.

Pressing her eyes closed, she steeled herself against the thought. She had learned years ago that wishes were like candy to a beggar man's child.

Ellie smoothed her skirt self-consciously. She wore a gown of ocean-blue silk, beautiful but simple. She had spent money she couldn't afford to spend on the dress. When she pulled it on for the first time, however, she had gasped her pleasure. Never had she owned such apparel. But standing in the midst of Nicholas's grand ballroom, New York's elite surrounding her with their creamy pearls and their startling rubies, Ellie realized her gown was acceptable at best. More proof, as if she needed more, that even if she wasn't Harry

Dillard's daughter, she didn't belong in this world. She wanted to melt into the long, flowing draperies and disappear, to hide her simple white lace gloves, and her neck that was bare of jewels. These were the things that Nicholas took for granted. The appropriate dress, the perfect gloves, the correct shoes. He had been so busy he had never given a thought that she wouldn't have the proper items for a gala—not even a gown.

But what did it matter what she wore? she admonished herself. She was not there to win a prize for fashion. Clasping her hands together, she knew her only purpose was to force Nicholas to believe that she couldn't marry him.

All around her people were talking, laughing. Some had started to dance. A fine formal dinner would be served at midnight. Pheasant, coq au vin, pâté de foie gras. The finest of champagnes. But Ellie would be gone by then. And standing there now, she wondered what she was doing there at all. Her plan had seemed so simple, the only thing left to do. But as she stood in the ballroom, anxiety and nervousness wrapping around her like a heavy cloak, she wondered how she ever could have thought her plan sane.

"Are you sure we should be here?" Charles Monroe asked uncertainly from her side.

Ellie turned to him with a start. "They let us in, didn't they?" She glanced quickly back at the door. "But maybe it's not such a good idea to be here after all. Let's go."

"Oh no, you don't. Not if we were invited," he stated with growing excitement. "Look. Over there. It's Theodore Roosevelt talking to the governor."

But Ellie was no longer listening. She knew the moment Nicholas became aware that she had arrived—the moment he saw her. He stood across the room, turning to face her, his smile made brighter by happiness and what she would have sworn was pride. Genuine pride. And love. He wasn't embarrassed by her gown, or by her. She saw it, felt it. She stood there, letting the unaccustomed feeling wash over her, taking it in, storing it in her mind, wanting to fold it up and tuck it away like the treasure that it was. Because she knew that in a mere matter of seconds the smile would disappear, and all that she would be left with was the memory. Maybe, she thought with one last futile burst of hope, she could still escape.

"Ellie," Charles said, "you're not listening to me."

It was then that she knew Nicholas became aware of the other man. Nicholas's smile faded into the brilliantly lit room, replaced by confusion. Right or wrong, sane or insane, she had come too far to turn back. Drawing a deep breath, making herself continue down the path she had chosen, she reached over and with shaking hands took Charles's arm.

The confusion on Nicholas's face alchemized into anger, deep, biting anger, before he started forward.

Ellie's breath caught. The time had come. But as he drew closer, her courage failed and she hurriedly said, "Let's dance, Charles."

They stepped out onto the highly polished floor, twirling amongst the other couples, Ellie doing her best to follow. She didn't hear the music, was unaware even of her feet moving through the formal steps of the waltz. She was only aware of Nicholas who had halted at the edge of the dance floor, his eyes burning into her soul.

Unfortunately, as was bound to happen, the music came to an end. But rather than let Charles lead her back where they had been, where Nicholas now stood, his tall frame rigid with anger, she guided him to the opposite side of the room.

"Miss Sinclair!"

Ellie's heart lodged in her throat until she realized the voice belonged to a woman. Turning, Ellie found Maisy Roberts. "Hello, Mrs. Roberts," she managed. "How nice to see you."

"Yes, of course. Who are you here with? I didn't realize that you'd be here," she stated, with a raised eyebrow.

Charles stepped forward. "I'm Miss Sinclair's escort,

hopefully soon to be her fiancé. Charles Monroe. And she . . . we were invited."

"Well," Maisy said, her accusatory tone receding, "how nice." She smiled, though stiffly. "Have you seen Deidra Carlisle?"

Ellie forced herself to be polite. "No, I haven't."

"Well, you should. I have to admit I was wrong about the veil. It's stunning. She has such peculiar ideas at times, but . . ." She shrugged her shoulders. "She needs a husband, and after tonight, looking as she does, no doubt she'll find one. Oh, look. There's Miriam Welton." Maisy tsked. "Such a shame about her."

Ellie started to ask why, but just then a woman came up to Maisy's side. "Maisy darling."

Faced with the choice of learning more about Miriam or making a quiet escape, when Ellie noted that Nicholas was walking their way she opted for escape. She took Charles's arm and slipped away just before Nicholas arrived at her side. When she glanced over her shoulder Maisy had taken Nicholas's arm. Nicholas only stared at Ellie, until Maisy said something that finally gained his attention. Ellie wondered what the woman had said when she saw the hard line of his jaw tighten furiously. Ellie stumbled, catching herself on a Chippendale chair.

"Are you all right?" Charles asked.

No, she wasn't all right. "Of course I am."

"Then let's dance again."

"I don't think—"

"Nonsense. A dance will do you good." Charles pulled Ellie back out onto the dance floor without waiting for an answer. The music swirled around her, glancing off her mind. She felt numb, simply allowed herself to be led along in a dance of someone else's making.

She was hardly aware that the music hadn't ended when Charles pulled them to a halt. Without warning, Charles let go of her hand and stepped away. She started to question him. But the words stuck in her throat when Nicholas stepped in and took his place.

"Nicky," she breathed.

The sensation was electric when he took her hand. He waited a heartbeat, his eyes boring into hers, before he placed his other hand around her waist. She stumbled when he began to move in time to the music. He steadied her with ease.

She wanted to press her cheek to the fine wool of his black formal jacket. She wanted to press her head to his heart. But most of all, she wanted to forget why she had come.

"Why are you doing this?" he asked.

The question was angry, startling her from her thoughts. But as much as there was anger, she knew his words were filled with hurt. She saw it in his eyes when she looked up at him. She saw it in his shoulders, the sudden shift when he tried to cover his pain. Most people wouldn't have noticed. But she had come to know Nicholas Drake too well. She had hurt him, as she had known she would. But she had failed to imagine how utterly devastated it would make her feel.

"Are you trying to get back at me for not spending time with you?" he added when she failed to answer.

"No," she whispered. "Of course not."

"Then why?" he demanded harshly. "Why have you come here telling people that you are engaged to that man?"

She flinched at the cold, ruthless fury in his eyes. But then she steeled herself, meeting his gaze, imploring him to an understanding that logically she knew was impossible. "I never said I was engaged to anyone."

"Maisy Roberts tells a different tale."

Ellie cringed. "That was Charles. He said he hoped to be my fiancé one day. But that hardly matters—"

"No?" he questioned. "Then what does matter? Why *have* you come here with another man?"

"I'm here with Charles because . . . I enjoy his company."

Nicholas's eyes narrowed ominously, his perfect step faltering for a moment. "You enjoy his company? You have come to the party to announce our engagement on the arm of another man because you enjoy his company? You are supposed to be here with me, Eliot."

He executed a sharp twirl, her skirts billowing about her ankles, and she clutched him for support.

"No, I'm not here with you, Nicholas. I'm here with Charles."

He pulled her close, too close for propriety's sake. "I don't know why you're doing this," he said, his voice low and deep, "but you're mine, Ellie. Mine."

Long minutes passed, and they came to a halt at the edge of the dance floor. "No, Nicky. I'm not yours." She glanced away, her throat tight and burning. "I'm not anyone's."

"What are you talking about?" he demanded.

"I told you long ago that I wouldn't marry you or anyone else, but you wouldn't believe me. Well, Nicholas, I *won't* marry you."

His breath hissed through his teeth. "This is a fine time to tell me."

Angry heat scorched her cheeks. "I've tried to tell you! Again and again. But you wouldn't listen."

His head jerked away sharply, his jaw clenched, and she knew he was remembering. When he looked back at her, his eyes were filled with white-hot anger mixed with despair. "Why?" he whispered, his voice catching with emotion. "Why are you betraying me?"

She sucked in her breath. Betraying him?

His hand gripped hers, tighter, his expression stricken. "God, I swore that I knew, as I knew nothing else, that you would never betray me—that you would be the one person in the world who I could count on to be constant and true, to be loyal."

God, she wanted to scream, she wasn't betraying him. But how to explain?

She watched helplessly as his emotions began to shift and

change, the despair glossing over with a practiced indifference, congealing into what she realized would soon be hate. Her heart clenched and tears burned in her eyes. If there had ever been a moment when she could have changed the course this night would take, it was gone. She knew, looking into Nicholas's eyes, that she had finally, completely, succeeded in achieving her goal. She had convinced him. She should have been pleased, but she only felt an utter emptiness of soul.

Her knees felt weak, and she wasn't certain she could breathe. She felt as if she were tearing a part of herself away. But what was done was done. They had shared an unexpected emotional bond that had woven them together, making them part of each other. The rending of that bond was bound to be painful.

Nicholas. His name fluttered through her mind, but she held her lips firmly closed.

"Nicholas!"

For a second, Ellie wasn't certain if she had spoken after all.

"Nicholas Drake! What a grand party you have put together."

Nicholas and Ellie turned and found Deidra Carlisle.

"Miss Carlisle," Nicholas said with a stiff smile. "I'm glad you're enjoying yourself."

She wore the veil of silk and pearls and, just as Maisy had said, Deidra looked stunning. "How did you ever manage to pull such a glorious affair together, you, a man alone?" She smiled. "Though I'm certain you hired all sorts of people to do it for you." She looked at Ellie. "What were you hired to do, Miss Sinclair?"

Ellie's shoulders came back. "I was invited. Now if you'll excuse me."

Ellie quickly stepped away, before Nicholas could hold her there. Deidra didn't appear to notice, she continued to talk, her hand resting on Nicholas's arm, holding him captive. Ellie could feel Nicholas watching her as she fled.

Only a few more steps, she told herself. One foot in front of the other. Faster. Please God, help me, she pleaded. But before she could make it to the door she felt a staying hand on her arm. Her eyes flew up. "Miriam?"

"Are you all right, Miss Sinclair?"

"I just need a bit of fresh air." Ellie tried to summon a smile unsuccessfully.

"Let me go with you."

"No!" Ellie took a deep breath. "No, thank you," she said more calmly. "I'll be fine. I just need to go."

But Miriam didn't release her. "I couldn't help but overhear your conversation with Nicholas." Miriam hesitated, before her voice grew odd, and she asked, "What did my brother do to make you hurt him so deeply?"

Ellie's breath caught, and she had to reach out to steady herself. She glanced from the long fingers that clutched her arm to the violet eyes that demanded an answer. But the look in Miriam's eyes didn't tell her if she was sympathetic or appalled. Ellie fought for control, swallowing to keep the tears back. "The only thing your brother did was to make the mistake of loving me."

And then she slipped out the door, down the steps, tears burning down her cheeks. She hated that she could still feel. She preferred the numbness, preferred the cold, empty center where nothing could touch her, as she fled out into the brilliant September night.

Chapter 24

"I'm leaving."

Barnard turned away from his painting in the nook and looked at Hannah. "Leaving?" His gaze traveled the length of her smartly clad form. "Where ya goin' all dressed up? Havin' a tryst, are ya? At nine in the mornin'?" He snickered and started to turn back to his work.

"I'm moving out."

His movements crystallized. His body, his breath. He stared straight ahead, not at the painting, not at Hannah, but at some place in between, at something only he could see.

At length his gaze focused on her face. "Movin' out? I've never heard of such a blame fool thing to do. Why the hell are you movin' out? Where the hell do you think you're going to go?"

She raised her chin a notch, hoping that he couldn't see the trembling of her hand that would betray her. "I love you, Barnard Webb, fool that I am. And since you don't return the sentiments, I find it impossible to live under the same roof as you any longer. And where I go is no business of yours."

"Bosh! Love! Women's romantic notions. Hogwash, I tell you."

Hannah stiffened, her white-gloved hands clasped together. "You are a heartless man, and how I ever came to love you I'll never know."

"You're just saying you're going to leave. A threat. That's what it is. A threat. You wouldn't leave here any more than you'd run through Central Park naked as the day you were born."

Gasping her outrage, Hannah tried to calm herself. "You are wrong, old man. I am leaving. Today. This morning."

He looked at her closely, long minutes counted off by the ticking clock on the mantel. "Then go," he muttered, the deep lines in his face hardening into a fierce mask. "Be gone with you. See if I care." He turned back to his painting with a jerk and a muttered curse.

Hannah stared at his rigid back, willing him to show some sign, any sign that he didn't want her to leave. But he only picked up the brush and started to paint. Perhaps Barnard was correct, she thought. She was a fool to believe, to hope for even a nugget of encouragement. She deserved better. She knew it, had known it for some time. But knowing something in the mind and knowing something in the heart had proved to be two very different things.

With a resigned sigh, for the first time in years feeling her age, she made her way up the stairs. She had expected Ellie to be up hours ago, had planned to talk to Ellie first. But Ellie's door had remained shut well past the time she normally got up. So Hannah had finally gone downstairs to tell Barnard.

It was Saturday, and Ellie had said the shop would be closed today. Hannah hated to wake Ellie on a day she could sleep in. Hannah considered waiting. But she couldn't wait. She had waited long enough—too long based on Barnard's heartless reaction.

She knocked briskly.

"Who is it?" she heard mumbled from behind the door.

"Ellie, dear, it's Hannah. I need to talk to you."

Silence.

"Ellie?" she called.

"Coming," Ellie groaned.

Hannah heard movement and held her breath until the door finally swung open. She gasped. "Ellie, dear! You look terrible! Are you ill?"

Ellie grimaced, then shook her head. "No. Just tired."

"I didn't hear you come in last night. Was it late?"

With a scoff, Ellie opened the door further. "No, not late at all."

"How was the party?"

Ellie's hand stilled in its task of brushing back her hair. "It was fine, Hannah," she said, suddenly impatient. But then she cringed, ashamed of herself. "I'm sorry. I'm just tired. What do you need to talk to me about?"

"I'm leaving."

Ellie wasn't certain why Hannah had felt it necessary to wake her up to tell her she was going out. For a second she wondered if they had made plans and she had forgotten. "What time is it? Where are you going?"

"I'm moving out, Ellie."

"Moving out?!"

"Yes. I'm leaving. For good."

At this, Ellie finally came fully awake. "Leaving? For good? What are you talking about, Hannah?"

"I've had another job offer. I wanted to tell you sooner, but one thing happened after another, the house business with Nicholas, then all the hat orders, and of course then we had the opportunity to go to Long Island. Foolishly, I had thought Barnard would see things differently if we got away from the city."

Ellie finally understood. "You're moving out because of Barnard."

"Yes, dear. I'm sorry. I know I should have given you notice, both for my apartment and for my position at the shop, but . . . once I drew up the courage I knew I wouldn't be able to wait. I hope you understand."

"Oh, Hannah," Ellie sighed. "You can't go. We'll work

things out." But of course, like Hannah, she didn't see how. Barnard would probably go to his grave believing that any day his son would come for him, hoping it would happen. And wasn't it *hope* that kept the spirit alive? How could she blame him?

"This is for the best," Hannah said. Abruptly, she started to go, leaving Ellie standing dumbstruck in the doorway. But then Hannah stopped and rushed back, pulling Ellie into a fierce hug. "For seven wonderful years you have been like a daughter to me. I'll miss you, child, more than I like to think about. I love you, just as I love dear, dear Jim. But I have to go. I can't stay here in a house with a man who clearly doesn't care for me when I care for him so deeply."

"Oh, Hannah, you can't leave. We love you, even Barnard, though he doesn't know how to show it. You know that."

"No, Ellie, I don't know that," she stated, then turned and headed down the stairs.

Ellie threw on a wrapper and followed, her mind racing, trying to come up with a solution. Hannah was like a mother to her. She couldn't lose Charlotte and Nicholas, and now Hannah, too. But her heart sank when she reached the bottom and saw the suitcases and crates lined up in the foyer, a hired coach waiting just beyond the open door.

"What's going on?" Jim demanded, coming up the front steps from the street.

Hannah reached over and took Jim's hand and squeezed. "I have to go, Jim."

"Where, Hannah? When will you be back?" His moon face filled with concern when he noticed the long line of suitcases. "Why do you need so much stuff?"

"I won't be back, Jim."

"What do you mean, Hannah? You gotta come back. You can't go!"

Hannah's eyes glistened with unshed tears. "Jim, I'm sorry. But I have to."

"Barnard!" Ellie demanded, making one last attempt. "Tell her she can't leave."

But Barnard never turned back to them. "If she wants to leave, who are we to stop her?"

"We are her loved ones, damn you!"

She saw Barnard flinch. She never used profanity. But if she thought her burst of emotion would prompt him to help, she was sadly mistaken. He simply continued on with his art, his crude colored lines and curves forming something only he could define.

Hannah seemed to have been waiting for Barnard's reaction as well. And when Ellie turned back to her the woman sighed, then called to the man who waited by the carriage.

Nothing Ellie said during the twenty minutes it took to load the coach, nor Jim's quiet tears changed Hannah's mind. Barnard's stiff-backed indifference held sway. By nine-forty-five on the first Saturday of September, Hannah Schurr was gone.

"Damn you, Barnard Webb," Ellie said heatedly, then turned away and started up the stairs.

She was halfway up the first flight when a knock sounded at the door. She turned with a start. She saw Barnard turn as well, with what she would have sworn was relief etched on his weathered face.

"She's back!" Jim announced, voicing everyone's thought.

But when Barnard leaned over and peered through the lace-covered window he said, "Nope. It's Nicholas."

"No," Ellie breathed. He couldn't be there. She couldn't see him. "I'm not here, do you understand," she hissed. She implored both Jim and Barnard with her eyes. "Do not let him know that I'm here."

Then she flew up the stairs and clicked her door shut just as she heard Jim chime, "Nicky!"

Nicholas stood in the doorway, looking tired, older than the hills. And angry. Very angry.

"Did you bring Charlotte?" Jim asked, forgetting Hannah for the moment, oblivious to Nicholas's anger.

"No, Jim—"

"Is she all right? How is she?"

The hard lines of Nicholas's face softened though only somewhat. "Much better. She's going to be just fine." He looked at Barnard, the fierce gleam returning to his eye. "I need to see Ellie."

Barnard shrugged as he walked over to the foyer. "Sorry, Nicholas," he said apologetically. "She's not here."

"Not here?" He glanced around the front room, then at Jim, who lowered his eyes and looked away. Nicholas's hand clenched at his side. "Damn it, Barnard. I need to talk to her."

"I'd like to help you, Nicholas, but I can't. Like I said, she's not here."

"Like hell she isn't." Taking Barnard and Jim by surprise, Nicholas stormed up the stairs two at a time, his breath barely broken when he reached her room.

Jim and Barnard followed in a confused rush, arriving just as Nicholas tried to open the door. But the brass knob wouldn't turn, the door firmly locked. Nicholas took a deep breath, pressing his eyes closed as if trying to calm himself. "Ellie," he demanded, as he knocked.

Ellie pressed her back against the door, the violence of his voice and pounding coming through the planks like an angry caress.

"Damn it, Ellie," he called, knocking harder, "let me in. We need to talk."

Ellie only breathed deeply, slowly. It was too late for words.

Nicholas's angry groan wafted up to the rafters, followed by the pounding, hard and fierce, on her door.

"What are you going to do?" Barnard demanded. "Break down the door?"

Ellie bit her knuckle to keep from crying out, from flinging open the door, and throwing herself in his arms.

"Damn it, Ellie," Nicholas called through the door.

But then he stopped. Long minutes of silence raged on the other side. She imagined him there, his height, his broad shoulders, his full lips that she would never again feel on her own.

"I don't know why you have done this," he said, his voice quiet, pained. "I only know that I would have given you the world if you had just been true."

Time hung suspended as her world crashed in around her. Then she heard the angry tread of his footsteps down the carpeted stairs. She tried to hold back the tears that burned in her eyes, but failed. With her back against the wall, her lips trembled as she slid down, sinking to the floor. And as the sound of the slamming front door rushed up the stairs to her, she was afraid that just as with little Charlotte, there weren't enough horsemen in the kingdom to put her back together again.

Chapter 25

Nicholas stood alone in his study. The doctor had just stepped out. There was nothing more to be done. All Nicholas's promises and determination were for naught. There was no help. No cures. Charlotte was going to die.

Oh, Ellie, he thought before he could stop himself. *Why aren't you here?*

Pressing his fingers to his temples, Nicholas rubbed, hard, willing the futile thoughts and pain to cease. But the pain went beyond the throbbing in his head, extended to a deep throbbing of his soul. He had tried to turn away from the truth. But this time he couldn't. His Will would be defeated. Ellie was gone forever, and Charlotte was truly going to die. There was nothing more he could do for her than to ease her pain.

When he opened the door to his study on his way upstairs, he found his brother-in-law coming down the steps, dressed, ready to go.

"Nicholas," William said, picking an imaginary piece of lint from his immaculate jacket. "I'm on my way out to the Metropolitan Club. Care to join me?"

The anger that was never far away began to seethe. "At noon?"

"Can't think of a better time for a drink."

Nicholas crossed the black-and-white marble floor in a few angry strides. In a brutal replay of the day in the hospital, Nicholas grabbed William by the collar and pinned him against the wall, the massive granite house seeming to shake from the force. "Your daughter is upstairs dying. Have you no heart?"

William Welton shifted his weight uncomfortably, but couldn't gain his freedom. "I'm no good at sickbeds. I'll visit with her tonight. Read her a story, and—"

"Damn it, man!" He banged William against the wall. "I don't care if you drink yourself into oblivion. But not today. Not now."

"What's going on here?" Miriam demanded from the stairway.

Her eyes were red-rimmed with dark half-moon circles underneath. Nicholas found it hard to believe his sister was finally feeling anything for her child. More than likely she was feeling sorry for herself—her glittering lifestyle coming to a standstill because of a responsibility she had never wanted.

He released her husband with disdain. William straightened his attire with a humph, before he looked at Nicholas, then slammed the front door on his way out.

Nicholas shook his head. "I didn't think it was possible that my opinion of him could sink any lower." He strode up the stairs, passing his sister whose violet eyes implored him, but to what he had no idea.

"Nicholas," she said.

He stopped at the landing and turned back to her, unaware of the fierce look on his face. "Yes, Miriam?" he asked tightly.

"Nothing," she whispered, pressing her handkerchief to her mouth, then dashed up the stairs past him.

Charlotte had been moved to a room with a southern exposure. A bright, colorful room of blooming flowers and bold stripes that she had always loved. When Nicholas quietly opened the door she lay very still on her side, her doll held tightly in her arms. He thought she was asleep. Carefully, as not to disturb her, he started to back out.

"Uncle Nicholas?"

His hand stilled. "Yes, princess. It's me."

"I know how busy you are, but will you sit with me, just for a little while?" she asked.

Bert had sent over the day's agenda, and every hour was accounted for. Meetings, planning sessions. He should have left for the office over an hour ago. "Of course I can."

His footfalls were muffled by the thick carpet as he strode across the room. She rolled over onto her back and smiled. But the smile couldn't mask her unnaturally pale skin or her labored breathing. He forced his own reciprocating smile. Pulling a blue velvet chair up beside her, he had no other thoughts than of his niece.

"Papa left, didn't he?"

Her smile had faded to sadness, and Nicholas felt a stinging bite of anger. "Yes, love. But he'll be back."

"When?"

"Soon. Real soon. I know he hated to leave, even for a second."

"Really?"

He could hardly remember those days when he existed in that place with no feeling. "Really," he lied, not caring that he did, only caring about the smile he had restored to her heart-shaped face.

"And Mother? Did she leave with him?"

Neither Charlotte nor Nicholas had heard the door open, and neither of them heard the Italian heels that stilled in the thick carpet.

"No, love, she didn't leave with him."

Charlotte sighed. "Do you think she's mad at me for being sick?"

"Of course not, Charlotte," he said emphatically, leaving no room for doubt. "She loves you very much."

"Really?" she whispered again.

His eyes burned oddly. "Yes, really."

Her contented sigh washed over him as she pulled her doll close to her chest, and though she tried to stay awake, her eyes drifted shut.

A few moments passed, then Nicholas was startled by an unexpected touch on his shoulder. He looked up and found his sister, tears glistening on her cheeks. "I know you didn't do that for me, but I thank you anyway," she said very softly, then walked across the room and sat in a chair on the other side of the bed.

They sat for hours, without speaking, each lost to their own thoughts, their own pain. The cloudy sky remained dark and foreboding, no sun to brighten the day. The doctor came in at intervals to check on Charlotte, his tight-lipped demeanor speaking volumes.

Charlotte woke at three.

She was weak, but she smiled at the sight of her mother. Miriam came over and sat on the bed, and Nicholas quietly left the room so they could share a moment alone. He found William in the foyer, staring up the stairs uncertainly.

"How's she doing?" William asked, his brow furrowed.

"As well as can be expected for a child whose father has little interest in her."

"What the hell do you want from me?" The outburst echoed in the ornate hall.

"You should ask your daughter that," Nicholas replied, having no sympathy for the man, before continuing down the stairs to his study.

The afternoon was difficult. Charlotte lost her breath again and again. The doctor raced to her side each time, until the sunless sky began to darken as the early fall day turned into night, leaving Charlotte spent and exhausted. After the last and most violent bout, Charlotte drifted off into a deep, unconscious sleep. The doctor went to Nicholas's study and said he wasn't sure she would wake again. Nicholas remained in his chair long after the doctor left, just sitting. When Nicholas finally walked into her room,

Charlotte lay in the bed, a wraith, her closed eyes dark sockets, a shadow of even the sick little girl who had come to him—was it possible that it had been only seven months before—a shadow even of the little girl he left this afternoon.

Miriam was asleep in her chair, her normally perfectly styled hair askew, her dreams obviously troubled. Jim sat huddled in the corner. When Jim had returned earlier, Nicholas had opened his mouth to ask where Ellie was, forgetting for the moment that she would never come to his house again. He had snapped his mouth shut angrily, but when Miriam had demanded that Jim leave, Nicholas had eyed his sister with all the pent-up fury he was feeling, then said, "He loves your daughter, Miriam, has been her friend while you chose to be away. He stays." He saw her flinch, but he didn't care. He was beyond caring about anything but Charlotte.

Now the room was quiet, and as Nicholas stood at the door he didn't want to wake anyone, but was unable to turn back and leave. He walked to the large window, staring out at the world beyond. If only Charlotte would wake, he beseeched a God he had not called upon since he was a boy. If only he would wake from a bad dream to find her violet eyes luminous, her laughter tumbling through the much too quiet halls of his house.

And when he turned back to her, as if that God had heard and was trying to make amends, her eyes fluttered open. Charlotte. Awake, as if she had only been resting.

For a second, one insane second, Nicholas felt a flash of intense relief—she was going to be fine. But then the second passed, reality surging back. Mercilessly.

Charlotte looked at him and their eyes held. Eyes so young, so innocent, eyes that hadn't seen enough, locked with ones so old, so cold, eyes that had seen so much. But somehow these two ill-matched souls had come together and forged a bond, had given each other something they hadn't had before they'd had each other.

Clearly mustering the energy, she smiled, so sweet, so lovely, hinting at the beauty she had been—and would have become had she been given the chance to live. Then she spoke, silently, with no sound, mouthing the words.

I love you. Silent but hard.

Nicholas couldn't speak. His ears buzzed as if she had shouted. So few people in this world had loved him, perhaps only Charlotte. He remembered the first day she had said she loved him, and he remembered as well the look of disappointment when he had been unable to return her words. She looked at him now in much the same way, hopeful but already forgiving him, as if she knew about the cold place in his heart.

I love you, too, he mouthed silently into the faint golden light of the room. *I love you forever.*

Her weak smile grew luminous, filling him with joy, and pride, and unbearable sadness, before slowly, inevitably, her eyes drifted closed. One last time. Before she was gone. Forever. A candle gutted, no wax or wick left to burn.

Chapter 26

Ellie woke with a start.

Slivers of moonlight seeped through the cloud-laden night, spilling into the room, filling her with a sense of icy finality.

Charlotte was dead.

She knew it, she felt it as if the moonbeams had brought a silent message.

Throwing off the covers, Ellie pulled herself out of bed and glanced at the clock. Midnight. Regardless of the hour, she pulled on her clothes. Sadness gripped her body, tearing at her as she thought of Charlotte. But once sleep completely relinquished her mind, she thought perhaps she was wrong. Perhaps it had been nothing more than a bad dream.

Ellie came down the stairs, not certain what she should do. Warm a glass of milk? Try to still her mind of what hopefully were only nightmares? But when she entered the front parlor, Jim sat slumped in a chair, silent tears sliding down his cheeks unchecked. Her breath stilled in her chest. She hadn't been wrong. Dear God, she hadn't been wrong.

"Oh, Jim," she murmured, putting her arms around his massive shoulders.

His tears came hard then, soaking through her gown when

he turned his face into her body. "I don't want her to go," he wailed. "I don't want her to go."

"I know, dear," she said gently. "No one wants her to go. But God had different plans for our angel."

"I don't like God! I don't like him at all!"

She rocked her giant friend through his tears and angry outbursts, until his tears began to subside, drying up to leave a vast chasm of pain. She ached for Jim, and she ached for Charlotte. But most of all she ached for Nicholas. How would he survive?

She realized then what had awakened her. His pain. And she realized as well why she had dressed. As if she had no will of her own, she kissed Jim on the head, found a woolen wrap, and slipped out into the night. She didn't think about what she was doing. Couldn't. She simply had to go.

The hired hack raced through the deserted cobbled streets, arriving in front of the house on Fifth Avenue. The windows were dark, no light to hint that anyone was inside. She started to leave, should have left. Instead, she went around to the back of the house, along the flagstone path that wound its way through the once bountiful garden now touched by fall. She moved slowly, almost reluctantly, but not knowing how to turn back. Straightening her spine with purpose, she climbed the curving granite staircase to the terrace off his bedroom.

Ellie knew he would be there, alone. Unable to reach out. She could feel it. Despite all that had happened, nothing changed the fact that she loved him, couldn't stand to know he was in pain.

Through the multi-paned glass doors at the top of the stairs she could see his room was lighted by a single tall candle—gothic, golden, a sentinel to the night—and a fire that burned behind the grate. With quaking fingers, she turned the brass knob. Her breath caught in a silent, aching gasp when she found him standing at the mantel, his back to her, staring at the flames, his grief washing over her as if it were her own. And with that, she forgot that she shouldn't be there. "Nicky?"

She saw his shoulders stiffen, then harden against her, but he never turned around.

"Nicky, please."

"Go away, Ellie."

His voice seared through the room like the sizzle of hot metal hitting water. She knew she should do as he said, but shoulds and shouldn'ts so often slipped away when she was near this man. "I can't seem to do that," she whispered, coming close until she stood behind him.

Tension radiated from his hard frame, a dangerous heat, and she knew his control was precarious at best. "Nicky, talk to me."

His rage grew, became nearly tangible in the high-ceilinged room. "Get out, Eliot."

But she couldn't. "I loved her, too."

She watched the muscle along the taut line of his jaw leap furiously, his shoulders so stiff she thought he would break into pieces. "Just as you loved her."

"Not enough!" he suddenly roared, his fist crashing down on the mantel. "I didn't love her enough!"

She had expected many things, but not this. "How can you say that? You loved her deeply."

"But I didn't do enough." The words were short and clipped. "I didn't do enough."

"You did everything possible!"

The sound of the crackling fire popped and hissed. "But I didn't save her."

Oh, Nicky, her mind cried, holding herself still. "No," she said quietly, "you didn't save her. No one could have. But you gave her your love. And she loved you in return."

His tormented groan echoed in the silent room, the haunted sound filled with despair and anger. "A gift I hardly deserved," he said, his voice strangled.

"No," she stated emphatically. "You're wrong, Nicholas. She gave, and you gave back. *You gave back!*"

"Oh God," he groaned.

Ellie came around to face him. "She loved you, Nicholas."

His eyes grew feral, and every muscle in his body grew tense as he tried to harden himself against her. But then she reached out and gently touched his cheek. "And you deserved her love."

The violence of his response shattered the silence of the dimly lit room. "She's gone!" he raged, pulling her to him in a fierce embrace.

His grief was real and heartbreaking, his tormented words tearing through her body. Without thought for possible consequences, Ellie wrapped her arms around him, holding him as the moon moved through the cloudy heavens.

"Oh, God," he whispered, choked. "Why someone so young and innocent?"

"Why so many things?" she wondered out loud. "It makes a person wonder if God truly has a plan, waving his hand to make things happen, his labor causing our pain."

It was long moments later when Nicholas pulled back and looked at her. "Why did you come?"

She looked away, but his strong, relentless fingers turned her back. "Why, Ellie?" he demanded.

"I couldn't stand to think of you . . . alone."

His saddened eyes grew dangerous. "Your hand has been nearly as painful as God's," he said coldly. "How could you imagine that I'd want you here?"

Ellie recoiled from his hard, unblinking gaze, and she knew a moment of uncertainty as she had never known before. The simple need that had led her there no longer seemed enough.

"Regrets?" he whispered sharply, his breath angry and savage against her cheek. "Isn't it a little late to regret impetuous actions? Too late to wish you hadn't snuck into the bedroom of a dangerous man?"

"Don't, Nicholas," she replied, trying to recover her composure. "You are no more dangerous than I am."

"How little you know of me." With menacing steps, he backed her against the wall, his strong arms trapping her. "No matter what you think I am, you actually know very little about me. I *am* a dangerous man, Eliot."

"That's not true," she retorted, her eyes burning with obstinacy, her misgivings forgotten in the face of his words. "You are a good man, Nicholas. You have showed that again and again."

"You're wrong," he countered, an untamed fire burning in his eyes as he drew her arms up above her head.

"No! *You* are wrong. You are kind as well as good, though you fail to believe that about yourself."

He leaned closer, his eyes lighted by menace, but she continued her pursuit. "You have been kind and good to Jim when you didn't have to be." She felt him flinch as if she had struck out. The fire in his eyes wavered. "You protected him against street derelicts. Even if you don't remember your swollen jaw and badly battered knuckles, I do."

His eyes burned into her, and she could see a battle wage within him. He wanted to lash out, he wanted to wound her—he wanted to wound anyone in this callous world which had allowed Charlotte to die.

"You won't hurt me, Nicky. Just as you couldn't hurt Jim, or let anyone else hurt him. You opened your heart to a man most people won't give the time of day." She took a deep breath. "Just as you opened your heart to Charlotte."

His moan was deep and savage, an animal in pain, caught in a trap with no means to loose himself. Anguished, she watched myriad emotions play havoc with the chiseled planes of his face, his burning anger melting back into despair. He started to push away.

"No, Nicky," she said, reaching out and holding on to him with surprising strength. "Don't!"

She could feel the tension in his body. And she knew that he hated the weakness, hated that he could be weak. "Charlotte loved you—because you are a good man."

And with a feral roar he gave in completely, his control

once and for all broken as he pulled Ellie into his arms, holding her with a fierceness that left her without breath. He cried then, as she was certain he had never cried before, his tears jagged and rough, sometimes silent, racking his body.

Later, it would be impossible for her to determine when the solace turned to something different, something more. It would be impossible to determine when the hands that clutched her in agony, loosened their hold and held her with a desperation that broke her heart. And as she succumbed to the feel of his touch, she wondered if she had gone there to love him. To learn where his kisses would lead. Using sweet Charlotte as an excuse.

His tears, hot and burning, seared her, mixing with her own. She tasted them, on his cheek, spilling onto her lips like a forbidden nectar. With their hands and eyes and bodies they wrote the age-old language of love, as they sank to the floor. They came together frantically. Each surrendering, each forgetting all else. He ran his hands over her body, testing, feeling, as if he was afraid she was only a figment of his tortured imagination.

"I'm here," she whispered.

She gasped as liquid heat suffused her body when his hard chest brushed every so lightly against her breasts, bringing them to taut peaks beneath her gown. The heel of his hand grazed the side of one breast, before he cupped the soft underswell.

He pushed at her chemise, his strong, lean, black-clad thigh moving between her own. He took in the rose-tipped peaks and she saw the awe light the deep blue depths of his eyes, the same awe that she had seen when he had found the painting she had created, hanging behind the thick glass window of the art gallery.

The Embrace. As he did now. So perfect. So lovely.

"Ellie," he murmured, his low, hoarse voice filled with raw desire.

But he said nothing else, simply came over her, his kisses hungry and desperate, searching for solace.

Boldly, she pulled at his shirt. Impatiently, he tossed it aside, allowing her to run her hands up his back, the hard, subtle ripple of muscles widening into broad shoulders. She took his kiss, then demanded more. With his tongue, he traced the outline of her lips, licking, laving, before plunging deep. She murmured and moaned, her body alive with molten blood singing in her veins.

"Tell me to stop, Ellie," he murmured thickly into her ear. "Tell me to stop now, or this time there will be no turning back."

"God help me, I don't want you to stop. Not again. Love me, Nicky," she cried, refusing to think about tomorrow and what it would bring.

But his eyes still searched hers, looking for an answer she couldn't discern. At length he whispered, "Only if it's forever."

Forever. Reason bade her to roll free, push him away. But the sweet elixir of his caress made her head spin, unable to think with sanity. She had no words with which to answer him. She kissed him instead, her touch a lie.

He groaned and came down on her, his mouth slanting across her lips, her cheeks, her jaw. Clearly he took her actions as answer enough. He devoured her, taking her in, nipping, biting. Licking. He wanted her intensely, she could feel it. Through skirts and trousers, she could feel the hard length of his desire pressed boldly against her thighs. He groaned as he pressed against her, kissing her ear, her neck, his tongue laving the hollow at the base of her throat. Lower and lower, his hands going first, a sweep across her collarbone before his lips followed. He covered her breast with his hand, kneading softly, slowly, the heel of his hand rubbing over her pink-tipped breast, pressing it high. And then his lips, his mouth, his tongue, before his hand lowered yet again. Skimming, caressing, seeking.

With the boldness of a man sure of his possession, he reached down and lifted the hem of her skirt, the soft material gathering against his wrist as his hand burned a path between her thighs.

Instinctively she flinched and tried to move away.

"No, Ellie. It's too late for that." He kissed her as he freed the tangle of skirt, deftly untying the silken bow of her pantaloons before tossing them aside, and she lay in all her splendor beneath him. "I have dreamed of this moment for months. You naked and open for me."

Her breath caught.

"Open your legs, Ellie," he repeated.

She lay motionlessly, staring up at him, amazing herself by longing to run her fingers through his hair, though feeling she should pull free. But slowly she discarded her once-resolute propriety. She wanted his touch, needed his touch. She allowed his hand to glide down her body, between her thighs, spreading them. She gasped, her breath catching, when he pulled one nipple deep into his mouth, at the same time sliding a deft finger deep inside her.

When he had caressed her so intimately, shamelessly, in the doorway of the art gallery, she had been amazed by the experience. But here, in the intimacy of his bedroom, the intensity was nearly devastating.

He stroked her, her body aching to his touch, his thumb teasing the nether lips that cleaved her body. His kisses were brushes of feather strokes against her skin—her lips, her neck—his fingers performing an exquisite torture. But then his lips seared a path down her ribs to the swell of her abdomen. And then he kissed her, his tongue tracing her secret opening.

"Nicholas!" she cried, startled, embarrassed.

"Shhhh," he murmured, gentling her like a wild mare needing to be tamed.

"Nicholas?"

"It's all right, love. Open for me. I don't want to hurt you. I want you wet when I take you."

He spread her thighs against her waning resistance, then kissed and licked until she writhed.

"Yes," he murmured against her, settling between her knees, his hands tilting her hips.

When he gently laved the terribly sensitive bud of her womanhood she cried out in both pleasure and mortification, and reached out to grab his head, to push him away.

"Shhhh," he commanded gently. "Let me love you."

With infinite patience he waited until her grip on his hair loosened, then he began to lave again, and her hands tangled in his midnight locks. She remembered the night he had made her feel such pleasure, and she knew deep down that she wanted to feel it again.

"Reach, Ellie," he demanded.

Her hips began to move, embarrassment a faint memory, sensation building in the core of her being, tingling in her legs, her breath short, until she seemed to explode, her body convulsing, her limbs trembling with her release. He cupped her woman's flesh, holding her body tight against him, safe, secure. Dear God, loved.

"You have so much passion," he said, coming up her body, looking into her eyes. And then he kissed her again, behind her ear.

Reaching between their bodies, he worked the fastenings of his clothes, then tossed them carelessly aside, the evidence of his desire free to press against her body. "Touch me," he murmured.

At first she wasn't certain what he meant. But when he groaned and took her hand, then guided it downwards, she knew. After an initial start of surprise, instead of the revulsion she might have expected, she felt only a budding excitement as she took the length of him in her hand. The velvety tip was moist.

"I want you, Ellie, as I have never wanted anything in my life. I have wanted you since the day I first saw you."

The words were an accusation, but she ignored the tone and relished the way she could control him with the mere touch of her hand. She stroked him, his guttural words growing incoherent, until he grabbed her hand, his breathing ragged.

"I can't wait," he said through his gasping breaths. "I'll try to be gentle."

He poised at the opening of her womanhood and she realized that they had come to a place where lives would be forever changed. His gaze told her he knew this was true.

Though his body was taut with barely maintained control, he pushed inside her with infinite patience, until he came to the barrier that marked her innocence. He stilled. They looked at each other for long moments, before he thrust one last time, entering her completely, breaking through the only gift she had to give the man whom she so desperately loved but couldn't have—her innocence lost as their bodies came together so completely, so perfectly, two parts of a whole. The bond that she had tried so hard to rend, she realized in that moment, was still intact, and now was finally complete, the missing thread woven into place. Was it possible to love someone so deeply? she wondered in the warmth of his embrace. Or to hurt so badly?

But then his body moved, and she thought no more, lost to her own desire before their bodies convulsed, and he spilled his seed deep within her womb. She held him fiercely, as if she would never let him go, wanting desperately to sear the feel of him into her mind.

Chapter 27

A vivid orange sun rose on the horizon. Barely. The clouds marring the way. Nicholas stood alone, a sheet of fine linen stationery held in his hand.

> *My dearest Nicholas,*
> *Forgive me.*
> *Ellie*

Nicholas stared at the note. One line. Nothing more. A haunting echo of so long ago, though all too clearly of the present, telling him something he didn't want to know, didn't want to believe.

He stood in his bedroom doorway, looking out over the garden. Ellie was gone. She wasn't in the kitchen sipping coffee. She wasn't picking early autumn flowers to present him as a gift. She was gone.

Under the cover of early morning darkness, she had clearly slipped out like a common thief, dashing away on silent feet as he slept, unaware, foolishly trusting a woman he had already learned couldn't be trusted.

His bitter laughter snaked through the room. He was a fool. He hadn't learned from his mistakes, and deserved what he got. Another note. Another betrayal. All by the women in his life he had dared to love, he raged, flinging the simple stationery into the fireplace, the white sheet slicing into the burned-out ashes of last night's fire to land like a solitary sail of a sinking ship on an indifferent sea.

He didn't have to find Ellie to ask what the note meant. He already knew. Her touch had been a lie. His obsession had turned out to be desire, deep-seated passion, and love that had been waiting for Ellie to come into his life. When he had decided to marry her, his life had come alive with golden purpose—not tarnished or sullied, but, for once, pure and good. And then when he had joined his flesh with hers he had known a completion he had never dreamed possible. Lying with Ellie in his arms, he had been certain that despite all that had passed between them they were still destined to be together. At that moment he would have forgiven her anything. But she didn't want to be the woman of his heart, she didn't want to be forgiven. She had betrayed their bond, again, spurning his love. She had proved that with her note.

And in that moment, standing in the grand doorway through which she had no doubt fled mere hours ago, he knew he hated her as he acknowledged hating only one other person in his life.

Chapter 28

Two days passed. Then three. Not until the seventh day did Ellie allow herself to believe that Nicholas had understood her message and wouldn't seek her out. Was she delivered or destroyed? she wondered, standing in the front parlor window, staring out.

Barnard sat in front of his easel, forever painting, though more quietly since Hannah had left. Jim had gone out, said he was going to the park since it was Sunday. Ellie looked forward to tomorrow. Monday. At this point, she would even welcome one of Charles Monroe's once again frequent visits. At least when she was busy taking orders, making hats, or even listening to Charles ply her with endless reasons as to why they should marry, especially now that he was a respectable businessman, she didn't have time to think.

Someone knocked at the door, brisk and impatient. Her heart lodged in her throat. Was it Nicholas? she wondered foolishly, before she could stop herself. What would she say if it was him? But then she noticed that Barnard had turned too, hope kindling in the gray eyes that had been washed clean of emotion since the day Hannah left.

Trying to remain calm, Ellie went to the door.

"Mr. Barnard Webb," a uniformed messenger announced brusquely. "I got letters here for a Mr. Barnard Webb."

Disappointment flashed through Ellie, then she cursed herself for a fool. Barnard rushed to the door, taking the letters with shaking hands. The messenger waited impatiently until Ellie realized that the man expected a tip. She found a coin and sent him on his way, then finally focused her attention on Barnard. But when she turned back and started to inquire about the letters, the words hung unspoken.

Barnard sat in an overstuffed chair, the missives littered around his feet as if they had fallen unheeded from his lap.

"Barnard, what is it? What's happened?"

Barnard didn't respond, only stared off into the bright fall day.

Hurrying to his side, her own concerns and heartaches pushed aside, she gathered the abandoned letters. One by one she picked them up. Each unopened. Addressed neatly, painstakingly. Some yellowed with age. All marked boldly. *Return to Sender.*

Barnard's letters, written over the years to his son. Coldly, callously, returned to sender.

Barnard deteriorated over the passing days. The once vibrant man turned into a hollow shell. Neither Jim's pleadings, nor Ellie's cajolings seemed to faze their friend. For the first time since Ellie had met Barnard, he acted like an old man at the end of his life.

During the nights, Ellie paced her room, trying not to think about Nicholas. During the days, she tried to show Barnard her love, sitting with him for hours—all to no avail. Barnard gave up, admitting defeat without putting up a fight. And that turned her concern into anger.

Slamming out of her room one afternoon, she marched down the stairs to Barnard's second-floor apartment with zealous determination. When he didn't respond to her knock, she threw the door wide open. But her anger abated when she saw him lying in bed, his craggy skin pale, his white hair limp. Jim sat at his side, rocking gently in a hard-backed chair. The sight broke her heart. But then she bolstered herself. Her sympathy had done him no good.

"Quit feeling sorry for yourself, Barnard!"

Jim gasped, but Ellie had seen Barnard's start of surprise, and was encouraged.

"So your son returned your letters. I'm sorry. But life is difficult. You know that. Why let it defeat you now?"

She could see that he wanted to respond, wanted to lash out at her, but he didn't.

"You can't undo what was done ages ago," she continued mercilessly. "Are you going to turn your back on the people who love you now? Are you going to take the easy way out by lying there, wasting away until you die?"

Still he didn't move, but Jim looked at her as if she had gone mad.

"Well, what about us, Barnard? What about Jim and me? We love you! And you're hurting us!" She paused. "And what about Hannah?"

"She's gone, damn it!" he shouted, wheeling out of bed, nearly toppling Jim from his seat. "She's gone, turned her back on me, just like my own son!"

Ellie's eyes widened incredulously. "She's gone because you showed her nothing but callousness and indifference. And as far as Hannah turning her back on you, as long as you live in my house I will not allow you to rewrite history. One meager word from you and she would have stayed. She wanted to stay. Was desperate to stay. She gave you every chance to change what she felt she had to do." Ellie gasped for breath. "But no! You were too proud, or just too stubborn! You'd rather let the woman you love go than utter a word of kindness or admit that you care for her. Well, Barnard Webb, we all know you. Every one of us knows that inside that crusty old shell there's a caring man, a very caring man!"

He stood like a tower of raging fury, his fists clenched at his sides, his lips pursed. But his eyes, pale gray orbs, glistened with betraying tears.

"You care about us, Barnard," she repeated doggedly. "Just admit it. Is that so difficult?"

His hands began to work at his sides. Jim began to cry silently, clearly hating how his life had fallen so far from what he knew. Barnard started to turn away.

"Admit it, Barnard," she persisted through clenched teeth. "Quit being so selfish."

He turned back sharply. "What do you want me to do? Admit that I was a lousy father? Admit that I'm a lousy friend? Admit that I was lousy to Hannah and that I don't deserve anyone's love in return?"

"No," she whispered. "Admit that you loved your son, and like so many others, made mistakes. Admit that you love your friends. Admit that you love Hannah and want her back."

"But what good will it do me! I'll never see my son again. And Hannah's gone."

"Go to her, Barnard. Go to Hannah and tell her of your love."

He scoffed at this.

"Oh, Barnard, take a chance."

He looked at her long and hard, his resolve wavering.

"What could it hurt?" she added softly.

A reluctant smile brought a glimmer of color back into his face. "Yeah," he said gruffly, though his smile grew. "What could it hurt?"

"Does this mean you're gonna go get Hannah?" Jim asked, running his sleeve across his wet eyes.

"I guess it does," he muttered cantankerously, but his eyes glistened with newfound excitement.

"When?" Jim demanded.

"As soon as I can get myself dressed and over to that blasted boardinghouse she's moved herself into."

"You know where she is?" Ellie asked astonished.

"Yeah, yeah. Been by there a couple of times."

"You never told us. What did she say?"

Barnard shuffled his feet. "She didn't exactly say anything." He hesitated.

"Go on."

"She didn't exactly know I was there."

"You've been spying on her?!"

"No, no, no. Just makin' sure she was all right, is all."

Ellie's eyes sparkled with overflowing amusement and love. "You are a fine man, Barnard Webb."

Jim launched himself onto Barnard, the tremendous strength of his hug the only thing that kept Barnard from falling under the onslaught. After a moment, Barnard returned his friend's affection, looking at Ellie around Jim's massive frame. "Thank you," he said quietly.

Ellie smiled. "Thank *you*."

She started to leave the room.

"Ellie," Barnard said.

"Yes?"

"Isn't it about time you took your own advice?"

Her eyes narrowed. "What are you talking about?"

"Isn't it time you took a chance yourself?"

"On what?" she asked crisply.

"On Nicholas Drake."

She stiffened, much as Barnard had earlier.

Barnard gave her a knowing look. "You're not so comfortable when the tables are turned."

"My situation is nothing like yours."

"Taking a chance is taking a chance, no matter what the situation. Hannah may tell me to go jump in the river. She may already had found herself some fancy beau to marry. But like you said, I'm going to take a gamble that she will return where she belongs and give me another opportunity to show her my feelings. It's time you take a chance on Nicholas. I told you before to tell him who you are, to be open and honest. But things happened with little Charlotte and all. I know that. But that precious angel is gone, Ellie." He hesitated. "Now it's time."

She turned with a jerk to the window. Tell Nicholas who

she was? Tell him she was the daughter of his most hated enemy? And if he didn't forgive her, how could she trust that he wouldn't tell the world who she was?

"Come on, Ellie," Barnard urged, his craggy voice softened with tenderness. "Take a chance that through his love, Nicholas will be able to see beyond the man who sired you."

"How?" she whispered, her hand to her mouth. "What can I tell him after all that's happened?"

"Tell him the truth. Plain and simple. He loves you, Ellie. Have faith in his love."

It was Monday morning, three weeks after Ellie had fled Nicholas's home under the cloak of darkness. She felt ill as she sat at her desk, wadded-up sheets of paper strewn about the floor. She had started her letter over again and again, not knowing what to say.

Dear Nicky . . .
Dearest Nicky . . .
Dear Nicholas . . .

And she hadn't even gotten to the actual missive. She groaned her frustration when she balled up yet another piece of paper. Come on, Ellie, she chided herself. You have to do this.

In the end she wrote a simple note.

Dear Nicholas,
*   At your house on Long Island I said that I needed to tell you something. I never got the chance. I would like the opportunity to tell you my story now.*

*   I await your response,*
*   Ellie*

Jim sped off with the note at noon.

Ellie paced the front parlor, glancing out the window every few minutes to see if he had returned. Minutes ticked by. She was hot and flushed. Tired and ill. Images of

Charlotte came to mind. The wasting away. But she wasn't sick, Ellie told herself firmly. She was just tired, nothing a good night's sleep wouldn't cure. But when she thought about eating she grew dizzy, her stomach roiling at the idea. She was weak an hour later when Jim finally returned.

"Here, Ellie," he said, handing her an envelope.

"But that's *my* letter, Jim! You were supposed to take it to Nicholas."

"I did. I really did. Look. Nicholas's assistant man, Bert, wrote on it then gave it back to me."

Nicholas had refused to see her, had refused even to read her note, she felt it in her bones. She had taken a chance and had lost. Clutching a chair back, she thanked God that Barnard had already left to retrieve Hannah so he couldn't be discouraged from his own path. Then, sick at heart, she took the unopened note and read the scrawl across the envelope.

> *Miss Sinclair, Mr. Drake has departed for the Caribbean indefinitely. I am closing the office here before I seek employment elsewhere. If there is anything I can do for you in the meantime please don't hesitate to ask.*
> *Sincerely,*
> *Bert Hall*

Her head swam. Her stomach roiled.

Nicholas had left.

She'd have no opportunity to tell her story, to be rebuffed—or forgiven.

"Ellie, dear!"

It was a moment before Hannah's voice seeped into her thoughts. As if in slow motion, Ellie turned. She tried to smile as she hugged Hannah who laughed and cried her joy. Ellie tried to cover her despair. And perhaps she would have ultimately been successful if just then Jim hadn't said, "Look! It's Nicky!"

Her breath caught as unexpected hope burgeoned in her

chest. But her hope turned to confusion when she realized Jim was pointing to the afternoon paper Barnard had set on the table when he came in.

"It's Nicky!" Jim repeated. "His photograph's right there." Startled, Barnard and Hannah looked down at the newspaper. Ellie picked up the newspaper before Barnard could retrieve it.

NEW YORK'S MOST ELIGIBLE BACHELOR TRAVELS TO CARIBBEAN TO MARRY

The bold headline was followed by an article.

Desolation swelled in Ellie's throat. With supreme effort she started to read. It was reported that Nicholas Drake had traveled to the Caribbean to marry one Miss Deidra Carlisle, the stunning heiress who had recently dazzled New York society.

The article went on but Ellie dropped the paper, the assorted pages falling to the floor.

"Ellie," Hannah said, wrapping an arm around her shoulders. "Ellie, talk to me."

"He's gone," she whispered. "I'm too late."

But before she could say another word, her stomach finally revolted, and she raced to the bathroom and was sick.

Two weeks later, Ellie had no choice but to admit she was pregnant. Pregnant with Nicholas's child. She had made love once—one time—and she ended up pregnant. She was shocked, stunned, desperate—and elated. She was going to have a baby. Nicholas's baby. But on the heels of elation came reality. Ellie had lived the life of an illegitimate child. And she could not submit a child of her own to what she had lived through. The question was, she thought over and over again as she paced her room, how to give her child a better life.

"Ellie, dear." Hannah knocked at the door. "Charles is here."

Charles Monroe. Ellie stopped where she stood as suddenly the *how* came clear.

Forcing herself to speak before she could think better of it, Ellie said, "Tell him I'll be right down, Hannah."

Ellie refused to think as, with hands shaking, she dressed with an attention to detail that was rare for her. The only chance her baby had stood downstairs, and Ellie had no intention of thinking of herself when her child's well-being was at stake.

"Charles," she said politely as she came down the stairs.

"Hello, Ellie. I need to talk to you."

His usual smiles and good humor were gone. Charles was as serious as she had ever seen him. "Of course. In fact, I need to talk to you as well."

They rode in silence along the streets in a covered carriage, up Seventh Avenue toward Central Park. Ellie's heart hammered in her chest.

"Ellie," Charles said, as the buildings began to recede. "We've known one another for a long time."

"Yes," she agreed, wondering suddenly where this could possibly be going.

"And during that time I've asked you to be my wife many times."

Her fingers curled around her reticule. Was he going to tell her his offer was rescinded? "And I've always been flattered, Charles."

"Have you? Have you been flattered or have you been laughing at me?"

"Of course I've never laughed at you. I've been frustrated with you, but never, never have I thought your proposal was a laughing matter. I cherished your friendship, always have."

"But recently, you've been . . . well . . . distant."

She took a deep breath. "Oh Charles, it's just that life has become . . . rather complicated."

"Then you still care for me?" he asked with pitifully hopeful eyes.

"Yes, I still care for you. You have been a good friend, and I will always appreciate that."

"Friend, Ellie? Is that all we are? Or, once and for all, will you marry me?"

She should have been elated. He had set before her exactly what she wanted, at exactly the right moment, like the perfect ending to a romantic tale. But this was no romantic tale, no story with perfect endings. "I would be honored to marry you, Charles."

His surprise overwhelmed his face. "You will?! I mean, that's wonderful!"

He reached out to hug her, but she put out her hand to stop him. "Before you say this is wonderful, I have something I must tell you."

"What is it?"

She didn't want to tell him, she didn't want to say the words out loud. But Charles was a decent man, and his only sin was caring for her. She couldn't go into marriage deceiving him. "I'm pregnant, Charles."

She watched him, her chin held high to counter her embarrassment. His face was so descriptive, his brow furrowing as he took in the words, the look that said surely he had misheard. Then finally, inevitably, the realization of the truth and what it meant.

"Who is the bastard?" he demanded. "I'll kill him!"

"I won't tell you, Charles. If you choose to toss me out of this carriage right now I'll understand. But if you still want to marry me, you must know that I will never, ever, tell you who the father of my child is."

Falling back against the plush seat cushion, Charles looked out at the passing scenery. "If that's the only way I can have you . . . then so be it."

"Don't marry me out of some convoluted sense of obligation. If you never see me again it is more than understandable."

"Convoluted sense of obligation?" He looked at her, his blond hair falling forward on his forehead, his brown eyes dull and lifeless. "No, none of that. I will marry you, Ellie Sinclair, because I love you."

Part Three

❧❧

Longing

What sweet thoughts, what longing
led them to the woeful pass.

— Dante

Chapter 29

March 1899

ELUSIVE PAINTER RETURNS
by Able Smythe

Two and a half years after his last painting, M. M. Jay has returned to the Art World. And what a return it is. Just as in the past, this latest painting appeared on the gallery doorstep, the painter as elusive as ever.

Given Jay's ingenious brush strokes and attention to detail, one might be tempted to believe that the artist's primary goal is *Art for Art's Sake*. However, no sooner does one make such a judgment than he steps back to take in the whole, finding a scene so real, so expressive that the beholder feels not like a connoisseur of Art, but like a voyeur to a scene well left without witness.

Erotic? many ask. Yes, even I must admit. Though when one truly studies the work, one realizes it is more erotic for the disturbing emotions it evokes than for what is actually on the canvas. Longing and desperation. Visible, nearly tangible. In bodies—only bodies, as always, no faces, never faces, as if somehow anonymity could be maintained.

My mind circles with wonder, but with curiosity as

well. Why did you return, M. M. Jay, if you are so intent
on staying in hiding?

"Good morning, good morning!"

Eliot Sinclair Monroe sailed into the dining room. With a
dazzling smile, she leaned down and placed a kiss on her
husband's forehead.

Charles Monroe tossed the *Times* aside, then pushed up
from his seat to pull out his wife's chair. "I trust you're well,
my dear?"

"I'm wonderful, simply wonderful," Ellie chimed as she
placed her napkin in her lap then sighed her delight over the
large plate overflowing with eggs, biscuits, grilled ham and
braised potatoes, that had been set before her.

Her blond hair was still silky, pulled away from her face,
secured in an elegant twist at the back of her head. Her form
was still svelte, belying the overly large breakfast that she
loved. Her gown was as simple as ever, a soft wool without
artifice, though now the simple style had become fashionable. With her natural grace, beauty, and charm, and now as
the wife of Charles Monroe, son of Rupert Monroe of the
now thriving Monroe Publishing, Ellie was much sought-
after by society. While the Monroes certainly had "new
money," they suddenly found themselves with plenty of it.
And Rupert Monroe guarded his family's "new respectability" like it was a priceless family heirloom. Ellie, in both her
husband's and father-in-law's opinions, was an asset.

"You're certainly bright and chipper this morning,"
Charles said, lowering his portly body back into his own
chair.

Ellie laughed. "It's a beautiful day. Cold but clear. And I
thought I would go over and visit with Hannah, Barnard
and Jim."

"Fine idea," he said, taking a bite of his unbuttered toast.

They ate in silence for a few minutes before Ellie asked,
"What is new in the world today, dear?"

"Nothing worthwhile. The newspaper is filled with garbage," he grumbled, eyeing a crystal dish of strawberry preserves. "After all these years, they're writing about that damned M. M. Jay again."

Ellie's hand stilled as she spread the preserves across a warm biscuit. *M. M. Jay?* After a moment, she forced a smile.

"Yes," Charles continued, unaware of the change in his wife, "apparently the degenerate painter has resurfaced. I saw one of his paintings a few years back. And let me tell you, what I saw was not art! It was indecent! I find it abhorrent that a respectable paper like the *Times* would lower itself to disseminate such tripe."

They sat in the breakfast room which overlooked the gardens of their recently completed Romanesque mansion on Fifty-ninth Street. A house, much to Ellie's secret dismay, that was no more than twenty yards from his parents' home where they had lived since their marriage. But if twenty yards' distance was all Ellie was going to get, then so be it. At least, she had told herself over and over again, she finally had a house of her own. Her life had been going so well, or as best as could be expected, until now.

How had an M. M. Jay painting appeared after all these years? she wondered, her heart lodged in her throat as the name M. M. Jay spun in her mind like a raging nor'easter. But she didn't have time to contemplate the matter further when she glanced up at the doorway. And found her son.

Her eyes burned with sudden, boundless joy. Never had she imagined she could love so intensely, so completely— without reservation. Her life was his, had been since the day she had given birth and held his precious body against her breast.

"Jonah," she said gaily, opening her arms to him.

The little boy toddled into the room, nearly losing his balance when he came to the fine oriental rug. Just when Ellie started to leap up, he caught his balance and laughed his delight.

"Mama!" he cried when she swept him up into her lap despite her elegant gown.

"How's my big boy?" she asked, ruffling his ink-black hair, laughing into his startling blue eyes.

"Where's that nanny of his?" Charles suddenly demanded from across the table.

Instantly, Jonah's jubilant smile dimmed to a wary glance as he pushed back into his mother's embrace.

"Here I am, here I am," Miss Hobart announced as she came around the corner. "A little devil he is," she laughed. "I turn my back for one minute and he's gone, he is, off searching out his mama."

The disgust over M. M. Jay turned to frustration on Charles's face at the sight of young Jonah. Ellie had come to recognize the frustration, she could see it, always did. And when her husband pushed up from his chair and strode from the room, the banging front door announcing that he had left for his office, Ellie pulled her son even closer, regret and frustration of her own suddenly marking her features.

If only things had worked out better, she thought for the thousandth time. She had tried, truly. Tried to love Charles as he wanted her to love him. What she had to offer him, however, had never been enough.

In the beginning, when she was pregnant, he had been wonderful, marrying her immediately. He had catered to her every need, promising that she would grow to love him as he loved her. And in her own way, she did love him. He had defended her to his parents, had never told anyone, even his mother and father, that the child she had borne was not his own. Everything had been going so well—until Jonah burst his way into the world, thankfully late, with a full head of black hair and blue eyes that had never changed color. Charles had taken one look at the child everyone thought of as his son and everything had changed.

Since Jonah's birth Ellie and Charles had lived together under the same roof, though they slept in separate bedrooms, maintaining a caring, though distant, relationship.

Once she had recovered from the rigors of labor and Charles had been able to exercise his conjugal rights, the reality of his wife having another man's child had clearly stopped him cold.

Thirty minutes after Charles left for the office, a fine maroon enamel coach was brought around. Ellie and Jonah went directly to the town house on Sixteenth Street. A month after Ellie had married Charles, Barnard and Hannah had married and had lived in the town house ever since.

"Ellie, Jonah," Hannah exclaimed with affection, her cheeks glowing with health and happiness.

"Nana! Nana!" Jonah cried, reaching out for a hug.

Barnard pushed up from his stool in the nook where he still painted. "There's my boy."

"Bapa!" Jonah squealed, launching himself into Barnard's arms.

"What brings the two of you here today?" Barnard asked gruffly, though he nuzzled Jonah's hair.

"We came," Ellie stated with a calm she didn't feel, "about a certain article that appeared in the *Times* this morning."

"What article?" Barnard asked, setting Jonah down and pulling a stick of peppermint from his pocket like a prize. Jonah squealed his delight.

"Barnard!" Ellie said. "Don't give him candy now. It's only ten o'clock in the morning. And don't play the innocent with me. I don't believe for one second that you didn't see the article by Able Smythe."

Barnard's head came up with a snap. "Able Smythe? I haven't seen the paper yet." He turned to his wife with an accusatory glare. "Hannah said it wasn't here."

Hannah cringed. "Well . . . I was going to show you, I was." Reluctantly, she dug out the morning paper from her knitting bag.

Barnard automatically turned to page three and read the article once, then twice. "Not bad," he mused.

"Barnard!" Ellie practically screeched. "How could this

have happened? You promised me you would never take another painting of mine."

"I didn't!"

"Then who did?"

"I did."

Everyone whirled around to the stairway.

"Yim!" Jonah called out, toddling over to his giant friend and wrapping his arms around Jim's leg.

"You did!?" Ellie asked, dumbfounded. "Jim, you took my painting to the art gallery?"

"Yeah," he pronounced proudly, lowering himself to the bottom step to give Jonah a hug.

Ellie felt faint. She couldn't seem to inhale deeply enough to get oxygen to her brain. Ever since Charles had mentioned the article, there had been a part of her that had hoped beyond hope that somehow it was a mistake. Or if not a mistake, at least had nothing to do with her. With every turn of the carriage wheels that had brought her closer to the town house she had imagined a hundred different explanations. Someone using the name, trying to capitalize on the notoriety. The gallery owner trying to gain business, using a painting from years before as a ploy. Surely the art gallery couldn't have gotten hold of the only work she had done in over two and a half years. But all hope had been dashed by Jim's simple declaration.

A creeping sense of unreality clouded her thoughts. Her world couldn't fall apart once again. Her life with Charles might be far from perfect—her parents-in-law might be overbearing, still treating their son like a child—but it was a life that she had worked hard at. And even though Charles had insisted she sell her hat shop, making her wholly dependent on him, her life was now as stable and safe as it had ever been—or had been until the *Times* had arrived that morning.

"Oh, Jim, why?" she asked, trying to remain calm.

Jim looked up. "I met a man, a nice man, who likes pretty, pretty paintings. He's got a shop where he puts 'em up for everybody to see. I told him *I* had a pretty painting at my house. When I took it over for him to see he said, Ooooooh." Jim smiled proudly. "He liked it a lot."

Her heart skipped a beat, pleasure rushing through her veins. But then she reined in her careening mind with the ease of a wagon master. It didn't matter what anyone thought of her work, what mattered was that she not ruin her life—yet again.

"Look at this, Ellie," Barnard interjected, pointing to the article. "He says you evoke emotions." Barnard whistled at the lofty wording. "I told you you're good. When are you going to accept that? And you know what else, in the last month since you started painting again, it's the first time in years that I've seen you . . . complete."

"It's true, Ellie," Hannah added. "Barnard and I have discussed it. You were lost without your art."

Ellie turned away, pressing her hand to her mouth. Until a month ago when she had been unexpectedly overwhelmed by the desperate need to hold a paintbrush and sit before a blank canvas that waited for her touch, she hadn't painted— not since her marriage. True, she'd been bereft without her art; her only joy had been her son. And that was enough, she had told herself firmly over and over again during the passing years. No woman needed more than the pleasure of raising her child.

But despite her admonitions, despite her boundless love for Jonah, she knew deep down it wasn't enough. She yearned for her art. And finally, that day a month ago, she had gone to the town house, walked up the three flights of stairs to her old apartment, and began to paint, the pieces of her world once again falling into place.

This morning, standing in the front parlor afraid her life might be threatened, she still couldn't deny that her return to her work had made her feel alive. But the reason for starting to paint again went beyond the joy it brought her. She had awakened on that day a month ago, startled, breathless, and had known she *had* to paint. "I don't understand it," she half whispered. "I don't understand why suddenly, for reasons I can't explain, I'm painting again."

"Whatever the reason," Barnard said, coming up behind her, resting his hands on her shoulders, "it's time you truly got back to your art. You need it, Ellie." He hesitated. "And I think you should seriously think about putting together a collection of work to show."

She whirled around. "What?"

"A show, Ellie. A true showing of your work. It has been your greatest dream since I've known you."

"I couldn't," she breathed, though the very idea set her blood humming in her veins.

"Of course you can. You see what your life has become. You no longer have your shop. Your life consists of little more than mindless social engagements."

"But I have my son, and you and Hannah and Jim."

"Not enough, Ellie. Yes, you love us all. But a part of you has wilted away these past years. Paint, Ellie. Then once and for all, truly show your work, even if it is as M. M. Jay."

Her breath hissed through her teeth. "But how?" she asked, tantalized as she shouldn't be.

"It would be easy. I'd take care of everything." Barnard glanced over at Jim. "And I promise you I'll watch Jim. No other paintings will leave this house unless I know about it."

"But—"

"And," he added, heading her off, "just like before, no one, I swear, no one, will know where the work is coming from."

"How can you make such promises?"

"Leave it to me, Ellie dear. I'm a master of secrecy. You just worry about painting. I'll do the rest. So what do you say?"

Ellie took a deep breath. Dear God, to paint again, truly paint with purpose. It was a heady thought, and for one fearless moment the possibility swirled unheeded through her mind. But if she did, would it put her on a reckless path to salvation—or destruction?

If the truth be told, she knew why she was painting again. It was because of Nicholas. On the morning that she had woken up with a start, she had woken up with the thought of Nicholas. Had felt Nicholas. As if he were there. Even though she hadn't seen or heard of him since he left Manhattan so long ago, she thought of him constantly. One look at her son made it impossible not to. Jonah looked just like his father. She loved the fact and hated it just as much. It had turned her into a liar. Anyone who questioned the fact that Jonah looked nothing like either she or Charles, forced Ellie to tell them that both her mother and father had dark hair and blue eyes. She was a liar because she didn't remember her mother, and because she knew her father's hair had been blond and his eyes hazel. But a liar she would be if that was what it took to protect her son.

As Jonah had gotten older she had stopped taking him places. He spent his days either at home or here on Sixteenth Street. With each month that passed, however, Ellie's fears grew stronger that someone would realize who Jonah's father truly was. Ellie had often wondered if Charles didn't secretly suspect. But if he did he never said the words, as if they had reached an unspoken understanding about the child who had another man's blood but his name.

Now she had come to a point where if she was truthful with herself, she couldn't imagine where this life she led could possibly lead. She couldn't imagine what kind of man her son would grow up to be if he wasn't allowed out of the house, allowed to be free. But she loved him with all her heart, just as she had loved the man who was his father, still loved him, she was afraid, even though he was thousands of miles away in the Caribbean, obviously married to Deidra Carlisle.

Ellie went down on her knees nightly, thanking God for Charles's help—but thankful as well that her husband wouldn't touch her. But while she was thankful, she longed to be touched, longed to feel the strength of strong arms holding her tightly. She longed to be held—by Nicholas.

God, how was it possible after all these years that she could still long for Nicholas as if it were only yesterday that he had made love to her? Giving her Jonah.

Oh, Nicholas, she whispered silently. If only you could see the perfection we created. In only you could see our son.

She took a deep breath and closed her eyes. Are you happy, Nicky? Do you have a family of your own, another son that looks like you?

Oh, Nicky, where are you?

Chapter 30

Nicholas folded the New York Times *and set the paper aside. The room was warm, the windows frosted on the outside from the late winter cold. Leaning back in the chair, he glanced around his study. His house on Fifth Avenue hadn't changed in his absence. A month ago, he had returned to find the city much the same, the streets crowded, the pace still hectic.

After being gone for so long he had foolishly assumed things would be different. But it was as if everything had continued along without him, unfazed, unaltered. He was the only one who had changed.

He caught sight of his reflection in the glass door on the book cabinet. He looked no different, he supposed; the slight graying at his temples didn't seem to make much difference in his appearance. But the glass doors didn't reflect what he felt inside.

Dead.

Cold and empty. A shell of a man, he had thought often. Just as he had been before meeting Ellie. Though a man who was even wealthier than when he had left. He had gone to the Caribbean and Italy, and had become involved in exports. Olive oil had proven to be a gold mine. The more money he made, the easier it was to make more.

He hadn't thought about a single building, neither the plans nor the construction of one in ages. While traveling in Europe he had marveled at the architecture, at times had even dreamed that one day he would build again. But somehow he never got any further than the thought. Deep down he didn't want to build any longer, he didn't want to remember.

But of course that was impossible. It was impossible to forget. Ellie. Always Ellie. Like a dream turned nightmare that plagued his mind, leaving him dead inside.

The first glimmer of feeling he'd had since he left the shores of America was only minutes before while reading the article about M. M. Jay. Why was that? he wondered. Why did he feel a flicker of interest flare to life in his breast at a short article on some elusive and scandalous artist?

His only answer was that it had always been that way, since the day he had read the first Able Smythe article. Something about the painter intrigued him.

A knock sounded at his study door.

"Come in," he called.

A thin man with a full head of thick red hair entered. "Good morning, sir. How are you today?"

Nicholas glanced at his new assistant with a wry look. In the short month Henry Brown had been working for him, Nicholas had found the man to be efficient, professional, a hard worker, and much too cheerful for his liking. But it was too late to make another choice now, and Nicholas couldn't quite bring himself to fire someone for being too happy. So Henry stayed, smiles and all.

"Where does the renovation stand?" Nicholas asked.

"Your office is nearly done. Another week and all should be ready. I've hired a receptionist, and I have several women lined up to be interviewed for the position of secretary."

They spoke of business matters for the next hour, until another knock sounded on the door.

"Mrs. Welton," Henry said, with a slight bow and huge smile, clearly enamored.

"Henry," Miriam said simply, and walked past him into the room.

Nicholas had seen his sister all of three times since his return. Looking at her now he was forced to concede not everything had stayed the same. Miriam had changed. And not for the better. But Nicholas refused to feel sympathy for her. If she had been a better mother her child might still be alive today.

He turned away from the thought that no one, not even a mother, could have saved Charlotte. He hadn't forgiven his sister for leaving her child alone, and couldn't imagine that he ever would. Not that Miriam had asked for forgiveness. She seemed totally unrepentant for her errant ways, or at least that was what he told himself, as he disregarded the years that suddenly lined her face, and the smile, like his own, that had disappeared. Disappeared like her husband.

William Welton had begun divorce proceedings against his wife within days after the death of their daughter. Then he had gone abroad, for good it was widely known, leaving his wife without a penny. Still, Nicholas had no room for sympathy. He might pay Miriam's bills and keep her in the latest gowns, but that was the extent of his involvement with his sister.

"Miriam," he said coolly in acknowledgment.

A weariness passed over her eyes, but then it was gone. "I guess you didn't get my note," she said.

"What note?"

"About dinner. I thought you might join me for dinner on Sunday."

"I have neither the time nor the patience for dinner parties, Miriam."

"It's not a party. It would be just you and me."

Nicholas raised a brow. "If you want something, Miriam, just ask. You don't need to ply me with food to gain favors."

She stood very still for a moment. "I don't want anything

from you, Nicholas," she said tightly. "You are more than kind as it is. I simply invited you over for a meal. That's all."

He looked at her, his face betraying no emotion. "Thank you for the invitation, but I must decline. Now if you'll excuse us, Henry and I have work to do."

Minutes after Miriam departed, Henry was dismissed. Nicholas wanted to get out of the house. He wanted to gallop through wide open fields on the back of a horse. But that was not nearly as easy to do in Manhattan as it had been in the Caribbean, where he had galloped day and night like a madman, the natives whispering that he was crazy. And for several months Nicholas was certain he had been.

For the most part while in the Caribbean, Nicholas had rarely seen anyone. His only caller had been Deidra Carlisle, who had plagued him at every turn. She had made it more than clear that they were perfectly suited to marry. He had made it perfectly clear that they were not. Eventually she had given up on him, marrying a newly widowed plantation owner.

Only a year after arriving in the Caribbean, Nicholas had left for Italy. But, as with the tropical island, the European country wasn't for him either. Ultimately, it was New York that was his home, New York to which he had returned.

Now, short of traveling north of Central Park where builders were only beginning to erect houses in number, Nicholas had no choice but to settle for a brisk walk through the snow-lined streets instead of a gallop.

Heading out in coat, hat, and gloves, Nicholas welcomed the harsh bite of winter wind against his skin. But as he walked block after block he realized with a muffled curse that his birthplace had become a town filled with memories of Eliot Sinclair. Frustrated, he caught a horsecar.

He dropped his nickel in the slot like everyone else, then leaned back against the hard seat as the gaunt horse and long carriage continued along the thoroughfare. Nicholas rode without thinking, welcoming the nearly deafening clatter of iron wheels on cobbled streets. When the noise finally got the better of him he jumped down the wooden steps to the pavement, ready to make his way on foot. But his step faltered when he realized where he was. At the same gallery that had shown *The Embrace*.

His eyes narrowed against the window through which he had seen the painting so long ago—the window against which he had pressed Ellie and discovered her passion. Ellie and *The Embrace*. He would always remember it that way. Together. Entwined.

That must explain why he had felt the flash of interest when he had read the article earlier that morning on M. M. Jay. Because of Ellie. And, as always, that was unacceptable.

"It's stunning, isn't it?"

Nicholas turned with a start and found a short, balding man standing next to him. "Yes," Nicholas said curtly, turning back to the window, noticing for the first time the artwork that hung there now, instead of seeing what had hung there years before. "Yes," he repeated.

"It's another work by M. M. Jay." The man shook his head. "Such a waste that no one knows who he is. What I'd give to meet him, just talk to the man, ask a few questions."

"You sound like Able Smythe," Nicholas responded dryly.

In the window's reflection Nicholas could see the man glance over at him.

"I *am* Able Smythe."

Nicholas turned to face him, studying the shorter man. "Really? I've read your articles on the artist."

Able's gaze turned speculative as he considered Nicholas. "And what do you think? Is M. M. Jay gifted, or merely obscene? Which camp do you fall in?"

Nicholas glanced back at the work, taking in the brazen though beautiful lines of the painting. "What is it called?"

"*Longing*. At least that's what I call it. They never arrive with titles. But how could it be anything else?"

Indeed, the work was filled with emotion—longing, Nicholas had to agree.

"But leave it to Jay," Smythe continued, "to outrage people by painting a woman swathed in nothing more than a sheer bit of material, touching her breast and . . . well . . . her fingers .sliding places left unsaid, looking as if she wished her hand was a lover's." Able Smythe actually blushed. "Still, I can only say that the artist grows with every work." He nodded his head for emphasis. "One of these days, mark my words, this artist will be great. Just look at this painting. It is as beautiful as it is haunting. Not a work that one is inclined to forget easily."

"No," Nicholas agreed.

"What did you say your name was?"

"I didn't," Nicholas said, returning his attention to the other man. "Nicholas Drake," he added after a moment's hesitation.

"Nicholas Drake? The builder, right?"

"Past tense."

"Oh yes, I remember something about you leaving New York, all kinds of plans for some big building left undone. Why—"

"Sorry," Nicholas said shortly, cutting him off. "I've got to go."

Nicholas walked away before the man could finish his question. Nicholas didn't want to be asked why he had left. He didn't want to be reminded of that time. But he scoffed at himself. As if by preventing someone else from mentioning the past he wouldn't think about it, or rather her, on his own. Her image tormented his mind with a reckless abandon that left him unsettled and filled with the emotion portrayed so clearly in the painting. Longing. Yes, he felt it. Hated that he did. Proving he wasn't as dead inside as he wanted to be.

Nicholas walked along the pedestrian-thick walkway, cursing himself with every step he took, because he knew where he was headed. Like a moth drawn to a flame, he had to see her.

He realized that this was what he had wanted since the day his ship sailed into New York Harbor. This was what he had wanted when he'd set out that morning, what he had wanted when he cut off Able Smythe. He didn't want to think about Ellie. He wanted to see her. Had to see her, though he cursed himself for a fool as he stood on the street looking up at the oval inset in the thick oak door.

Every muscle in his body screamed at him to run, fast and far. Instead he took the steps and knocked. Minutes passed without a sound, and just when he raised his hand to knock again the door swung open.

Silence.

Then, "Nicky!"

Jim lurched forward and wrapped Nicholas in an all-consuming hug that nearly toppled them both right down the hard steps to the walkway.

"Hello, Jim," he said, a faint memory of a smile hinting at his lips.

"Oh, Nicky, Nicky! I missed you *sooo* much."

"Well, yes. Fine," he replied uncomfortably.

"I think about you and Charlotte every single day. I talk to Charlotte in my prayers every night. I asked her to bring you home. And here you are!" He hugged Nicholas again.

Nicholas couldn't speak, and not solely due to Jim's hug which would have crushed a lesser man.

"I bet you miss Charlotte too, don't you, Nicky?"

Only every single day. "Yes," he said shortly, not knowing what else to say.

"Barnard and Hannah went to the market." Without inviting Nicholas in, Jim went into the house, talking the whole way.

After a moment's hesitation, his heart beating hard, Nicholas followed. The house smelled of baked bread and sunshine, despite the freezing cold. A home. Family. Was Ellie upstairs? he wondered.

Jim went to a table where he started to rummage through a tin of marbles.

"Shouldn't you be at work?" Nicholas asked, dragging his gaze away from the stairway.

"Work?"

"At the hat shop."

"Oh, no," he said with grave seriousness, as if Nicholas didn't have a brain in his head. "We don't got the shop anymore. We sold it. No more hats."

"Really?" Nicholas cocked his head, then noticed the nook filled with easel and supplies. "I see Barnard's still painting."

Jim glanced over and seemed to notice it for the first time. "Oh, yeah," he laughed. "He's always painting. Says he's gonna be famous some day."

But Jim's laughter cut short when Nicholas reached down and picked up a small painting that leaned against the wall behind the table where Jim sat.

"No, Nicky!" Jim cried, reaching out. "Put that back! I'm supposed to put that away. Barnard made me promise."

"I'll let you put it away," Nicholas said, moving beyond Jim's frantic reach. "Just let me see it."

Jim fell back into his chair with a groan as Nicholas studied the painting. It was small, but stunning. "Good Lord, I didn't realize Barnard was this good."

Jim's round face grew troubled, his joy at seeing Nicholas vanished. He jumped up from the table, accidentally knocking the tin to the floor. Marbles clattered and rolled in every direction. But Jim hardly noticed. "Give me that, Nicky!"

"Jim? What's wrong?"

"You gotta go, Nicky. You gotta give me that thing, then go."

Nicholas straightened with surprise at the curt tone.

"You can't stay here, Nicky. Ellie would be mad if she knew. You gotta go."

Nicholas's eyes narrowed, but he was at a loss for what to say. He knew he shouldn't be there, didn't need to be reminded, and having it pointed out to him by Jim didn't sit well. "Actually, I've come here to see Ellie."

"Oh, no!" Jim said with wide eyes, taking hold of the painting and pressing it to his broad chest. "You can't. You can't see her. It'll make her mad."

"If you'll just tell her I'm here," Nicholas persisted coldly.

"She's not here, Nicky! Now go! I don't wanna get in trouble."

Nicholas hesitated, desire to see Ellie battling with reason. But suddenly he felt foolish. Why had he come? What purpose did it serve? None. None at all.

Once outside, Nicholas walked to Sixth Avenue, then headed north. He hadn't needed proof that Ellie wanted nothing to do with him, but had gotten it anyway. He felt nothing, or so he told himself. He felt nothing that she had clearly stricken him from her life—as he had been unable to do with her.

With hands thrust deep in his coat pockets, Nicholas walked on until he came to the shopping district, past B. Altman, past Siegel-Cooper. A brand-new, smartly fitted maroon enamel carriage had pulled up to the curb, and a liveried footman was helping a woman down. Later, Nicholas would curse his decision to walk, lament not hailing a hired hack, or even taking the elevated train. But just then, as the elegantly clad woman stepped down and started to turn back to the carriage, saying something to someone inside, stopping in mid-turn when she saw him, he could only stare.

"Nicky," she breathed, her breath a white puff in the cold air.

"Hello, Ellie."

They stood on the walkway, passersby walking around them.

"You're back," she said.

The same soft smile that he had longed so often to see pulled at her lips.

"I didn't realize you knew that I was gone," he said.

The bloom of red roses stained her cheeks. How long had

it been since he had seen a woman blush? Since Ellie. Since Ellie had slipped into his life and his heart.

Despite long years of hurt and anger, her beauty washed over him like a soothing balm. He was captivated by her emerald eyes, mesmerized by the hair beneath her hat that was still as silky, and her form that was still as slender beneath her simple gown. She was still a beauty that had the power to take his breath away. "How have you been?"

"Fine, I suppose," she responded like a shy schoolgirl. "And you?"

They stood on the walkway, oblivious to the hurried crush of pedestrians around them.

He shrugged his shoulders. "Fine."

"You look wonderful."

He could tell that she was sincere. As always she spoke frankly. Straightforward. Bold, brave. Dear God, how he had missed her.

The past slipped away and he took a step closer, started to reach out. He wanted to touch her, to feel her, wrap her in his arms and never let her go. He could tell that she realized his intent when her breath seemed to still in her breast, her lips slightly parting. He could see in her eyes that she longed for his touch as much as he longed for her.

"Uh-hum," the footman said, starting for the carriage doorway. "Excuse me, Mrs. Monroe, should I help young—"

Too many emotions hit Nicholas at once to make sense of them all. But mostly he was suffused with two simple words. *Mrs. Monroe.* He was hardly aware of the sudden panic that etched Ellie's face, or that she suddenly reached out and slammed the carriage door shut.

"Mrs. Monroe?" Nicholas asked with deadly eyes.

When she merely stood with her back stiff and her eyes wide, failing to respond, he reached out and firmly took her hand. He ignored the footman's objections and Ellie's weak protest as he pulled her fine leather glove free.

The solid gold band was like a blow. He couldn't think, much less speak. At length, he looked up from her delicate fingers, one boldly encircled by another man's ring. "Did you find yourself a knight in shining armor to build you a castle by the sea?" His deep blue eyes went metallic, as did his voice. "Or was it just me that you didn't want?"

Nicholas released her with disdain. His anger returned, though shifting, changing—in that moment crystallizing into something beyond simple hate. "To think I believed your fanciful story."

"What are you talking about?" she asked, her voice strained.

He stared at her, then scoffed. "Nothing. Just foolish words uttered by a foolish woman, taken to heart by a foolish man." His words were mocking and hateful, though he mocked himself as much as her. God, he wanted to scream, to lash out.

"Oh, Nicky."

"No! No, Mrs. Monroe," he said sharply, his teeth suddenly clenched. "It is Nicholas. Nicholas Drake."

They stood scant inches apart, their breaths touching, mingling like lovers.

"I'm sorry," she said finally, resignation replacing her schoolgirl's blush. "So sorry."

He saw the softness in her eyes and that made him even angrier. Angry because she would never be his. Angry because she had betrayed him. Angry that he cared. "Are you?" he demanded, venom lacing his words. "Are you sorry that it's not me when you lay in another man's arms?"

Her gasp didn't stop him, neither did the shocked countenance of the footman. "Are you sorry when you feel his hands—"

"Stop it! Stop it, Nicholas. Don't do this."

"Don't do what, love?" he asked with marked coldness, the endearment a slap. "You have never been one to mince words. Do you expect something different from others?"

"Why are you doing this?" she cried in a whisper.

But her emotion only served to stoke the fire of his anger.

"You have to ask?" He laughed, though the sound was void of mirth. "Think back, little one, if you can't remember."

She started to turn away. But he caught her arm, staying her. The footman started forward, but Nicholas's gimlet gaze quailed whatever obligations the man felt. "Think back to a ballroom filled with guests. Or a secret night of illicit—"

"Stop," she whispered, her voice choked.

But then she drew a deep breath, and he watched as she raised her chin defiantly. "I don't need to be reminded," she stated. "I remember on my own quite well enough."

Her eyes locked with his, and the intensity and disappointment he saw there nearly made him cringe—nearly. But he was beyond caring, or so he told himself as he abruptly released her arm. She was out of his reach forever now. If their past had ever been surmountable, her marriage was not.

"Whether you believe me or not," she said stiffly, "I am sorry."

And then she slammed herself back into the carriage with finality, before the driver jumped into his seat, cracked the whip in the air, and the maroon enamel carriage lurched away in a burst of speed.

Chapter 31

A month later Nicholas sat in his now-completed office. Though it was eight o'clock in the evening, he was still there, busy, with no time to think, and he liked it that way. But this night he had seen a posting in the *Times*. A full gallery showing of the work of M. M. Jay. That night. As always, Nicholas was intrigued, but amazed as well. There had never been more than a single painting at a time, and rarely, at that.

Nicholas left the office, then had his driver drop him off at the gallery. Yet again, Nicholas experienced a moment's hesitation when he came to the front door set back in the little alcove. Images flooded his mind. The sweet feel of her skin, warm against his. Her unexpected passion. But then he steeled himself against emotion and pushed through the door.

The gallery was crowded, patrons talking, laughing. A Bohemian crowd. Artists, dancers, poets. Not the elite of New York society. If they wanted to see the work, they'd arrange for a private showing. But it was the artwork lining the walls that commanded Nicholas's attention. Demanded his attention. Paintings—some large and bold, some small, almost shy, all alive with undeniable passion. Making him feel.

"What do you think?"

With effort, Nicholas turned his head to find Able Smythe at his side. But he didn't respond, couldn't really. His heart hammered oddly in his chest.

"I can tell you feel about M. M. Jay as I do," Able answered for him. "But I become more puzzled by the minute. This group of paintings arrived with a note. *For a showing.* That's all. Damn," he added with great feeling. "When will we ever learn who the man is?"

"Maybe never," Nicholas managed, not understanding the strange buzz that echoed in his head.

"If only I could find him."

"Yes," Nicholas said distractedly, blocking out the newspaperman, concentrating instead on the paintings that lined the walls.

Nicholas took in each piece, the color, the texture, the image. He felt as if he knew the work, had known it forever. The buzz grew louder, and his eyes narrowed against the unexplainable feelings. It made no sense.

But then he turned, and found a painting, one small painting to the side, out of the way, nearly lost.

"No Nicky! Put that back!"

The sound of Jim's fear and his words welled up in Nicholas's mind as if the giant man stood next to him. But Jim wasn't there, only the painting—the painting Nicholas had picked up and studied at Ellie's town house.

Confusion washed over him. Nicholas remembered the day he had first gone over to the house on Sixteenth Street. *"There are those who say I am M. M. Jay."* Barnard's words. Though followed by Hannah. *"This old goat couldn't paint a three-inch square of plaster wall white to save his life."*

Nicholas's heart pounded, the sound of his blood rushing through his ears. Able Smythe asked another question, but Nicholas didn't answer, didn't hear. He turned on his heels and quit the gallery. He walked, faster and faster, until he was nearly running. Within minutes he was on Sixteenth Street, pounding on the door.

The house wasn't dark; in fact it blazed with light. He glanced at his pocket watch. Eight-forty-five. He pounded again. What seemed like hours later, Barnard pulled open the door.

"Nicholas!"

Barnard's surprise was genuine. But Nicholas hardly noticed. He pushed past the older man with little regard for proprieties, and strode directly to the little nook that held the man's paints.

"What the hell are you doing?" Barnard demanded, his surprise giving way to outrage, and perhaps concern.

Nicholas ripped the covering white sheet from the easel, his eyes dark and wild. It took a moment for Nicholas to absorb the painting that rested on the easel. "I've been a fool," Nicholas ground out at length.

Suddenly everything came clear. *The Embrace*. It was familiar because it was Ellie. With him. Dear God, in the rain. He remembered the looks of panic whenever he had spoken of M. M. Jay. The paint on her fingers. The feeling that somehow he knew the artist's work.

His stomach clenched, his head pounded much as he had pounded on the front door. And as if he had willed her there, the front door burst open, and her chiming laughter floated over to him. "Barnard, I can't believe it!"

Nicholas turned slowly to face her. She saw him instantly, and he watched as the laughter changed to horror in her eyes.

"Nicky!" she gasped.

"Yes," he answered, his voice marked with a barely maintained control, "it's me. Are you surprised?"

"What are you doing here?"

"Call it curiosity."

He saw her glance flicker over Barnard's painting. "Yes." He answered her unspoken question. "I've come to look at Barnard's work."

"I think you should leave," she said firmly, regaining her composure.

"But I can't. Not yet. My curiosity has yet to be appeased. You wouldn't want me to leave . . . unfulfilled, would you?"

He walked toward her, his stride a predator's gait, until he stood scant inches before her. Unexpectedly, he reached out and took her hand, his grip anything but gentle. When she resisted he held firm, their eyes locked. Without a word, very slowly, he uncurled her fingers and found the telltale sign. He nearly laughed at himself when he realized he was disappointed. He had hoped he was wrong. More the fool he.

"Paint," he remarked simply, his voice laden with contempt. "Helping Barnard?"

She didn't look away, nor did she answer.

"No," he said for her, tracing her nails. "Not helping Barnard."

Then suddenly he was overwhelmed, the nearness of her body, the softness of her skin, the sweet scent of her hair, wrapping around him, strangling him. "Is that what you used me for, *Mrs. Monroe*?" he demanded, his words searing the room with their malice as he dropped her hand.

Barnard stepped forward. "Get out of here, Drake, right now before I call the authorities."

But Nicholas ignored him, his face shifting into a hideous mask. "Did you touch my body so you could paint what you felt?"

Her cheeks blanched.

"And to think I believed you came to me in the middle of the night to offer comfort." His laughter was haunted. "Did you let me make love to you so you could paint what we shared?"

He saw her delicate hand reach out and grasp a chair back. Barnard choked and sputtered his outrage. "Is that what I was to you," Nicholas persisted ruthlessly. "An artist's inspiration?"

"Damn you, Drake. Leave her alone!"

"I will not leave her alone!" he said, his voice slashing through the room.

Barnard's face suffused with red, his hands clenched. Then he raced out the front door, and Nicholas knew the older man had gone for the authorities. But he didn't care. He stared at Ellie. "Just tell me this, was I the only one to inspire you, or were there others?"

Her hand snaked out and connected with his cheek before he realized what had happened. The surprise on her face at her actions matched his own. But then he smiled, a cold, hard smile that was chilling, as he touched the stinging imprint on his face. "A little late for maidenly gestures I would think."

"Get out," she said, trembling.

"Have I made you angry, M.M.? Or do you prefer Miss Jay?"

"I didn't think it was possible to hate you. Ever. But now I know I was wrong."

His glacial smile disappeared. "Good. I'd hate to think my feelings weren't reciprocated."

Her eyes closed and her body wavered. "Just leave."

A shot of concern passed through him. He felt a stinging need to reach out, ask if she was all right. But he bit the need back, emotions flailing his mind.

"Please," she whispered, drawing a tortured breath. "Please just leave me alone."

With lightning speed he reached out and angrily grabbed her arms, pulling her so close that he could feel her pounding heart against his chest. "Why didn't you leave *me* alone?" he demanded, his voice choked. "Even if you had to use me for your paintings, why did you have to make me love you?"

What little fear that had glistened in her eyes evaporated, strength from some deep well within her surging forth. "I didn't pursue you! I told you again and again there could be no future for us. You were the one who wouldn't take my words to heart. You're equally to blame for bringing us to this pass. Be man enough to shoulder some of the responsibility."

"I may have pursued you in the beginning, but once you made . . . your grand statement at the gala, making it perfectly clear you wanted nothing to do with me, I left you alone. But as always with you, you say one thing, but your actions say another. You, you, Eliot, came to my house in the middle of the night. And when I told you I would only make love to you if it was forever, you simply pulled me close, your touch a lie. Everything about you has been a lie!"

"That's him, officers!"

Nicholas's head snapped up, and he found two policemen coming forward, Barnard standing in the doorway behind them. When they started to reach out, Nicholas stepped back, his hands extended, holding them off. When he spoke, the dangerous edge of his anger had been contained. "No need, gentlemen." He pulled himself together. "I was just leaving."

He glanced one last time at Ellie, his mind flashing with a shudder of emotion, before he strode from the room, his boot heels ringing on the foyer tile, before he slammed out the door.

He walked mindlessly until hailing a hired hack on Sixth Avenue. He snapped directions, then vaulted into the tiny carriage and fell back against the seat. He ran his hand across his face, through his hair. The rattle and sway of the carriage ran up his body, jarring his mind. He pressed his forehead against the door, the wooden side biting into his skin.

When the carriage rolled to a stop, he didn't realize it had until the driver banged on the side with a stick. "I don't got all night, mister," the driver yelled down.

Nicholas stepped down, handed the man a coin, then went straight to his study. Nicholas wasn't a drinking man. But tonight, for reasons he didn't care to examine, he pulled the stopper from the crystal decanter, and determinedly set out to get drunk. He drank to ease his mind, to cease his thoughts. But as the minutes ticked by, the liquor didn't help. His mind still whirled, and his thoughts still raged.

"Excuse me, sir."

Nicholas turned toward the doorway. He wasn't drunk yet, or so he told himself as he poured another glass to the brim. "What is it, Albert?"

"There is a man here to see you, sir."

"Tell him I'm not in."

"Sorry, sir, but he says it's urgent. Says he needs to talk to you about someone called M. M. Jay."

Nicholas's fingers stilled around the crystal tumbler. After a moment he said, "Send him in."

Able Smythe entered the study, looking both pleased with himself and leery. "Mr. Drake. Sorry to bother you so late, but . . ."

"But what, Mr. Smythe?"

"But I was passing by and I saw your light."

"Passing by? Where do you live, Smythe? Next door to the Vanderbilts?"

Smythe had the good grace to blush. "I'm sorry. If you must know, I came up here solely because I . . . feel certain you know something about M. M. Jay." Suddenly he groaned in frustration. "I've been trying to learn about M. M. Jay for years."

Nicholas threw back a long swallow of amber liquid, before he grimaced. "Yes. And tell me, Smythe, what have you learned about the . . . infamous M. M. Jay?"

"Nothing actually. I'm no closer now than before to learning the man's identity. It's as if he doesn't exist."

Nicholas scoffed, then took another swallow of his drink. "Oh, M. M. Jay exists."

"I knew it!" Able came forward, his small eyes lighted with excitement. "I knew that you must know something. The way you looked at the paintings, the interest you have shown. Something told me you were intrigued for a reason."

"Intrigued, Smythe?" Harsh, biting laughter rang through the room. "Hell, I used to *love* M. M. Jay."

It took a moment for Able to assimilate the information, but when he did his eyes bulged and he grew flustered. "You . . . you . . . loved M. M. Jay?"

Nicholas laughed sardonically, relishing his unwelcomed guest's discomfort. "Yes, more's the pity." He eyed the man over his crystal glass, before finishing off the last of the bottle. "But it's not what you think." Nicholas looked around the room for more liquor, forgetting the other man.

"Then what is it?" Able blurted out.

Nicholas glanced back, his head spinning at the quick movement. "What is what?"

"You said," Able prompted, "that it's not what I think about M. M. Jay."

M. M. Jay. A liar, a betrayer. Anger sizzled down Nicholas's spine. "You haven't found your artist, Mr. Smythe, because you've been looking for the wrong person."

"Wrong person? Whatever do you mean?"

"I mean that you've been looking for a man."

"And . . . ?"

Nicholas found another crystal decanter, this time of port. He didn't bother with a new glass; he poured the rich, heavy wine into the one he already held. "M. M. Jay is a woman. A woman, Smythe." Nicholas grew very still and his voice lowered painfully. "A beautiful woman with white-blond hair and emerald green eyes."

Able gasped. "Eliot Sinclair! Now Eliot Monroe!"

Nicholas turned sharply to stare at him, the deep burgundy port sloshing over the side of the glass.

Able shrugged. "I'm a reporter. Years ago I heard rumors about you and Miss Sinclair. I tried to follow them up. But then when you left the country and she married someone else, I assumed I was wrong. I haven't thought about it since. Until now." Able whistled through his teeth. "Jesus! Charles Monroe's wife is M. M. Jay." He looked at Nicholas. "Do you still love her? Is that why you came back?"

Nicholas's countenance grew cold and dangerous. "You have worn out your welcome, Smythe."

"Yes, of course," he mumbled hurriedly. "I'm sorry to have bothered you."

Then he turned and fled, leaving Nicholas alone, his head throbbing, his heart a knot in his chest.

Good God, what had he done? he raged silently, before he threw his glass into the dormant fireplace, crystal shattering into a mosaic of jagged pieces, wine running like dark rivulets of blood in the gray ash.

Chapter 32

M. M. JAY REVEALED
by Able Smythe

For those of us who have searched the world wide to learn the identity of M. M. Jay, search no further. Our elusive artist has turned up—and turned out to be none other than Eliot Monroe, wife of prominent New Yorker, Charles Monroe, daughter-in-law of Rupert Monroe.

It was revealed to this reporter by a reliable source that the active society woman has been painting in secret for years. Is it possible that Rupert Monroe condones his daughter-in-law's clandestine activities? Has he seen the provocative work of his son's wife? . . .

"How could you?"

Miriam stood in the doorway of the dining room. Nicholas sat at the head of the table, his head throbbing. He told himself that he felt horrible because of all the liquor he had consumed the night before. And in part this was true. But he had just read the *Times* and didn't want to think about what he felt after reading Smythe's article. Guilt? Shame? He didn't think it was that simple. He felt a much deeper reproach, as if in revealing M. M. Jay's identity he had wounded Ellie in ways that he did not understand.

"How could I what, Miriam?" he asked impatiently.

She strode into the room, eyes intent, jaw set. "This," she hissed, thrusting a copy of the newspaper in his face. "How could you have done this?"

"I have my own, thank you."

"Oh, so you have a copy of your betrayal?"

"*My* betrayal!" he suddenly roared, pushing up from his seat, the heavy ball-and-claw chair falling back with a clatter.

"Yes, your betrayal!" she shouted back, unintimidated. "You're the only person who possibly could have, or should I say, *would* have revealed this information."

"You knew?"

"No, I learned like everyone else, this morning, in the paper. But it didn't take a genius to realize who the *reliable* source must have been. You. You did this!"

"You can't possibly know that it was me."

"Of course I can, because you're the only person hateful enough to want to hurt her."

The muscles in his jaw began to work. "I wasn't trying to hurt her, though what does it matter if I was?"

Miriam looked him in the eye. "I've regretted many times that we were related. But I have never felt it so intensely as I feel it now. You, Nicholas Drake, are reprehensible." She jerked her head away, gazing out through the windows. But then the angry lines of her face shifted and her shoulders rounded in defeat. "How could one family turn out so badly, produce so many cold, heartless people?" She glanced back at her brother, her eyes imploring him. "Why did she do it, Nicholas?"

Confusion marred his brow, and a strange heat rushed up his spine.

"Mother," she explained. "Why did Mother kill herself? You know the answer."

The room closed in around him. He looked at his sister.

"Why would I know?" he asked, his tone stiff and unyielding.

"Because I saw it in your eyes when we were young. I might only have been a child, but I knew you, I worshipped you . . . I loved you."

Love.

Had she? he wondered unexpectedly.

"Nicholas, please. I could always tell when something was wrong with you. Tell me what you knew. Tell me what you *know*."

Long moments ticked by on the mantel clock. "You're wrong," Nicholas lied. "I have no idea why Mother killed herself."

Ellie sat in her room, staring out through the sheer window draperies at the crowd in front of the granite-and-marble mansion she had put so much energy into creating. Reporters surrounded the house, men trampling evergreens and newly planted topiary at will. But she hardly noticed. She was numb.

Nicholas had told.

She knew she shouldn't be surprised; he hated her, and rightfully so. She had hurt him, terribly. And now he had his revenge. But by lashing out at her, so many others were hurt as well. For the first time she was forced to concede that he had been correct when he said she didn't really know him. How could she have been so wrong about the only man she had ever loved?

She had thought, foolishly, that she had suffered the extent of the consequences of having loved him. She had thought her life had been put back together. Her son had a name, and she had gained a bit of herself back by starting to paint again.

Yes, she was a fool, she thought, ignoring the summons of her husband. And she would never forgive herself if her folly ended up hurting her son.

"Ellie!" Charles demanded.

But Ellie didn't respond, simply stared out the window, looking at the faces of the curious, all vying for a glimpse of M. M. Jay. How strange, she mused through the fog in her mind. Me, a notorious woman.

"Talk to me," Charles raged.

When she realized he wasn't going to leave her alone, she dragged her gaze away from the masses in the yard below, and looked at her husband. "What would you like me to say, Charles?"

His face suffused with red. "Tell me this isn't true!"

She sighed, turning back to the window. "I can't do that. I can't lie to you."

"Why not?" he roared. "You've been lying to me for years. What is so different now?"

Actually, she had never said she didn't paint. But she had no desire to argue technicalities. By omission, she supposed, she had lied. Regardless, the truth was out, there was no turning back.

Unexpectedly, Charles dropped to his knees before her and took her hands. "Tell them it isn't true. We'll brazen it out. It will be your word against Able Smythe's." His eyes pleaded with her. "I love you, Ellie. I'll stand by you, if only you'll deny the article."

She reached out and touched his cheek. "Oh, Charles . . ."

"Ellie! Ellie!"

Jim burst into the room, panting as if he had run the whole way from Sixteenth Street.

"Jim?"

"It must have been the delivery boy!"

Charles stood and went to Jim. "What are you talking about?" he demanded.

"Paintings! From the basement! The delivery boy must have stolen them this morning."

"What are you talking about?" Charles repeated.

Ellie sat frozen.

"The delivery boy who brought Hannah the food from the market. She told him to put it in the kitchen like always.

And now Ellie's pretty paintings are gone. Barnard told me to come quick to warn you."

"Damn!" Charles cursed. "There are more paintings?" He turned on Jim. "Why didn't you watch him?"

Jim shrank away.

"Jim is not to blame, Charles. I am."

"God, what a mess!" her husband cried, holding his head in his hands. "I'll have to tell Father. He's going to be furious."

Ellie wanted to scream at her husband to make decisions on his own, quit running to papa. But what did it matter. It was much too late to change a full-grown man, she thought, settling back into that place where fog surrounded her mind.

For days Ellie rarely spoke, only held little Jonah tightly when he came to her, cooing in his ear. Indeed, what little chance there had been to deny the report was vanquished when the missing paintings turned up at the gallery.

At Charles's behest a doctor came and went, pronouncing her sane, or insane, she didn't know, didn't care. She couldn't think.

Nicholas had told.

The knowledge circled in her head, pushing at all else, leaving no room for anything but the image of Nicholas's face when he had confronted her. *Have I made you angry, M. M.? Or do you prefer Miss Jay?*

As the days passed, her father-in-law came and went, arguing with his son, shouting about reputations, the possibility of cancelled business contracts, respectability attained after long years of hard work jeopardized. Though it was hard for Ellie to care.

A week after the article appeared, the family solicitor was brought before her. The man tried to talk to her, explain things. But she couldn't make sense of his words. At length, he pushed up and slammed out the door, leaving a thick stack of papers behind.

The next morning, Ellie was packed. Charles didn't come

down to say good-bye. She knew he was too stunned and hurt for that. It was his father who was angry. It was his father who had insisted that Charles divorce her. Rupert Monroe was a man obsessed with his newfound status. And Ellie had tarnished their name.

Shame riddled her body. A divorced woman. More proof that she was her father's daughter. She was a fool to have let Barnard talk her into a showing. But she knew that wasn't true. She had wanted that showing, had wanted to paint again. But most shameful of all, she had wanted her work hanging for the world to see.

She took Jonah by the hand and hailed a hired hack. Only Jonah's nanny, Miss Hobart, stood on the doorstep to tearfully wave good-bye. Ellie and Jonah rode to the town house on Sixteenth Street, and, as if they had expected them, Hannah and Jim were waiting at the door.

"It was that father of Charles who sent you away, I'll bet," Hannah stated, pulling Jonah into her arms.

"With reason," Ellie said, eerily emotionless.

"Families are supposed to stick together."

"But families are not supposed to be deceived."

Hannah pursed her lips. "How can you defend them?"

"How can I not? They didn't do anything wrong. I did."

Barnard stood in the foyer, looking every one of his sixty-eight years.

"I'm sorry," he whispered.

"Don't be sorry, Barnard. It wasn't your fault."

"But I'm the one who started all this!"

"I'm a grown woman. I didn't have to say yes."

"But I started it by taking the paintings out in the first place without your permission."

"That's not what got me into trouble, and we both know it."

"Ellie," he moaned.

But Ellie wouldn't listen. She walked up the stairs to the fourth floor, to the room she had never entirely given up. Had she known that one day she would return? she wondered, as she sat down in a chair by the window. Perhaps it was inevitable. She had tempted the gods by having the child of one man, but marrying another. How could they have resisted the chance to balance the scales?

Days passed. A pallor fell over the occupants of Sixteenth Street. For three years Charles had supported Ellie, and in turn she had supported everyone else. Barnard knew that Charles had taken the money from the sale of her milliner's shop and had "invested" it, though not in Ellie's name. At the time when Barnard had questioned her, she had been too grateful to Charles to care.

Now, with money no longer coming in, Barnard realized that the household would have to adjust. In short order, Barnard went out and got a job delivering groceries. Jim began collecting and selling rags for pennies, Hannah took care of Jonah.

And Ellie cleaned.

She dusted and mopped and scrubbed. Nothing more. She never left the house, rarely spoke. Just cleaned. And when she finished, the house sparkling like a jewel, she simply started all over again. Dusting and mopping and scrubbing.

"Ellie," Barnard said one day. "You've got to pull yourself out of this." He shifted his weight uncomfortably. Ellie had always been the strong one, stalwart, holding on so the rest of them wouldn't be swept away. But now the tables had turned. Ellie had broken down, pretending that everything was fine, when in truth nothing was fine at all.

"Please, Ellie love," Barnard said, watching her go to work on the floor, "we've got to think of a way to make more money. Jim and I can't bring in enough to support us all."

"We'll be fine, Barnard," she said with a distant smile, before she reapplied her stiff bristle brush to the tiles that had come perfectly clean days before. "Yes, we'll be fine."

• • •

When it was discovered that Ellie had moved, reporters and onlookers switched their vigil from the mansion on Fifty-ninth Street to the town house on Sixteenth. A month after the article appeared, Miriam pushed through the mix of reporters and curious.

Surprise showed on Jim's face when he opened the door a crack and found Miriam. "Miz Welton? What're you doing here?" He opened the door and let her in, announcing excitedly, "Charlotte's mama is here."

"What do you want, Mrs. Welton?" Barnard demanded.

Miriam forced a smile. She had expected they would be less than friendly. She was Nicholas's sister after all, and beyond that, she conceded that she hadn't been particularly kind to them when Charlotte was alive. "I would like to speak to Ellie. Please."

"What could you possibly have to say to her?" Barnard asked belligerently.

Miriam had asked herself the very same question time and time again. She had been reading the papers. New York had turned the M. M. Jay matter into the scandal of the decade. Turf bosses and crime paled in comparison to a society woman painting scandalous artwork. And with every article that Miriam read, her heart ached a little more. That afternoon, without thinking about the right or wrong of it, she had made the decision to come. "I would like to help, Mr. Webb."

Barnard scoffed. "Ellie doesn't need any more help from the Drakes."

"Please, sir. Let me talk to Ellie."

"I told you no! Now leave!"

Just then Hannah stepped into the room. "Barnard, what's all the racket . . . ? Oh, Mrs. Welton."

"Hello, Mrs. Schurr," Miriam said politely.

"She says she's come to help," Barnard snapped sarcastically. "I told her to get out."

Miriam felt Hannah's considering gaze.

"Barnard, dear," Hannah said finally. "I'd like to have a

word with Mrs. Welton. Why don't you go upstairs and see to . . . *things* up there. Make sure my door is shut." She looked back at Miriam. "It's such a mess."

"What are you talking about, woman?" Barnard demanded.

But then Miriam saw some silent message pass between the two, after which he nodded his head, then hurried up the stairs. Miriam was given no opportunity to examine the strange interaction before Hannah said, "None of us have been able to help her, Mrs. Welton. You'll have to excuse Barnard. He's just being protective, doesn't want our Ellie hurt any more than she already has been."

"Yes, I'm sure. And truly I'm not here to hurt her."

"No, I don't suppose you are. And maybe you can help Ellie in a way the rest of us haven't been able to help her."

"Thank you," Miriam said. "I'll try."

Miriam climbed the stairs and knocked on what Hannah had said was Ellie's door. When she gained no response, she took a deep breath, then simply turned the knob and walked inside. Ellie stood by the window, staring out, a dust cloth forgotten in her hand. "Hello, Ellie."

Ellie didn't respond, simply gazed out the window.

Miriam sighed. "Surely you realize that you're letting him win."

She could see that Ellie tensed, but still she remained silent. "Ellie, you're allowing others to destroy your life."

"No," Ellie said suddenly into the quiet room. "*I* have destroyed my life."

"Your life is not destroyed! Not yet! Not if you don't allow it. You're not the only person in this world who's been touched by scandal."

Ellie turned slowly, and looked at Miriam for the first time.

"I know all about scandal and devastation," Miriam continued, "and I know the taste of bitter regret." She took a deep breath. "As you well know, I left my child alone with an uncle she hardly knew so I could selfishly sail off to

Europe and live the life without responsibility I thought I deserved." Her laughter was filled with self-loathing. "I returned to a dying child."

"Charlotte's illness wasn't your fault," Ellie said with a tired sigh.

"Wasn't it? If I had taken her to a doctor earlier would she still be alive? If I had even noticed that she was not well, what would be different today?"

"The doctors said there was no cure. Charlotte didn't have ordinary consumption. You know that, Miriam."

"Do you think that helps? My child is dead! She became extremely ill. And I wasn't there until the very end! And I was only there at all because I was dragged back by Nicholas, kicking and screaming, I might add. Even if there wasn't anything I could have done to save her, I should have been there. For that I blame myself, just as Nicholas blames me, just as William blames me."

"Charlotte loved you, and she certainly didn't blame you."

Lines of heartache ravaged Miriam's face, and tears suddenly glistened in her eyes. "I know she loved me. The memory of that sweet little face looking up at me with unconditional love rips my heart apart every day." She pulled her shoulders back. "Did you know that William divorced me?"

"Yes, and I'm sorry. It was terribly unfair of him. *He* wasn't there for Charlotte."

"But he's a man! The rules are different for men. I would think you'd have realized that by now. There were those who celebrated you as a male artist, but even they scorn you now that they know you're a woman—for the very same paintings!" She shook her head. "But I can't turn back the clock . . ."

Ellie glanced away.

"And neither can you, Ellie. It doesn't do anyone any good for you to hide in this house."

"What do you expect me to do? Invite the reporters in? Charge admittance to the curious?"

"Just get out of the house. Resume your life. Hold your head high. Where is that brave woman who walked into Nicholas's grand gala on the arm of another man?"

Ellie closed her eyes briefly. "She's gone."

"No, she's not! She's here, alive, and it's time she got back to doing what she does best! Painting!"

"Painting?" Ellie cried. "Good God, that's what got me into this mess."

"And it's what will get you out of it." Miriam's eyes blazed with purpose. "Ellie, you're good. Everybody is talking about your showing."

"They're talking about how scandalous it is, not how good I am."

"You're wrong. Regardless of what they think of you as a person, as an artist. They say you're good, with all the potential in the world. It's time you stopped hiding. Show them your strength. It's time you got back to painting . . . and it's time you started selling your work."

Ellie whirled back to her. "Good Lord, Miriam. Who would buy a painting of mine?"

Miriam smiled then. "Who wouldn't. Who wouldn't want a painting by the scandalous M. M. Jay? They may look down their wealthy noses at you now, but once you get back out there and let them know you haven't been defeated, they will come around. And then they will hang your work in their galleries."

"I refuse to profit from my notoriety."

"You will profit from your talent. You will paint. For money. People's portraits, commissioned works. Society has money to spare, as well you know."

Silence filled the room as Ellie studied Miriam. "Why are you doing this?" Ellie finally asked.

This time it was Miriam who looked away. "Perhaps because I don't know how to fight for myself. And if you fight—no, *when* you fight, and *when* you win—you win for all of us who have been less than perfect in society's eyes." She looked back. "But also, I know how I felt when Charlotte died and William divorced me. I know how much I wished there was someone who understood, not someone who could only offer empty condolences. I wanted to know that someone else out there had made a mistake, that I wasn't the only one." She hesitated. "And I wanted to know that someone else had survived."

Silent moments ticked by. "Have you survived, Miriam?"

She shrugged her shoulders. "I'm trying," she whispered. "I take it one day at a time."

Ellie reached out and took Miriam's hand. How strange, Ellie thought, to find strength from such an unexpected source. "Thank you."

"No, thank *you*. It helps a little to think that maybe I can make a difference at something."

"You have. And I truly will think about your suggestion."

"Only think about it?"

"For now, it's the best I can do."

"Good enough." Miriam turned to go, then stopped. "If it's any consolation, as far as I'm concerned, what my brother did was unforgivable."

For a moment Ellie didn't respond. "He was hurt and he lashed out at the person who had caused his pain. He's been hurt badly in his life."

"You're too kind, Ellie," Miriam replied, suddenly bitter. "We've all been hurt in life. Nicholas is no different from the rest of us. He just has greater power to wound."

Chapter 33

Nicholas wanted to see her.

After everything that had come to pass—all the lies, all the deceit—he still wanted to see her. Needed to see her.

He closed his eyes against the weakness.

As the days had passed, again and again he thought he saw her. Suddenly, unexpectedly. Gazing in a shop window. Laughing with a flower vendor. But again and again he was proven wrong. The flash of emerald green eyes, or glimmer of white-blond hair was nothing more than a figment of his imagination. He saw her in the street like a mirage in the desert.

Despite everything.

He wasn't even clear as to why he wanted to see her. Was it possible that after all these years he still sought answers? Was it possible finally to come to understand what about her drew him to her like a moth is drawn to a flame? Could he learn why he couldn't forget her? Could learning the answers finally cleanse her from his mind?

Too many questions and so few answers. And beyond that, there was a part of him, he knew, that said he wanted to punish her—to punish her for betraying him, for lying.

Seeing her to punish her? The fact that this made little or

no sense didn't change the simple fact that he wanted to see her. And he would. He would see her. Make her see him—face him, look into his eyes. Not on a street corner. Not in her front parlor with Barnard calling for the authorities. He wanted to see her someplace where she couldn't escape his gaze, where she couldn't turn her head away.

Yes, he would see her. Though he had no idea how to go about it. He knew he could simply go to the town house, but undoubtedly Barnard would be there like a warrior guarding a citadel.

Nicholas refused to think about what he had been reading in the papers. The scandal. The divorce. Instead, he took a deep, calming breath and left for his office.

The days were growing warmer as spring turned into summer. Nicholas knew Henry didn't expect him at the office today. Nicholas was supposed to be traveling to New Jersey to see a prospective buyer who wanted to distribute olive oil throughout Canada. But Nicholas wanted to take a file on another prospective buyer with him to read during the ride back that evening. So he stopped at the office on his way out of the city.

At the sound of a woman's voice, Nicholas halted outside his assistant's office.

"Just a select list, Henry."

Miriam's voice. What did she want now? he wondered, as he started forward, only to stop again at her words.

"Just a few names of people in the city who might be interested in commissioning artwork."

"Why do you need me to make up a list?" Henry asked.

"Because you know everything about everybody in town. I don't. I don't know who likes what, much less who collects art. And you have to promise me you won't tell my brother."

"You're trying to help Mrs. Monroe, aren't you?"

"What if I am?"

There was a silent pause, and Nicholas knew his assistant

was trying to determine if he should put the list together or not.

"Henry," he called, stepping into the room.

Miriam whirled around.

"Miriam," he said simply. "I trust you are well."

"How long have you been standing there?"

"Standing there?" Nicholas asked innocently. "What are you talking about? I just got here."

He saw his sister's relief, and he nearly smiled. A strange elation filled him. "Henry, I need the file on Vanderweer. I want to take it with me."

Henry pushed up from his desk and retrieved the file. "Anything else, sir?"

"No, I'll be on my way," he said in surprisingly good humor.

And suddenly he was in good spirits. For his sister, unknowingly, had provided him with the means to see Ellie.

"I said no, Barnard!"

"Now, Ellie—"

"No! I said no, and I mean it. I will not accept commissioned work."

It was a week later and Ellie and Barnard stood in the front parlor, as angry at each other as ever before.

"Ellie, this doesn't make any sense. You love to paint."

Ellie spun around to face him, her eyes wild. "Painting has ruined my life. Don't you understand that? I am going to work—at something respectable. I will forge an acceptable path. My son deserves that!"

Barnard scoffed. "And what, pray tell, are you going to do? Clean people's houses? Take in laundry? What, Ellie? What can you do to make enough money to support your son?"

"I'll make hats again. My hats were in demand. I'll start here, working upstairs. And as soon as things start going, I'll rent space."

"Who's going to buy a hat from you?"

"Women loved my hats!"

"*Society* women loved your hats! Society women with money loved to buy your hats!"

"And they'll buy them again!"

Barnard squeezed the bridge of his nose with his fingers as if searching for patience. "How can you possibly think that the very women who spurn you now are going to come to your house or even your shop to buy your hats?"

"You said they'd buy my artwork," she reasoned. "Why not my hats?"

"Because M. M. Jay doesn't make hats! M. M. Jay paints, has been written up in the *Times*, has nearly everyone in town—perhaps everyone in the art world—wondering and talking. They are intrigued by the painter, not the milliner."

Ellie jerked away, biting her knuckle to keep from crying out. He was right, she knew he was. The reporters and onlookers didn't shout out, "Let us see some more of your hats." They wanted to see her paintings.

She closed her eyes. People commissioning her to paint for them. How could she do it? How could she paint a commissioned landscape to match some society matron's decor? How could she paint portraits of the very people who had so easily stricken her from their lives? But if she was truthful with herself, she knew she was afraid.

People were intrigued with her now because she was a notorious woman. Even those who had been intrigued with her before they had learned who she was no doubt had been intrigued in part because of how the paintings had arrived, intrigued by her anonymity. Her work had never been shown truthfully, without any other consideration besides the work itself. Even Able Smythe, at the height of his support, had said her work was restrained.

And now everyone knew that she was the artist. They were aware of her work. She could no longer hide behind a name that had circled through her head since she was a child like a nursery rhyme. If she painted again, expectations high, how could she possibly live up to their expectations—or perhaps her own? And what would that do to her if she fell short?

"What am I going to do?" she whispered.

"You are going to do what you do best. You are going to paint."

"I can't," she pleaded.

"You can! And you will. Just once. This one commission."

"I told you to tell the agent no."

"I did, but he came back and said his client would pay five thousand dollars. Five thousand dollars, Ellie! More than enough to allow you some choices. Do the commission. Then decide about the rest of your life later."

"Dear Lord, who in their right mind would pay five thousand dollars to have me paint their portrait?"

Barnard shrugged. "I don't know. The agent handling the transaction wouldn't say. But I'd guess it's some society woman who wants to have the notorious M. M. Jay paint her portrait. She'll be the envy of every woman in town."

"You sound like Miriam."

"Miriam knows her own kind of people. She knows that they wouldn't give you the time of day, but to have your work in their homes would be a coup."

Ellie groaned and stared out the window as if searching for some sign as to how she should answer. But truly, what were her choices? "All right," she said, biting her full lower lip. "Just this once."

"Good girl. The agent is bringing his client by in an hour."

"Barnard!"

"What?" he asked, pretending innocence.

"You were obviously quite sure of yourself."

"No, Ellie dear. I simply knew that if nothing else, you would listen to reason."

Indeed, exactly one hour later, the doorbell sounded. Ellie took a deep breath. She sat in Hannah's favorite chair, wondering who it would be. One of the women she had worked alongside for nearly two years at charity events? Would the woman treat her like a servant? What would she say?

"I'll get it," Barnard called.

It was all Ellie could do not to leap up, grab Barnard's arm, and tell him she had changed her mind. She would find another means to make money. They could survive. Surely.

But she knew this wasn't true. Charles still hadn't given her a cent, wouldn't even talk to her about the money from the sale of her milliner's shop, not to mention the sale of the building in which the shop had been housed. And the law was against her.

She pulled back her shoulders, smoothing her shirt, determined to brazen this through no matter how awful it turned out to be. But awful didn't come close to what she felt when it wasn't a woman she had worked next to at a charity ball who walked through the door, or a woman at all.

"Nicholas," she breathed.

"Mrs. Monroe," he replied with a crisp nod of his head, his slice of lips that might have been called a smile sadly lacking in humor.

"Lord have mercy on my soul," Barnard muttered, his hand still on the brass knob, clearly uncertain if he should slam the door or invite the man in.

Nicholas made the decision for him by stepping into the foyer. "I take it you remember me, Mr. Webb," he stated, his gaze fixed on Ellie.

"You know damn well I remember you. The only question is why are you here?"

Nicholas looked at Barnard for the first time, amusement flickering across his face. "I think we both know the answer to that."

"You conniving bastard."

"If using an agent to commission a work is considered conniving, then conniving I am. But if my mother were alive I'm certain she would take issue with you calling me a bastard." His eyes grew dark and dangerous. "Alas, I am irrefutably my father's son."

Ellie watched, mesmerized, as Nicholas turned back to her, his arctic eyes washed clean of emotion. If possible he was taller than she remembered. He stood before her, collected, elegant, his black hair longer than was fashionable, but silky. His blue eyes were pale in contrast, startling, as always looking at her, as if he could see into her soul.

She might have fainted had she been the fainting type. And just then she wished she were. Anything to take her away from the nightmare that was unfolding in her parlor.

"Get out!"

One slash of black brow rose in response. "Now, Mrs. Monroe," he said, his tone metallic, "is that any way to treat a paying client?"

"I mean it, Nicholas. Get out of my house." The words were spoken low, but clear.

He merely handed his hat over to Barnard. "You were never very good with welcomes. But I'll forgive you."

Forgive you.

His eyes widened unexpectedly, as if he was surprised by what he had said. She saw it, felt it. She saw as well when his eyes narrowed. No, he would never forgive her. Not for her lack of welcome or anything else he felt she had done to him.

She realized then that he was there in some perverse way to punish her. He didn't care one whit for art, for his portrait. It was nothing more than an excuse. To punish her. She knew him so well. Hadn't revealing her identity to the world been punishment enough? she wanted to demand. But then she remembered his obsessive pursuit of her father, and she knew the answer. His obsession now seemed to have been redirected towards her.

When Nicholas regained his composure, his eyes once again pools of calm blue sea, he managed a smile as if excavated from within at considerable cost. Then he shrugged. "Where will we work?"

"*We* won't be working anywhere. I am not going to paint your portrait!"

"Temper, temper. I realize that temper is said to be a most common trait among artists, but can you really afford one?"

"What I can or cannot afford is none of your business."

"Be that as it may, I'm here, I've paid—an outrageous sum I might add—and I expect to get my money's worth."

"You don't have enough money in the world to buy me, Drake."

"Ah, so it's back to Drake. So be it. Drake, Mr. Drake, Nicholas, Ni . . ."

They both knew he almost said Nicky.

". . . whatever," he continued, unable to hide his momentary loss of balance, "it doesn't matter. You're an artist. You paint. Now I'm paying you to paint me." His cold gaze met hers. "You weren't paid for the work before."

She met his gaze with blazing animosity. "I have never met anyone as ill-mannered and rude in my entire life."

He laughed out loud. "You certainly aren't an arbiter of propriety I would think."

His words stung more than they should have. She knew he hated her, knew he thought she was the lowest of women. But his words hurt nonetheless. "Why are you doing this?" she asked, trying to keep the quiver of emotion from her voice. "Why can't you just leave me alone?"

He looked at her then, truly looked at her. She saw his pain, just a flicker before it was gone, but enough. He was hurting, and he wanted her to hurt, too. She nearly laughed out loud, bitterly, at the irony of this deplorable situation. She hurt, oh yes, she hurt. But she'd be damned if she gave him the satisfaction of knowing it.

"A deal is a deal, Mrs. Monroe. I have commissioned a work, a portrait. You have accepted. Now I expect you to fulfill your side of the agreement."

"I can't," she said, her voice tight.

"Of course you can, Ellie. And you will." He glanced at

his pocket watch, then looked back. "Perhaps not today. But you'll change your mind," he said. "You have no choice."

The following day, Ellie was startled when the doorbell rang. What if it was Nicholas? She had hoped he would stay away, prayed that he would. And perhaps he was doing just that, she thought with equal measures of relief and disappointment, when Miriam, not Nicholas, blew into the house, her eyes burning with purpose.

"Ellie!"

Ellie looked across the room at the other woman, unsure what to think. Had it all been planned, Nicholas and Miriam sitting up at night finding yet another way to hurt her?

"I know what you're thinking, Ellie, and who could blame you? But you have to believe me, I had nothing to do with my brother's appearance here yesterday. I only found out about it an hour ago."

The late morning sun poured through the window like a spill of gold, and Ellie could see the genuine anguish on Miriam's face. "I believe you." And she did.

Miriam breathed a deep sigh of relief. "He's a monster," she said, when she had regained her composure.

"Whether he is or isn't hardly matters. I'm not going to accept his commission."

"But you already have!"

"I'll return the money, it's as simple as that."

"My brother never makes anything simple, Ellie, as well you know. Besides, you should do the work. Let him pay you that outrageous sum."

"I don't want his money."

"But you need the money!" Miriam hesitated, seeming to consider. "I know Charles has washed his hands of you, and won't give you a cent."

Mortification stung Ellie's cheeks. "How did you know?"

"Word travels fast."

Ellie felt that at any moment she might simply wither away. But she couldn't afford such a luxury. She had Jonah to think of and Barnard and Hannah and Jim. "Regardless, Miriam, nothing changes. I won't paint Nicholas."

"He owes you, Ellie. Let him pay."

It was then that fortune dealt Ellie another blow.

"Mama, Mama!"

Ellie lunged for the door, intent on slamming it shut. But her effort was for naught when Jonah toddled in, his balance precarious, his smile rapturous at the sight of his mother. Before Ellie could utter a word, Hannah rushed in behind him, swooping him up with an energy that belied her years.

"I'm sorry," Hannah mumbled. "What with all his walking these days, he's everywhere, harder and harder to keep my eye on."

Hannah whisked Jonah off as quickly as possible. Ellie turned back, but knew that it was too late.

"Dear God in heaven," Miriam breathed. She stood, stunned, staring at the empty doorway through which Hannah had carried Jonah away. Tears pooled in Miriam's eyes. "I didn't know."

"Very few people do. Charles was such a protective father," she lied.

Miriam glanced as if Ellie had said nothing. "He looks just like Charlotte."

Ellie couldn't respond, couldn't speak.

"Ellie . . ." But at the look in Ellie's eyes, Miriam's words trailed off.

"You said you wanted to be my friend, Miriam."

"Yes. I do."

"Then prove it to me, to my son, by swearing that you'll never tell Nicholas."

"But Ellie—"

"No, Miriam! No buts. Nicholas can never know."

"Why? Why can't you tell the child's father?"

"*Not* his father! Do you understand? Jonah is mine. Mine!" Ellie turned away, not wanting Miriam to see how scared she was.

"Tell him Ellie. Tell Nicholas of his . . . Tell Nicholas. He'll help you."

"He will not help me! And I will not hand him the means to once and for all destroy me completely."

"He would never do that to you."

"Of course he would, Miriam. You said yourself he is a monster. He wants to ruin me, just as he ruined my—" Ellie staggered. Her world was collapsing, her mind out of control, her mouth spewing out secrets. "You can't tell, Miriam," she finally managed. "Please. I can stand Nicholas's disdain, and the Monroe's disdain, even society's disdain. But I couldn't bear to lose my son."

Miriam seemed to search her soul, seemed to ask and answer questions to which only she was privy. But in the end she nodded. "All right, Ellie. I won't tell Nicholas about Jonah. But only if you paint Nicholas's portrait."

Disbelief flashed through Ellie's eyes.

"Face it, Ellie. You need the money. If not for yourself, then for your son. Don't punish Jonah because you are angry at Nicholas. Take the money, then leave New York. Start a new life somewhere else. Give Jonah a chance."

"What are you talking about? How can I leave here?"

"How can you not? You've obviously been hiding Jonah since his birth. I understand why. There are enough people in town who would take one look at the boy and know Nicholas is the father."

Ellie's stomach knotted. She knew it was true, but to hear her suspicions confirmed made her sick at heart. But how could she leave? Where would she go? And yet she realized now that Miriam was correct. How could she stay?

"Paint Nicholas, Ellie. There is time enough for decisions and plans after that."

The doorbell rang again that afternoon. Ellie had spent hours pacing her room, trying to make sense of her thoughts. She had told Barnard she wouldn't see anyone. She needed time to think.

But her wish was not to be granted when her door opened without so much as a knock, and not Barnard but Nicholas stood in the doorway. For a moment she was speechless. But only for a moment.

"Get out!"

"I would expect something a little more original from you, Eliot."

Barnard came up behind Nicholas as if he had been forced to run up three flights of stairs. "I told him . . . he couldn't . . . come up here . . . I did . . . but he wouldn't listen."

"He did," Nicholas agreed with an infuriating grin. "And no I didn't—listen, that is."

"Get out!" she repeated through clenched teeth.

Nicholas hung his head. "Really, Ellie, we've been over this already. I'm here to have my portrait painted."

There were sounds in the distance, downstairs, and Ellie's eyes suddenly widened. "Barnard, go help Hannah. In fact, why don't you all go out for a while."

Barnard hesitated, but then suddenly, as if remembering something, hurried back down the stairs.

"So," Nicholas said, "you want to be alone with me."

"In your dreams, Drake."

"Perhaps, but in reality as well."

"I want you out of my house."

Nicholas considered her. "Are you afraid to paint me, Ellie? Is that it?"

She opened her mouth to speak, but what could she say? Anger boiled inside her. She wasn't afraid, she told herself, but that wasn't true. She *was* afraid. Afraid of what she might do if she had to spend time with him—reach out and touch him. Kiss him.

Love him once again.

Her jaw cemented with a strangled cry. "You obviously take great pleasure in hurting me."

She saw the change in him, the shift in his eyes as all smiles and humor fled.

He shrugged. "Neither pleasure nor anything else. What you feel or don't feel doesn't touch me."

It was a lie, and Nicholas knew it. And that was part of the problem. He *was* affected. He found it hard to believe that this was the same woman he had known before. She looked the same in all the superficial ways. Her hair, her body, her clothes. It was her eyes that had changed. The difference hadn't been there when he had seen her before— before he had revealed M. M. Jay's identity. Her eyes no longer shone with innocence, or infinite depths of giving. No fire or outrageousness. And he hated that it bothered him.

"You can't afford to turn me away, Ellie. You need the money."

"Why does everyone keep telling me what I do and don't need?!"

Why indeed? Nicholas wondered. But just then answers didn't matter. He wanted to be there. He wanted to sit with her. To punish her, he reiterated irrationally in his head. Nothing more. "Perhaps everyone keeps telling you because you seem to be the only person who doesn't recognize easy money when you see it."

"Easy?" she asked wryly, a flash of her former irreverent self. "I think not."

Nicholas gave a burst of surprised laughter. But then he contained himself. "Easy or not, can you stand there and tell me, or even tell yourself, that you don't need the money?"

Her eyes narrowed to slits of jade. "You know I can't."

He merely gave an arrogant quirk of brow as if to say, *See, I told you.* And of course she didn't need telling. She did need the money, as everyone kept reminding her. Damn him for being correct. But what were her alternatives? "All right," she stated coldly, her fists clenched. "I'll do it. In the afternoons. Only afternoons."

Nicholas stared at her for a long while, and she wasn't certain if he was gloating or relieved.

"Good," he said simply, then started forward.

"We'll start tomorrow. I'm not ready today."

He hesitated, starting to argue. Then he shrugged. "Fine. Tomorrow it is."

He left the room without another word or even a look back over his shoulder. Thankfully. For if he had, no doubt he would have seen her fear, and used it against her.

Nicholas arrived promptly at three the following afternoon. For the time it would take to paint the portrait, Hannah and Barnard had agreed to keep Jonah out of the house. Ellie should have felt safe. But didn't. Not with Nicholas standing there, his face an unreadable mask.

"How do you expect me to work with you staring at me like that?" she snapped, hating the situation, hating that she didn't know how to handle it.

"What do you want me to do?" he asked with an infuriatingly tilted slash of dark brow.

"Read a book, look out the window. Just do something besides stare at me. I have to think. I have to study you, take in your features if I'm going to paint your portrait." Though she knew that as long as she lived she wouldn't be able to forget the exact curve of his cheekbone, or angle of his jaw—or the sweet feel of his skin beneath her fingers. Her heart ached. "Just sit!" she demanded, when he still stood staring. "Over there where the lighting is best."

After a curious glance he strode to the window, lowered himself into the chair, and looked out onto the street below. As soon as he did, she realized it was a mistake to have him sit in the light that illuminated him. Her breath caught painfully. He was so beautiful, staring out at the world beyond. What was he thinking? she wondered helplessly, wanting to know.

He opened a window without asking, letting the warm summer breeze in to wrap around them. At any second, Ellie felt as if she would suffocate. The heat, his presence. But then he surprised her by pulling out a cheroot from his pocket. Mesmerized, she watched as he made little ceremony of clipping the end, lighting a match, and inhaling deeply. His long, strong fingers held the small cigar with a masculine grace. He sat there, a man at ease, relaxed. But she knew that beneath his calm exterior was a power and forcefulness that lay deceptively contained. "I didn't realize you smoked."

Exhaling, he studied the cigar, then said, "I rarely do. Does it bother you?"

"No," she said, turning away abruptly.

Since Ellie no longer had to hide her work, she kept all her supplies in her room now. No more running to the basement for turpentine or linseed oil that might give her away. And canvases. Of all sizes. Not just the ones that could fit behind the folding screen.

She busied herself with supplies, choosing colors, pulling out a canvas, wiping down brushes. All tasks that didn't need to be done, not yet. She still needed to take him in, to sketch, to pull her thoughts together. But her thoughts were in disarray. She could hardly breathe, much less put a coherent thought down on canvas or paper. How did she possibly think she could do this?

He didn't seem to be having any of the problems she was having. He sat there, his thoughts elsewhere, certainly not on her, she thought. No, not on her. She took a deep breath and forced herself to concentrate.

How would she paint him?

She had lain awake for hours thinking about it, knowing it had to be perfect, knowing it had to take the breath away. Nothing less would be good enough. She hadn't drifted off until nearly morning, only to wake paralyzed with the impossibility of her task.

To be with Nicholas, and to paint him. Beautifully. As his perfect body deserved to be painted. It was hard enough when she thought about nameless faces being aware of her as the artist. But it was no longer a nameless face. It was Nicholas. And foolishly, she didn't want to disappoint him.

An hour passed, though she didn't know how. When she

looked down she had a multitude of sketches before her. Different angles. Different shading. None good enough. None that captured the essence of the man. But it was a beginning.

"There," she stated into the quiet. "Enough for today."

He glanced up, startled from his reverie, glancing at the clock that stood on the fireplace mantel. "We've hardly begun."

"But we have. That's all that matters."

For a second she thought he would argue. After a moment, however, he merely pushed up from the chair, his cheroot long spent, and walked toward her. "Let me see."

"Absolutely not."

"Why not?"

"You can't see anything until it's done. Now good-bye."

She walked to the door and opened it, holding it wide as he stood there, staring at her from the middle of the room, no longer at the window, not yet at the easel.

At length he walked to the door. As he came nearer she could feel the heat of him emanating, burning. And just when she thought that he would simply pass by and she could breathe a sigh of relief he paused. He turned to her, so close that if she shifted her weight she would touch him.

Her breath caught when his fingers brushed against her jaw, barely, gently, then down her throat to her collarbone just beneath her gown. With one touch her body came to life as it hadn't since she had known him years before. Their breaths grew hard, together, each lost. He was going to kiss her, she realized when she felt his breath against her cheek, and she wanted nothing else.

"Are you happy that I can't forget you?" he whispered harshly, his eyes for the moment lighted by naked yearning.

It seemed like forever before her mind comprehended the change—forever before she completely realized his meaning. He blamed her for yet another real or imagined sin. One more transgression for which she could never atone.

She drew a deep breath and tensed, the liquid heat of her

body solidifying into stone. "Happy? No," she whispered, swallowing painfully over the aching lump in her throat. "I'm not certain I even know what happy is anymore."

His jaw tightened, and his eyes burned with angry desire. She thought for a moment that he might still pull her close. Instead, after a timeless space of silence, he stepped back, turned on his heel, and departed, leaving her in the doorway, thinking not about his words, but about the feel of his fingers drifting across her skin.

Chapter 34

Nicholas returned the next day.

Ellie had prayed all night that he would cease this folly. To no avail. He strode into her apartment at the top of the house as if he had come for tea. Calm, self-possessed, while she stood near the window, her hands trembling, her heart pounding so hard she was certain he must hear. And if she thought she could convince him to leave her alone, she was mistaken.

He returned the next day, and the day after that. No reprieve. Every time he left she was more shaken. He had touched her arm, held a tendril of her hair that had escaped from her chignon, had even brushed one finger across her lower lip.

He wanted her. She could see it in his eyes. Disturbing. Primitive. She could feel the heat. His desire frightened her because it matched her own. An intense fire. Dangerous if allowed to burn.

"You're late," she snapped on the fifth day, angered by the heat that welled up inside her at the sight of him.

Ellie saw Nicholas glance at the clock, and she knew that the traitorous timepiece on the mantel was just then tolling the hour—the hour in which he was supposed to arrive.

"Hmmm," was his only response as he glanced back at her.

His presence filled the room, flooding its white walls, pooling at her feet, very nearly overwhelming her. She wanted to race out the door and never look back. But as he looked at her now, she was certain he knew exactly what she was thinking. A small smile pulled at his lips as if he were pleased. She raised her chin and pulled back her shoulders. He would not get the better of her.

"Are you just going to stand there," she demanded, "or are you going to take a seat?"

"For you Mrs. Monroe," he offered with a galiant, mocking bow, "anything."

His tone was sarcastic. Her cheeks flared red with anger. "If you're willing to do *anything* for me, Mr. Drake, then why don't you leave."

His smile faltered, though his eyes glittered with what she would have sworn was appreciation. "Not *anything*. I lied."

"Why am I not surprised?"

Their eyes locked. "I was unaware that you were in a position to cast stones . . . M. M. Jay." Whatever lightness of soul he had brought in with him dissipated into the sunny whiteness of the room. The lines of his face grew hard, harsh, and she hated that she regretted her words.

She broke their gaze and took a deep breath, trying to step away, to steel herself against his presence, and was all too aware when he finally took his place by the window.

Forcing herself to the task at hand, she picked up a piece of slender charcoal, and tried to concentrate. She had been unable to put on paper the image she sought. This day, however, slowly, painfully, the image began to emerge. Faint, distant. Nearly unrecognizable. But a glimmer of truth, bringing a hint of relief. She hadn't forgotten how to work. Not entirely.

Her mind relaxed, eased, if only just a bit. For a moment she managed to lose herself to the art. She had missed her work, and a bud of excitement crept up inside her as her hand began to move effortlessly across the pad of paper. A thrill of blood surged through her veins, a sweetness filled her mind, and somehow she forgot—somehow she immersed herself in the world of line and proportion, moved beyond reality.

With eyes focused and mind soaring, Ellie sketched until she realized the lighting wasn't quite right. She walked across the room to stand before Nicholas. As he stared out at the world, she studied his profile, forgetting it was him. Determined to get better shading from his sharp features, she very carefully reached out, touching his cheek. He flinched as if struck, his harsh gaze meeting hers, shattering what little distance she had managed to find. Her mind came crashing down, the excitement crushed like a flower into a gravel path beneath a thoughtless boot heel.

"I'm sorry," she murmured automatically, stepping away.

But his hand came up and took hers, staying her.

His touch was like fire and her hand began to tremble. He exhaled sharply, pressing her fingers against his cheek. "Why," he breathed harshly. "Why can't I forget you?"

"Please," she whispered, choked. Though even she wasn't certain what she wanted him to do.

"Do you ever think about my touch?" he asked, his voice desolate. "Do you ever think about what we once shared?"

Of course she did. Every day of her life. "No," she answered simply, unable to say anything else.

She tried to jerk free but he held her captive. "Liar," he hissed against her skin, kissing her wrist as he pulled her closer still. "I can tell from the trembling of your hand that you do. Often. Just as I think of you." He kissed her palm. "Often."

"No, Nicky," she said, not thinking.

Her mind told her to flee. But some emotion, stronger than intellect, kept her there. She watched, helplessly, as he reached up and touched her jaw. The feel of his hand flooded her mind.

"Nicky," he chuckled, the sound haunted. "I dream of that, you calling out to me."

"No," she murmured.

He only pushed up from his seat to stand before her, and looked deep into her eyes. What did he see? she wondered. But her thoughts stilled when he leaned down and pressed his lips against her hair. His fingers trailed back to her ear, sweeping a long tendril of white-blond hair back, before he traced a path along the line of her jaw. Her breath came to her in a rasping shudder.

"No," she breathed again, pushing at his chest.

"Why," he demanded. "God, why not?"

He felt as much as saw her intake of breath. He noticed as well the wild flutter of her pulse in her neck that betrayed her. She was here now, with him, not lost somewhere in the recesses of her mind while she worked. She was aware of him, him, as a man, not an object to be painted. He could see it. And childishly he was pleased that he could pull her back from that distant place that he envied.

She reached out and touched him, though only to brace herself, he knew. The simple touch was like wind to a raging fire. But still he knew he should leave her alone. He should slam out of the door and never come back, for he played at a game that wasn't a game. No winner possible.

Frustration assailed him, his hand clenching by her jaw. But he failed to take his hand away—he simply continued his perilous course, until his fingers reached her chin. He forced her to turn her head, to look at him. Tears shimmered in the green depths. And then he was lost, the fire consuming him.

He pulled her close, crushing her to him. "Stop," he demanded, kissing her forehead. "Stop pushing me away."

"I can't."

"You can't, Ellie?" His strong hands seared a path up her arms, over her shoulders, to the delicate curve of her neck. With his thumb he tilted her chin to look into her eyes. "Or you won't?" He didn't wait for an answer. He lowered his head to hers, capturing her lips in a kiss. One strong hand traced a path down her back, pressing them close as the kiss became a demand—long and slow, deep, unyielding.

With a defeated moan, she encircled his shoulders, clinging to him with a fierceness that startled him, left him breathless. He kissed her temple and felt her tears, before his mouth slanted over hers hungrily. She opened to him, then nipped at his full lower lip, clearly not caring that she was being bold. He groaned into her mouth, his tongue tangling with hers.

His lips trailed down her neck until he kissed the ripe swell of her breast beneath the fabric of her dress. "So beautiful," he murmured, pushing the fullness up against his palm.

But then his fingers began to work the fastenings of her bodice, and she felt a caress of summer air against her skin. "No!" She wrenched herself free. "No," she repeated, this time a whisper. "I can't. I can't do this! I'll give you your money back, whatever, just leave me alone!"

She whirled away, but he reached out and grabbed her arm. "No. I won't leave you alone." He pulled her back to him. "I can't," he said, his touch sending her thoughts into wild confusion.

She had dreamed of him holding her again, dreamed that she would feel his lips against her own. And now that her dreams were coming true she had little will to hold out against him.

"You plague me at every turn, Eliot. I've resisted. But I can't any longer. I want you," he murmured ominously, "just as you want me."

"No."

But when he ran his tongue along the pulse in her neck, her head fell back.

"Yes, Ellie. You want me. Accept that."

"No," she cried brokenly, her eyes closed against any sight of his desire.

"You want me," he repeated. Very slowly he kissed her, a

sensual dance of lips and tongue tangling with hers, tantalizing, tempting, coaxing her to surrender. He felt her inner battle, until finally he felt her resistance melt away. He gathered the hem of her skirts, bringing his hand between her thighs. "Yes," he said softly, "you want me."

His intimate touch surprised her, and her eyes flashed open. He only kissed them closed, his hand moving magically between her legs. "I can feel your desire," he murmured, then pulled her underclothes free.

"We can't."

"Of course we can," he said, as he slipped his fingers deep between the nether lips that cleaved her body, capturing her gasp of pleasure in his mouth.

She stiffened then melted in turn, her delicate hands clutching the white lawn of his shirtsleeves.

"Yes, Ellie." He nudged her knees apart with his own, one hand stroking, one hand pressed to her back, holding her close. He felt her body begin to move, knew that she was yearning. Then he stopped.

"Nicholas?"

Her tone was questioning, though what she questioned he didn't know. "Shhh," he murmured, kissing her reassuringly, as he gathered her in his arms and crossed the floor with determined strides to the far end of the room where her bed stood, white and pristine.

Bracing his knee against the mattress, he lowered her gently, then followed in her wake. He came down on top of her, pinning her down when she tried to roll free. His eyes met hers, his elbows planted on either side of her, his large hands framing her face, the gesture gentle and caring, before his eyes suddenly darkened. "Let me make love to you, Ellie." But before she could answer, he kissed her once again, his mouth slanting hungrily over hers, unable to get enough.

She clung to him, reveling in the feel of his hard body pressed to hers. He pulled her gown and the rest of her underclothes free, tossing them aside.

"Sweet Jesus, you are so beautiful," he murmured, awe in his eyes. "More beautiful even than I remembered."

Her fingers found purchase in the over-long cloud of his hair. His mouth licked and sucked, biting and kissing, making her yearn impatiently. She tore at his shirt, wanting to feel his skin next to hers. Willingly, he obliged, standing up next to the bed, tossing his shirt aside, working the fastening of his trousers until they fell free and he stood in all his startling glory, more stunning than Michelangelo had sculpted *David*.

His bold sex was hard and heavy with arousal, the muscles along his chest and abdomen quivering with his barely maintained control. He came between her knees, almost reverently, lowering himself slowly until the swollen tip of his manhood brushed against her. Their bodies pressed together until there was nothing between them, joining in a centuries-old caress. Their eyes met and held, until she moved, her body stirring, yearning, no longer able to wait, and he groaned, plunging into her with a single hard thrust, deep into her womb. He cried out with the intensity, murmuring her name, grasping her tightly as he buried his face in her hair.

The sun moved through the sky, spilling into the room through the open windows. Slowly, reluctantly, Ellie became aware of their surroundings—the sketch pad and pencil that lay forgotten; their clothes, shirts and trousers, but no sign of her lucky red stockings. Suddenly she remembered the day she had discarded them so long ago after learning that Nicholas had left New York, taking all hope with him. Why did she remember the stockings now? she wondered.

The sounds of the streets below began to intrude on their precarious world. Nicholas held her close in the aftermath of their love. They lay together for long minutes, neither speaking, neither moving.

At length, Nicholas looked down into her eyes as her

tears spilled down her cheeks. Every trace of his coolness and hard edge had disappeared long ago. Only despair remained. "Why, Ellie?" he demanded.

Of course she knew what he meant. *Why had she betrayed him?* She looked at him forever. "I have no answer for you," she said finally.

"You have no answer," he asked, the anger beginning to burn, "or is it that you're not brave enough to tell me?"

She looked at him, with a calm that amazed her. "If I had an answer, would it change things? My guess is that if you still have to ask, any answer I could provide would be irrelevant—only the betrayal matters."

She saw that he recognized the truth of her words, and she hated the pain that flared to life in her breast. If only . . .

With a curse, he rolled free and pulled on his clothes, before he finally looked back at her. Their eyes met, and in that moment, she saw him more clearly than she ever had before. She saw that, like her, he was shattered by what they had done—startled and empty—because in the end, as she had said, nothing had changed. Too much had gone on before, too much had happened to be surmounted. Yes, he desired her, and no, he couldn't forget her, but she saw in his eyes that even their all-consuming passion couldn't wipe clean the betrayals of the past. Desire wasn't enough. He couldn't forgive her for arriving at their engagement party on the arm of another man. He couldn't forgive her for marrying someone else. Beyond that, he couldn't forgive her for being M. M. Jay, for putting to canvas their intimate moments, making it impossible for him to trust that she truly loved him, not certain if she simply loved what they had shared. And as she returned his anguished gaze, she wasn't certain she could ever wholly forgive him either, for betraying her to the world.

She longed to wash their hearts clean, but how? And if she couldn't, she knew with a sinking certainty, that there could be no future in a relationship forever subverted by doubt and mistrust.

Ellie realized then why she had remembered the stockings. There was no hope of washing their hearts clean, just as there had been no hope of telling Nicholas her story once he had left Manhattan years before.

All hope for them had been discarded long ago, just like her red stockings.

"I'm sorry," he said.

The words echoed in her mind, round and round. He was sorry? For what? For making love to her—or for ever having loved her at all? But when her thoughts cleared and she would have asked him which he had meant, she found that he was gone. Once again she was alone.

Chapter 35

Tears coursed down her cheeks. She closed her eyes, light all around. The paintbrush felt foreign in her hand.

Nicholas had asked before if she was afraid to paint him. Was she afraid? she wondered.

Images swirled, making her light-headed. She saw in her mind's eye the touch—his touch that she had thought she would never know again. The intensity. The burning. But most of all, she saw the image of him standing, framed by the window, alone, lost, his blue eyes desolate as if all the hope and Will he believed in was gone. The memory of being a boy, before, and now. Unbearable longing. Longing for so many things. Childhood returned. Charlotte. And Ellie knew that he longed, as well, for the innocent love they'd had but a glimpse of during an idyllic time in August so long ago.

Her hand began to move of its own volition, filling the bristles of the brush with color, then painting, slowly at first then faster. No sketches. No preparations. Just the strokes, truthful and real, an extension of herself. And as she painted she realized that she *was* afraid, but not simply of the surface fears about which she had thought Nicholas spoke. Her fear was not solely of being unable to live up to expectations. It was a fear of a much deeper inadequacy. Fear not just that she was the illegitimate daughter of a horrid man—but fear that she could never be anything more.

And that fear, no longer nameless, rushed in through the crumbling dam that had been her protective wall, overwhelming her. And she realized as well that she had raised the white flag of surrender long ago, *ensuring* that she would be nothing more than Harry Dillard's daughter.

Past and present blurred, became indistinguishable.

With a strangled cry, she dragged her sleeve across her face and tried to focus, tried to empty the raging thoughts from her mind.

Slowly, almost painfully, lines and curves began to take over. Faster then slower, her mind finally set free. And she forgot. She painted as she had never painted before, painting for the lost child who was Nicholas. Painting for the lost soul of herself.

Color streaked her cheek, splattered her smock. But she didn't notice. Her hair fell free, wild to tumble down her back. She felt no constraints. She felt nothing but the work as the brush moved in desperate strokes.

Painting, creating. Living through her art.

Whether it was hours or minutes she would never know. But when she stepped away, stood back and took in the canvas, her breath caught in her throat.

A portrait of Nicholas? No. Rather a life, captured on canvas, and even she knew it was the best work she had ever done.

Chapter 36

The following day there was no sign of Nicholas. Nor the day after that. It was as if he knew the painting was done. No need for him to return. Or perhaps as she had suspected, like her, he had recognized the futility of their meetings. She knew she should be thankful. She told herself she only wanted to see him one more time to show him the portrait, to see his reaction. But now that he was gone, seemingly for good, she couldn't ask him to come back. She would simply have to send the painting to his house. Obligation complete. The story at an end.

Indeed, after days passed with no word from Nicholas and the portrait was dry enough to wrap in brown paper, Ellie had Jim take it to Nicholas's house. She waited for hours, hoping against hope that once Nicholas saw the work he would send a message. He loved it. He hated it. Anything. Just something to acknowledge that he had seen it. But by nightfall with no word, she realized no word was coming. She might never know what he thought.

The next morning, when sunlight had just begun to paint the world in shades of dark blue and violet, a hard pounding on Ellie's door brought her out of a deep sleep.

"Ellie! Wake up!"

Barnard's voice came through to her, and suddenly she came awake. Something must be wrong with Jonah. She flew to the door, throwing it wide. "What has happened?"

"Look! Here! In the morning paper."

Dread washed her concern away.

"Page three," he added.

Her eyes fluttered closed and she had to grab the doorjamb to keep from falling.

"Damn it, girl. Read!"

With shaking hands, Ellie took the *Times* which was folded open to page three.

M. M. JAY PROVES MASTERFUL
by Able Smythe

Think what you will about the propriety of the infamous M. M. Jay. But make no mistake about the artist's talent. Years ago I said Jay held back. Well no longer is this true.

Her most recent work is undeniably a *pièce de résistance*. The artist has captured the true essence of a man on canvas, beautiful in his starkness and power, his animal mask having slipped for just a moment, revealing a hypnotic beauty and deep, normally unsee-able wounds. It is the portrayal of a man in anguish, a man caught between hate and longing.

The work would be impressive if painted by a man. There is no denying the exceptional use of stroke and line, color and dimension. But could a man have done this work, I ask? Could a man have seen beneath his own mask? Does he allow himself to see?

Undoubtedly the answer is no, as most men are blinded, or blind themselves to their inner feelings. It is M. M. Jay, as a woman, who has glimpsed beneath the controlled surface every man works his whole life to perfect.

Regardless of who M. M. Jay is, and no matter what

one thinks of her as a woman, we must accept that she is a painter of startling depth and talent worthy of our respect. One day, and one day soon, her paintings will be worth a king's ransom.

Ellie stood perfectly still, unable to move as tears of searing joy burned in her eyes.

"I told you!" Barnard exclaimed. "I said you could do it. And now you have. No buts or falling short. You have done it. You have proven to the world that you can paint!"

But all Ellie could think was that she hadn't failed. No, she truly hadn't failed, she thought, laughter mixing with her tears.

"Just wait," Barnard added with a firm nod. "You'll see. Your life is about to change."

Within hours it began to happen. Everyone, it seemed, wanted a painting by M. M. Jay. Overnight Ellie found herself in demand. Her past seemed miraculously to have disappeared. Barnard was victorious, Hannah was maternal, Miriam quiet but supportive, while Jim was simply happy. Only Ellie didn't share in the celebration. She held Jonah with a fierceness that frightened her.

After the initial elation over her success had settled, it had finally dawned on her that this sudden good fortune had come about because Nicholas had obviously shown Able Smythe the painting. A ripple of fear crashed through her body. Why had he done it? she had to wonder. Had it been an effort to make amends—or another attempt to hurt her that had gone awry? She remembered all too well his hatred for her father, and the extraordinary ends to which he had gone to bring him down. Was Nicholas trying to punish her still? And if he was, when would it end? Dear God, how would it end?

"Ellie, what is it?"

Ellie looked up and saw the concern in Miriam's eyes. "Nothing, Miriam, really."

Jonah scrambled down from Ellie's lap, his laughter ringing throughout the room. Everyone was so happy, so relieved. Jonah obviously sensed it. If only *she* could be happy, too. If only she could trust her sudden good fortune. But she had lived at the mercy of men for too long to believe so easily.

With a muttered excuse, Ellie hurried from the room, needing time to think. She walked endlessly through the hot, muggy streets of New York. Without realizing it, she ended up at the tower Nicholas had taken her to the night she had thwarted his efforts to buy other houses on her street. Taking the hard granite steps, she climbed to the top.

Isolation surrounded her. She had lived in a world of isolation, connecting with others who were isolated, too. But then Nicholas had come into her life, offering her a glimpse of so much more—so much more that she couldn't have.

But was that true? she suddenly wondered, looking out into the blistering hot August sky.

She had lived through her art all her life, losing herself in a world she could control. Was it possible to live beyond the art, live life itself, and not vicariously? Not as a slave to her fears? Could she allow herself to feel in life the emotions she allowed herself to feel in her work?

True, Nicholas had shown her a love she couldn't have. But she had also believed she would never know the love of her own child. Now, she couldn't imagine a day that her son wouldn't wrap his arms around her neck and hold her with a vibrant love.

She had a child—against all odds.

A tiny shiver of excitement raced down her spine, excitement she had been afraid to feel.

And Miriam, Ellie suddenly realized. Miriam had survived. Bruised and battered. But still there. And now her friend. Truly a friend, not someone who was dependent upon her.

Ellie realized then, with a startling rush of breath into her lungs, that she wasn't just her father's daughter anymore. She was an artist, a mother, a friend—a successful woman in her own right. She had become something more than Eliot Sinclair, bastard daughter of Harry Dillard.

The thought left her breathless, a miraculous sense of pleasure washing over her. How odd that she had been pushed to it by Nicholas betraying her identity. Had he not told, no one ever would have known she was M. M. Jay. Had he not told, she would still be with Charles, hiding her art. Had he not told, she never would have painted him. And if she had never painted him, would she ever have been able to prove to the world—prove to herself—that she could be something more?

And then it came to her, more clearly than the blue summer sky, as clear as his pain had come to her on the night of Charlotte's death. Nicholas hadn't tried to hurt her. On the last day he had come to her, the day they had made love, she had seen in his eyes the final, devastating acceptance that they had no future together—that while he loved her in some way he didn't understand, they couldn't move beyond the past. And she knew now deep in her soul, that he had shown Able Smythe the portrait as one final, parting gift to her. He might hate her in some insatiable place in his being, but he loved her as well. And for that he gave her a gift.

The stinging bite of sadness filled her at the realization of what he had done, but more importantly, at the realization that truly their story had come to an end. No more possibilities, however slight. No happily ever afters.

How would she survive?

But then she quelled the piercing sadness that she felt at his loss. She quelled the fear that she could never be whole without him. She promised herself there and then on top of the granite tower, that she would not be ruled by fear. No longer.

A glimmer of hope sprang to life in her heart. She would paint. And she would survive. Even without Nicholas. She was Eliot Sinclair, a woman who was more than just the parts, a person in her own right.

Unexpectedly, Nicholas's words from long ago suddenly rang in her ears. *Will it, and it shall be. Hard work and perseverance.* She wasn't afraid of hard work, never had been. She had only been afraid of who she was.

Her excitement resurfaced over prospects that she had never dreamed possible. And with a determined start, she turned, wanting to hurry home to join the celebration with those who loved her, wanting to begin her new journey. But with her mind so filled with the anticipated taste of life, she hadn't realized that she was no longer alone.

Three men stood a mere twenty feet from her, smiles on their faces that made her blood run cold.

"Well, my friends," the tallest of the men said, "it's been long in coming. But after all these years it looks like fate has finally smiled on us."

A tremor of fear visibly shuddered through Ellie's slim frame. The man only chuckled. "Boys, where are our manners? We didn't introduce ourselves. My name is Rudy." He wrapped a large meaty arm around the man next to him. "And this is Billy, and that's Bo."

Ellie took a step to the side, toward the stairs. She knew without having to be told that this was the kind of element that needed to be wiped from the streets.

Rudy raised a brow. "It seems the little lady is in a hurry to leave. Alas," he shrugged, "we can't let that happen."

She took another step, but so did the men. "No pretty lady, we can't let you go. We've been following you for days now, and this is the first time we've caught you alone. We've finally been presented with an opportunity to even the score. Can't pass that up now, can we?"

"What are you talking about? I don't even know you."

"Well, unfortunately for you, we know a friend of yours. Nicholas Drake. And you see, he up and disappeared on us. Then lo and behold, he turned back up and Bo here happened to see him coming out of your place a week or so ago." Rudy shrugged again. "We thought he was simply visiting our old pal Jim, but as—"

"You!" Ellie suddenly blurted, forgetting her own predicament. "You were the ones who were giving Jim trouble!"

"We don't like to think of it as trouble. Isn't that right, boys?"

"Right, boss."

Anger burned Ellie's cheeks. "No, not trouble. It was worse. You and your friends are weaklings who try to make yourselves feel better by preying on people who are weaker than you. You're cowards, that's what you are. Cowards who don't stand a chance against a man like Nicholas Drake. And you know it. So you gain your vengeance by hurting a woman." Ellie scoffed, ignoring the rising anger of the men. "You're probably even too weak to take on me."

In a burst of angry speed, Rudy lashed out at her. But Ellie jerked free, racing to the stairs, nearly making it to safety. But when she took the top step, her long skirts tangled in her legs. Her foot slipped. She gasped and reached out, grabbing for something to save her. But there was nothing to take hold of, nothing to grasp, before she tumbled to the bottom of the unrelenting stairs.

Part Four

Castles by the Sea

Suns that set may rise again . . .

— BEN JOHNSON

Chapter 37

Nicholas flew through the doors of Bellevue. He had raced like a madman across town to a hospital he swore he'd never set foot in again. But on this day, the past, be it Ellie's transgressions or little Charlotte's battle for life, was forgotten. There was only the soul-searing need to see Ellie. The need to see Jim's words proven false.

"Where is she?" Nicholas demanded of a nurse.

The woman blinked back her astonishment at the sudden appearance of the raving man. "Where is who, sir?"

"Ellie Sincl—Monroe."

"Ah," she murmured, her brown eyes softening with sympathy. "You must be Mr. Monroe."

He started to correct her, but before he could she added that only family was allowed to see Ellie, and not for long at that. With no thought of conscience, Nicholas became a man he despised.

Nicholas was ushered into a grim room of no windows and stark walls. A pain he couldn't describe impaled his heart as he took in the small, nearly childlike frame of Ellie, so vulnerable as she lay in the middle of the narrow bed. If he hadn't believed Jim's words before, he had no choice but to accept the truth now. Her eyes were closed, her chest barely stirring with breath. What could be seen of her white-blond hair was back, melting into the sheets and bandages. But the cuts and bruises that she had sustained were clearly visible as he took the remaining steps that separated them. She looked as if she had been beaten within an inch of her life.

"No," he stated, as if his simple command could change what he saw. "No, Ellie."

"They don't expect her to live."

Nicholas spun around to find Barnard in the doorway. "What do you mean?"

"Just that," Barnard said, clearly trying to hold emotion back. "Her injuries are severe. She's hit her head terribly."

"How?" Nicholas demanded through clenched teeth, agony torturing his mind. "How did it happen?"

"She fell down the stairway of that granite building not far from the house. You know the one, don't you?"

Of course he did, Nicholas thought as he turned back and took Ellie's hand in his own, so small and fragile in contrast. *Why were you there?* he asked silently, a wrenching pain filling his heart. *And how did you fall?* But her lips remained unmoving, no answer supplied.

Nicholas spoke with the doctor in charge, then sent for a specialist who arrived within the hour. The short, wiry man only confirmed the initial prognosis. Severe injury to the head. Not expected to live.

After the doctor left, Nicholas sat next to Ellie for hours after having to threaten the nurse when she tried to make him leave. He sat, then paced, then sat again, talking all the while. But Ellie didn't respond.

It was late afternoon when Miriam came into the room. "Nicholas?"

At first, he didn't respond. "Please leave, Miriam."

Miriam stood in the doorway, unmoving, amazed at the ravaged form that was her brother. She realized then, with a sinking certainty, that she had misjudged him. All this time she had believed he hated Ellie, when in truth it was clear

that he loved her more than life itself. Deeply, though
painfully. He simply didn't know how to move beyond all
the lies and betrayals. And as Miriam stood there, she
remembered the day he had told Charlotte how much her
mother loved her. A simple gift. For Charlotte. But one
Miriam would always be grateful for. And with that thought,
Miriam made a decision. She took a deep breath, then said,
"Go to Ellie's house."

Nicholas was startled from his thoughts. "What?"

"There is . . . information at Ellie's house that the
doctor needs," she clarified.

"Then go get it," he snapped hotly.

"I'm sorry. I can't." She bit her lip, then added, "I have
other plans that can't wait."

Nicholas gritted his teeth. "A date? Hoping to snare a rich
man?"

The words stung, and Miriam swallowed back her tears.
She knew that he hated her, but just then that mattered little.
All that mattered was Nicholas, and giving a gift of her own.
"Yes. A rich man. Otherwise I'd go to Ellie's house myself."

"Send Barnard or Jim."

"Jim wouldn't be able to find . . . what the doctor
needs, Nicholas. It's too important, and Barnard is out in the
reception room sound asleep. He's an old man, Nicholas,
and this is killing him. Go to Ellie's house, it won't take
long." Her heart pounded as she looked down at the small
table next to the bed. Ellie's belongings. Shoes, clothes. And
her keys.

"I'll send a messenger."

"No!" she blurted out, then calmed. "This is a . . . file,
yes, a file, that I know Ellie wants no one to see."

Nicholas eyed his sister curiously. "Then how do you
know about it?"

"Because she's my friend."

"You, Miriam?"

"Just go to her house, Nicholas! And just go in. Just . . .
look around. No doubt Hannah is in bed sick with worry."

"You expect me to go to Ellie's house and 'just look around' for some file?" he asked incredulously.

Her mind raced. "Her desk," she said, unable to think of anything else. She picked up the keys and held them out. "Yes, a medical file in her desk." That would get him in the house. Beyond that, her conscience would allow her to do no more.

Nicholas didn't want to leave Ellie's side, but saw no alternative if the doctors needed the information. He cursed his sister, then pushed up from the chair he had occupied for hours. He glanced at Ellie one last time, then kissed her gently, and strode from the room.

Before Nicholas left the hospital, however, he gave Jim a note to take to an old friend who had sat with him on the police commission years before. He couldn't shake the uneasy feeling that plagued him about Ellie's fall.

The house on Sixteenth Street was quiet when Nicholas entered. He walked up the stairs to the fourth floor and was flooded with memories when he pushed open the door. Fading summer light dusted the room in gold. This room, where he had made love to Ellie, her pleasure ringing in his ears. Dear God, how was it possible that he could love one woman so much?

A desk stood against a wall next to the door. He couldn't imagine what kind of medical information the doctor could need unless Ellie had some condition about which he had been unaware.

Drawer by drawer, he searched. Slowly at first. Carefully. But drawer after drawer he found nothing that resembled a medical file. Frustration began to mount. Paper after paper. File after file. Still nothing. And just as he unlocked the last drawer a violent anger assailed him when he determined that his sister must have sent him over there to get him away from Ellie—in some small way to gain revenge.

Fury seared him, and he started to push up from the chair.

But his mind froze when a name on a piece of paper leaped out at him from a page in the last drawer.

Harry Dillard.

He had not allowed himself to think of his thwarted efforts in once and for all wiping the man from the face of New York. He had been deterred. By Ellie. And now to find his name in her desk . . . what did it mean?

With his anger building by the second, he ripped the paper from the drawer. His eyes narrowed in confusion as he read the document. A deed. The thought-to-be-lost deed to her house. Leading him to one undeniable truth.

Ellie was Harry Dillard's daughter. His illegitimate daughter.

Nicholas's mind reeled. Ellie was his most hated enemy's daughter.

He sat, stunned and confused. Propelled by the need to know, the need to understand, Nicholas began to search her desk again, frantically trying to find additional pieces to the puzzle. His hand stilled over a letter addressed to him, yellowed with age, and a note scrawled across the top by his former assistant Bert. *Miss Sinclair, Mr. Drake has departed for the Caribbean.* . . . There was also an old article. NEW YORK'S MOST ELIGIBLE BACHELOR TRAVELS TO CARIBBEAN TO MARRY. He skimmed the article with a curse before, with trembling fingers. Nicholas tore open the seal. A letter finally delivered, though nearly three years late.

Dear Nicholas,

At your house on Long Island I said that I needed to tell you something. I never got the chance. I would like the opportunity to tell you my story now.

I await your response,
Ellie

What had she wanted to say? Suddenly, he remembered that day on the pier. She *had* been trying to tell him something. Instead he had told her the story of his past—told her

of his insatiable need to destroy everything that was of
Harry Dillard.

Nicholas didn't realize that he groaned out loud until the
agonized sound wrapped around and stung his ears. His face
twisted into a wretched mask. Dear God, how could he have
been so blind? He turned away with a jerk, and when he did
his life changed forever.

He found a little boy peeking out from around the
doorjamb. Nicholas could only stare. How long ago had he
seen that sight? Three years past when Charlotte had peeked
her head around the doorway of his dining room, and then
had asked for coffee. *Little Charlotte*. His heart tore into
pieces. For the little boy, though younger than his niece,
looked just like her.

Just like him.

With Ellie's white-blond hair and green eyes, and Charles
Monroe's blond hair and brown eyes, the sight of the little
boy could only mean one thing. He, Nicholas, was the
father.

His mind reeled with sudden, brutal understanding as to
why Ellie had never been able to sell her house, or give
herself to him fully, and why finally she had married
someone else.

And as he sat there, the innocent gaze of the little boy's
blue eyes on him, he understood for the first time that Ellie
hadn't betrayed him. She had done what she'd had to do in
the face of his all-consuming anger at her father in order to
give her son—no, their son—a name.

God, he wanted to scream, cry out. How could he have
been so blind? And he realized then that in his maddened
attempts to punish her for her perceived betrayal, he had
betrayed her—again and again and again. He was no better
than men like Harry Dillard who hurt people weaker than
themselves. Because of his single-minded pursuit of his
own selfish desires, he had destroyed Ellie, as well as what
could have been of their love. Perhaps, he thought, he was
even worse than her father. Harry Dillard, at least, had been

honest about who he was. Nicholas had espoused righteous-
ness, all the while inflicting pain.

He couldn't move, couldn't speak. But he was saved from
doing anything when he heard Hannah's voice call out.

"Jonah, love. Where are you?"

Jonah. His child's name was Jonah. A tremor of emotion
raced down his spine.

But Jonah didn't answer the summons. The boy stared
back at Nicholas, bold blue gaze locked with bold blue gaze.
Nicholas would have chuckled proudly at the child's un-
flinching stare had he not been so sick with grief.

"Jonah. What are you doing up here?" Hannah huffed as
she climbed the steps. "Heavens, you can barely walk, much
less take the stairs. We have enough people in the hospital
without you taking a tumble your—"

Hannah froze in the doorway at the sight of Nicholas.

"Lord have mercy," she gasped, glancing between Jonah
and his father. "You can't be here!"

"But I am," he whispered brokenly. "I am."

"This can't be happening! This can't be happening," she
wailed.

The sound of the slamming front door wafted up to them.
In minutes Barnard had hurried up the stairs, doubled over
from lack of breath. When finally he could breathe, he
stammered, "Damn you, man. Haven't you caused enough
trouble in Ellie's life? Why can't you leave her alone?"

"I didn't come here to cause trouble. I didn't even
know . . . Jonah was here."

"It was Miriam!" Barnard exclaimed. "Miriam did this!"

And Nicholas realized in that moment that she had. She
had led him to his son and, perhaps unknowingly, to an
understanding of what he had done. Shame riddled his mind
when he remembered thinking she had sent him here to gain
revenge. "Don't worry, Barnard. I won't do anything to hurt
Ellie . . . not any more than I already have."

Barnard glanced at the papers and documents littered
across the desktop. "I take it you know everything now."

"Yes. The whole sorry tale. God, how could I have been so stupid?" His voice rose with panic and anger, and his eyes closed. "Answers staring me in the face from the beginning. I wonder if I was truly so stupid, or just didn't want to know." After a moment he opened his eyes, and saw his son. Nicholas stood and walked to the doorway. Jonah watched his approach. Curious, not scared. Nicholas lowered himself on his haunches.

"Hullo," Jonah said, slowly reaching out with his toddler's hand to very carefully touch Nicholas's cheek.

Nicholas trembled. "Hello to you, too."

Jonah's eyes lighted with joy.

Very gently, Nicholas reached out and took Jonah's hand, looking down at the fingers that seemed impossibly tiny. Unexpected tears burned at Nicholas's eyes. "God, if I had only known."

"What, Nicholas?" Barnard demanded. "What would you have done?"

"I don't know, Barnard," he answered truthfully. He looked into his son's eyes. "The only thing I know is that in this life I have failed. Buildings and money and power don't mean anything. At life and loving I am a very poor man."

Barnard's gaze narrowed. "If only you had realized that before, Ellie wouldn't be dying."

Suddenly Nicholas grew fierce, his eyes burning with silver-blue fire. "Ellie is not going to die. I won't let her. I might not have been able to save Charlotte . . . or my mother, but by God, I'll save Ellie."

He kissed his son's fingers, then stood. "I have to. I need a second chance to make things right."

Chapter 38

Nicholas pushed through the hospital doors, with Hannah and Barnard behind him. Miriam stood in the waiting room, staring out a murky window. She turned at the sound, and her eyes opened wide at the sight of Jonah in her brother's arms.

Her heart seemed to stop. Had she done the right thing? she wondered. Nicholas's face certainly didn't provide her with an answer. His glacial eyes found her across the room, and he could have been feeling any number of emotions, and she wouldn't have known.

He walked straight towards her, his hard gaze fixed on her. When he reached her he just stood. At length his eyes softened, like ice melting in the sun. "Thank you," he said quietly, much as she had said to him years before.

He reached out and took her hand. "Thank you," he repeated.

"Nicky!" Jim raced through the doors, waving a sealed letter. "I got a message from your friend."

Nicholas handed Jonah to Jim, who took him over to a scraggly sofa to play. Then Nicholas tore open the missive, read the few lines, then swore savagely.

"What is it, Nicholas?" Barnard asked.

"They've taken in some men thought to be involved with Ellie's fall.

"Who are they?"

"Three fellows I had a run-in with years before." He crumbled up the paper. "I'm going to kill them." He started to turn back towards the entry. But Hannah stood in the way.

"When will it stop, Nicholas?" she demanded.

His dark brow narrowed ominously.

"This insatiable need for vengeance," she explained. "This endless circle that spins out of control, growing larger, encompassing more. Haven't you seen enough revenge for a lifetime, Nicholas? You said you wanted to make things right. Then start now, today. Let the police handle those men. It's Ellie and Jonah who need you now."

And standing there, with Hannah's gently lined hand resting on his arm, Nicholas knew that she was correct. The circle of vengeance was endless. Consuming. If he had learned nothing else, he had learned that. For now he had to leave Rudy, Billy, and Bo in the hands of the police. It was time he thought of Ellie and their son. Nothing else.

With that thought, he turned abruptly and called for the man in charge. Within minutes the doctor taking care of Ellie was standing in front of Nicholas.

"But you can't take Mrs. Monroe out of here." The man swallowed. "She's a gravely ill woman."

"So you've said." Nicholas's blue-eyed gaze was glacial. "But you've also said there is nothing else you can do for her."

The doctor shifted his weight. "Well, this is true—"

"Then you should have no objections that I take her with me."

"But—"

"No buts." Nicholas strode down the hall to Ellie's room, chaos erupting behind him. But Nicholas didn't notice. The sight of Ellie washed every other thought from his mind, for she still lay on the bed, deathly pale except for the red and blue-black of her cuts and rapidly forming bruises. When he thought about her falling, he knew it was a miracle that she was alive at all. And the miracle, he believed, had to believe, was meant to give him a second chance—give them a second chance.

"I'm here, little one," he whispered, coming up next to her, speaking as if she could hear him. "I've met Jonah. And now I'm going to take you and our son away from here."

Her silence didn't deter him as he gathered her up in his strong arms. Within minutes, Nicholas had this newly found, makeshift family piled into the carriage. Hannah and Barnard, Miriam and Jim. Jonah. And Ellie.

"Where are we going?" Jim demanded.

Nicholas pulled Ellie close, pressing his lips to her temple. "To the house on Long Island." Yes, he thought, to the place she had once called magical, where the power of sunshine and the power of the sea surely would heal her.

Nicholas had always been a man of action, not one to sit back to be tossed about by the vagaries of life. He took hold of the things he wanted, obsessively, and wouldn't let go. Today, he took hold of Ellie's fate. And wouldn't let her go. He had failed his mother. He had failed Charlotte. He had failed Ellie in so many ways. But he wouldn't fail her again.

Days passed. In the room at the top of the house which Ellie had so loved, she lay unmoving on the bed. Nicholas sat by her side day after day. Jonah was there most of the time, the two of them who looked so much alike, talking to Ellie as if she were listening. Only when his son was not nearby did Nicholas allow his emotions to seep through. Nicholas alternately cajoled and berated the woman he loved to wake up. But Ellie merely lay there, lost to a world he couldn't seem to breech despite his belief that he could.

On the seventh day, when everyone else had lost all hope, Nicholas sat by Ellie's side late into the night. Towards dawn a voice from the doorway jarred him. Nicholas turned to find his sister. He gave her a tired, awkward smile. They hadn't spoken since the hospital. "Come in."

"Why don't you get some sleep. I'll sit with Ellie."

"No. Thank you, though."

Miriam sighed. "Do you mind if I sit with you awhile?"

"Please," was all he said.

Minutes ticked by. "I'm sorry, Miriam," Nicholas said, breaking the silence, "for so many years of being . . . callous. If only I could find a way to make it up to you."

Miriam reached over and took his hand. "You already have, Nicholas."

"But—"

"Shhh. There's nothing else to say. The past is gone, and we've found each other."

Nicholas squeezed her hand, his throat tight, before he settled back in his chair.

They sat in a newly comfortable silence as the sun rose over the ocean. It was nearly seven in the morning when Nicholas suddenly leaped from his seat. "Did you see that?"

"What? See what?"

"Ellie. Ellie just moved."

"Oh, Nicholas," Miriam said with a sigh. "How long is this going to go on? It's time you started making plans."

Nicholas turned sharply. "What are you talking about?"

"Ellie, Nicholas. And Jonah. It's time you started thinking about . . . the future."

"The only thing I can think about now is Ellie and making her well."

"But you have a son, Nicholas. And one of these days you're going to have to face the fact that Ellie isn't going to get better."

"She will get better!" he stated emphatically. "She has to."

After that morning, Nicholas began talking to Ellie obsessively. He *had* seen movement. He was sure of it.

He stayed with her constantly, working her muscles, massaging her skin, brushing her limp hair until it shone. As days passed, Nicholas knew that Barnard and the others thought he was going mad. But while everyone else was wringing their hands and trying to determine what to do, Nicholas began to see the change. Ellie was groping her way out of the dark, murky place in her mind that held her captive.

He took her outside on a Tuesday, bright, hot August sun spilling down from the cerulean blue sky. He had set up a makeshift bed on the beach despite Bernard's shout of outrage and Hannah's cry of concern. But Nicholas was certain that the sound of the waves and smell of the ocean Ellie had so cherished would seep into her mind, finally coaxing her from the final vestiges of her deep sleep.

Jonah was there, insisting that Nicholas play with him in the sand. And when long minutes ticked by and Ellie's eyes didn't open as Nicholas had been so certain they would, he turned away sharply. Maybe Barnard, Hannah, and Miriam were right. Maybe he *was* going mad, he thought suddenly, feeling the same anguished defeat he had experienced when he had heard the telling gunshot, then again, when he had realized Charlotte was going to die. He hadn't saved his mother, and he hadn't saved his niece. Perhaps his efforts to save the woman he loved were in vain as well.

"Play!" Jonah demanded, banging his little shovel against the beach. "I want to play!"

Ellie woke to the feel of bright, hot sun kissing her skin. And light. Bold and beckoning. Willing her to seek it out. She was alive.

Inhaling deeply, she breathed in the salty air.

Dear God, she was alive.

The events of the past tried to tumble down on her, but she pushed them out of her fog-laden mind. Stiffly, she turned her head as if turning away from the unwelcome thoughts, and she saw them—as clear and vivid as any painting, but this time what she saw was real. It was life, not an image captured on canvas. Jonah, her precious son, kneeling next to Nicholas, building a sand castle on the beach, the sun shining silver behind them. The pain in her body was forgotten.

Only seconds passed before Nicholas glanced up as if he had heard her silent thoughts. His hand stilled in its task. He looked haggard, and tired, his chiseled features hard with anguish. But she saw in his eyes the depths of loving and caring that she had seen years before, though now the hate was no longer there to subdue it. And she knew deep down as the waves spilled onto the beach that Nicholas had learned her story. And loved her still.

Her heart burgeoned with a joy she could hardly fathom. And then, as if finally sensing the change, Jonah turned as well and noticed Ellie. His eyes lighted with a pleasure that brought a surge of elation to her heart. "Mama!" he squealed, then pushed himself up awkwardly and wobbled over to where she lay. "Mama!" he cried again, throwing himself into her arms.

She didn't grimace at the pain. She was overwhelmed by the pleasure of holding her son, the feel of his tiny arms and legs, his sweet kisses—and she was overwhelmed by the presence of his father.

Her eyes met Nicholas's over Jonah's shoulder. Nicholas, strong and powerful as ever, kneeling in the sand, unexpected tears glistening in his eyes. She saw an uncertainty in him that she would have sworn was impossible in such a confident man. And she realized that not only had he come to understand her past, but he tormented himself for the part he had played in it.

"To think how I've wasted my life," he said, his voice ravaged. "Chasing demons that only existed in my head. I've hurt you unbearably." He sighed raggedly. "But still I'm a selfish man. I know I should leave you alone as you have asked before, leave you to those who haven't hurt you. But I can't. At least not until I've told you that I'm sorry—desperately sorry," he said, the words choked, his expression stating clearly that he was afraid she wouldn't believe him.

He squared his shoulders and took a deep breath. "Now it's up to you. If you ask me now, I'll leave."

She saw his pain, saw his regret. And she understood as the sun caressed her skin and the waves lapped at the beach, that she would know laughter once again. Her life was starting anew, full of promise, full of purpose just as she had determined before she fell. But as she had never dreamed possible, her life would be full of Nicholas, too. A tremulous smile pulled at her lips, and she reached out to him.

It was all Nicholas needed. He came to her side, the bucket falling away, revealing the final turret of the sand castle. With a reverence that brought tears to Ellie's eyes, he wrapped her and Jonah in his embrace, burying his face in her neck.

"Who would have believed," she whispered, her voice soft and hoarse, but strangely strong, "that my dreams would come true and my knight in shining armor would build me a silver castle by the sea?"